'Brilliant. Dark, haunting, heartbreaking and utterly compulsive'
Kia Abdullah

'I've just finished *Strange Sally Diamond* and I'm in that dizzy
aftermath when you feel you have been through an out-of-body
experience . . . Many readers, consciously or not, may feel an
identification with Sally Diamond. I certainly did. We might also
be thankful that, unlike her, we can draw our bucket back up out
of the dark, toxic well she has been assigned. Maybe it doesn't
matter if it's Liz's best book; it probably is. But the sheer mastery
of the whole thing, the modulated propulsion, her sentences as
right as right can be. She is as excellent a writer as anyone living I
can think of, and most likely a better novelist. It is all just a
perfected dance and how she does it no mortal soul can know'
Sebastian Barry

'Utterly compelling and so beautifully written! Believe
the hype – this is so good' Louise Beech

'Chilling in parts, bittersweet in others, this is a big read
that will have you thinking and urging Sally on long after
the novel has ended' *Belfast Telegraph*

'Such an incredible book' Sonali Bendre Behl, Sonali's Book Club

'Brilliantly witty and extremely moving, the character of Sally will
capture your heart' *Best* magazine, Book of the Month

'Simply magnificent. Call it a crime novel if you want but
it's so much more than that. A hugely disturbing yet deeply
moving portrait of damage that I can't recommend highly
enough' Mark Billingham

'Dark, thrilling, absorbing, funny, happy, sad, obsessive,
compelling, twisted, shocking, sensitive and moving.
Sheer perfection!' *Books By Your Bedside* blog

'A thrilling, utterly immersive mystery that, paired with Sally's
unique, unforgettable voice, makes it a true winner . . . Nugent
is at the top of her game' Bookreporter

'Original, gripping, heartbreaking and utterly brilliant. Loved it more than I can put into words. I urge you to go out and read this amazing book. Book of the year contender!' @thebookshopman, X

'Nobody writes quite like her . . . a dextrous plotter who delights in keeping her readers off balance . . . in Sally Diamond she may have created her most empathetic character yet . . . another gem in the queen of crime's crown' *Business Post*

'What a brave, funny, disquieting, riveting book. By the end, I felt I knew Sally Diamond's mind better than I did my own' Louise Candlish

'In a stellar writing career, this really is Liz Nugent's finest hour. I put my whole life on hold for it. What a character, what a story' Claudia Carroll

'I was blown away by *Strange Sally Diamond* . . . Utterly chilling and impossible to put down' Andrea Carter

'There are no words to describe *Strange Sally Diamond* . . . any description, any word, would not come close to doing this masterpiece justice. Fourteen hours after opening the first page, I closed it. Gripped until the very end. Just wow' Dr Jennifer Cassidy

'If you are lucky enough to get Liz Nugent's latest book do NOT start reading it at bedtime if you need to get up the next morning!' *Chapter in my Life* blog

'Dark, heartbreaking, funny, brilliant – *Strange Sally Diamond* will stay with you well beyond the final page' Paul Cleave

'It's both heartbreaking and it'll make you laugh' Harlan Coben

'I absolutely loved this book. Liz Nugent does not put a foot wrong. It's tense, it's creepy, it's foreboding and unflinching. It's such a joy to read a book like this, to be completely assured that you are in the hands of a brilliant storyteller and to just be able to give yourself over to a story because you know it's going to be so good. Liz is a rare and gifted storyteller and writer, and a gift to readers – so clever, insightful and psychologically brilliant' Edel Coffey

'If you like quirky, twisted and dark then you will LOVE this book' Tracy Fenton, *Compulsive Readers* blog

'An incredible read. A truly wonderful central character and captivating story. I devoured this book' *Fran McBookface* blog

'Incredibly page-turning . . . riveting'
Adam Garcia, *Between the Covers*

'I devoured *Strange Sally Diamond* and it is still going around in my head days after I finished it. I loved it!'
Patricia Gibney

'I was absolutely gripped and desperate to get back to reading every time I had to put it down!' @GlasgowBookworm, X

'So compelling that I found myself reading non-stop. She's got unforgettable characters, the prose is crisp and there's real wit in the pages. Sally, damaged and alone, intelligent and isolated in her own head, made me laugh, right until I cried . . . one of the best books of the year' *Globe and Mail*

'FIVE STARS. Finally out: the novel I first read during the depths of winter, and that I have not been able to shake since. As sinister and subversive as expected from Liz Nugent, but also [. . .] incredibly empathetic and wrenching and surprisingly funny, and just plain human. It zigs where you think it is going to zag – its two perspectives, its two different timelines and the voice of Sally itself, unlike any I've come across in fiction. Utterly ABSORBING' Shinan Govani

'Utterly fabulous . . . Deserves every plaudit'
C. S. Green

'Her best yet . . . a heartbreaking but humane tale of people damaged beyond repair' *Guardian*

'Mesmerizing, shocking yet uplifting. Sally is a character you can't help but love. This book is destined to be HUGE!'
Debbie Hart, *Reading For Leisure* blog

'Dark, disturbing and touching all at once. And the moral complexities have kept me pondering' Robyn Harding

'Utterly captivating . . . an all too believable, almost mundane, world of cunningly planned evil and the age-old debate about nature versus nurture . . . This is a really striking and immersive construct, with perhaps the faintest of echoes of Emma Donoghue's *Room* and John Fowles' 1960s thriller *The Collector,* but delivered brilliantly in Nugent's distinctive voice' *Irish Independent*

'Nugent understands brilliantly the way the macabre and the comic combine; she has a flair for the bravura curtain raiser; and she is drawn repeatedly to socially and psychologically non-conforming characters . . . This is harrowing territory, yet the narrative strands are suffused with energy and texture. Above all, at the centre of this troubling, ingeniously conceived, utterly absorbing novel, Sally is a terrific, protean creation, imbued with immense life force and a kind of naïve charm. It is never less than enthralling to spend time in her company and the novel's soaring coda is a tribute to her spirit' *Irish Times*

'An outstanding achievement which transforms the dark psychological thriller map with both bravura and delicacy. One for the ages' Maxim Jakubowski

'I've loved all of Liz Nugent's novels and this was no exception. *Strange Sally Diamond* is clever, compelling, chilling, disturbing and soooooo dark!' Diane Jeffrey

'The best book I've read this year. A truly incredible reading experience' Lisa Jewell

'No one gets into damaged people's heads like Liz Nugent – I'd have known this was her writing even if her name had been deleted from the cover. Moving, thrilling, enraging and impossible to put down' Erin Kelly

'I'm lost in admiration. *Strange Sally Diamond* transcends genre and deserves to win literary prizes. It's vivid, pacy, taut but so very moving. It's written with enormous compassion, and I LOVED the character of Sally, my heart absolutely broke for her. This novel feels *different,* it seems to me that it defies categorization. It's dark certainly and the ending is chilling yet it's written with incredible heart' Marian Keyes

'Possibly my favourite Liz Nugent book so far. I LOVED IT! Strange Sally strides onto the page, fully formed and funny as hell (this is Liz: we're talking dark funny). I was hooked from the first paragraph. I held my breath, gasped, laughed and cried. This is twisty, original and pitch-black. I'll go anywhere with Liz – but only in daylight' Nikki May

'I finished it in two sittings . . . you just cannot put it down . . . astonishing' Katie Melua, *Between the Covers*

'Another bloody scorcher from Liz Nugent that kept me up to the wee hours to finish. Liz is one of the most intelligent, original, twisty crime writers working in the genre today' Adrian McKinty

'Compassionate and challenging, letting us imagine the lives that are forgotten when the news cycle moves on . . . a very special book' Val McDermid

'Utterly compelling. Brilliant writing and memorable characters. Genuinely unputdownable' Dervla McTiernan

'An intense book, a page-turner . . . a riveting mystery, with puzzles piling up . . . Nugent's spectacular novel gives us both despair and hope' *Minneapolis Star Tribune*

'Sally is one of the best, most compelling characters I've read in a long time' Dr Liz Mistry

'I absolutely devoured this. Liz Nugent has created a dark, twisted, gripping, intriguing, heart-stopping tale full of characters who, despite the horrors they inflict, are victims in their own right. Sally is a character that will stay embedded under my skin for a long time' Sinead Moriarty

'One of the most original and spine-tingling books I've read in ages, Liz Nugent's *Strange Sally Diamond* draws you in to the close, claustrophobic world of rural Ireland and the life of an emotionally withdrawn woman whose dark, hidden past is coming back to haunt her. Crackling with tension, this book with have you turning the pages late into the night. An absolute triumph' Abir Mukherjee

'Reading *Strange Sally Diamond* is like plugging yourself into the mains; shock relentlessly follows shock. A heroine you won't forget in a characteristically dark tale. Liz Nugent has written her masterpiece' Philip Nolan

'Liz Nugent has outdone herself. Twisted and twisty, dark and gripping, no one will forget Sally Diamond in a hurry!' Graham Norton

'A shockingly smart, dark and twisted psychological thriller. I was compelled to continue reading (beyond bedtime!) and often laughed out loud, only to be shocked again as the chilling story continued to unfold. Although heartbreaking, it is a compassionate story of people damaged beyond repair' NZ Booklovers

'The elevator pitch for *Strange Sally Diamond* could go: *Room* meets *Eleanor Oliphant,* but this dark gem of a novel is so much more' *Observer*

'A brilliant book, it's just so good' Muireann O'Connell, *Ireland AM*

'The queen of Irish suspense strikes again! A book that had me compelled, wanting to read on ferociously whilst at the same time being deeply unsettled as the prospect of what might befall some of the characters next. Her best yet!' Damien O'Meara

'Twisted, shocking and very, very dark, Liz Nugent has created a character for the ages in Sally Diamond' Louise O'Neill

'This book is fantastic – I couldn't stop thinking about Sally for weeks!' Hollie Overton

'I absolutely LOVED *Strange Sally Diamond*. A truly unique voice that smacks you in the face (in the very best way) from the first page. So dark. So absorbing. So disquieting. It's *Eleanor Oliphant* meets *Room*. I'm in awe' Lizzie Pook

'One of the year's boldest and most original offerings, Nugent's off-kilter latest novel grabs hold and won't let go' *Publishers Weekly*, Best Mystery/Thriller Books of 2023

'It creeped me out (in a good way). Think *Room* and
The Collector but add a dazzling/unique main character and
encroaching dread. Terrific' Ian Rankin

'A meaty psychological thriller with a compelling central
character . . . both touching and terrifying, showing both the
good and evil of humanity as well as the legacy inflicted on
future generations . . . her best yet' *RTÉ Guide*

'This book will stay with you for a very long time!' Amanda Ross

'Creepy, absorbing and, yes, funny and sweet . . . Block out
plenty of time for this one' *St. Louis Post-Dispatch*

'It has been six weeks since I read *Strange Sally Diamond*
and still about twice a day a scene will flash before me and
make my insides curdle' Eithne Shortall

'Absolutely superb. I was so enthralled with Sally in the present – but
the Peter flashbacks, *oh my God*. I couldn't read it fast enough. And in
true Liz style, what a twisted, unexpected ending' Jo Spain

'Compelling, shocking and unlike anything you've read before'
Stellar Magazine

'This edge-of-the-seat thriller will leave you with bated
breath anticipating what's going to happen next'
Surjit Reads and Recommends blog

'Magnificent, genre-defying . . . a triumph. Unputdownable'
Summers & Swan, X

'Truly outstanding – clever, compelling and intricately crafted.
FIVE STARS' @susiesbookrevs, X

'Be prepared for a roller coaster ride – Sally Diamond
is going to get under your skin' Vanda Symon

'Liz Nugent is a genius of an author and *Strange Sally Diamond* is
one of the best crime novels I've read in years. Sally is a character
who will initially shock you, perplex you and then win your heart.
Dark, intriguing, heartbreaking and surprising, if I wasn't biting my
nails, I was smiling to myself. It's absolutely brilliant. If this book
does't win every prize in 2023, I will be very surprised' C. L. Taylor

'Strikingly well-observed and consistently surprising' *The Times*

'Disturbing yet touching' *Times of India*

'Fab. Gripping. Compelling. Enthralling. Would recommend the following: 1. Buy the book, 2. Cancel all other plans. Truly world-class storytelling' Eirin Thompson

'It's a cracker, you will absolutely love this and you'll want to get it today. This book is dark as hell with lovely touches of comedy . . . so engaging' Ryan Tubridy

'Absolutely loved *Strange Sally Diamond*. It reminded me in parts of John Fowles' *The Collector*. Highly recommend!' Laure van Rensburg

'Dark, compelling and emotional, a real page-turner' *VIP Magazine*

'Oh my GOODNESS talk about "this book will keep you up all night" – *Strange Sally Diamond* is literally electric. Picked it up because I loved the cover, twenty-three hours later, yes honest, I finished one of the most compelling reads EVER!' Waterstones Horsham, X

'Dark, disturbing and compelling . . . make sure you have a window of time to read it because once you're in, you'll want to keep going' Angela Watt, *Little Write Space* blog

'I marvel at the imagination . . . labyrinthine . . . fiendish' Bill Whelan

'In Sally Diamond, Nugent has given us an astounding creation with a singular voice . . . it is an absorbing, twisty, compulsive psychological thriller with surprising humour and pathos' Sophie White, *Sunday Independent*

'Liz Nugent dares to go where many won't. What a compelling storyteller she is. Always challenging. I laughed out loud only to recoil from my laughter as the story unfolded. For this is wickedly dark territory. And yet amidst the darkness, she allows a light to glimmer – that of a diamond. Sally Diamond, to be precise' Sarah Winman

'*Strange Sally Diamond* has more heart than nearly any thriller I've read. Nugent continues to prove herself a master at eliciting empathy for her characters, even – especially – the ones you really want to hate. An absolutely brilliant concept and flawless execution. I will be thinking about this story for months to come'
Stephanie Wrobel

'Nugent's new novel and its title character are wonderfully, almost indescribably strange indeed . . . dark, funny, twist-and-turn-filled'
The Zoomer Book Club, *Zoomer* magazine

Strange Sally Diamond

LIZ NUGENT

PENGUIN BOOKS

PENGUIN BOOKS

UK | USA | Canada | Ireland | Australia
India | New Zealand | South Africa

Penguin Books is part of the Penguin Random House group of companies
whose addresses can be found at global.penguinrandomhouse.com.

First published by Sandycove 2023
Published in Penguin Books 2024
001

Typeset by Jouve (UK), Milton Keynes
Printed and bound in Great Britain by Clays Ltd, Elcograf S.p.A.

The authorized representative in the EEA is Penguin Random House Ireland,
Morrison Chambers, 32 Nassau Street, Dublin D02 YH68

A CIP catalogue record for this book is available from the British Library

ISBN: 978–0–241–99357–6

www.greenpenguin.co.uk

MIX
Paper | Supporting
responsible forestry
FSC® C018179

Penguin Random House is committed to a
sustainable future for our business, our readers
and our planet. This book is made from Forest
Stewardship Council® certified paper.

For Richard, with even more love

Away, away, from men and towns,
To the wild wood and the downs —
To the silent wilderness
Where the soul need not repress
Its music . . .

– Percy Bysshe Shelley

PART I

I

'Put me out with the bins,' he said, regularly. 'When I die, put me out with the bins. I'll be dead, so I won't know any different. You'll be crying your eyes out,' and he would laugh and I'd laugh too because we both knew that I wouldn't be crying my eyes out. I never cry.

When the time came, on Wednesday 29th November 2017, I followed his instructions. He was small and frail and eighty-two years old by then, so it was easy to get him into one large garden waste bag.

It was a month since he'd been up and about. 'No doctors,' he said. 'I know what they're like.' And he did, because he was a doctor, of psychiatry. He was still able to write prescriptions, though, and would send me to Roscommon to get those filled out.

I didn't kill him; it wasn't like that. I brought him in tea that morning and he was cold in his bed. Eyes closed, thank God. I hate it on those TV dramas when corpses stare up at the detective inspector. Maybe you only have your eyes open if you've been murdered?

'Dad?' I said, though I knew he was gone.

I sat on the end of the bed, took the lid off his beaker and drank the tea, missing the sugar I put in mine. I checked his pulse first, but I could tell by the waxiness of his skin. Only, waxy isn't the right word. It was more like . . . his skin didn't belong to him any more, or he didn't belong to it.

Dragging the waste bag across the yard to the barn was hard. The ground was frosted so I had to heave the bag up on to my shoulder every few minutes so that it wouldn't rip. Once a month, when he was well, Dad would empty the bins into the incinerator. He refused to pay the bin charges and we lived in such a secluded spot that the council didn't chase us about it.

I knew that corpses decomposed and began to rot and smell, so I carefully placed the bag into the incinerator barrel. I splashed some petrol over the top and set it going. I didn't stay to hear it burn. He was no longer he, it was a body, an 'it', in a domestic incinerator beside a barn in a field beside a house at the end of a lane, off a minor road.

Sometimes, when describing where we lived over the phone, Dad would say, 'I'm off the middle of nowhere. If you go to the middle of nowhere and then take a left, a right, another left until you come to a roundabout, take the second exit.'

He didn't like visitors. Apart from our doctor, Angela, we had callers maybe once every two years since Mum died. The last few fixed the car or installed a computer, and then a few years later, another man came and gave Dad the internet and a newer computer, and the last one came to improve our broadband. I stayed in my room on those occasions.

He never offered to teach me how to use the computer, but explained all the things it could do. I watched enough television to know what computers could do. They could bomb countries. They could spy on people. They could do brain surgery. They could reunite old friends and enemies and solve crimes. But I didn't want to do any of those things. Television was what I liked, documentaries, nature and history programmes, and I loved dramas, fantasy ones set in the future or Victorian ones set in great houses and beautiful dresses, and even the modern ones. I liked watching people with their exciting lives, their passionate love affairs, their unhappy families and their dark secrets. It's ironic, I suppose, because I didn't like people in real life. Most people.

I preferred to stay at home. Dad understood that. School had been horrendous. I went to all the classes, tried to avoid other girls and went straight home afterwards. They said I was autistic, even though my psychiatrist dad had told me I definitely wasn't. I joined no clubs or societies, despite Mum's pleading. When I did my final exams, I got two As and two Bs and two Cs in Honours subjects and a pass in Maths and Irish. That was twenty-five years ago, after which we moved again, to a bungalow at the end of a tiny lane, a mile outside the village of Carricksheedy.

Weekly shopping trips were always an ordeal. I sometimes pretended to be deaf to avoid conversation, but I could hear the schoolchildren's comments. 'Here she comes, Strange Sally Diamond, the weirdo.' Dad said there was no malice in it. Children are mean. Most of them. I was glad I was no longer a child. I was a forty-two-year-old woman.

I would collect Dad's pension and my long-term illness benefit from the post office. Years ago, the post office wanted us to set up direct debits to our bank accounts for our bene-fits and pension, but Dad said we should at least try to maintain some relationships with the villagers, so we ignored the advice. The bank was all the way over in Roscommon, eleven miles away. There was no ATM in Carricksheedy, though with most businesses, you could pay with your bank card and get cash back.

I also collected Dad's post because Dad said he didn't want a postman poking his nose into our business. Mrs Sul-livan, the postmistress, would shout, 'How is your dad, Sally?' Maybe she thought I could lip-read. I nodded and smiled, and she would put her head to one side in sympathy as if a tragedy had occurred, and then I would go to the large Tex-aco garage. I would buy what we needed for the week and get home again, nerves abating as I turned into the lane. The round trip never took longer than an hour.

When he was well, Dad would help unpack the shopping. We ate three meals every day. We cooked for each other. So, I prepared two meals and he prepared one, but the division of labour was even between us. We swapped duties as age took its toll on him. I did the hoovering and he unloaded the dishwasher. I did the ironing and the bins and he cleaned the shower.

And then he stopped coming out of his room, and he wrote his prescriptions with a shakier hand, and he only picked at food. Towards the end, it was ice cream. I fed it to him sometimes when his hands shook too much and I changed his bed linen on the days when he could no longer control himself and didn't make it to the chamber pot under his bed, which I emptied every morning and rinsed out with bleach. He had a bell beside his bed, but I couldn't hear it from the back kitchen, and in the last days, he was too feeble to lift it.

'You're a good girl,' he said weakly.

'You're the best dad,' I'd say, though I knew that wasn't exactly true. But it made him smile when I said it. Mum had taught me to say that. The best dad was the dad in *Little House on the Prairie*. And he was handsome.

My mum used to ask me to play this game in my head. To imagine what other people were thinking. It was a curious thing. Isn't it easier to ask them what they think? And is it any of my business? I know what I think. And I can use my imagination to pretend things that I could do, like the people on television, solving crimes and having passionate love affairs. But sometimes I try to think what the villagers see when they look at me. According to a magazine I read one time in

Angela's waiting room, I am half a stone overweight for my height, five foot eight inches. Angela laughed when I showed her the magazine, but she did encourage me to eat more fruit and vegetables and fewer carbs. My hair is long and auburn, but I keep it in a loose bun, slightly below the crown of my head. I wash it once a week in the bath. The rest of the week, I wear a shower cap and have a quick shower.

I wear one of my four skirts. I have two for winter and two for summer. I have seven blouses, three sweaters and a cardigan, and I still have a lot of Mum's old clothes, dresses and jackets, all good quality, even though they are old. Mum liked to go shopping with her sister, Aunt Christine, in Dublin two or three times a year 'for the sales'. Dad didn't approve but she said she would spend her money how she liked.

I don't wear bras. They are uncomfortable and I don't understand why so many women insist on them. When the clothes wore out, Dad bought me second-hand ones on the internet, except for the underwear. That was always new. 'You hate shopping and there's no point in wasting money,' he would say.

My skin is clear and clean. I have some lines on my forehead and around my eyes. I don't wear make-up. Dad bought me some once and suggested that I should try it out. My old friend television and the advertisements meant that I knew what to do with it, but I didn't look like me, with blackened eyes and pink lipstick. Dad agreed. He offered to get different types but he sensed my lack of enthusiasm and we didn't mention it again.

I think the villagers see a forty-two-year-old 'deaf' woman walking in and out of the village and occasionally driving an ancient Fiat. They must assume I can't work because of the deafness and that's why I get benefits. I get benefits because Dad said I am socially deficient.

2

Thomas Diamond wasn't my real dad. I was nine years old when he first told me. I didn't even know what my real name was, but he and my mum, who was also not my mum, told me that they had found me in a forest when I was a baby.

At first, I was upset. In the stories I had read, babies found in forests were changelings who wreaked havoc on the families they invaded. I do have an imagination, despite what Dad often said. But Mum took me on to her knee and assured me that those stories were made-up fairy tales. I hated sitting on Mum's knee, or on Dad's knee, so I wrestled myself away from her and asked for a biscuit. I got two. I believed in Santa Claus right up until I was twelve years old and Dad sat me down and told me the sorry truth.

'But why would you make up such a thing?' I asked.

'It's a fun thing for children to believe, but you're not a little girl any more.'

And that was true. I had begun to bleed. The pain of the periods replaced the Tooth Fairy and the Easter Bunny, and Mum and Dad began to explain other things. 'If Santa Claus doesn't exist, does God, or the devil?' Mum looked to Dad and he said, 'Nobody knows.' I found that concept difficult. If they knew for a fact that Santa Claus didn't exist, why didn't they know for sure about God?

My childhood was replaced by duller, less colourful teenage years. Mum explained that boys might take an interest in me, that they might try to kiss me. They never did, except one time when I was fourteen and an old man tried to force

8

his mouth on to mine and crept his hand up my skirt at a bus shelter. I punched him in the face, kicked him to the ground and stamped on his head. Then the bus came and I got on, and was annoyed by the delay as the bus driver got off to help the old man. I watched him rise slowly to his feet, blood trickling from his head. The driver asked me what had happened, but I stayed silent and pretended that I couldn't hear him. I got home twenty minutes late and missed the start of *Blue Peter*.

When I was fifteen, I heard a girl in my class telling two others that I had been a feral child, found on the side of a mountain and then adopted by the Diamonds. She said this in the toilets. I was sitting on the cistern, my feet on the lid of the toilet in a cubicle, eating my lunch. 'You can't tell anyone,' she said. 'My ma heard it through a friend of hers who used to work for Dr Diamond when it happened. That's why she's so weird.'

The other girls did not keep it a secret. For a few weeks, they tried talking to me, asking me if I liked mountain climbing and if I ate grass. Stella Coughlan told them all to leave me alone, that it was none of their business. I ignored them all. I didn't ask Mum and Dad about it. I already knew I was adopted and I also knew that babies can't survive on mountains and that stupid girls make up things to be spiteful.

Mum died the year after I left school. We had been fighting a lot. She had wanted me to go to university. She had filled out my university application forms against my wishes. She thought I should study Music or the sciences. I love music and playing the piano is probably my favourite thing to do. Mum had a teacher come to the house to give me lessons when I was nine. I liked Mrs Mooney. She said I was a gifted pianist. She died when I was in my teens and I didn't want another teacher, so I taught myself to get better at it. I didn't want to take any exams. I just liked playing.

Mum said there were many options open to me. But I did not want to meet strangers and I did not want to leave our new home. Dad said I could do an Open University degree, but Mum said I needed to be 'socialized' because I would never leave the house or get a job if I wasn't pushed. I said I didn't want to leave the house, and she was angry.

The week after that argument, she had a stroke, while working in her GP practice in the village, and died in hospital. The funeral was in Dublin because that's where all her family and old friends lived. She had always visited them regularly. On the few occasions her sister, Christine, had visited us, I had followed her around like a dog. She was like a glamorous version of Mum. Dad would stay in his study when she visited. Mum said that Dad made Aunt Christine feel unwelcome. After Mum died, she stopped visiting but always sent me birthday cards with money in them.

Dad asked me with wet eyes if I would come to Mum's funeral, but I declined. I needed to sort out Mum's clothes and see which could fit me and which would go to the charity shop. I asked Dad to bring back a recipe book from Dublin because Mum had done most of the cooking and, while I was excellent at helping her peel vegetables, I wasn't so adept at pulling together a full meal. But I knew I could learn from books.

When Dad returned after two days in Dublin, he asked me if I was sad and if I missed Mum, and I reassured him that I didn't and he wasn't to worry about me. Dad looked at me in that funny way he had sometimes and said that I was probably lucky to be the way I was, that I could probably avoid heartache for my whole life.

I know I don't think in the way that other people do, but if I could stay away from them, then what did it matter? Dad said I was unique. I don't mind. I have been called so many things, but my name is Sally. At least, that's the name Mum and Dad gave me.

3

In the days after Dad died, it was quiet. Maybe I did miss him? I had nobody to talk to, nobody to make tea for, nobody to spoon-feed ice cream to. Nobody to wash and change. What was I for? I wandered around the house and, on the third day, I went into his office and idly opened his drawers, found a lot of cash and Mum's old jewellery in a metal box. Lots of notebooks documenting my weight and height and development going back decades. A fat envelope addressed to me on his desk. Files and files with my name on them in different categories: communication, emotional development, empathy, comprehension, health, medication, deficiencies, diet, etc. Too many to ever read. I looked at their wedding photo on the mantelpiece, and remembered how Mum said they never felt like a complete family until they found me. I had long since been disabused of the notion that I was a foundling child. They had adopted me in the ordinary way, Mum said. She had asked if I was curious about my birth parents, and when I said no, she beamed at me. I felt good when I made my parents smile.

I looked at Dad's old photos of his working days, presenting papers at conferences in Zurich. Photos of him with other earnest-looking men in suits. Dad mostly studied and wrote academic papers but sometimes, if called upon in an emergency by Mum, he might attend to a local patient in Carricksheedy or beyond.

He studied the human mind. He told me that my mind worked perfectly but that I was emotionally disconnected. I was his life's work, he said. I asked him if he could reconnect the emotions and he said that all he and Mum could do was love me and hope that, one day, I would learn to love them back. I cared about them. I didn't want any harm to come to them. I didn't like to see them upset. I thought that was love. I kept asking Dad, but he said I shouldn't worry, that whatever I felt was enough, but I don't think he understood me. I got anxious sometimes, if there were too many people around, or if I didn't know answers to questions, or if a noise was too loud. I thought I could recognize love from books and TV, but I remember watching *Titanic* one Christmas Day and thinking that Jack would have died anyway because he was a third-class passenger and a man, and Rose would most likely have survived because she was rich and it was 'women and children first', so what was the point of adding in the love story that wasn't even factually true. Dad was sobbing.

I didn't like hugging, or to be touched. But I never stopped wondering about love. Was that my emotional disconnection? I should have asked Dad when he was alive.

Five days after Dad died, a knock on the door came from Ger McCarthy, a neighbour who leased a field behind our barn. I was used to him coming and going up the lane. He was a man of few words and, as Dad used to say, he was 'a great man for asking no questions and making no small talk'.

'Sally,' he said, 'there's a wild smell out of that barn of yours. My cattle are all accounted for, but I'm after thinking that a sheep strayed in and got caught in there and died or something. Would you like me to take a look, or is your dad up to it?'

I assured him I could deal with it. He went on his way, whistling tunelessly, his overalls splattered with mud.

When I got out to the barn, the smell from the incinerator barrel made me gag. I wrapped my scarf around my mouth and opened the door. It hadn't burned properly. I could see the full shape of the body. There was an oily substance around the bottom of the barrel. Flies and maggots swarmed around it. I set the fire going again with rolled-up newspapers from the house and logs from the barn.

I felt disappointed with myself. Dad should have been more specific with his instructions. We burned organic matter regularly. Corpses were organic matter, weren't they? Maybe crematoriums were hotter. I would look it up in the encyclopaedia later. I poured in the rest of the petrol to get the fire started, hoping that a second burning would do the job. I pulled at my hair to calm myself.

I went to the post office to collect my benefits, and Mrs Sullivan tried to give me Dad's pension too. I pushed the cash back towards her and she looked at me quizzically and shouted, 'Your dad will be needing his pension.'

'He won't,' I said, 'because he died.' Her eyebrows went up and her mouth opened.

'Oh my God! You can speak. I never knew. Now, what did you say?' and I had to repeat that I wouldn't be needing Dad's pension any more because he was dead.

She looked behind me at the butcher's wife. 'She can speak,' she said, and the butcher's wife said, 'I'm amazed!'

'I am so sorry,' Mrs Sullivan continued to shout, and the butcher's wife reached out and put her hand on my elbow. I flinched and shrugged off her touch.

'When is the funeral?' she said. 'I never saw it on the death notices.'

'There's no funeral,' I said. 'I cremated him myself.'

'What do you mean?' said Mrs Butcher and I told her that

14

I had put him in the incinerator because he had told me to put him out with the bins when he died.

There was a silence, and I was turning to leave when Mrs Butcher said, with a tremor in her voice, 'How did you know he was dead?' And then Mrs Sullivan said to Mrs Butcher, 'I don't know who to call. The guards or a doctor?'

I turned back to her and said, 'It's too late for a doctor, he's dead. Why would you call the guards?'

'Sally, when somebody dies, the authorities have to be notified.'

'But it's none of their business,' I protested. They were making me confused.

When I got home, I played the piano for a while. Then I went into the kitchen and made a cup of tea. I took the tea into Dad's office. The phone began to ring and I turned it off. I looked at the envelope on his laptop with 'Sally' written on the front, and 'to be opened after my death' in Dad's shaky handwriting. It didn't say how long after his death I should open it, and I wondered if it might contain a birthday card. My birthday wasn't for another nine days, so I was going to wait until then. I would be forty-three years old. I felt like it was going to be a good year.

It was a large envelope and, when I picked it up, I could feel that it was thick and that it contained many pages. Maybe it wasn't a birthday card. I put it into the pocket of my skirt. I would read it after *Murder She Wrote* and *Judge Judy*. I settled myself into the living room on the sofa I used to share with Mum. I looked at Dad's empty armchair and thought about him for a few minutes.

I was soon distracted by the goings-on in Cabot Cove. This time Jessica Fletcher's gardener had been up to no good with the rich lawyer's widow and she killed him when he refused to leave his wife. As usual, Jessica outsmarted the Sheriff in solving the crime. During one of the ad breaks in *Judge Judy*, I heard a knock on the front door.

I was shocked. Who could it be? Perhaps Dad had ordered something on his computer, though that was unlikely because he hadn't used it for about a month before he died. I turned up the television loud as the knocking continued. It stopped and I had to rewind the TV because *Judge Judy* had started again and I'd missed a bit. Then a head appeared at the window to my left. I screamed. But it was only Angela.

4

Dr Angela Caffrey had been Mum's business partner and took over the practice after Mum died. I had visited the practice many times over the years. I didn't mind Angela touching me or examining me, because she always explained clearly what was going to happen. And she always made me better. Dad liked her and so did I.

'Sally! Are you all right? Mrs Sullivan told me Tom has died, is that right?'

I stood awkwardly at the door to Dad's study in the hall. In the past, Dad always invited Angela into the sitting room and offered her tea, but I didn't want her to stay long. Angela had other ideas.

'Shall we go through to the kitchen, and you can tell me all about it?'

I led her down the steps to the kitchen.

'Oh, you have the place spotless, your mum would be so proud. You know, I haven't been here for ages.' She pulled out Dad's chair from the table and sat down on it. I stood with my back to the range.

'So, Sally, did your father die?'

'Yes.'

'Oh, poor Tom! Was he ill for a long time?'

'He slowed down a lot and then he went to bed about a month ago and didn't get up.'

'I wonder why he didn't call me? I'd have come straight out. I could have made sure he was comfortable.'

'He wrote pain med prescriptions for me to get filled in Roscommon.'

'He wrote prescriptions for himself? That's not exactly legal.'

'He put them in my name. He said he wouldn't go to jail and neither would I.'

'I see.' She paused. 'And when exactly did he pass away?'

'I found him dead on Wednesday when I brought him in his tea in the morning.'

'Oh my dear, that must have been so distressing. Now, I don't want to pry but Maureen Kenny –'

'Who?'

'Maureen, the butcher's wife? She said that you said there was no funeral and that you had him cremated on your own.'

'Yes.'

'And where was this cremation held?'

'In the green barn.'

'Sorry?'

'The green barn.'

'Here? Behind the house?'

'Yes.'

'Did you not think to call someone? Me, the hospital, an undertaker?'

I felt like I was in trouble, like I'd done something wrong.

'He told me to put him out with the bins.'

'He . . . what? He was joking, he didn't mean that!'

'He didn't tell me it was a joke.'

'But how can you be sure he was dead?'

'He wasn't breathing. Do you want to see the incinerator?' I asked.

Her eyes opened wide. 'That's not the way to dispose of . . . Sally, this is serious. Only a medical professional can certify a death. Didn't he leave any instructions about his funeral?'

'No, I don't . . .' and then I remembered about the enve-lope. 'He left this for me.' I pulled it out of my pocket.

'And what does it say?'

'I haven't opened it yet.'

I was getting bothered with all of this talking. Either I don't talk at all, or I talk too much and I say things that don't make sense to anyone but me.

I put my hands over my ears and Angela moderated her voice.

'Would you like me to open it? May I read it?'

I threw the envelope at her and went to the piano, but it didn't calm me. I went to my room and crawled under the duvet and the soft blue blanket. I began to pull hair from my head. I didn't know what to do. I wondered when Angela would leave. I listened to hear the front door shut.

5

A soft knocking sound woke me up. It was dusk outside. I must have blacked out. It happens when I am distressed, though it hadn't happened in many years.

'Sally?' Angela whispered. I looked at my watch. She had been there for three hours and twenty-five minutes.

'Yes?'

'I've made some tea and beans on toast. You should get up because we have to talk.'

'Is there sugar in the tea?'

'Not yet,' she said, 'but I'll add some.'

'Which mug did you use?'

'I . . . I'm not sure.'

I opened the door and followed Angela down the hall.

She gave me my tea in Dad's Scrabble mug. I added a spoon and a half of sugar and an extra teaspoon of milk. She had made herself tea in a china mug that neither Dad nor I had ever used.

'So, I've read your dad's letters —'

'There's more than one?'

'Yes. It's okay, love. The thing is, I have to call the guards, and they will want to talk to you. But I don't want you to worry because I'm going to be with you, and I'll explain your condition to them and I'll make sure they are gentle with you. But, and this is the hard bit, they will probably want to search the house and you should come and stay with Nadine and me for a little bit, while they carry out their enquiries.'

'What enquiries?'

'It's just that . . . it's . . . unusual to burn a body of a family member, it's not legal, and I'm so sorry to tell you this, love, but there were funeral instructions in his letter . . . among other things.'

'Oh. Why would the guards want to search the house? On TV, they always leave a terrible mess.'

'They'd want to reassure themselves that your dad died of natural causes, but it's clear in his letter that he knew he had little time left. It's obvious that he trusted you, and that he loved you. I'm confident the post-mortem will show that he was already dead.'

'I don't want visitors and I don't want to come to your house.'

'Sally, if I can't control this, you might end up in a prison cell for a few nights or more. Please believe me. Your mum and dad would have wanted me to help you. In the letter, your dad said you should ring me when he died.'

I pulled at my hair again. She reached out but I flinched away from her. 'Sorry, I'm sorry, I wasn't thinking,' she said.

'But he didn't say when to open the letter. He just wrote to open it after he died. I didn't know I was supposed to open it that same day.'

'I know, but I'm afraid there is going to be a lot of fuss now. I'm going to call the guards, and they will want to interview you. You might need a solicitor. But I will be with you and I'll explain anything that your dad hasn't explained in the letters, although he was thorough.' She paused. 'There are things in the letters that you may find . . . upsetting. But we will take it slowly. Your dad only wanted you to read one section per week. There are three different parts.'

'Why?'

'Well, there's . . . a lot to take in. I thought your mum and dad were open with me about your circumstances, but it seems there was a lot they kept hidden from everyone.'

'About me?'

'Yes, Sally. But we can discuss that another time. I have to call the guards now. Would you like a mild sedative before they come? To help you stay calm?'

'Yes please.'

6

Two guards came, not one. One man, one woman. I didn't look at their faces. They were nice and calm until I told them I'd put my dad in a refuse sack and then into the incinerator. The smaller one raised her voice. 'What in the name of God did you do –'

Angela asked her to lower her voice. The pill that Angela gave me made me feel like I was in a kind of dream world. They said they would have to get a forensics team straight away and that I needed to pack a bag and leave the house, but that I must leave out the clothes I had worn the day my father died. They groaned when I presented them with a neat pile, freshly laundered. Angela said she needed to give a copy of Dad's letter to the guards and she photocopied it in his office while I went to my room to pack a bag. The woman guard followed me, tutting. I used Dad's suitcase. I didn't have one of my own. He wouldn't mind. It was dark, and it was after my bedtime.

'Will you please not make a mess?' I said. The man said they'd do their best and the woman made a harrumphing noise and said, 'You'll be lucky.' Angela gave the man the photocopied pages and asked him to make sure that they were given to the highest-ranking officers in the investigation. He nodded. He said little. He asked for the keys of the Fiat. I gave them to him but asked him to make sure they repositioned the seat when they were finished going wherever they needed to go in it. They said they would need me to come to the station in Roscommon in the morning. Angela said that she would bring me there herself.

As I left the house, I heard the woman guard say 'Fucking psycho' to the man, but he noted that I heard and shushed her. She turned to look at me and I was able to read disgust on her face.

I don't know why she was disgusted. The house was spotless. As I walked towards Angela's car, four patrol cars arrived through our gateway and people started putting on white plastic suits over their clothes. They set up these huge light beacons pointing towards the house and barn. Angela said they were treating it as a crime scene.

I was feeling a little drowsy but I wanted to stay. In lots of dramas, police planted evidence or contaminated the scene. I needed to make sure that wouldn't happen. Angela assured me that it wouldn't.

We didn't say much on the drive to her house, but I looked at her then while she watched the road. She was a nice rounded shape. Like grannies in old TV shows. She had curly grey hair. She wore a check shirt and a denim skirt and black ankle boots. I liked the way she looked. She glanced over at me and smiled and frowned at the same time. Dad always warned me about mistaking people for how they look with how they act, but we both liked Angela.

7

I woke up in a strange bed in a strange house, although my own blue blanket was on the bed. I had packed it last night. I opened my mouth to scream, but Dad had always said that I mustn't do that unless I was in danger. Was I in danger? I would shortly have to explain again why I had disposed of my dad. I shut my mouth and didn't scream. I remember Mum saying that if you tell the truth, nothing bad can happen to you.

I heard some commotion outside the bedroom door. 'Hello?' I called.

'Sally, I'm leaving some green towels inside the bathroom for you. The shower is easy to use. We'll see you downstairs for breakfast in about twenty minutes, okay?'

It was Nadine's voice. Nadine was Angela's wife. I had met her around Carricksheedy several times. She was younger than Angela and wore her long blonde hair in a ponytail. She walked their dogs and tended to their chickens and designed furniture for her job. I didn't like the dogs and always crossed the road. 'We've put the dogs outside so you don't have to worry, okay?'

Dad went to their wedding. I was invited too but I didn't go. Too much fuss.

Their bathroom was like you'd see in a hotel in a film, or in an ad for bathrooms. I sat on the toilet and then washed my hands and brushed my teeth before stepping into the large shower stall with one glass wall. We had one family bathroom at home and a separate toilet, and the shower was a rubber hose attached to the bath taps. Because of the electricity bills Dad didn't like us to take baths, except for once a week, so we made do with the shower. Angela and Nadine's shower was great. When I was finished, I combed out my hair in my room, pinned it up and got dressed, made the bed and went downstairs.

It was bright. The sun streamed in through glass doors and it was open plan. Modern. Every wall was straight, corners were sharp. I'd seen homes like this on TV in the 'afters' of a home-improvement show. Dad loved those. He always laughed at the homeowners. 'More money than sense!' he'd say, or 'Notions!'

Angela stood at the grill, flipping sausages and bacon. 'Will you have a fry, Sally?'

I was hungry. I hadn't eaten the beans on toast the night before because I'd been so disturbed.

'Yes, thank you.'

Two dogs were outside the window staring up at Angela as she turned the rashers once more.

'The boys look hungry,' said Nadine, and she grinned and waved at them. They barked in response.

'What boys?' I asked.

'The dogs, Harry and Paul.'

'They're funny names for dogs.'

Angela grinned, 'We called them after our ex-husbands,' and then they both laughed. I grinned too even though I thought it was a bit rude to their ex-husbands.

I was seven hours and fifteen minutes in the garda station. They took my photograph and fingerprints. They left me in a room by myself for the first forty-seven minutes and then two women came in, wearing suits, Detective Sergeant Catherine Mara and Detective Inspector Andrea Howard, shortly followed by a grumpy man who introduced himself as Geoff Barrington, my solicitor. Howard turned on a tape recorder and they introduced themselves for the tape. I didn't want to look at them, so I looked at the wooden table and the scratches in it. Someone had engraved the word 'cunt' into the table in spiky capitals. That was an extremely rude word.

They asked me three times to tell the story of my dad's death, and I got a bit annoyed at having to say the same thing over and over again. Geoff sighed deeply and said the best thing for me to do was to answer their questions. They asked me why I didn't know that a domestic incinerator wouldn't be hot enough to burn human remains. I shook my head. And they asked me to speak out loud for the record. I said I didn't know because we burned everything else that wasn't plastic.

Then they asked me about the letters and why I hadn't read them. One of them laughed when I said I'd been considering waiting for my birthday. I got angry then. 'Why are you laughing?' I shouted. Geoff put his hand on my arm, and I shook it off.

'Sally, do you wait for your birthday to open all of your mail?'

'I don't get any mail,' I answered.

He scribbled in his notebook again and asked them to refrain from laughing as it triggered his client. I stared at him then. He looked as tired as I felt.

Mara asked me my date of birth even though I'd been asked that twice already. They asked me about my real date of birth, and I wasn't sure what they meant. Then they asked me about my adoption and if I knew who my birth parents were and I was surprised because I didn't understand how this was relevant. I told them that Mum and Dad had adopted me from an agency when I was six years old and that I knew nothing about my birth parents. They asked me what my earliest memories were and I told them that it was when I blew out candles on my seventh birthday. They asked in several different ways if I remembered anything before that and I said no, and then they asked me to try to remember and I told them that my dad had always told me that I didn't have to remember things I didn't want to.

'But,' said Howard, 'you must remember something from early childhood?' I shook my head. They asked me to speak out loud for the record. 'I don't remember anything before my seventh birthday,' I said. Geoff asked to speak to them outside the room.

Shortly after that, Angela came in with a burger and chips from Supermacs. Another guard stood in the corner of the room. I offered him some chips but he refused. 'You're all right,' he said. I liked him. He looked a little bit like Harrison Ford when he was young. I would have liked to talk to him. But he went back to saying nothing, and looking at his shoes. I look at my shoes when I'm uncomfortable too.

Angela told me that the police would be at my house for a few more days and that I might be charged with a crime.

'What crime?' I asked.

She didn't answer. 'Let Geoff do his job. Honestly, he has your best interests at heart.'

8

I spent five nights in Nadine and Angela's house. Geoff talked mostly to Angela and ignored me, which most of the time suited me, but all the time, they were talking about me. Angela would check occasionally that I understood what was being said, but he didn't address anything to me, except the last time when we were in his office in Roscommon town, and he tried to shake my hand as he said goodbye, and I snapped mine away. It's easier to look at someone when they're not looking at you. He was handsome and I suppose he did his job properly because he said that the charges of Illegal Disposal of Human Remains would most likely be dropped under the circumstances. Angela said it was because of my condition.

Geoff and Angela agreed that it would not be lawfully possible for her to become my legal guardian or me to be made a ward of court as I was an adult and I had nearly always made my own decisions, even if some of them were 'misguided'. But Geoff said it might be a condition of the court that if I had a serious dilemma in the future I would ask Angela or a guard. Like, for example, if I ever thought of incinerating a body again, Angela would assess the situation and tell me what to do. I thought that wasn't a good example to give. I was hardly going to endure this kind of fuss again.

Geoff said my father left me money in his will. He didn't know exactly how much, because a lot of it was tied up in shares and bonds, and he was going to unravel it all, but 'Enough to keep you going for a good while, if you're careful,' he said. But I have to pay bin charges from now on and divide up my rubbish into compostable, recyclable, soft plastics and glass, and I will have different-coloured bins for each one and I will leave them at the gate on alternate weeks and bin men will come and take them away in their smelly truck. The postman will deliver post to the house, but I was assured he would never come into it. Angela says it will be much more convenient.

I didn't like staying at home on my own then because people kept turning up at my door. They wanted to interview me, or to get my 'side of the story'. They are a lot more interested in my adoption than my setting my dad on fire. I was confused by this. What could one have to do with the other?

Now everyone in Carricksheedy stared at me. A few of them smiled and put their heads to one side. Sympathetic. Some of them crossed the road when they saw me coming, and that was fine with me. Some of them began to say hello, even the young ones from the Texaco when they lifted their heads from their phones. They said, 'Hi, Mary!'

My name is Sally, no matter what they called me.

The police made a terrible mess of the house. I couldn't help screaming when I saw it. Angela and Nadine were with me. Angela made me breathe and count until I could find my centre and, when I did, we set about putting the house in order. After a while, I asked them to leave because they didn't know the exact place for everything, and it was easier to do it myself.

When she left on the third night after I came home, Angela said that she would call in twice a week to see me and that I was always welcome in her house. She handed me the first part of Dad's letter. She told me that I wasn't to feel sorry or sad. I knew by then that trying to burn Dad's body was the wrong thing to do. Everyone had told me so. When I am told something once clearly, without jokes or ambiguity, I understand completely. You'd think it was something I'd been doing for years, casually burning bodies, the way they went on about it. It was one body, and he had told me to do it, more or less.

When the house was finally set to rights, it was 13th December at 8 p.m. and I sat down to watch *Holby City*. In this episode, it was Essie's birthday, and I remembered that it was my birthday. I paused the television. How could I have forgotten? I never forget. But there had been so much distraction.

Over the past decade, I had made my own birthday cake from the Delia Smith recipe book. Even though I knew the recipe off by heart I liked to take down the cookery book. I liked Delia. Her photo on the cover was smiling and she was wearing a red blouse. I had always had at least one blouse like hers. Bright red and buttoned to the neck. She was reliable. I thought if I ever had a best friend, she'd be somebody like Delia.

It was too late to start cooking a birthday cake but I was forty-three. I decided to read Dad's first letter after *Holby City* was over. When it finished, I turned off the television. There were two pages. Every time Dad got a big letter, he used to drink a glass of whiskey while he read it. Now I was in charge of the house and it was time to do things like Dad did them, except for burning the rubbish obviously.

1st November 2017

Dearest Sally

I guess we both knew that this day would come soon and I'm sorry if you're sad about it, but I understand if you're not.

The first thing you should do is ring Dr Angela Caffrey. Her number is 085-5513792. Let her know that I have died. She might be surprised as I've kept away from her for so long but, like yourself, I don't like fuss and the prescriptions you've been filling for me in Roscommon have kept me pain-free. I worried that my mind might start to go, but when I go to bed tonight, I think I might stay there until the end. Getting up and dressed has caused me a degree of discomfort this last while, and I know you'll be a good girl for bringing me my meals and taking care of me.

I have pancreatic cancer. It started out as back pain a few months ago and a consultant in Dublin confirmed it was terminal. I think it's very advanced now, so you shouldn't have to mind me for long. If it goes on longer than six weeks, I'll ask you to ring Angela to get me moved to some godawful palliative care unit. Also, if I lose consciousness, you will call her. I know you don't like speaking on the phone but you'll do it because you're a smart girl.

As regards my funeral arrangements, I realize that I was never clear about the details so please ring O'Donovan's undertakers in Roscommon. Angela will help you with that. Ordinarily, I should be buried with your mother above in Dublin, in Glasnevin, but you know I don't like Dublin much. You and I are alike in that way.

The accounts are all up to date. You have a bank account with the AIB in Roscommon town. The manager there is Stuart Lynch. He'll be understanding and there is more than enough money in that account to tide you over until probate goes through and you inherit everything. Your mother came from a wealthy family, and we have lived frugally specifically so that you could enjoy a debt-free life after my death. Our solicitor is Geoff Barrington at Shannonbridge. He knows everything he needs to know about you, and he'll make sure you are well looked after. He knows things that you don't know, but we'll get to that later.

I'd like the funeral service to be held in St John's Church of Ireland in Lanesborough. It's such a pretty church and the graveyard

is a nice spot. I'm not going to make too many demands, but I'd love
if you could arrange for the choir to sing 'Be Thou My Vision'. I
was in the school choir when I was a little boy. That was my favourite
song, because we used to change some of the words around to make
each other laugh. Oh dear, we got up to some mischief in those days.
I am rambling.

You don't have to attend the funeral if you don't want to, but I
would like you to be there if you think you can manage it. I don't
think there'll be more than ten people there and you'll know all of
them. Some of the nosey parkers from Carricksheedy might show up
but you could ignore them. I think I have given you enough trouble
already and you will have a busy week, so I'd like you to take things
slowly. Please don't read the next part of the letter until next week.

Your loving Dad

I finished the whiskey and rang Angela. 'There has to be a
funeral,' I said.

'I know, love. If you don't mind, I've already set things in
motion? I have a copy of your dad's letter here. I rang the
undertakers. The coroner has agreed to release the remains
as soon as we want so we don't have to do much planning.
The only thing is that St John's doesn't have a choir. I didn't
know that your dad was a churchgoer?'

'He wasn't, but sometimes in the summer, when Mum was
alive, we'd go out and have a picnic out there.'

'In the graveyard?'

'Sometimes.'

'Do you want to go, Sally?'

'No, but I will.'

'It's just that, because it was a national story, there might
be —'

'He wanted me to go.'

'I know, but –'

'I'm going. Will you and Nadine come too, please?'

'Of course we will. But –'

'Thank you. Have you got a date yet?'

'I was waiting for you to read the letter and decide.'

'Can we have it tomorrow?'

'I'm afraid that's too soon to arrange everything. Perhaps next Tuesday?'

'That's nearly a week away.'

'I don't think it can be done sooner. I'll have to warn the guards.'

'Why?'

'Lots of people are interested in you, Sally. I guess you don't realize how unusual it is to burn your father's body, and there are other things . . . in the letters.'

'I guess my birth name is Mary? A few people have greeted me on the street.'

'Please, don't buy any newspapers or listen to the radio or watch the news.'

'Why?'

'You are headline news and so much of what they are saying is speculation. It would be impossible for anyone to glean the truth. The facts are in your dad's letters.'

'I'm not allowed to read another one until next week.'

Angela sighed deeply.

'I have to go now. *Line of Duty* is on,' I said.

'Okay, love, do you want me to call around tomorrow? Do you need anything?'

'No, thank you.' I hung up.

9

The next Saturday morning, I was mopping the kitchen floor when I heard a noise outside and saw a boy on a bicycle passing the kitchen window at the back of the house, cycling over rough grass, heading towards the barn. He was followed moments later by two more boys and a smaller girl who was sitting on the back carrier of one of the boy's bicycles. It didn't look safe to me. I'm not good at guessing ages but I thought the boys might be somewhere between twelve and eighteen. Lanky ones and Black ones and freckly ones.

I opened the back door and stepped outside.

'What are you doing here?' I called out.

'Shit, it's her!' shouted the lanky one and the small girl screamed. The boys swerved their bikes and pedalled furiously towards the side of the house. 'Strange Sally Diamond, the weirdo!' shouted the freckled boy as he disappeared from view. The Black boy was barely looking where he was going and bumped over the shovel lying in the grass. As he did, the girl fell off the back of his bike and banged her head on the shovel's handle as it lifted against the weight of him and his bicycle. It was like something I had seen on a Bugs Bunny cartoon. He didn't stop. The boys all sped off.

I expected the girl to cry. She had been screaming hysterically since she saw me. But she lay flat on the grass, still and silent.

I moved towards her cautiously. Her eyes were closed. I put my hand on her face and it was hot. I put my arm around her narrow chest and it rose and fell with her heartbeat. She wasn't dead. I suspected concussion. Dad had given me a course in first aid, and every year on 1st October we refreshed it. It was to protect myself, he'd said, but he also said I could help other people if I happened upon an accident. I had never happened upon an accident before. I lifted her head and, sure enough, I could feel a swelling at the back of her head underneath her hair. There was no blood. No immediate need for alarm. I picked her up from the grass and carried her, one arm under her bottom, the other cradling her head over my shoulder. I took her inside and laid her down on the sofa in the sitting room. I covered her with a rug to keep her warm, as I hadn't lit the fire yet, and then went to get ice from the freezer in the kitchen. I emptied a full tray of ice cubes into a clean hand towel and returned to the sitting room. I gently lifted her head and applied the home-made ice pack to the swelling. Her eyes fluttered open, and they widened in shock when they saw me. She screamed again and I knew that she was frightened.

'Does it hurt?' I asked.

She scrambled backwards from my touch, and I realized that I hadn't minded touching or holding or carrying this girl while she'd been knocked out. I held out the ice pack and said, 'You should hold that to the back of your head and lie still for a while. You are concussed. I'll have to ring Dr Caffrey. Would you like a glass of brandy?'

She shook her head and then winced.

'You must try to keep still. Are you pretending not to be able to talk? I do that all the time. Are you like me?'

She stared at me and her eyes filled with tears. She had a pretty little face. After a few moments, her lips trembled and then she said, 'I want my mum.'

I sighed. 'So do I, but I only noticed recently, after my dad died. Is your mum alive?'

'Yes.' Her voice grew more high-pitched. 'Will you ring her, please?'

Ah. A question. A question I didn't like. I didn't like speaking on the phone to strangers.

'I'll ring Dr Caffrey and she can ring your mum, okay?'

'Okay.'

I remembered that children love sweet things. 'Would you like a chocolate biscuit?'

'Can you ring my mum first?'

'Fine.'

I went to get the phone from Dad's study and brought it back into the sitting room. She was sitting up now on Dad's chair on the other side of the room, but she held the towel of ice to her head.

As I was about to ask for her number, she asked, 'Can I ring Mum myself?'

That seemed like a good idea. I passed her the phone. She dialled furtively. I don't think she wanted me to see the number.

'Mum, can you come and get me, please? . . . I'm in –' she looked up at me – 'Strange Sally Diamond's house . . . Yes, I know. She's here . . . In the room with me. I was on Maduka's bike. He cycled away and I fell off . . . I don't know where he is . . . please come and get me . . . hurry . . . no,' she whispered, 'but she asked me if you were dead . . . I don't know . . . Maduka and Fergus and Sean wanted to see where she – you know –' she looked up at me again – 'where she did it . . .'

Then a stone came crashing through the window of the room and landed at my feet. I looked out to see the two white boys picking up stones from the gravel drive and hurling them towards the window. The girl ducked down in the chair. The back of the chair would shield her from flying glass.

I ran to the front door.

'Let her go!' said the freckled boy.

'She is concussed because you, Maduka,' I pointed to the Black one, 'dropped her off your bike and she hit her head. She's on the phone to her mother right now.'

'Oh man, I'm going to be in so much trouble.'

'You've broken my window. Drop those stones right now.'

'Killer Sally Diamond!' said the lanky one, but they dropped their stones.

The girl came to the door. She still had the phone in her hand. She looked up at me and handed me the phone. 'Mum wants the address.' I didn't want to talk to her mum. I didn't want any of these children on my property and I didn't want a broken window. 'You,' I said, pointing to Maduka, 'tell her where I live.' Maduka approached and I could read fear in his face too.

He took the phone from me. 'Hi, Mum,' he said in a low voice and wandered away with the phone. I didn't look at the other two boys' faces but I noticed them picking up their bikes and edging slowly up the driveway towards the gate. By the time Maduka handed back the phone, they were gone.

Maduka and the girl sat on the sofa together while I cleaned up the broken glass and set the fire going. They whispered to each other as I cut up a piece of cardboard and taped it to the window.

Then I gave them chocolate biscuits and they took one each, sniffing them first, and then Maduka licked his and nodded to the girl and they both ate their biscuits in a hurry, dropping crumbs into their laps. We sat in silence.

Eventually, Maduka coughed and said, 'Did you do it?'

I avoided looking at him.

'Do what?' I'm not normally good at guessing but I had a good idea what he was going to ask.

'Kill your own dad and then burn him? I mean, did you burn him alive?'

'No. I did not. He was dead that morning when I brought him his cup of tea, so I put him out with the bins and we always incinerate most of our rubbish so I thought it was the best thing to do.'

'Are you absolutely sure that you did not kill him?'

'One hundred per cent. I took his pulse. Nothing. The guards agreed that I didn't kill him. I made a mistake by burning his body. I didn't know that I wasn't supposed to do that. If I had killed him, I'd be in jail, wouldn't I?'

'That's not what they said at school.'

'Schools are full of liars. When I was at school, everybody lied about me. It was a dreadful place.'

The children looked at each other. Maduka said, 'Fergus said that I smell.'

'Of what?'

'I don't know . . . I guess that I smell . . . bad.'

I approached him without getting too close and sniffed the air.

'See? They are liars. You don't smell of anything. Why are you hanging around with eejits like Fergus? Was he the freckly one?'

'No, he's the tall one.'

The girl smiled. 'My name is Abebi.'

'You don't look like a baby.'

She giggled and spelled her name. I smiled back at her.

'Do they say that you smell too?'

'No, but some girls say I should keep washing so that my face would be white.'

'Stupid girls.'

Their mum came to collect them. I heard and then saw the car in the driveway. I told them to go on out. The boy said, 'I will make Sean and Fergus pay for your window. I told them not to throw stones, but they wouldn't listen.'

'Do they have jobs?'

'No, we're only twelve,' he said.

'I'll pay for the window, then. I have lots of money now.' He smiled. 'Thank you.'

'Do you want to come to my dad's funeral on Tuesday?'

Abebi looked up at me with her big eyes. 'We have school.'

'I wouldn't bother going to school if I were you,' I said. 'Waste of time.'

The mother was outside putting the boy's bicycle into the boot of her car. She did not approach the doorway but she was craning her neck to see me. I stood back behind the door, out of sight. She was a white lady. I heard her shouting at the children, 'Hurry up! Get out of here! Wait until I get you home!'

I played Mum's game of trying to imagine what she thought of me and I realized that she must be scared. Maybe a lot of people were scared of me. Except perhaps those two children. I liked them. Maduka and Abebi. I forgot to ask Abebi what age she was. I wanted to know. I wanted to know what house they lived in and what TV shows they watched and if their dad was nice like mine.

10

The next day, early, there was a knock on the door. It was Angela. Her eyebrows were furrowed and her lips were thin. This meant she was annoyed.

'Sally! What were you thinking? You can't take strange children into your house!'

'I did not invite them. They trespassed. I treated one of them for concussion and I gave them chocolate biscuits.'

'You told them not to go to school!'

'I liked them.'

'Yes, well, it took me a while to calm down their mother and explain your situation. Sally, please, try to think about the consequences of your words and actions, especially with children. I'm a full-time GP. I had to get a locum in last week while I dealt with your crisis.'

'What crisis?'

Her face was red, but then she cracked a smile and then laughed out loud. 'Sally, you are a crisis. You don't mean to be, but if you have doubts about anything, you must ask me, okay?'

'But I don't have doubts about anything.'

'That's what I'm afraid of. Mrs Adebayo understands everything now, but all she had heard were the rumours that you'd killed your dad. I talked her around and, luckily, the children did say you were nice to them.'

'The white boys broke my window.'

I showed Angela the damage and asked her to call a glazier.

'Sally, I know it's hard for you, but you are going to have to learn to do things for yourself. Like calling a glazier. Oh God, you don't have a smartphone, do you? Or a laptop. But you know how to look up the Golden Pages? You still have one, don't you? I saw it on the hall table.'

I nodded.

'Well, find one that's local to here and ask them to come out and fix it.'

I started to pace the room.

'Sally, I know your dad meant well, but he was overprotective. You should have gone to college. Jean was right.' Jean was my mother's name. She and Dad had argued over whether I should go to university. Dad won.

'I don't like talking to strangers.'

'Well, you brought two strangers into your house yesterday, and you had no problem talking to them. Did you invite them to your dad's funeral?'

'Yes.'

'Why? They are children.'

'I liked them.'

'Well, there you go. So you don't dislike all strangers.'

I hadn't thought of it like that.

'So, find a glazier in Roscommon and ask them to come out and fix the window, okay?'

'But what if he's mean, or if he attacks me, or if he's one of those that thinks I killed my dad?'

'Most people know the truth, and the ones that don't are, well . . .'

'They're scared of me?'

'I'd say the glazier will come out, fix the window and get out as soon as he can.'

'So I won't have to make him a cup of tea?'

'You won't have to do anything except pay him.'

'In cash?'

'Yes, he'll probably prefer that. Look, I have to go. I'll be late for work. Ring me only if there are any problems. Put your phone back on the hook, so that I don't have to keep coming out to the house. I'll see you on Tuesday at the funeral, but I am busy.'

I knew I should say sorry. 'Sorry, Angela.'

'Fortunately, you're yesterday's news. The media circus has moved on. A county councillor has been accused of taking six million euro in bribes and a man in Knockcroghery murdered his best friend yesterday. I have to go. Bye!' And she left, leaving a whiff of antiseptic after her. I liked that smell. She was always clean.

As she was getting into the car, she called out, 'Oh, and we'll have to do something about Christmas. You'll come to us.'

The initial phone call to the glazier was not as difficult as I imagined. I practised a few times before I lifted the phone. The directions to the house were the most difficult part. There would be a call-out fee of €80 since I lived so far out of Roscommon and then I'd have to pay for the glass and the time spent to fit it, and I would have to measure the window and call them back. The woman's voice was pleasant and foreign, though I couldn't place it.

I measured the window and called the lady back. This time, her attitude was different, and because I couldn't see her face, I could not tell her mood. She verified my name and the address again, and then asked if I was the daughter of Thomas Diamond.

'Yes,' I answered.

'Fine,' she said. 'Alex will be there in the morning about ten a.m.'

Alex arrived promptly, fitted the window and was gone in less than an hour. He barely spoke to me and I stayed in the kitchen. I counted out the cash and then he said, or mumbled, 'I'm sorry about your father.'

'I shouldn't have tried to burn him. That was a misunderstanding.'

He said nothing more and got into his van and drove away.

Tuesday 19th December was the funeral service. I drove myself to the church despite Angela's offer. She said it was normal to travel in a cortège behind the hearse, but I couldn't see the point. Two guards stood at the gates and kept the photographers at bay. Contrary to what Angela had predicted, I was still news. I noticed people with mobile phones holding them up towards me as I approached the church. The whole village must have shut down because everyone was there. I didn't know most of their names, but I recognized all the faces.

I wore the black coat that Mum had worn for funerals. I had a green dress on under that (also Mum's) because she'd been buried in her black dress. I also wore my black boots and a red sequinned beret that Dad said was for special occasions. I'd worn it once when we went to Fota Island Wildlife Park when Mum was alive. That was a good weekend. But this was a special occasion too.

The faces I recognized all wanted to take my hand and shake it. I snatched it back each time, but then Angela was by my side. 'Shaking hands is a way of them sympathizing with your loss. Please try and let them. Nice hat, by the way. I think your dad would have approved.' I had seen funerals on television. I knew shaking hands and crying and blowing your nose were expected. I asked Angela for one of her pills.

I let my hand be shaken by about forty people then. In the middle of it, Angela hissed at me, 'You're supposed to shake their hands too.'

I didn't like it. I didn't like all these people being there. I'm sure some of them barely knew my dad, but they all had something to say about him.

'He was good to us when Mammy had her breakdown, God rest her soul.'

'He always had his eye out for a bargain.'

'If it wasn't for your dad, I'd be in the river,' said one rheumy-eyed old man. I knew that Dad had very occasionally seen patients of Mum's when she begged him back in the day.

Nadine led me away by the elbow. I don't mind people touching my elbow. 'Some friends of yours have come,' she said and I didn't know who she was talking about, but behind the mob of locals, I spotted Abebi and Maduka and their mother and, I assume, their father.

I ignored the other mourners and went straight over to them. Mr Adebayo said, 'My name is Udo and you've seen my wife, Martha. I want to offer my condolences and to apologize for my children trespassing on your property on Saturday. Maduka admitted on the way here that his friends broke your window. Please let us reimburse you for your costs.' He spoke fast. I think his accent was Nigerian. So, the children were not adopted like me. Maduka's face was tear-stained.

Martha spoke then. 'We have warned them never to bother you again.'

'You don't have to pay me for the window. It's already fixed and paid for. The glazier was scared of me. I think the boys were worried that I'd put Abebi into the incinerator. Not their fault.'

Here I was, talking too much. And then I did something else unusual. I put my hand out and rubbed Maduka's face. 'They are good children. I don't think their friends were. Sean and Fergus.' I have an excellent memory.

'I'm not allowed to play with them any more,' said Maduka. Martha muttered about them being a bad influence.

'I thought the least ours could do is come here to show how sorry they are about everything,' Martha said. Abebi let go of her mother's hand and looked up at me. 'We are doing the nativity play on Thursday. I'm playing the Virgin Mary. Will you come and see us?' I was considering the invitation when we were distracted by the arrival of the hearse.

I tried to think what kind of mess was in the coffin. Poor Dad. I should have called Angela that day. But he should have written 'Open on the Day I Die' on the envelope. In capital letters. Underlined.

Everyone in the churchyard went quiet and Angela guided me to the back of the hearse where they were unloading the coffin on to a clever fold-up trolley. We walked behind the undertakers and followed them into the small, pretty church. Nadine told me she had organized flowers. I thought it was a waste to buy flowers for a dead man but I also knew not to voice all my thoughts. The ruddy-cheeked vicar came to shake my hand. I put them both in my pockets.

He had asked me to visit him the night before, but I told him over the phone that I didn't like meeting strange men. He reminded me that he had met me several times when I was a young girl when I used to go to church with Mum. I told him he still qualified as a strange man, so he agreed to discuss the arrangements over the phone. He asked some questions about Dad and I told him the answers.

'Our numbers are dwindling every year. I don't suppose you would consider attending, even on an irregular basis?'

'No,' I'd said, 'it's very boring.'

The church was stiflingly warm. I don't think it had ever seen so many Catholics in it. I was an Anglican technically, but Dad and I agreed some years ago that we were atheists.

We took our seats at the front pew, Nadine and Angela on

either side of me. Mrs Sullivan, the postmistress, and Maureen Kenny and her husband, the butcher, stood behind us. Ger McCarthy stood in the pew opposite ours. I had never seen him in a suit before. And he was clean-shaven. I looked for Maduka and Abebi but they must have been down the back.

It was the usual boring stuff except that the coffin was in front of us. The vicar made a sermon about how my father had been such a big part of the community, which was a surprise because Dad avoided the community as much as I did. Angela made a speech in which she remembered my mother and said that no matter what mistakes had been made after my father's death, he would be proud of me today. There was a smattering of applause after that, and I knew Angela was right, because Dad often said how proud he was of me. I grinned at Angela.

After the ceremony, we went out to the graveyard where we used to picnic, and a hole had been dug for my dad's coffin. Half of the people left then. Ger McCarthy shook my hand and said he was sorry for my trouble. Quite a lot of people said those same words before they drifted away. But I spotted the Adebayo family and I was glad they'd stayed. It started to rain heavily like it does at funerals on TV. The coffin was lowered into the hole and finally we could leave.

Angela had said those who attended the funeral might expect to have been invited back to the house. Some neighbours had given her food, sandwiches, pies and cakes. It was traditional, apparently. But I didn't know them. Why would I invite them to my house? I was told the villagers were now going to the pub. Nadine and Angela invited me to their house, but I was tired and wanted to go home to bed.

As I approached the car, Abebi came up beside me and said, 'We're sorry about your daddy and we're sorry about trespassing.'

Her family were behind her. Udo said, 'If there is anything you need doing around the house, I'm sure Maduka would be happy to attend to it, or I can if it's too difficult for him.'

'Just . . . please . . .' said Martha, 'don't tell them not to go to school. They like it.'

I said nothing for a moment and then I asked, 'Could they come for afternoon tea one day after school?'

Martha looked at Udo. Abebi put her soft little hand in mine and I didn't pull away.

'I'm not sure. They have homework . . .' said Martha.

'I was excellent at homework. Maybe I could help them?'

'We'll see, after the holidays?'

'How are you spending Christmas?' It seemed like the question I heard most people asking. I wanted to keep the conversation going. Most unusual for me.

'The regular family day. Church in the morning. Then Santa Claus and turkey and hyper chocolate-filled children and a TV film in the evening.'

'May I come?' I asked.

Angela was behind me. She laughed and touched me on the elbow. 'You're so funny, Sally. Don't worry, Martha, she's coming to us for Christmas.'

I hate it when people laugh at me. I pulled at my hair.

'I don't always say the right thing.' I knew I'd got it wrong somehow. 'I'm socially deficient, you know.'

'I wish you'd stop describing yourself that way,' Angela said.

I had learned that those two words were useful in situations of confrontation or confusion. There was a pause in the conversation. Martha and Angela were both blushing. I stared at them each in turn.

'I like your hat,' said Martha.

'Thank you, it's for special occasions.'

I played the piano when I got home. It's calming. But I felt tired and went for a nap. I woke as dusk was settling, remembering it was almost the shortest day of the year. I hadn't eaten since breakfast. I put some of the food from the neighbours in the fridge and freezer. I thought about how they must see me. The people who prepared food weren't scared of me. I doubt that most of the people in the church were scared of me. Nadine said that I'd made a mistake and they knew I was unusual. I know she meant socially deficient.

As I put a beef stroganoff into the microwave (it came with helpful instructions from 'Caroline in the Texaco'), I realized it was nearly a week since I'd read the first of Dad's letters. I ate my dinner and poured a glass of whiskey. The food was tasty. I was surprised. Dad had always said there was no point in me trying new things because I was so set in my ways. I'd have to find Caroline in the Texaco and ask her for the recipe. I am good at following recipes.

I opened the envelope and pulled out the second part of Dad's letter.

Dearest Sally,

I have spent most of your life keeping you away from psychotherapists, psychiatrists (apart from me) and psychologists.

My profession would never admit this but most of what we do is not very scientific, more like guesswork. Every decade or so, we come up with new labels to categorize people. You could have been diagnosed with anxiety disorder or PTSD. Some might even have said you had Autistic Spectrum Disorder, or that you had an attachment disorder. The fact is that you are a bit odd, that's all.

You are you. As unique and different as every other person on the planet. Your oddities are not disabilities (although we call them disabilities to get your welfare allowance), they are mere quirks of your personality. You don't like talking on the phone and I don't like cauliflower. Are we so different?

I have never been able to diagnose you because none of those categories make sense of the person you are. No label would be able to account for all the contradictions of your behaviour. Sometimes, you are curious. Other times, you couldn't care less. You are emotional about things that wouldn't matter to other people but can be unmoved by things that would devastate others. You don't like talking to strangers, but occasionally I cannot stop you talking to them; remember when the Jehovah's Witnesses came to the house?

Most of the time, you don't like when people look at you, but sometimes you stare people in the face, examining them. (I guess that you want to know more about them. I need to remind you that makes people a little uncomfortable.) Your behaviour has always been inconsistent. It is not bad. But you don't fit any diagnosis of which I am aware.

The issue now is that I don't think it's wise for you to live alone out here. I may have been unwise to indulge your self-isolation. I'm not sure that you ever feel lonely. Your decision-making processes aren't always what we refer to as 'normal' and that can lead to trouble and uncomfortable situations. I think you need guidance. Sometimes, you become confused about issues that are important. Your reluctance to approach people is to your detriment. I know that you like and trust Angela, but you cannot depend on her for everything. She runs a busy practice. And she and Nadine need time with each other also so you can't go running to them with every question. I have made you dependent. That was my mistake.

I feel responsible for you being such a loner and this house doesn't help. It has already begun to deteriorate here and there, like me. And it is too isolated, like you.

The car isn't going to last forever and, while you could easily get another car, I think your mother was right all those years ago when she said we should find a way to socialize you. I know you hated living in Roscommon town but you need to be around more people. Would you consider moving into Carricksheedy village? Also, you don't need a three-bedroom house. It was selfish of me to allow you to spend your time alone in this house with only me for company.

We have let the back field grow wild and unkempt. Do you remember when your mother maintained it as a wildflower meadow? It hummed with bees and butterflies in the summertime. It is one of my many regrets that we did not keep that up. You made up a song about it. Please keep up that singing and playing the piano for the rest of your life, it brings you peace and no doubt could bring joy to others.

I think Ger McCarthy has had his eye on the land for a while. He asked me about it a few years back but I was afraid to make changes that might upset you. I treated you like a child. I'm sorry, my love. He'd probably renovate the house and farm the land that adjoins his own. He's already leasing the second back field, as you know. I'd advise you to sell to him, but be guided by the estate agent. This house is a good-sized bungalow with big rooms, although neglected. But the acres surrounding it are fertile and ideal for cattle grazing. As secluded as we are, the village is spreading outwards. There are apartments on the main street now. Who would have thought it? Maybe you should see if there is one for sale?

Would you consider getting a job? I can't think of anything that would suit you but I think getting away from home on a regular basis would be good for you.

By the way, you don't have to worry about the bills, they all are on a direct debit and Geoff Barrington will see to it that they continue to be paid while probate is processed.

In the beginning I thought it was funny that you pretended to be deaf. But now, I think it was unwise. You should talk to people. Ask them about themselves. A simple 'How are you?' is enough to start a conversation. Try to look them in the face. Even if you don't want to know the answer, you will eventually develop friendships. The only opportunity you had to do that was in school and, despite your unhappy experience there, there were some nice girls who tried to help you. Remember them? In the outside world, you will find more people who are kind than people who are not. Seek them out.

Janet Roche runs a painting class and it would be a nice way to get to know people. Ian and Sandra in the library in Roscommon run all kinds of groups and I know they run a class to teach people how to use computers. It doesn't cost anything. I'd start with that if I were you.

That is all for now, my love. Have a good week. Before you open the last letter next week, I want you to have a good meal and a small whiskey. There is a lot of information to take in and I don't want to bombard you with everything all at once.

Your loving Dad

Why would I move house? I liked living here. I didn't want to be in the village, and I certainly didn't want to socialize. I could be a childminder perhaps. To Abebi and Maduka. Martha and Udo might let me look after them sometimes. They wouldn't have to pay me.

Another curious thing. Dad had said PTSD in his letter. I knew that meant Post-traumatic Stress Disorder. What trauma was he talking about?

13

The next day, I went to the post office. There was a long queue of people chattering as I opened the door but, as they turned and saw me, a hush descended. The woman in front of me had been at the funeral. 'We never knew you could talk,' she said.

'How are you?' I asked, as Dad had suggested, but instead of answering, she said, 'I'm Caroline from the Texaco, I dropped a casserole to your door a few days ago. It must be hard to prepare meals or to think straight when you're grieving.'

'It was delicious,' I said. 'May I have the recipe?'

I looked her in the face. Her lipstick was red and her eyes were blue, and I think she might have been a bit younger than me, but I am not good at guessing ages.

'Sure, will I email it to you?'

'I don't use a computer, but I'm going to take some classes after Christmas in the library. They are free.' I had ascertained this by phoning the library that morning and the conversation was easy and the man, Ian, was nice.

'Do you have a mobile? I could text it to you?'

'No.'

'I'll write it out, then, and you come see me in the Texaco and I'll give it to you.'

'Thank you. I think straight, by the way, but I am emotionally disconnected so I don't process grief in the normal way. How are you?' I thought I'd try again.

'Busy,' she said and held out a sheaf of envelopes. 'Trying to get Christmas cards into the post before it's too late.'

The postman had delivered cards to the house over previous weeks. Some were addressed to Dad and some were addressed to me. I thought I should probably open them.

I couldn't think of anything else to say to Caroline.

The queue had moved slowly, many customers pushing unwieldy parcels through Mrs Sullivan's open window at the counter.

'So, where will you be spending Christmas?' Caroline asked.

'Angela and Nadine have sort of invited me, but I'm not sure if I'll go. I might stay at home.'

'The lesbians?' she said.

'Yes,' and I looked into her face again and there was a frown on it. What had I said that was wrong?

'You wouldn't want to be hanging out with them much. I go to a doctor in Roscommon since your mum died. People might think you're one of them.'

'One of what?'

'You know. Lesbians.' She whispered the word.

'Well, I'm theoretically heterosexual,' I said.

She stared at me and gave me a confused face.

'I've never had sex, so I can't be one hundred per cent sure.'

She turned away then and it seemed like the conversation was over. But that had been an actual chat and I was proud of myself. She took her phone out of her pocket and started scrolling. After she had been served, she nodded at me before leaving. 'Goodbye,' I said, 'it was nice to chat,' but she didn't reply.

At the window, Mrs Sullivan put her head to one side. 'Sally,' she said, 'how have you been?' She still shouted as if I was deaf.

'Fine, thank you. I need to get an address for Martha Adebayo, please. She isn't in the phone book.'

'Martha the yoga teacher?' she shouted.

'I don't know what she does. She has a husband called Udo and two children.'

'I know who you mean. Her studio is down Bracken Lane by the butcher's,' she said. 'Sunflower Studio. I don't think I can give out her home address. Why do you want it?'

I pretended to be deaf again and turned around and left. 'Happy Christmas!' she called after me. I didn't return the greeting.

'Poor thing,' she said to the man behind me. 'I think her hearing comes and goes.'

I walked up the hill and turned left on to Bracken Lane at the butcher's shop. The Sunflower Studio was right next door. I remember when it used to be a florist, but then a supermarket opened up in the village of Knocktoom, five miles away, and gradually the florist, the grocer's and the bakery all closed, leaving only the small Gala supermarket and the Texaco.

A large glass shop window revealed six women and one man with their backs to it, legs stretched, bums in the air, arms reaching forward. Martha stood with her back to them, and they all rose and reached their hands to the ceiling with splayed fingers and then bent forward as she did, dropping their arms and shoulders and shaking their hands to release tension. I had followed an exercise class like this on morning TV a few years ago. Dad used to join in sometimes. He said it was good for me to get exercise, but apart from long walks around our land, I hadn't done that much recently.

The class was over. The students all retrieved layers of clothes from neat piles on a shelved unit and started to put them on. I guessed there were no shower facilities here and I thought again about Angela and Nadine's perfect shower.

I heard Martha's voice then. 'Sally! Come in. Did you want to sign up for a class?'

I pushed through the door as the others passed me. I didn't look up until we were alone. 'How are you?' I said.

'Not bad. A bit sweaty.' The room was warm and I could see the florist's counter was still there. She went to a water fountain. 'That's the last class before Christmas, but you'd be welcome to join us on 4th January. A hundred euro for eight classes. I'm sure you could do with some loosening up?'

'Would you like a childminder for free?'

'Sorry?'

'I know I have no experience but my mum always said I should get a job and your children are the first children that I've met that I liked. I could feed them, and I've done a first-aid course so they'd be perfectly safe, and I was a good student so perhaps I could help them with their homework.'

All the words rushed out of me and I looked into her face to see if she understood me.

'And I've stocked up on chocolate biscuits and I promise I won't tell them not to go to school. I would do exactly what you tell me. You could write it down for me. I'm excellent with instructions. I could collect them and drive them home, as often as you like.'

She was grinning. This was a good sign. We sat on two chairs while she drank a plastic glass of water.

'I'm so glad you like my children.'

'So, about the childminding?'

'Look, no offence, Sally, but I'm not sure you're the right . . . fit for that kind of job. Besides, I only work part-time, I can be home when school finishes. We don't need a childminder.'

I was annoyed. 'Why do you think I'm not the right fit?'

'Sally, you have no proper qualifications. I'm glad you like my kids but the fact that they are the only kids you like is . . .

weird. What if they misbehaved with you? I don't know how you would handle discipline if you were angry with them.'

'Usually, when I am angry or depressed, I pull my hair out,' I said.

'Oh my God! Don't you see how that would upset them?'

'I wouldn't pull their hair out, and sometimes I play the piano to calm myself.'

'I'm sorry, Sally. If you're looking for a job, I don't think childminding is right for you. But, you know, I honestly think yoga might help you to cope with stress. Think about it. First two classes for free. What do you say?'

She was smiling again. 'I'll think about it,' I said and turned to leave. 'Will you tell Abebi that I'm not coming to the nativity play? Children are usually terrible actors.'

She laughed. I guess she thought I was joking. 'I understand. Well, I suppose you wouldn't be missing much.'

I went towards the door.

'Hey, happy Christmas, Sally!' she said.

'Happy Christmas, especially to the children,' I said.

14

On Friday 22nd December, in the afternoon, there was a knock on the door. It was the postman, with a parcel delivery, a small enough box, but too big to fit into the letter box. I put it with all the cards and letters. Later that evening, it occurred to me that I should open them all. What was I waiting for? Waiting to open envelopes had already caused me enough trouble. There were ten or twelve cards addressed to Dad – some were postmarked before his death – and a few were addressed to me.

3rd December

Christmas greetings to you and Sally, love from Christine and Donald! X
   P.S. I hope another year doesn't go by before we get to see you. Please visit us soon, and bring Sally. I bet she hardly remembers us but we'd love to see her again. She should know she has other family.

Christine was Mum's sister, the glamorous lady who looked like a film star. I remembered Mum used to go on foreign holidays with her and visit her in Dublin, and their long phone conversations. There was a phone number and an address in Donnybrook, Dublin 4.

Then another card addressed to me in the same handwriting:

16th December
Dear Sally,

*We were so sorry to hear of Tom's death. I have tried phoning you
many times, but perhaps you have changed your number. We last saw
you when you were a teenager, you may not remember. I am your
mother's sister. Jean and I were close but your dad seemed to withdraw
from the world after Jean died and, although I tried to keep in touch,
he was reluctant to maintain contact.*

*We often thought of you both but respected your father's wish for
privacy. Unfortunately, Donald is not in good health, and we cannot
make it to the funeral, but he is convalescing at home now. We would
love to come and see you and help in any way we can.*

*I saw from the newspaper coverage that you must have been
confused at the time of Tom's death. We were in touch with the
guards to explain that you have a condition and were so relieved
that the matter was resolved. I also spoke to Dr Angela Caffrey
and I was happy that you had a loyal and trusted friend of Jean's
to speak on your behalf. PLEASE do call. We would love to
see you as soon as possible. You might consider joining us for
Christmas?*

She signed off with love and her phone number.

There was a letter, handwritten, one page, ripped out of a
copybook. The handwriting was terrible. The address was
incomplete too, but the letter had found me.

Saly Dimond

*You are the spawn of the devil and you wil get your punishmen. How
dere you burn the good man like that after he tuk you in and saved
you from hell. Hell is were you belong. Im prayin to the Virgin Mary
that you go there soon, you bich. Its to late for repentesne. The appel
dusnt fall far frum the tree.*

No signature and the paper was almost torn in places where the biro had been dug into the page. Dad and I had agreed long ago that hell didn't exist but the writer obviously hated me and that made me feel anxious. The next card took my anxiety away.

Dear Sally,

You might not remember me but we were in school together in Roscommon from 1st Year to 6th Year and we often sat beside each other in class (because nobody else wanted to sit with us!).

I am terribly sorry to hear what happened with your dad. Because I remember how you were, I can totally understand how you made such a mistake and I want you to know that most people would feel the same way as me, if they knew you like I did.

We never spoke much in school but I tried not to speak to anyone because my stutter was so bad. I am much improved since then. Shortly after I graduated from college, my grandmother died and my mum inherited some money and she spent a small fortune on private speech and language therapy for me. I won't ever be making public speeches, but I can hold a conversation now without getting totally stuck and I guess that with age and the love of a husband and two great kids, I have grown in confidence.

I often thought about you over the years and was surprised that you didn't go on to study music. You were the most incredible pianist. I used to sit outside the music room sometimes to listen to you play, and I wasn't the only one. But I'm guessing that perhaps you were afraid of leaving your parents, or maybe social anxiety kept you home? I don't blame you. I was terrified to go, but it was so much better than school. We were both targeted by bullies there.

In college, I found friends for the first time who were much more understanding. I got involved in social justice societies and I now

*work as a fundraiser for homeless services. It's tough now, the
campaigning is endless.*

*I don't want to bring you down by revisiting your early memories. I
had no idea that all that shit had happened to you before we met in
school. I mean, it's no surprise that you are the way you are, but I
never saw any harm or malice in you – you were a bit unusual,
that's all. If you ever want to get in touch, my deets are below. I guess
I wanted you to know that there are plenty of people like me, who
admire you, firstly for surviving such horrific adversity as a child, and
secondly, for living your life on your own terms. I came to your dad's
funeral and I thought the red hat was a classy touch – a bit unusual
for a funeral, but that's you! I remembered you well enough not to try
to approach you or shake hands. You were looking at the ground the
whole time, like in school. I just want you to know I was there, I
guess.*

*I wish you well, old pal. (Is it okay to say that? I feel like we were
sort of pals back in the day!)*

*All the best
Stella Coughlan*

I remembered Stella perfectly well. Her stutter was bad. She
would turn crimson when anyone tried to talk to her, and if a
teacher asked her a question, I could smell the sweat gather
under her arms. She shared chocolate with me sometimes,
wordlessly. She was not unkind. And yes, the bullies targeted
her mercilessly. She got it worse than me because I rarely
reacted. Mum taught me that. Stella often cried silently beside
me. I could tell by the way her shoulders shook, but I didn't
know what to say to her. Would I call her some day? Maybe.

There was another nasty one, accusing me of patricide,
but offering to pray for my soul, with perfect spelling and a

signature. The other cards were mostly a range of condolence and Christmas cards from people who I half knew or names I had heard Dad mention. That left two more letters and the parcel. Both letters were from journalists, asking for my 'story' and making implications about my tragic childhood. 'The nation deserves answers,' said one. The other offered me €5,000 for an 'exclusive'.

What had happened to me before Mum and Dad adopted me? And how did 'the nation' know all about it when I didn't? I was tempted to ring Angela, even though she might be annoyed. It must have been something bad. Whatever it was should not matter as I couldn't remember it. I had not ever tried. But now I recalled how the guards seemed to find it unusual that my first memory was my seventh birthday party. Did other people have memories earlier than that? My memory is excellent. I felt a strange buzzing in my head. My hands were shaking. I think this was nervousness. I played the piano for a little while until I felt better.

Then I picked up the box. I unwrapped it carefully and put the paper in the drawer where we kept all the paper for lighting fires or rewrapping.

It was a long shoebox and, when I opened the lid, I immediately felt a warm glow in my stomach. A small teddy bear lay in tissue paper and I grabbed him out of the box and hugged him to my chest. The warmth in my stomach reached all the way to my fingers and toes. I held him out in front of me. He was old and well worn, missing an eye, stained and patched, but he made me feel so . . . something. I clutched him again, confused. Why did he have this effect on me? Why was I so immediately warmed by his presence? Why was I calling it 'him' in my mind?

'Toby,' I said. He didn't reply.

I rummaged through the box, looking for a letter or a card. On a yellow Post-it note was written:

I thought you'd like to have him back.
S.

15

I knew this bear. I knew his name was Toby. Did Mum give him to me? I have an excellent memory. Why couldn't I remember? He smelled musty and dirty but also of something familiar. I was overrun by emotions I couldn't understand. I was laughing and excited and agitated. I wanted to find 'S' and make him or her explain. I badly wanted to ring Angela, but I heeded Dad's warning. Who could I talk to about this? Dad said that he would explain more in the next letter, but I wasn't allowed to open it until Tuesday. This was one of those situations when I needed guidance. It was late. Dad always said it was not proper to phone anyone after 9 p.m.

I stood up and stumbled to my bedroom, feeling dizzy but in a good way. I got ready for bed without letting go of Toby. I talked to him, explaining what I was doing, welcoming him to his new home. I hoped he'd be happy here. I imagined his answers. I wrapped my arms around him and felt so light-headed that I don't know whether I fainted or drifted off to sleep.

I had dreams that night, vivid, of a thin woman with long hair. I was sitting on her lap. This was strange because I never sat on anyone's lap. It was also strange because I'd never had a dream before.

The next day, I rang my aunt, Christine.

'Oh, my darling,' she said, 'it is so good to hear from you, we have been so worried about you.'

'Do you still have that red coat?' I asked.

'What? Oh . . . that was such a long time ago. I'm delighted you remember. It must be twenty years since I saw you.'

'You looked like a film star. I loved that coat. Aunt Christine, do you remember anything that happened to you before you were seven years old?'

There was a pause.

'Well, yes, I have a few memories – getting an ice-cream cone from my dad, your grandfather –'

'What age were you?'

'Maybe three or four?'

'I thought people's memories only started when they were seven?'

'Well, it's different for everyone.'

'I think something bad happened to me when I was younger than that.'

There was another pause.

'Sally, may I come and visit you?'

'Why?'

'I think it would be best if I could speak to you face to face.'

I warmed up at the thought of seeing her again.

'I could be there by lunchtime today?'

'Will you want lunch?'

'No, a cup of tea –'

'I can make ham sandwiches.'

'That would be lovely.'

'Don't bring Donald, okay?'

'Well, fine, he's recovering from an operation, but why don't you want to see him?'

'Dad said he was a lazy oaf who married you for your money.'

She laughed.

'Why are you laughing?'

'Your dad. Talk about projecting . . .'

'I don't understand. I don't like it when people laugh at me.'

'Goodness, I'm not laughing at you. Look, don't worry, I won't bring Donald.'

I hung up shortly after we had done the goodbye thing that annoys me: 'Goodbye,' 'Bye,' 'Goodbye,' 'See you later,' 'Yes, goodbye,' 'Bye, then.' So tedious.

Two hours later, I went to the kitchen to make the sandwiches. I had fashioned a sling out of an old scarf of Dad's to carry Toby as close to my heart as I could. I told him about our expected visitor. I asked him again who 'S' was. I didn't expect an answer, but it was nice to talk to him. I didn't feel alone.

When I answered the door, Aunt Christine was there, carrying a large bouquet of flowers.

'Darling! Oh my, it's been too long. You are so tall! And beautiful!'

Aunt Christine used to look like a stylish version of my mum. But now, she was disappointingly old. I nearly said it. The skin around her face had all fallen downwards, though her eyes were bright with golden eyeshadow and spiky lashes. That made sense. Mum was dead so long. I felt comfortable with her until she reached out to touch me and I backed away. 'Sorry!' she said, putting her hands in the air as if she were under arrest. 'You used to let me hold your hand, you know.' This was true, but I was out of practice.

We went to the kitchen and I turned on the kettle and set about making tea. I watched her. She looked at me and smiled. 'How are you? I see you don't have any decorations up?'

'No, Dad and I agreed they were for children.' Aunt Christine frowned.

'I got all these letters,' I said. 'Some people want to be my friend. Some people hate me. They wrote that I was a spawn of the devil.'

'May I see?'

I showed her the assorted mail.

'Well, these can go straight into the bin,' she said, lifting the nasty notes and the letters from journalists. I agreed. I didn't want to keep any of them, except the letter from Stella, my classmate, and the note from 'S'.

'How are you feeling?'

'I'm fine. Dad said I should move into the village. He says it's unhealthy for me to live here on my own.'

'Aren't you lonely here?'

'I've got Toby,' I said, pointing to my bear.

'Toby isn't a person, darling.'

'I know. I'm not stupid.'

She said nothing. We stared at each other. Her head was to one side and her eyes were soft.

'What happened to me before I was adopted?'

She looked away then, out of the window, at the floor and then back at my face. She asked, 'May I take your hand?'

'What for?'

'Touch can be comforting, you know. And it's not a nice story.'

I let her take my hand and put it between hers.

'Jean said that you . . . were medicated, that you don't remember anything at all?'

I shook my head.

'Your mother, your real mother, I mean, she . . . died.'

'What did she die of?'

'She was kidnapped by a man, when she was young, when she was . . . a child.'

I had seen films and dramas about men who kidnapped young women.

'Did he lock her in a cellar?'

'Yes, well, no, it was an extension at the back of his house. He lived in a large house on a half-acre of land in South Dublin. He kept her there for fourteen years.'

My head started to buzz. 'Stop talking, please.'

She stroked my hand.

I turned away to refill the teapot. I picked up a sandwich and ate it. Aunt Christine sat silently.

'Would you like one?'

'Sorry?'

'Would you like a sandwich?'

'No. Darling, I'm so sorry. It's a terrible story. Is there a friend I can call? What about Angela?'

'Yes, I'll call her.'

I picked up the phone. Angela didn't work at weekends so I thought I wouldn't be disturbing her.

'Angela? My Aunt Christine is here. She told me that my real mother was kidnapped –'

'Fuck.'

'What?'

'I wanted to be with you when you opened the last letter from your dad. It explains everything . . . well, most things. May I speak to Christine?'

Aunt Christine took the phone out to the hall. I couldn't hear exactly what she was saying but I could hear her voice getting high-pitched. And then I heard her hang up the phone. When she returned to the kitchen table, her eyes were wet with tears.

'Sally, I'm afraid I've made a mess of this. Angela is on her way. Let's talk about other things until she gets here.'

'Do you think she loved me? My real mother.'

She picked up a sandwich. 'Oh, I think she loved you with all her heart.'

'How do you know?'

'These sandwiches are delicious. Let's wait for Angela, will we? Shall I make more sandwiches for her?'

'I'll make them. It's lucky that Toby doesn't eat, otherwise we'd run out of bread.'

'What age are you now, Sally?'

'Forty-three. What age are you?'

'Sixty-seven.'

'Did my real mum get married?'

'No . . . let's wait for Angela.'

'Okay. Do you want to hold Toby?'

She hadn't seen him properly and I wanted to show him off.

'Goodness, he is a little battered, isn't he?'

'Yes, he's getting in the bath with me tonight.'

'Oh, that might not be a good idea, to immerse him. It could destroy him. He's old. Shall we try to give him a scrub now? A gentle one, while we wait for Angela?'

Aunt Christine filled the washing-up basin with sudsy water and used a nail brush with light strokes while I held out Toby's arms and legs. The water swirled with brown foam.

'I wonder where he's been?' she said.

'I don't know. He came in the post yesterday with that note, signed "S", but I knew at once that he was mine, and that his name was Toby. But I don't know where I got him. Maybe Mum gave him to me, but I don't remember, and my memory is normally excellent.'

'"S"?' she said, and I moved over to find the note again.

'Do you know who "S" is?'

Aunt Christine almost dropped Toby into the water, and I caught him just in time.

'Oh God, we shouldn't have touched him, or washed him!'

'Why? He was dirty. He needed it.' I took over the gentle washing now, rubbing his little face and his soft brown snout with a J-Cloth. Aunt Christine began to pace the room, wringing her hands together.

When the doorbell rang again, Aunt Christine leapt up to answer it. I could hear them whispering in the hallway as Angela embraced her. How easily they seemed to hug one another, even though it must have been years since they'd met.

Angela strode into the room. 'Sally, I think you shouldn't touch that bear.'

'Why?'

'Put it down, please.' Her voice was firm.

'He's mine. His name is Toby.'

'How do you know that?'

'I don't know how. I just do. I love him.'

I startled myself with the strength of my words. I had a strong need to protect this toy and to keep him close. I could see Angela was surprised.

'You shouldn't have touched it.' She looked at the scrubbed bear. 'I think it's too late now. He's been handled and washed.'

Aunt Christine's voice went high. 'I'm sorry, I didn't know until after we started washing it. I haven't seen Sally in over twenty years. I thought it was hers.'

I began to feel anxious. 'He is mine. I can . . . feel it. I'm keeping him.' I clutched his damp body to mine and felt the wetness on my chest.

'It may be evidence,' said Angela. 'Do you have the wrapping paper it came in?'

'I don't understand!' I shrieked. 'You're not making sense.'

I felt utterly lost and the buzzing in my head had not stopped. I began to pull at my hair, as Angela softly asked me how and when he was delivered. 'May I put my arm around you, Sally?' I nodded, and it felt warm and natural to have an arm around my shoulders as I held Toby tight. We stayed like that for a little while until my anger subsided.

'We should go into the sitting room and relax a bit. It's been a shock, and we have more information for you,' said Aunt Christine.

'First, I need the wrapping paper,' said Angela.

'There was a box as well,' I said.

I found the box and the paper. 'The stamps on this are from New Zealand. Express post,' said Angela 'The box comes from a shoe shop. The guards will finally have a lead.'

'What are you talking about?'

'I think you need to read your dad's last letter, and then I'll answer the questions that I'm able to answer, okay?'

We all went into the sitting room. I was so dizzy. Aunt Christine asked Angela if she might have some medication that would pacify me.

'Sally needs to be fully able to absorb this news.'

I retrieved Dad's letter from his office. 'I'm supposed to wait until –'

'Your dad would be okay with it, Sally, honestly,' said Aunt Christine.

They guided me to the sofa and sat either side of me. I asked them to sit on the other chairs.

PART II

16

Peter, 1974

I remember when I was small, being in a grand room over-looking the sea. There was a wall of books behind me, and I sat at a long dining table opposite my dad. Before he left for work every weekday, Dad would have breakfast with me, and we would listen to the radio. And then he would give me biscuits, fruit and a colouring book with crayons. He gave me my homework instructions and then he locked me into my white bedroom in the annexe. There was a large window which looked on to the back garden, and a potty under the bed, a shelf with my four books and a cupboard which contained my clothes.

The days seemed endless then, but when he came home, he would unlock the door and scoop me up into his arms and carry me into the main house. He would cook me a hot meal and then he would check my work, reading and writing and sums, and then we would watch television until my bedtime, but he could never explain how those tiny people got into the television box. I often heard him playing the piano, or sometimes I woke to the sound of him unlocking the room next door.

On Saturdays and Sundays when the weather was fine, I was allowed out into the garden, where I would help him with the weeding. I'd make little hills out of the cut grass, or bird's nests, and then he might put them on a bonfire.

The annexe was in a funny-shaped building on the side of the house. There was a door into it from the downstairs pantry. There was another door beside my bedroom door too. Occasionally, I would hear noises coming from behind the other door. Often, the sound of crying or howling. Dad said that's where he kept the ghost, and that I mustn't worry because she could never get out. And he was right, because she never did. But the noise could be frightening sometimes. When it got bad, Dad told me to stay under the covers with my hands over my ears and I think he must have gone into the room next door and told the ghost to be quiet, because there wouldn't be a peep out of it for days.

At bedtime, Dad would read me a story and kiss my forehead and tell me he loved me and we would say our prayers together and then he would lock the door again to keep me safe until morning.

Every year on my birthday, 7th August, we had a Special Day. Dad didn't go to work. The first one I remember, Dad brought home a tent and we pitched it in the garden. He made a bonfire and we cooked sausages on it. We slept in sleeping bags in the tent. And then, later, he woke me up and it was dark. He led me outside and lit fireworks and the summer ink sky burst into colour and noise and it was the most exciting thing that ever happened to me.

The next birthday was scary. I was seven years old, I think. I was frightened when we went through the gates at the bottom of our garden in Dad's car and turned out on to the road. I was dizzy. I hadn't been in his car before although I helped him wash it on Sundays. He had put cushions on the front seat so that I could see out of the window. And he gave me a bag to get sick into, in case the dizziness didn't pass. It went away quickly. Outside the gates, there were people – the same size as Dad and me – and there were women. I'd only seen them on TV and in books, but these were life-size.

We had a long journey in the car to the zoo. I was worried

that we would never find our way home, but Dad said he would always be able to find home.

I was so terrified of letting go of Dad's hand. I was more intrigued by the people than by the animals. They walked around in groups, mothers with children and babies in prams, mums and dads walking arm in arm. Groups of children, girls and boys, running around together. Dad was trying to get me to look at the chimpanzees and the elephants, but I was listening to the people talking to each other. Dad bought me an ice pop and told me not to look at the other people, but I couldn't help it. A man stopped Dad and talked to him. I hid behind Dad's legs. Dad told the man I was his godson. I could tell he didn't want to talk to the other man, and we moved along quickly, and then Dad said it was time to go home. I was glad.

I had lots of questions. I asked him what the difference between a son and a godson was and he said a godson was a child who believed in God. And I certainly did.

I asked Dad if women were bad. He said most of them were. I said that there were nice ones on television and in my books, but he said that television and my stories were make-believe. I asked if I had a mum and he said I did but that she was a ghost. There was a big padlock on the door of the room next to mine in the annexe. Now, I asked if my mother was the ghost who lived in that room, if she was the one who made the howling noises, and he said that she was, but that I shouldn't worry because I wouldn't ever have to see her.

17

Sally

I opened the letter with trembling hands.

Dearest Sally

I hope by now that you have recovered a little from my death.

These are things I should have told you gradually long ago, perhaps over a period of time. I don't want you to be upset by this news. It is all in the past and nothing will change for you now, unless you want it to, but I think you are a creature of habit and you will go on as you have.

Your birth name is Mary Norton. Norton is your birth mother's name. We believe it would not have been her choice to use your birth father's name. All of the original medical reports and some newspaper clippings are in the box under my desk in a file marked PRIVATE. When you came to us, we decided that you were a new person. You were our Sally Diamond.

The reason you are a bit odd is not because there is anything wrong with your brain, but because you were raised in disturbing circumstances, until you were discovered.

At the age of eleven in 1966, your mother, Denise Norton, was kidnapped by Conor Geary. He abused her mentally and sexually for the next fourteen years. As far as we are able to tell, you were born eight years after her abduction. Your birth mother could not be certain of the date or even the year, but that was her best guess, and my medical colleagues agreed that you were probably born sometime in the latter half of 1974. Your birth was not registered, for obvious reasons, so the birth date on your adoption certificate may not be correct. I am sorry to tell you that Conor Geary, the kidnapper, is your birth father.

Denise Norton's family searched for her for years. She was not found until March 1980, after an anonymous tip-off to the guards. You and your birth mother were discovered within a matter of days. You were both in appalling condition in a home-made extension at the back of Conor Geary's house in Killiney, Co. Dublin. The window of your mother's room was boarded up. It was dark and dank. There was a hot plate and a fridge. There was a mattress on the floor in one main room with a toilet and washbasin adjacent. Your small bedroom next door was bright and airy with a large window looking out to the garden. You were both terribly emaciated and although you were almost completely silent, and obviously distressed on your release, Denise was suffering from severe mental health issues. I am not sure it would do you any good to try to imagine her state of mind. In the beginning, she was feral, and would attack anyone who approached her. You both had to be anaesthetized in order for doctors to physically examine you. Normal sedatives were not strong enough. It was never initially intended that she would be permanently separated from you.

Your mum was well qualified. Jean had done an additional specialist rotation in child and adolescent psychiatry before finishing her GP training at the time of your discovery. You and your birth mother were both admitted to St Mary's Psychiatric Hospital, where I was Medical Director. A special unit was set up and I assigned a dedicated team of staff to look after you. Given the concerns about your development and physical health, I requested that Jean be seconded to work alongside me at St Mary's and, because we were a married couple, it suited everybody. We worked as a team around the clock, living in the unit with you, along with the support staff.

I never gained Denise's trust, though in my defence, I tried extremely hard, and if I had had longer with her, I am sure that

I could have helped her to adjust. I don't think she could ever have lived a 'normal' life, given all of the horrors she had experienced. My initial aim was to get her to a place where she could live in an open facility with access to the outside world and twenty-four-hour medical and psychiatric assistance. This facility would not have been an appropriate long-term place for you, however, and it was my strong suggestion then that you should be separated from your mother at some stage when Denise was ready. You were still being breastfed. Unheard of for a five-year-old. Jean showed Denise how to bottle feed you, but your birth mother strongly resisted. We failed, and you screamed and pulled your hair out, but eventually we had to make a drastic decision. One that I will always regret, but not in every way.

I feel now that it was a crude and possibly cruel thing to do, but we were concerned for your future. I was convinced that you were young enough to be retrained, as it were, and that you might have a chance at a normal life. You and your mother stayed in the unit for fourteen months together and, in that time, we were never able to separate you from Denise. It was a harrowing time and nobody who treated either of you could have been unaffected.

I saw you with your birth mother almost every day. She refused to talk about Conor Geary but strenuously denied that he had ever sexually assaulted you, or that you witnessed any of her abuse. You would be locked in the toilet when the assaults took place. Medical examinations also suggested that he did not sexually abuse you and I think you must assume that is the case. We cannot rule out that he may have physically harmed you, though, as he had definitely left your mother with physical as well as emotional scars. He removed her teeth as punishment. Conor Geary was a dentist.

Your mother took her own life in May 1981 after you had spent one night in a separate room with Jean. We made terrible mistakes, but there was no intention to harm either of you. Until my dying day, which will shortly come, I will feel responsibility for your mother's death. There was a brief hospital inquiry and I was cleared of medical negligence, but I do hold myself accountable, Sally. I should have found another way.

Jean and I approached the Adoption Board and the Minister for Health together. We had not had any luck having children of our own. They agreed that a home with a psychiatrist and a qualified GP who intended to move away from Dublin was for the best. We felt that we could provide a safe and stable home for you and I hope that we did that and that you have always felt safe with us. Losing Jean so young was a tragedy, but I think we managed, you and I, did we not?

It is because of your very early experiences that you are sometimes socially and emotionally disconnected. Your tendency to take things literally is a hangover from your early years of social isolation in captivity. It is most fortunate that you have no memory of that time before we brought you home. I would strongly advise you to do nothing at all to try to revive those memories as I know they could only be traumatizing.

So, now you know. I agonized over writing this letter. I wondered if it were better that you never got to know these details. Nobody in Carricksheedy knows your background, not even Angela. Jean told her own family, but everyone else was sworn to lifetime secrecy. Your discovery in 1980 was huge news as you can imagine, and we did everything in our power to keep you away from the media.

Thankfully, my name was not released in the news coverage. The department agreed to put out a press release to say that you had been adopted in the UK. I moved us out of Dublin as soon as you could leave the unit.

So now I finally say goodbye, my love, leaving you with lots to think about. You are under no obligation to do anything at all with this information. But if you need to talk to anyone, you could show Angela this letter. She will be shocked, but will be of practical or emotional support if you need it.

I wish you good health and happiness and a peaceful life.

Your loving Dad

When I finally stopped reading, I noticed that Angela and Aunt Christine were muttering to each other.

'Do you have any questions you'd like to ask us?'

I had so many questions that I didn't know where to start. 'May I have some whiskey, please?'

Aunt Christine looked to Angela and Angela nodded. She smiled at me.

'I think we should all have a whiskey.'

'This is the trauma Dad was talking about when he mentioned PTSD.'

'Sally, do you think I might stay the night? Would that be okay with you?' said Aunt Christine.

'I think that's a good idea, you should reconnect with the family you have,' said Angela. 'Christine can stay in your dad's room. I'll go and make up the bed.'

'No need,' I said. 'I changed the sheets after the police were here that time. Yes, she can stay. But, Angela, Aunt Christine isn't my real family.'

I had done the maths in my head. 'If my birth mother was nineteen years old when I was born, what about her mother and father, my grandparents? Are they alive? Do I have any real aunts and uncles? What about cousins?'

Angela looked at Aunt Christine. 'I'd like to know the answers to that too. I can't believe I worked alongside Jean for eight years and she never told me any of this. She told me she had specialized in child psychiatry as part of her GP training, but never that she was involved in the Denise Norton case. I knew that Tom was a psychiatrist, but he no longer practised. I assumed he was writing academic papers and contributing to medical journals. Occasionally, Jean would bring him in to talk to a patient, but just to assess them for referral.' She sighed before continuing.

'Sally, I didn't know any of this until I read the letters the day . . . the day the police came. I had to photocopy them and hand them over. Back in the day, the Denise Norton case was notorious but your identity was kept secret. The guards read your dad's letters and they have copies of his files so someone then leaked the information that you are Mary Norton. That's why the press and photographers were there at the funeral, and why they found the house and your phone number. Christine tells me they've been writing to you as well.'

'There were pictures of you in the paper, Sally, at your dad's funeral. That's why I've been so worried about you,' said Aunt Christine. 'I always knew the truth. But Jean and Tom were desperate to protect your privacy. Jean wanted to tell you once you turned eighteen, but Tom . . . he disagreed. And then she died so shortly afterwards.'

'You haven't answered my question about other relatives?' I stared at Aunt Christine as I sipped the whiskey and she took a large gulp of hers.

'Denise's parents were desperate to reconnect with her. But from what Jean told me, the reunion did not go well. When your real grandparents, Sam and Jacqueline Norton, were first reunited with Denise, she physically attacked them, particularly her father. The anger of fourteen years all came tumbling out in resentment against the people who loved her the most. Also, and this might disturb you, they believed they could bring Denise home after her treatment, but they would not countenance taking you. You were his child. You have to look at it from their point of view. If they took you into their home, they would be taking part of Conor Geary too.'

I thought of the vicious letter calling me the spawn of the devil.

'After Denise's death in the psychiatric unit, they were broken people. They moved away to France.'

'Didn't they ever get in contact to find out what happened to me, Aunt Christine?'

'I assume they considered it many times, but perhaps you might have only been a reminder of the daughter they'd lost. Sally, are you absolutely sure you recognize that bear, you know for sure that he's yours?'

'He's mine,' I said, squeezing him tighter.

They kept changing the subject, hopping around from one thing to the next. I poured more whiskey. So did Aunt Christine. She offered some to Angela, but Angela shook her head.

'Darling,' said Aunt Christine in a soft voice, 'your birth father fled days before the guards discovered you and Denise. He cleared his bank account and abandoned his car at the East Pier in Dún Laoghaire. He could have drowned himself, but no body was ever recovered. They think he got on a ferry to Holyhead. He certainly left the country. He didn't have a passport – you didn't need one to get to the UK in those days – but he had money. Why would he take all of his money out of his accounts if he intended to kill himself? Nobody knows where he went. He was never caught.'

'I think he sent you the bear,' said Angela.

My hands flew automatically to my hair, but then back to Toby. I couldn't let go of him.

18

Peter, 1974

Dad was wrong about me never having to see the ghost in the room next door. In mid-September, Dad said he had to go away for the weekend and that I had to stay in her room while he was away.

'With the ghost?'

'Yes, but she won't hurt you. She's your mother.'

I was terrified at the prospect.

'Don't worry,' he said, 'it's only two days, and you're in charge of her. She has to do whatever you say, and if she doesn't, you can take her food away. If she does anything you don't like, you have my permission to kick her. Do not answer any of her questions. That's the only rule.'

'I thought it was naughty to kick people.'

'She's not a person, she's a ghost. It's fine.'

I became upset. 'I don't want to stay with the ghost,' I cried.

'You're too small to be on your own for a whole weekend, and besides, the ghost wants to see you. She's been begging me to see you for . . . years.'

'Why?'

'Because she's your mother.'

'Will she try to hurt me?'

'Definitely not.'

'Is she dead?' I had a vague notion that ghosts were dead people.

'No, not really.'

'But why is she in that room?'

'You're too young to understand some things. No more questions. I'm going to put a camp bed in there and you can bring your favourite blanket, and two of your books. You can have your bedside lamp as well.'

None of this did anything to allay my fears.

On the Friday after dinner, Dad led me into her room. It was dark and quiet, until he plugged my lamp into a socket beside the door. Then I heard the ghost. 'Peter? Is that you?' Her voice was trembling, and she emerged from under a blanket and reached out towards me. Dad went right over and smacked her across the face. 'See? That's what you do if she does anything you don't like. She won't hurt you. She knows what will happen if she does anything to upset you.' His voice was light and even and comforting to me.

He set down a large paper bag full of food beside me. 'That's for you, not for her, okay? She has her own food.' She crawled back under the blanket and I didn't get to see her face properly. He showed me the camp bed, which was right beside the door we had entered. He showed me the light switch for the toilet and the washbasin and reminded me to brush my teeth and wash my face each night. He showed me the fridge and the cooker in the corner of the room and told me she would make mashed potatoes with peas and bacon for my dinner tomorrow. He would be back on Sunday morning.

'I don't like it here,' I said. It was smelly and dark and stuffy. Dad lifted me up into his arms. 'You have nothing to worry about, I promise.' He kissed the top of my head and went to the door and I heard the lock switch as he got to the other side of it. I immediately ran to the door and hammered my small fists against it. 'Please don't leave me here. I'm scared of the ghost!' I screamed. But I heard nothing from the other side of the door. He was gone.

She stuck her head up out of the blanket again. She sat up. 'Peter, don't be scared. I've missed you so much,' she said. Her hair was long and tangled, and some of her teeth were missing, but her eyes sparkled. A dark bruise covered the lower half of one side of her face. 'I'm your mummy, don't you remember me?' I cowered against the door.

There was something familiar about her, but she terrified me.

'You lived here with me, until he took you away, as soon as you could walk and talk and were toilet trained. He forced me to wean you eventually, but I had no idea he'd take you from me. I haven't been outside this room in . . . I don't even know how many years –'

She was speaking so fast, her words tumbled on top of each other. She stood up and I saw that one of her ankles was chained to a bolt in the wall. She could get to the toilet and kitchen area, but she couldn't reach me. Her arms and legs were thin but her belly was large and she dropped her arms to place her two hands underneath it. She wore a shirt that was too big for her, and a skirt that lifted up at the front. She wore a pair of woollen socks on her feet.

'What date is it?'

I didn't want to speak to her. I quickly ran to the toilet and turned the light on and left the door open and weed into the toilet bowl. When I came out, she was within reaching distance of me. She held out her hand to me. 'I wanted to call you Sam after my dad, but he said it had to be Peter. I gave birth to you, right here in this room.'

I pushed her hand away roughly. Dad said I could kick her. I lashed out with my right foot and hit her on the shin.

'Owww,' she said, but she didn't cry.

87

'Open the curtains,' I said.

She looked at me with big eyes. 'There aren't any. There isn't a window.'

I smacked her across the face like Dad did.

'Please don't hit me,' she said. 'Did he not teach you that it's bad to hit people?'

'Dad said I could hit you. Why isn't there a window? I have a window in my room.'

'He likes to keep me in the dark. There was a window the day I came but he boarded it up from the outside.' I knew where on the outside the window was boarded up, but I couldn't make sense of it now in the gloom. The only light came from the toilet and my bedside lamp.

'Why did he do that?'

'As punishment.'

'What did you do?'

'I can't remember.'

'It must have been bad.'

'I tried to escape and he caught me so I bit him!'

'Oh.' I ran back to my side of the room.

'I'd never bite you. I love you.'

I didn't reply.

'It's so nice and warm here now. I'm glad he didn't bring you in the winter. It's summer now, right?'

I bit back the answer. It was September.

'You don't remember me at all? Do you know what year this is? Or what month?'

'Yes.'

'Will you tell me?'

'No.'

'Please. It's important. I've been here since June of 1966. I was eleven. I think you were born a year later, but I don't know how long ago that was.'

'Dad told me not to tell you anything.'

'What age are you?'

'Where were you before?'

'I had a family and school and friends and my own bedroom and windows. He says it's my imagination, but I remember.'

'Who says?'

'The man.'

'My dad?'

She nodded.

'What's his name?' she asked.

I knew it was Conor Geary but I wasn't going to tell her.

'I don't know.'

'You can call me mummy. I'd love to hug you, you know, to hold your hand? You were only learning to talk when he took you away. You had a few words: Mama, bed, biscuit and milk. That's when he took you. Don't you remember?'

I had a shadow of a memory. I used to sleep beside her on that mattress.

'Shut up.'

She was quiet for a while but she stared at me through the gloom.

'Could you bring that lamp a little closer? So that I can see you properly?'

'No.'

'I want to show you something.' She took a teddy bear from a shelf behind her. 'Do you remember Toby?' He was a cute bear with a red bow around his neck. 'He was mine,' she said, 'and then when you were born, he was yours. Would you like to have him back?'

I remembered Toby more than I remembered her. He was dirty now, and one eye was missing. It disturbed me to look at him. I desperately wanted to hold him, but it meant getting closer to her.

'No, thank you.'

'I thought I'd never see you again.'

'Why is your belly so big?'

'I guess I'm having another baby. You were in my belly once, the same as this one. You're going to have a little brother or sister.'

'How did the baby get in there?'

'He put it there.'

'How?'

She said nothing for a while.

'Dad locks me in my bedroom during the day on weekdays.'

'So, is it the weekend now?'

'It's Friday.' And then I clamped my hand over my mouth because I had broken Dad's rule by answering a question.

'Or it could be Tuesday,' I said.

'It doesn't matter. I'd never tell him anything you told me. I hope he never punishes you. I'm sorry that he locks you up too.'

I needed to be the boss like Dad said. 'He doesn't lock me in a place like this. I have a huge window and I can see the garden and I have books and toys.'

'Are we near the sea? Sometimes, I think I can hear it?'

Not answering all these questions was hard. I realized that you couldn't hear the sea from this room. There was lots of torn cardboard nailed to the walls.

'If you ask me any more questions, I'll kick you again.'

'Okay. Do you want to ask me any questions?'

'No. I want you to be quiet. I don't want to be in here. I wish I was back in my own room.'

She moved back on to her mattress and groaned loudly.

'Stop making that noise.'

'I can't help it. Being pregnant is painful sometimes. It's the baby, your brother or sister.'

'Which is it?'

'I don't know.'

'Why not?'

'You can't tell whether it's a boy or a girl until it's born.'

'I don't want a sister.'

'I wanted to keep you so much.'

'Here?'

'No, at home with my family.'

I didn't say anything. I didn't want her to be my mum.

I took an apple from my bag. Dad always said I had to eat the healthy things before I could eat the sweet things. I took a big bite out of it and chewed. She stared at me.

'Get back under the blanket.'

She did, but there was a tiny gap and I could tell she was looking at me through the blanket. I went over and kicked at it. There was a gasp, and she rose again, but this time there was blood on her face.

'I'm sorry, I'm sorry,' she said and began to cry.

I didn't like her bleeding face. 'Get back under the blanket and don't look at me. Stupid woman.'

19

Sally

'I think we need to take the teddy bear with the note and the box and wrapping paper to the guards. They might be able to get some DNA from it,' said Aunt Christine.

'Unlikely,' said Angela. 'You two have washed most of the evidence away. All three of us have handled the box and wrapping paper. Postal workers in New Zealand and Ireland too, and everywhere in between, but I suppose they might be able to get some information.'

Aunt Christine said, 'Judging by the style and age of the bear, I'm guessing it was Denise's. It's like something from fifty or sixty years ago. Parts of it seem to have been attacked by moths.'

Angela agreed. 'What did the note say again?'

'"I thought you'd like to have him back." No signature. Just a letter "S".'

'Maybe Sally had a nickname for her father? Do you remember, Sally?'

Angela put her hand up. 'I don't think Sally needs those questions, Christine.'

'Sorry, you're right.'

'I'd like to go to bed to rest for a while,' I said. 'With Toby.'

It was five o'clock now and pitch-dark. The two women began to apologize, saying it must be a terrible shock, that I must feel overwhelmed by all of the revelations. Aunt Christine said she would nip into the village to get some provisions and that she would wake me for dinner later. I went to my room and left them to talk about me and my terrible past. I took Toby with me. I was tired of their talking and I wanted time and space to think.

In my room, with the old flowery wallpaper Mum had chosen all those years ago, I tried to think about what I should do. So many questions floated around my head.

Later, I woke to delicious smells coming from the kitchen. I went to the bathroom and washed my face.

Aunt Christine greeted me in the kitchen. 'Darling, did you have a nice nap? Angela is staying for dinner. I hope you don't mind. I've roasted a chicken.'

'For three of us?'

'Yes, you can use leftovers for sandwiches or soup if you like.'

She had also made mashed potato and a carrot and parsnip puree, like something from a TV cookery show. 'Will you set the table, darling?'

I pulled the table out from the wall and unhinged the flap to make it as big as it used to be when Mum was alive. Dad and I always ate dinner in front of the television on trays. But we always had lunch in the kitchen. This was the wrong way around.

Although it made me a little nervous, Aunt Christine talked in a soothing way, describing how she had prepared the dinner, recalling when she and Jean had gone shopping in Arnotts and had bought the same set of plates, how she was glad to see they were still in use. She sounded like Mum, and if I closed my eyes, I could almost imagine that Mum was back, though I knew it wasn't possible. It was nice to think about.

'Where is Angela?'

'She had to pop home to feed the dogs and do a few things. But she's coming straight back.'

'Shall I get some wine from the cabinet?'

'Oh, I think we had enough alcohol earlier. Do you have sparkling water?' I did.

On my way out to the sitting room to get it, I stopped dead in my tracks and then ran to my bedroom. I pulled the bedclothes apart. I ran back to the kitchen.

'Where's Toby?' I shouted at her.

'Darling, I –'

'Where is he?' My cheeks were getting hot. My head was spinning.

The doorbell rang.

'That will be Angela. She can explain.'

I let Angela in. 'Where's Toby?'

'Calm down, Sally, breathe in for four –'

'Did you take him when I was asleep?'

'Yes, I did. Toby is a toy, Sally, but it might be possible to find out where he came from. I went to the garda station in Roscommon with the bear, the box and all the wrapping. They will send it to a lab in Dublin and a forensic team will –'

'He was mine!'

'Sally, be reasonable, you –'

I lashed out at Angela with my fists, punching her in the face, the stomach, her arms. She folded her upper body into a ball, leaning forward, putting her hands over her head and her elbows in front of her face. Aunt Christine dragged me away.

'Sally! Stop this at once.' Aunt Christine had my mum's angry tone.

My temper abated as quickly as it had surfaced. I sat in the chair in the hall. Aunt Christine led Angela into the kitchen. I heard the two of them whispering. I had done a bad thing. Again. Really bad. I rocked back and forth in the chair. I could not control my emotions. Maybe I should be locked up.

'Angela, I'm sorry, I'm so sorry. I lost my temper.'

She was holding a bag of frozen peas to her jaw. Aunt Christine was standing over her. Thank God there was no blood.

Angela put her hand up to stop me talking, shook her head and winced with pain.

'Jesus, Sally! You were out of control. I had no idea that you could be so violent. That kind of behaviour is completely unacceptable.'

I could tell Aunt Christine was angry, and as I moved towards her, she stepped back. She was also afraid.

'I don't know why I did that, I don't even know why.'

I could feel the heat rising in my face again.

'Something about the bear has triggered you, Sally,' said Angela. 'That's why it has to be investigated. If your birth father sent it to you, it may be possible to trace him. We don't know, but we must try. Think of the damage he did to your birth mother, and to you. I will be fine, but you could have seriously injured me. How often have you had violent outbursts like this before?'

I described the seven incidents in detail, three when I was seven, one when I was eight, one when I was nine: Mum had later said they were childish tantrums. Once when I was fourteen with the man at the bus shelter, and the last time in school a year later when a girl at the desk behind me cut off one of my pigtails. I was nearly expelled but got away with a week's suspension. I broke her arm. I had to write her a letter to say how sorry I was.

'And nothing like that between then and today?'

'No, I swear. Can we please get Toby back?'

'No,' said Angela, 'absolutely not, look at the effect it had on you.'

'It's not a good idea,' agreed Aunt Christine.

'Am I going to jail?'

'No. But you have to understand how serious this is, Sally. You are an adult woman. If I went to the guards, they could lock you up. You must never, ever strike another person again. Do you understand?'

'Yes, Angela, but –'

'Do you understand?'

'Yes.'

'Under the circumstances, Christine, I don't think I can stay for dinner. I need to go and lie down at home. Would you mind driving me? I walked out here from the village.'

'Yes, no problem.'

'Thank you. It will only take a few minutes.'

They both ignored me. A sizzling sound came from the oven as the front door shut behind them. I turned it off. The chicken was slightly burnt on top.

I tried to put things into perspective. I was not going to jail. Angela was going to be fine. Aunt Christine was now scared of me. Why had I lost control like that?

I carved the chicken and served up the vegetables on two plates and opened a bottle of sparkling water and was pouring some into Aunt Christine's glass when she returned.

'I don't know what to say to you, Sally. I think Jean was right to be worried about some decisions Tom made regarding your development. But Angela thinks it's not too late.'

'What's not too late?'

'You need a lot of therapy, darling, because you can't go on like this. It's not normal.'

'My life is normal to me.'

'That's the problem. Tom never pushed you to make . . . corrections. You should have friends, a social life, a job, a partner if you want. There is so much you have missed out on and you don't even realize it.'

'Dad said that in his last letter, that he had made mistakes, but there's nothing wrong with me, except that I'm a bit odd.'

'You just physically attacked the one person who has always been there for you. You will need to make it up to her. How do you think you will do that?'

'I could buy her flowers and write her a letter.'

'That is a good place to start, but how can you ensure that you won't attack anyone again? You need help.'

I knew she was talking about psychotherapy. That's what Mum wanted me to do when I was in school.

'I guess I could try seeing a therapist?'

'Angela will be relieved to hear that. Make sure you put it in the letter.'

That night I went to bed and thought about Toby and where he might be.

It was Christmas Eve the next day and I just wanted to be on my own. I had allowed Aunt Christine to hug me when she said goodbye. I apologized again. She said we would keep in touch and that I should visit them in Dublin after Christmas when I had a few therapy sessions under my belt. I wasn't sure about that.

I sat down to write a letter of apology to Angela. I added that I would agree to go to therapy if she thought it would stop me from harming people I cared about. I told her not to worry about the bag of peas. I could easily replace them at the Texaco. I wished her and Nadine a happy Christmas and told her I'd stay on my own for Christmas Day.

I walked into the village. There was noise and people and Christmas lights twinkling everywhere. I put in my earplugs and went to buy flowers in the Texaco. I got out of there as soon as I could and walked down to Angela's house. I pushed the card through the door and put the flowers on the doormat and left in a hurry. I understood what shame meant. It was one of the emotions I was in touch with.

20

Peter, 1974

'*Stupid woman*' were the words Dad often said when we were watching television. The mums on television were nice-looking, clean and well dressed mostly, baking apple pies for their children and tending to the cuts on their knees. This ghost was useless. She was a terrible mother, so bad that she had to be chained up like a wild dog.

We didn't speak for a long time, but there were things I wanted to know. She popped her head out bit by bit but didn't look at me. She wiped the blood from her eye with the blanket. It didn't bleed much after that.

'How will the baby get out of your tummy?'

'The last time, you came out through here.' She pointed to the area between her legs. 'It was quick and painful. There was a kind of rope around your neck, but he pulled it away.'

'Dad?'

'Yes. He was pleased about you. He was good to me for a while after that. But I didn't know then he was going to steal you from me. I was twelve years old then, I think, but I don't know how old I am now. I've lost track.'

'You don't know how old you are? You're stupid.'

'I suppose you're in school now. I'd say you're clever.'

'I'm not in school. Dad teaches me here.'

'Oh, I bet your friends miss you.'

'I don't have any friends. Dad is my best friend.'

'Don't you miss having other children your own age to play with?'

I remembered the day at the zoo. Lots of groups of children chattering excitedly to each other.

'You are not to ask questions. Stupid woman.'

I took out my bottle of milk and poured it into a glass on the tray Dad had prepared. The way she stared at the bottle was so strange.

'Haven't you seen milk before?'

'Not since you were a baby. He gave me milk then so that I could breastfeed you, but when he took you, I didn't get milk again.'

I refilled the glass with milk and handed it carefully to her. Her hands were shaking so much that I was afraid she'd spill it, but she clamped her mouth down on to the glass and drank it down in one go, like a greedy pig.

She started to cry. 'Thank you. Thank you so much. I know you're a good boy. Half of you is me. The good half.'

I snatched the glass back from her. 'You have no manners,' I said. 'It's rude to drink like that.'

She looked down at the floor. 'I'm sorry, it's been . . . so long.'

I walked over to the fridge and put the bacon in there along with the rest of the milk and some butter and cheese. I left the potato, bread, banana, cornflakes and tin of peas on the top with the chocolate and crisps which were my Saturday-night treat.

There were four bottles of clear liquid in the fridge already.

'What's that?'

'My water.'

'Where's your food?' I asked her.

She ruffled under her blanket and brought out half a packet of custard cream biscuits.

'That's all he gives me. May I . . . may I have your apple core?'

'I put it in the bin.'

'I don't mind.'

She went to the bin and took out the apple core.

'That's disgusting, eating out of a bin.'

'I'm hungry. That food you have. Is there enough for us to share?'

'He said that food was for me.'

'But if there was too much for you, can I have the left-overs? Please?' Her eyes were filling with tears again and I didn't know what I should feel.

'No,' I said, 'it's against the rules.'

I tried to ignore her by reading my books, but she wanted to see them. I wouldn't let her, so she asked me to read out loud to her. I read five pages of *Gulliver's Travels* and she said I was an excellent reader and that she was proud of me and that it was a brilliant story. I was wary. I started to cry. 'I want my dad.'

'Oh, my lovely boy. He is a bad man. Do you think it's right that he keeps me locked up out here with barely any food, in the dark, with no books?'

'There's no television here either.'

'Our neighbours had a television. Do you have one here? In this house?'

I nodded. It wasn't answering questions if I didn't say anything.

'Wow. Is the house big?'

I wondered about that. I suppose it was. There were lots of rooms. That day we went to the zoo, we passed lots of houses but most of them were all crammed together. On television, I saw big houses and small ones. I decided our house was big, but I wasn't going to tell her that.

I went to the pile of clothes that Dad had laid out on the single chair beside my bed and found my pyjamas.

'Do you need any help getting undressed?' she asked.

I ignored her and took off my clothes. I looked at my

watch. The small hand was between seven and eight. I was late for bed.

'Oh, you have a watch! What time is it?'

'Bedtime.' It was twenty-five past seven. I had just learned to tell the time and I wanted to show off, but there was no point in showing off to somebody as stupid as her. Dad was a bit fed up of me showing off. He said I didn't have to tell him the time every five minutes.

'Okay.'

'I need to brush my teeth.' I passed her to get to the toilet and, this time, I closed the door.

I did another wee and brushed my teeth. There was no mirror here and one thin towel. When I opened the door, she was kneeling in front of it. She had her arms stretched out wide. I tried to jump past her, but she quickly wrapped her arms around me, pushing her face down on to my head and kissing it. I struggled violently.

'Let me go, let go of me!'

'I love you so much, I can't help it. I thought I heard you through the door sometimes, but he's put up all this insulation on the walls and I didn't know if it was my imagination. He never told me anything about you. He said if I tried to talk to you through the wall, he would punish you. I'm so glad you're here.' Her arms tightened and I screamed into her armpit.

She released me then and I ran to my corner.

'I'm sorry, Peter, I'm so sorry. I just wanted to hold you for a moment.'

'I'm telling Dad. He's going to punish you so badly.'

'I need –'

'I don't care. Shut up. Don't say anything else. You're bad and you're mean.'

I got into the camp bed and turned the lamp off.

*

I was afraid to go to sleep, but I must have been tired, because I woke to see faint shafts of light coming through the boarded windows. I didn't know where I was for a moment, but then the horror of it all came back to me. I switched on the bed-side lamp and saw that she was as close to me as she could get, staring at me again.

'Peter? I'm sorry. Can we please start again? I'm so sorry.'

'I'm hungry.'

'Let me get you some cornflakes?'

I looked to the shelf above the fridge. The chocolate was gone. I was saving it for that evening, as Dad had instructed. The loaf of bread was half eaten too. The banana was missing. And there was only half a carrot left.

'You ate my food! You ate my chocolate.'

'I did. I had to. Can't you see? He starves me here. There's still enough for your dinner.'

I said nothing, but I put on my clothes quickly and tied my shoelaces, before I went over and kicked her as hard as I could with my leather shoes, repeatedly, in the face, in the head, in her fat belly. She rolled herself into a ball, whimper-ing and crying. Dad was right. She knew I was in charge now. She didn't try to talk to me again for ages. She got under her blanket and sobbed there, and every so often she would cry out in pain.

I shouted at her to shut up.

I got my own cornflakes and sat on my camp bed. I tried not to cry. I wanted my dad. I hated the ghost. I rattled at the door and looked at where the window had been. There was no glass in it. Just planks of wood. I could see chinks of light coming through but could not see the garden. I read my book and played with my matchbox cars and tried to forget where I was. I missed television. I wondered if Dad had sent me here as punishment. But what had I done to deserve it?

21

Sally

On Christmas Day, I got up early and lit the fire in the sitting room. Our Christmas Days after Mum died were usually the same: a turkey lunch, mostly prepared by me. I would drink a glass or three of red wine, which made me feel warm and giddy and then sleepy. We ate in front of the television because there was so much to watch. We both liked *Raiders of the Lost Ark* and that was on most years on some channel. Indiana Jones was handsome and when I thought hard about him, I felt a tingle in my knickers. I asked Dad what that meant, and he said it meant that I was heterosexual, theoretically.

On this first Christmas morning without Dad, an old Abbott and Costello film was on TV. I had my tea and toast in front of the television. Dad used to laugh out loud at these films and I would join in laughing even though I found the antics of the two men stupid, but Dad liked it when I laughed. Sometimes I laughed spontaneously. There used to be a show called *You've Been Framed* and it was full of short videos of people falling over in stupid ways and hurting themselves. That was funny.

But I realized nothing was funny when you watched it on your own.

At 11 a.m., the phone rang. It was Nadine. 'You were invited for Christmas lunch and the invitation still stands, but if you ever hurt Angela again, I'll hit you so hard that you won't know what day it is.'

'I think that's fair,' I said.

'And another thing,' she said. 'That stupid teddy bear is not to be mentioned in this house.'

'Okay.'

'Can you be here in half an hour?'

'Yes, thank you.'

When Nadine answered the door, I put my hand out to shake hers, and she took it and I shook very firmly to show I meant I was very sorry indeed.

'It's all right,' she said. 'You're a nutcase, but you're our nutcase.' She laughed and I laughed because she was right and it was nice to feel that I belonged to someone. I apologized again to Angela. The frozen peas had worked because her face was unmarked.

I asked a lot of questions that day but I didn't get many answers. Angela didn't know anything except that I'd been adopted. She had looked up my story on the internet and could glean bare facts. The date my birth mother was abducted, the date we were discovered. Conor Geary's date of birth and family circumstances (he had one sister from whom he had been estranged). The date of my mother's death. She did not know how exactly she died but that it was ruled a suicide. The reports that I had been adopted abroad.

Apart from that, we had a nice day. I hadn't thought to buy them gifts, but Angela and Nadine had bought me a purple sweater that was soft and bright. I was amazed that they didn't turn the television on at all. They played with Spotify and tried to get me to join them in dancing. They drank a lot. I drank three glasses of wine and that is my absolute limit. Even then, I was feeling sleepy, but I was glad to walk home.

The minute I got in, I turned on the central heating and the television. I was disappointed not to get answers from Angela about what had happened to me. I went into Dad's office and opened the box marked PRIVATE. There were old

Polaroids labelled 'Denise and Mary Norton'. My birth mother was so young and frail, and in most photos she looked terrified. In photos where her mouth was open, I could see that she had no visible teeth. In the majority of them, she had her arms wrapped around a small child. In bed, on an office chair, standing by a radiator. She wore clothes that were mismatched and seemed to swamp her emaciated body. It took me a moment to realize the child was me, despite the label. I did not, do not, resemble Denise, although she must have been young when she died. I compared photographs of me when I was in my late teens and early twenties. There was no likeness. In the photographs where she was on her own, her face was tear-stained and her arms reached out. For me?

I didn't recognize her, but with close inspection, I recognized me. My face was taut and pinched, unlike the photos of my seventh birthday party, where I looked well fed, albeit unhappy. Denise looked gaunt. In some of the photos, we are smiling at each other and she appears to be talking to me. I don't look at the camera. Despite the circumstances, I look like my smile is genuine and voluntary. My sunken eyes sparkle. Toby isn't in any of the photos.

I went to the mirror and tried to replicate the smile, but I am an adult woman. It is stupid to try to smile like a child.

In the box, also, there were small cassette tapes and a Dictaphone. The tapes were numbered and dated. I slipped the first numbered tape, dated 11/04/80, into the slot, but the batteries were long dead. I replaced them and pressed play. I recognized Dad's voice immediately.

Tom: Denise, come in, no need to be afraid, this is a safe place. Nobody is going to hurt you here. And this is your little girl, Mary?

Me!

Denise: [*screaming*] Leave the door open, please open the
    door!
Child: [*whimpering*]
Tom: I'm so sorry. Jean, will you leave the door open wide,
    please?
Denise: Where is she going? I don't want her to go!
Jean: Tom, it might be better if I stay?

My mum's voice!

Tom: You're right. Now, Denise, is that better? Jean will
    stay and the door is open. Would you like to sit down
    there, and Mary can sit – oh I see, well, you can sit
    together. Wherever you are comfortable.
Denise: [*mumbles*]
Tom: Did you sleep last night, Denise? I know everything
    must be strange to you after being . . . away for so long.
Denise: [*mumbles a question*]
Child: [*whispers an answer*]
Tom: There is no need to whisper any more, Mary.
Denise: Don't talk to her!
Jean: Will I take Mary over here to the play area?
Denise: No!
Tom: It's just a few steps away. You can watch.
Denise: No. I said no!
[*A long silence. Jean coughs*]
Tom: You saw your mother and father last night, Denise,
    how did that feel?
Denise: They look old.
Tom: It's been fourteen years. People age. Do you think you
    look different to the way you looked fourteen years ago?

Denise: I suppose.

Tom: Jean, can you check that file and see if there are any photos of Denise before . . .

Jean: Yes, there are some right here.

Tom: Denise, would you like to see what you looked like fourteen years ago?

Tom: Are you nodding your head or shaking it?

Denise: I want to see.

[*Sounds of movement*]

I think the tape has stopped, but it is just another long silence. Then there is the sound of tearing and scuffling and the child, me, whimpering. Dad is calm.

Tom: Why did you tear up those photos, Denise?

Denise: They want her. They don't want me.

Tom: Who?

Denise: My mammy and daddy. They want that girl back.

Tom: That girl is you, Denise.

Denise: I don't know her.

Tom: Jean told me that it was a stressful visit, Denise. You're twenty-five now, isn't that right? Can you imagine what it was like for your mammy and daddy, missing you for all those years, wondering what had happened to you?

Denise: Why didn't they keep looking for me?

Tom: Well, it's . . .

Jean: They never gave up hope that you were alive. Didn't your mammy say that last night?

Denise: They didn't try hard enough.

Tom: You know, Denise, it's not possible to keep looking for someone forever.

[*The sound of a child's whispering*]

Jean: What did you say, Mary?

Denise: Don't talk to her.

Jean: I'm sorry.

Denise: Give me that.

Tom: The doll?

Denise: Give it to me.

[*Noise of movement*]

Tom: Mary might like to play with a doll. Has she seen one
  before?

Jean: What are you doing with the doll, Denise?

Denise: I'm doing up all the buttons. She shouldn't be a
  little slut.

I stopped the tape. I knew what had happened to Denise.
How she had protected me. I did not remember her voice or
her face in the photographs, but I was incredibly sad for this
stranger. Dad used to say that I had empathy in abundance,
but I didn't use it often enough.

I turned to Dad's notes and took out a file at random.

Denise Norton D.O.B 05.04.55
26/09/80 WEEK 24
Hard to know if I am making any progress with Denise. Her mental capacity is severely diminished, and
I would estimate her mental age at little more than
when she was kidnapped: eleven years old. The contra-
diction is that she is an extremely overprotective
mother. Mary can walk and talk, although she never
uses her full voice and only whispers. Jean says there
is no physical reason for this. She is toilet trained
but will only go when her mother is present. Mary is
approximately five or six years old according to the
doctors and still has not been in the presence of

other children. Denise holds her hand and must be in physical contact with her at all times. We have tried a cot bed beside Denise's bed, but Denise refuses to let go of the child. Mary, sensing her mother's fear, is also unwilling to let go. There was a mattress in one room and a child's bedroom in the extension where they were kept, though maybe they always slept together on the mattress. The small bedroom looked uninhabited from the photos I saw. Denise rarely answers questions about their circumstances in Killiney. Jean has some half-baked theories but no evidence of anything.

Mary and Denise read the same books. Denise shows no interest in adult books or newspapers (this may be a blessing!) but this means that Mary's reading is advanced for her age. Denise's handwriting has not progressed beyond the year of her abduction. Mary's reading ability is way ahead of her peers, not that she has ever met any peers.

We had another attempt at a family therapy session with Denise and her parents yesterday. Denise was uncommunicative and struck her father when he kissed the top of her head when leaving. Medication has only taken the edge off her anger and volatility. Mr and Mrs Norton are distraught and have repeatedly asked when will we be able to 'fix' Denise. They think we can magically restore her to normal and that they will then be able to take her home. They are keen, as are we, that we separate mother and child. They want to see their daughter unencumbered with Mary. In consultation with her parents, we have all agreed to tell Denise that Conor Geary is dead and there is no way she will ever see him again. Security at this site is high and the manhunt for the psychopath who has destroyed at least one life is under way. Sightings have been reported and clairvoyants are cashing in, but there have been no solid leads.

Denise did not respond when we told her he was dead and could never harm her. She does not trust any of us.

Both Jean and I have tried to open conversations about him, but we are met with screams which upset her and the child. I don't know how we can ever broach the subject of what he might have done to her. My honest belief is that Denise is so damaged and has been brutalized for so long that any kind of normal life will be extremely unlikely.

She talks to Jean sometimes when they go out to walk around the grounds. She has allowed Jean to take Mary's other hand when they are walking. So, in a way, Jean has made more progress than I. Denise wants to know what each flower is called and teaches little Mary the names and spellings. Jean reports that Mary constantly asks for Toby. Denise has told Jean that Toby is a toy bear. Denise's parents have confirmed that when Denise was abducted from their garden in 1966, she was in possession of a teddy bear that she called Toby.

Denise has physically attacked me only once in the last week. The child was crying, so I instinctively reached out to console her. Denise charged at me like a pit bull and bit at my arm, while never letting go of the child. Again, we had to end the session early and Jean led them back to their quarters.

On the positive side, Denise and Mary have physically improved. They have both gained weight. Denise eats everything put before her and Mary copies everything Denise does. Denise is a striking-looking young woman, apart from the missing teeth, but she has the mind of a child. They both enjoy bath time and cry when they have to get out. But they look better. Denise's hair has been cut short to stop her pulling it out, but she still tries, several times a day, and Mary copies her.

They are completely isolated here. Jean and I are both of the opinion that it is still too soon to introduce Denise to other people.

As for us, we are a bit sick of living on campus. There are four nurses and one other female paediatrician who attend Denise and Mary in our unit, but Jean and I need a break soon. It is exhausting to put so much effort into one case with so little reward.

The thing is, there is hope for the little one, if we can get both her and her mother to allow some gradual separation. We will keep trying. But this is the most gruelling case I have ever worked on and it's the same for Jean. If we don't make a breakthrough with Denise soon, she might break us all.

Toby was my bear, and my mother's bear. My mother pulled her hair out too when she was distressed.

22

Peter, 1974

Hours passed, and she slept, I think. I pulled apart some bread and smeared some butter on it for my lunch. I took the rest of the food and put it under the chair beside my camp bed.

When my watch said five o'clock, I shouted at her to wake up. She had to make my dinner. Bacon, mashed potato and peas.

She lifted her head and said, 'There's something wrong with the baby. I can feel it.'

'I don't care, make my dinner.'

She struggled to stand up and her face was red and sweaty. Her legs were shaking.

'You hurt me. I think you hurt the baby.'

'Dad told me I could.' Dad hadn't said anything about a baby. She could have been making up the whole baby thing. She was a thief anyway. I was cross about the chocolate.

She started to talk again but kept stopping to take deep breaths. 'He used to make potatoes for me, years ago . . . I only get them now every few months . . . I can't remember the last time I had a carrot.'

She squealed again and held her belly. 'It's not time yet. He said I had about six weeks, but when was that? It's hard to keep track of the days here.'

I didn't know what she was talking about. But I felt mean about kicking her so much.

'I'm sorry,' I said.

She looked at me and she was crying and smiling at the same time.

'It's not your fault, baby. You live with a monster. How could you be normal? What kind of man would tell you that it's okay to kick and punch a pregnant woman?'

'Dad is not a monster! He's the best!'

'But he keeps you locked up. You have no friends, you don't go to school. Have you even met other children?'

'No, and I never met a woman, and I'm glad.'

'But what about when you go to the shops? Or if you got sick? Haven't you ever seen a nurse?'

'Dad knows how to fix me. He's a dentist.'

She bent over in pain again. 'Is he? . . . I never knew . . . I should have . . .'

She put her fingers in the gaps where her teeth should have been. She obviously did not brush her teeth.

'You have to make my dinner. I'm hungry!'

Her face was wet with sweat. She straightened up and lifted a frying pan and fried some rashers. The smell was delicious. She mashed the potatoes with a fork and opened the tin of peas and poured them into another battered pot to heat. She slopped it all on to a plate and pushed it across the floor to me, moaning and groaning.

'Stop making those noises.'

'I wouldn't be making noise if you hadn't hurt me. I thought you were sorry.'

'Not any more. You're a thief and you stole my food and the bacon isn't even crispy the way I like it.'

She stopped, breathed aloud a little and steadied herself against the sink. 'Oh my God, you're just like him. He'll turn you into a monster too if you don't escape.'

She fell back against the wall and slid down it. She fell asleep again, right there.

I ate my dinner and then the crisps.

At some stage, she crawled across the floor to her mattress and pulled the blanket over herself and cried.

I cried then too. What a terrible mother I had. This was all like a bad dream.

We didn't speak for the rest of the evening, not even when I passed her to wash and brush my teeth and do my wees.

In the middle of the night, she woke me, crying out, 'Help me! Please God, help me!' but I didn't want to help her and I didn't know how.

'Shush!' I said.

In the morning, she went to the toilet. I could hear her weeing and then filling the basin with water. There was the sound of splashing and moaning.

I got dressed and ate my cornflakes while she was in there.

She came out of the toilet soaking wet from head to toe. She had no clothes on. She was still shaking. I stared at her naked body, the roundness of her belly, and the two breasts, drooping bags of flesh above it. I hadn't wondered what naked ladies looked like. Her bottom was kind of normal, but wide, and she had hair between her legs and under her arms. I couldn't help staring. She saw me looking. 'I'm burning up. I can't put my clothes on, it's too hot.'

'Cover yourself up, you stupid woman.'

'Aahhhhhhhhhhhh!' She screamed and clutched her belly and, before she half fell on to the mattress, I could see blood pouring down her legs.

I was terrified. I didn't know how to help her, but I wanted it to stop.

'Stop it,' I ordered her, but she was wailing now. Dad had said he'd be home by eleven this morning. It was nine thirty.

'I think the baby is dying. I might die too.' She was gasping and taking deep breaths. 'Is that what you want? You have to tell somebody that I'm here . . . My name is Denise Norton. Please remember that . . . I used to think that people would come looking for me, but I think they have given up now. You're the only person who knows I'm here. Please, as soon as you get out today you must tell somebody that I'm here. Denise Norton. Denise Norton. You're my son.'

'Who would I tell?'

She sobbed then. 'You could run outside to the road and tell the first person you met.'

'I'm not allowed outside the garden.'

'Don't you see? If only you were old enough to understand . . . we are both prisoners.' Her breathing was becoming shallower. She fell asleep again. I could see blood spreading across the blanket. What if she died? Would Dad be angry with me? I went to the fridge and filled a glass with milk. I went to her and held it to her face.

'Milk is good for you,' I said and I tried to lift her head. She roused slightly and tried to drink the milk but most of it spilled on to the mattress. 'Do you want my cheese?' I tore the packet open, and she gnawed at it.

'Denise Norton,' she said over and over again. 'You must tell someone. If I die here, they won't know who I was.'

'Stop saying things.'

'Does anyone know you exist? It's not normal to be locked behind gates. He's a monster. Can't you see?'

I shouted then and pulled away from her. 'He is not. You're a monster and I hate you!' I aimed another kick at her but struck the corner of the wall instead.

'You know what? I think I hate you too,' she said. 'I'm ashamed of what he has made you.'

*

Dad arrived at five to eleven. When he saw the mess and the blood, he told me to go to my room and stay there.

'But it's Sunday,' I complained.

'Go to your room,' he roared at me and I scurried into the room next door.

He hadn't even said hello or hugged me. What if he put me in her room as punishment for killing her? What if he chained me to the bolt in the wall? I stayed in my room for hours and hours, afraid to leave even though the door wasn't locked and I was hungry. I blocked my ears when I heard, or thought I heard, some muffled screams.

Eventually, Dad came in and I tried to judge by the set of his jaw whether he was angry or not. He opened the door and kneeled down to my level.

'I'm so sorry, little man, I should never have put you through that. I promise, I'll never leave you there again. I didn't think it would be fair to leave you on your own for two whole nights, but you might have been better off.'

'Is she dead?'

'What? No. She had a baby.'

'My brother or sister?'

'It's a girl.' His lip curled.

'Are they all right?'

'Yes. You kicked her?'

'You said I could.'

'I suppose I did. I guess I didn't realize you could kick that hard. She'll be all right eventually. Let's go and get some food, okay?'

I watched television while Dad prepared dinner in the kitchen.

I couldn't stop thinking about Denise Norton and my baby sister.

'Dad, she said I lived with her for the first few years and then you took me away. Is that true?'

'Not entirely. I needed her to breastfeed you. You know what that is, right?'

I nodded. Dad got *National Geographic* magazines. I'd seen photos.

'But as soon as you were ready, I brought you out here to spend time with me. She was of no use to you after that. I taught you how to read and write.'

'She doesn't have any books. Will you give her some of mine?'

Dad didn't say anything and I could tell by the way his jaw clenched that he didn't like me asking that. I couldn't stop thinking, though. As Dad presented me with beef and onion pie, I said, 'Dad, what did she do?'

He understood what I meant.

'Terrible things. I'll tell you when you're older.'

'I think you should give her some new blankets.'

He reached over and took my hand. 'Peter, she's a nasty bitch and now she has pushed out another nasty bitch. They don't deserve your consideration. I wish you had a better mother.'

I nodded eagerly. 'Me too.' And then, 'What's a bitch?'

'A female dog,' he said, and laughed, and then he tickled me and I laughed too.

'She said that I was a prisoner like her. Is that true, Dad?'

'Of course not, you're so precious to me. I want to keep you safe.'

'Do you want to keep her safe?'

'Ah now, Peter, you saw what she was like. Would you want her walking around the house with us?'

'No way!'

'Exactly. Now forget all about her. I'm sorry you had to suffer that. It won't happen again.' I went to my room and I wrote down the date on the wall behind my bed with a crayon. *September 15th 1974.* I don't know why I did that, but it's a date I never forgot.

Over the following weeks, I tried to forget about the bitch and the baby. Sometimes, at night, when everything else was silent, I could hear the baby crying from the room next door. I could hear my dad visiting to give them food and stuff.

I had lots more questions for Dad about why I didn't go to school, and why I couldn't have friends, and why I wasn't allowed down to the front gate, but he got sad when I asked those questions. He said it was hurtful to him, and that he was doing his best.

Months later, I raised it again. 'I'd like to go to school and meet other children. On television, children are always playing together. At the zoo that time, there were loads of children and families, like on television.'

This time, he shook his head and bid me to come and sit beside him. 'I didn't want to tell you this until you were older, Peter, but you have a disease.'

'What do you mean?'

'It's called necrotic hominoid contagion. If you touched another person, you would get sick and you could die, a painful death. Remember when we went to the zoo? I never let go of your hand. It's too dangerous for you. You must never mix with other people. It's the only way I can save your life. That's why I had to leave you with her the time I went away for work. You cannot get the disease from your parents. There is nobody else I can leave you with. They might kill you.'

'But what about when I grow up?'

'I don't know. I'm hoping some treatment might be

available, but there isn't a lot of research on the condition at the moment.'

'What would happen if I touched somebody else?'

'You would gradually turn to stone, like in the story of Medusa. Remember? The woman with snakes for hair? It's an agonizing death. Whoever she gazed upon would turn to stone. You see, women and girls are particularly dangerous, but touching anyone at all would put you at considerable risk.'

This explained why Dad was so sad when I asked all those questions.

'So will I stay here for the rest of my life?'

'My poor boy, we will have Special Days Out on your birthday, but we must exercise extreme caution. You are happy here, aren't you?'

'I get lonely sometimes.'

'And that's why you have specially chosen books in your room. You can have extravagant adventures with Homer, or scale mountains with Sir Edmund Hillary, or fly a plane like Biggles.'

'My favourite books are the ones about children who are friends with each other.'

He ruffled my hair fondly. 'Your reading is advanced for your age. Alas, your taste is not.'

'So . . . I'll stay here for the rest of my life, with you?'

'Let's take it a day at a time. You never know when there might be a cure.'

'What about my baby sister?'

He took his hands away from my hands. 'What about her?'

'Would I die if I touched her? Couldn't she live with us?'

'Absolutely not. All women are dangerous.'

'Even babies?'

He didn't answer. I said nothing more.

23

Sally

As one year ended and a new one began, I read through all of the files and listened to all of the tapes. Some of Dad's writings were medical records, but some were personal diaries. There was no further mention of Toby. The records confirmed that Mum and Dad were living with Denise and me in a specialist unit in the grounds of St Mary's and were on call around the clock. We were a psychiatric enigma. No case like ours had ever arisen in Ireland before. Dad corresponded with psychiatrists in the USA, but none of their cases exactly matched mine and my birth mother's. Dad was warned that it could take years of work to undo the damage and he was advised to take it slowly.

Denise was sedated at night-time but, even under sedation, she would not release me from her grip. She eventually became more talkative and she quickly learned to read longer words, alongside me. An educational psychologist joined the support team but admitted it was hard to teach both mother and daughter at the same time as they were 'a constant distraction to each other'.

At one time, Mum and Dad took a week's holiday from the unit. When they returned, it was three weeks before Denise or I would talk to them again.

Dad tried 'every single thing one can think of' to get Denise to talk to him or Mum about Conor Geary, but she either cried, which made me cry, or she was silent and pulled at her hair. Dad did ask her if more than one man had attacked her and forced her to do things that she didn't like with her body. On that occasion she was completely silent, although the tape suggested that she shook her head.

Through official channels, my birth had to be registered and Mum and Dad got to decide on which day I was born. They chose 13th December 1974. They tried to hold a small party for my sixth birthday with all the staff, but Denise didn't like the singing and I didn't understand the concept of blowing out candles on a cake. Dad guessed that Conor Geary must have threatened us at some time with fire. Denise screamed and threw the cake at the wall. I'm glad I don't remember that birthday.

Reading about my birth mother was ... odd. She was angry, aggressive and violent. She was unable or unwilling to articulate any of the terrible experiences we had suffered. It was clear that Dad was frustrated with her. She could not understand that he was there to help her. She did not display any sign of affection or softness, except to me. I could glean from his notes that the longer Dad spent with Denise, the less he liked her.

Dad decided eventually that Denise and I must be separated. I had begun to progress and was no longer whispering. I was starting to show 'normal signs of curiosity' consistent with my age. At that stage, Denise had occasionally let go of my hand, and in the sessions in Dad's office, she would allow me to play with the toys in the corner, but never took her eyes off me. In consultation with the team, Dad concluded that I would never be able to develop naturally under Denise's shadow. Her violence and aggression were often mimicked by me. The plan was a trial separation at night when we were asleep. Denise's parents gave their consent, even though it wasn't technically needed. She was a ward of court.

Denise was heavily sedated on 15th May 1981. We had been in the unit for over a year at that stage. Denise would have just turned twenty-six. I was placed in a separate room next door to hers with Jean, and a nurse was to stay in a pull-out bed in Denise's room. Dad slept upstairs. Nurse Crawley was primed to give Denise further sedation if required that night, but that she was not, under any circumstances, to reunite us.

Everyone in the unit was on high alert, but Dad said nobody could have predicted what happened. Mum and Dad were awake most of the night, but Dad eventually drifted off to sleep about 5 a.m. At 5.30, Denise's screaming started. Dad did not intervene. Twenty minutes later, the nurse began to scream. When he entered her room, Denise was already half dead. She had banged her head repeatedly off the wall with such ferocity that she suffered a brain haemorrhage. She died later that morning in hospital without regaining consciousness. The nurse had tried her best to restrain her, but Denise had unnatural strength. Nurse Crawley was distraught, as were Mum and Dad.

An inquiry was held. Dad was exonerated, although he expressed terrible guilt. Dad wrote that Denise's parents, although devastated, may have been relieved. Their visits over the previous fourteen months had been extremely difficult for them and had become more infrequent as time went by. Denise's father had given up coming altogether. Denise saw all adult men as a threat. Their daughter was gone long before she died. She had never allowed her mother to hug or hold her. She recoiled from her father. Dad was the only man she ever saw. In retrospect, Dad thought that a female psychiatrist should have been appointed to take the Norton case, but he was the only person with the appropriate experience of dealing with deeply traumatized patients at the time and took us on as a special project. Aunt Christine had said that men made all of the decisions in those days.

Jean took over my primary care and development. On the morning of my mother's death, I too had woken and fought my way into Denise's room. I saw her unconscious body and her bloodied head. Jean grabbed and hugged me and tried to soothe me, but I kicked and screamed and fought and escaped her grasp and curled up beside my dying mother until the ambulance came to take her.

I barely ate or spoke for the first three months after Denise's death. Denise's parents no longer visited. They did not want to see me. They officially declared they would not be taking me home in the event that I would be released. I was a ward of court. Gradually, I became more attached to Jean; not in a physical sense, but I would confide my worries in her. I told her that Mummy had gone with Toby and that I was afraid I would be on my own. Dad noted individual sessions with me and, over time, 'despite Mary's deficiencies', he speculated that I might be rehabilitated.

The Eastern Health Board issued a press release announcing that Denise Norton had tragically committed suicide. No details of the circumstances were given. Mum and Dad's names were withheld too. The newspapers of the time said that Conor Geary now had a death on his hands. He might as well have murdered Denise.

Even though Dad was exonerated by the inquiry, he knew that his reputation in the small field of Irish psychiatry was irreparably damaged. By mutual agreement, he resigned his position.

It was Mum's idea that they should adopt me. They had been married for five years by then and Mum had fertility issues. She would not be able to have children of her own. Dad saw a chance to redeem himself with me. He said in his notes that raising me might go towards 'assuaging the shame' he felt over Denise's death. In consultation with the Eastern Health Board and the Adoption Board, it was agreed that Mum and Dad could formally adopt me. 'It was pushing an open door,' Dad wrote. 'Jean and I were the only adults Mary had responded to, and despite my handling of her mother's case, I was still a senior psychiatrist and kept up my licence. Jean was a medical doctor. Who better to manage such a damaged child?' That's what he called me. A damaged child.

Mum had applied to take over a GP practice in Co. Roscommon and Dad would opt out of practice and instead work on research from home. The adoption papers were signed on 30th November 1981. I was given a new name: Sally Diamond. I was reborn and moved to Roscommon town with my new parents.

I wished I had Mum's notes from that time. I scoured the house looking for anything she had written, but I remember Dad destroying a lot of stuff in the incinerator after Mum's death.

I gave Angela Dad's notes to read too, after I had read them. She said she found them deeply disturbing. I was fascinated by them. It was like reading or watching a documentary on somebody's life in a faraway place at a faraway time.

I wanted to know where Conor Geary was. 'S' had to be him. 'S' knew who I was and where I was and he had been in my life from birth to age five. The guards had compared the writing on the short note signed 'S' with Conor Geary's handwriting in dental files they had from nearly forty years ago and found no comparison but who else could it be? I knew he must be alive.

I wanted nothing to do with Toby now.

*

In February 2018, I began intensive therapy with Tina, a psychotherapist in Roscommon. She was a little older than me, with dark hair greying slightly at the temples. She wore orange lipstick and white nail polish. We sat in matching armchairs. From the first session, she insisted that I look at her face when I talked to her. The first few appointments were difficult. How did I feel about this, that and the other?

'Fine,' I said.

'Fine is not an emotion.'

I began to explore my emotions. I found that I was angry, resentful, hurt and anxious as well as grateful, warm, kind, considerate and lonely. Tina said that trust was my number-one issue, but that given my background, it was entirely reasonable. I liked that. I was reasonable.

Sometime in March, the guards got in touch. The Director of Public Prosecutions was not going to proceed with a prosecution over my illegal disposal of human remains. I had no case to answer. I'd not been worried about it. Detective Inspector Howard was shocked when I said this to her. 'You weren't worried that you had criminal charges hanging over you?'

'Not really. I mean, it was a simple misunderstanding. Thank you very much.'

'It wasn't my decision. You should thank your lawyer.'

'I will write to him this evening.'

Howard also informed me that the bear had finally been forensically examined. Despite our cleaning, they were able to find pollen spores in the seam on its back. The pollen had been found to be indigenous to flowers only grown on the North Island of New Zealand. The shoebox came from a shop in Wellington. The box was somewhere between eight and ten years old. The guards were reopening the cold case of Conor Geary's disappearance and Interpol were now involved in the search. A forty-three-year-old photograph of my birth father was circulated and published in newspapers in New Zealand and Ireland.

All my dad's files and tapes were taken away, though I was given copies of everything.

A further flurry of media activity ensued. More phone calls and letters from international journalists. I hung up or closed the door in their faces. Martha started a local Whats-App group to deter journalists from finding me. And to give them false leads as to where I was and what I was doing.

I completed my computer course by the end of June 2018. There were five people in my class. They all knew exactly who I was, but they were a lot older than me. When they asked me questions, I became anxious. Tina suggested that I should tell them the truth: I had no memory of the abduction or anything of that time. That worked. My fellow students lost interest and treated me normally. They took it in turns to bring cake every week. I made brownies from my Delia Smith recipe book. Everyone said they were lovely.

Under Tina's guidance, I tried out conversation with them before and after classes. It amazed me how much they wanted to talk, about their drug-addicted grandchildren, their in-grown toenails, that week's bargains in Lidl. I didn't have that much to say but they didn't seem to notice and I didn't mind listening. They laughed a lot. I rarely knew what they were laughing at, but I don't think it was me.

I now had an email address and could google whatever I wanted. I watched the news every night and I registered to vote. I got rid of the house phone and learned to use a smartphone.

I found several articles written about Conor Geary over

the years in newspaper archives through the library services. He was compared to Lord Lucan, an aristocrat who had murdered a nanny and then vanished off the face of the earth. There were true crime websites that speculated as to where he went and what had happened to me, all now updated with the news of my incineration of my father and photographs of me at his funeral.

There were old black-and-white photographs of the small extension we had lived in. The bolts on the outside of the doors, the boarded-up window. The grim-looking toilet and washbasin. The mattress with its thin blankets. My small, empty bedroom. None of it looked familiar. Former dental patients of Conor Geary described him as quiet and anti-social. 'He kept himself to himself,' they said.

24

Peter, 1980

Years passed. I regularly asked Dad if there was a cure for my disease but, each time, he shook his head sadly. As I was twelve now, he explained more about it. I wouldn't turn to stone, but human touch from somebody unrelated would rot the skin all the way through to my bone and the necrotic tissue would spread quickly throughout my body until it reached my inner organs. I would simply decay from the outside and the pain would be fierce. Dad guessed that it would be quick, but when I asked if he meant five minutes or ten hours, he said that I shouldn't think about it.

I did have other Special Days Out but I was terrified when we went to the circus, not of the lions but because of the children and parents who sat either side of me. I crawled into Dad's lap, even though I was far too old for that, and he wrapped me in his coat. Other children laughed at me.

Knowing of my disease gave me nightmares. I begged Dad to have our Special Days on our own, and he hired a projector and we watched cowboy films on a big screen. Another time, he bought me a catalogue of books and I could choose whatever I wanted. I picked books about Neil Armstrong, and World War Two, and an illustrated encyclopaedia of dinosaurs. Dad thought they were great choices. The best time ever, we left the house on foot and walked down a long winding avenue to a train track. Underneath the train track was a tunnel that led to a beach and the sea. Dad had bought me swimming togs. We sat on a rug on the gravelly sand until Dad suggested that he could teach me to swim. I noticed strange marks on his stomach and shoulders, but when I asked Dad about them, he just shook his head and I knew that meant they were not to be discussed.

I squealed when my toes hit the cold water and Dad carried me in on his shoulders and then gently immersed me, while I screamed with fright and excitement.

'Peter! Don't scream like a girl.'

That was always the worst insult Dad could throw at me and, for a moment, I cried, but the salt water disguised my tears and soon we were splashing around and I was in the water up to my neck, laughing with my dad. I learned to swim that day. I could float on my back and look at the whispering clouds in the blue, blue sky. Afterwards, we went back and dried off with towels and sat on the rug. Nobody came near us, and it felt normal. I asked if we could do this every year, and he said 'we surely can' and I felt like the luckiest boy alive.

Shortly after my eighth birthday, Dad stopped locking me into my bedroom when he went to work. I began to help with preparing meals. Dad rotated my books often, so that I only ever had two or three at a time. He said I had grown out of toys and when they disappeared along with the clothing I had outgrown, I wondered if my sister had them next door. Dad was strict about me keeping all of my belongings in my room. I didn't have many, just books and clothing and copybooks, and a few toy soldiers I kept hidden because I was afraid Dad would say I was too old for them.

I began to realize that our lives were far from normal, mine and Dad's, as well as the two in the room next door. I could hear them all the time, moving around. I could hear my dad visiting at night. The sound was always muffled and I could never make out the words. The ghost often shrieked and the child often cried. I read hundreds of books and nobody in them lived like we did, or like my mother and sister. I asked Dad about this. Why couldn't I sleep in one of the bedrooms upstairs? Why did I have to sleep in the room in the annexe next door to her? Why did he not have any friends? Why didn't we have a telephone? He said he had lots of friends that he saw every day at work. I asked him about his work as a dentist, what exactly he did, and he explained about fillings and dentures. My teeth were in excellent condition because I was diligent about brushing first thing in the morning, after dinner and before bed. I asked him did he not want to go to the pub with his friends after work. He replied that he didn't drink alcohol, and that he would rather not leave me on my own in the house for any longer than he had to. I wondered why there were no other mad and dangerous women locked away and he gave me a book called *Jane Eyre* to read. 'It's written by a woman, but you'll see what I mean.'

Indeed, Bertha Mason was terrifying, but Jane was nice. I had never read books about women. Denise Norton hadn't tried to hurt me, I said, and then Dad said, 'I didn't want to ever have to explain, but . . .' He pulled up his sweater and there was a scar all the way across his stomach. 'She stabbed me.' He reminded me of the bruises and black eyes he would sometimes have in the mornings. He had told me they were a result of his clumsiness, but now he admitted it was her who had inflicted his wounds. He pulled down the collar of his shirt and showed me the latest, a bite mark on his shoulder. He was like poor Mr Rochester in the book. I was shocked, and surer than ever that I never wanted to see my mother again.

Later, he gave me *Medea* to read and *Macbeth*. 'You see what she made him do? He was a weak man. That's why a man has to be in charge. We have to show our superiority.'

I asked Dad why he didn't have my mother arrested. She could go to jail or a mental hospital. He stared at me for a long time and then said, 'I couldn't put my own wife in jail. It would be too cruel. You have no idea what goes on in places like that.' If Denise was of no use, why didn't Dad let her go? 'A man has needs,' was all he said in response to that.

'Dad, she said she's been here since she was eleven. Is that true? Did you marry her when she was eleven?'

He tossed his head back and laughed. 'She is so stupid, she doesn't know what age she is.'

'What age is she? Her teeth have fallen out, so I guess she must be old.'

'Exactly.' He grinned at me.

I was beginning to discover for myself what a man's needs might be. I had a certain reaction when I saw beautiful girls on TV and I knew it had something to do with my penis, because when I thought about those girls on my own in bed, I couldn't help playing with myself, resulting in what one of the encyclopaedias called 'ejaculation'. I even did it in my sleep. I was afraid of asking Dad about this. I wasn't sure what his reaction might be. He had mentioned in passing a few months previously that masturbation was against the laws of God. I hadn't known what the word meant then, but I certainly knew now.

I kept my new discovery to myself, but in Dad's library I discovered books on human anatomy with drawings of naked men and women, arrows pointing to their various body parts. I was going through puberty. The only naked woman I had ever seen was my stupid mother. Vulva and vagina were the words that stayed in my mind. I learned how babies were made. Dad put his penis into her vagina and vulva and pushed his seed into her. Why would he do that when he hated her and she disgusted him so much? He must have done it twice. 'A man has needs,' he'd said. Now I understood.

That was not the only thing that changed that year. Everything did. One spring afternoon, I was at my desk in the sitting room studying some Greek texts when, from my window, I saw a man climb through the undergrowth below the high wall on the left-hand side of the garden. I was startled. I had never seen anyone enter our grounds before without it being prearranged. Occasionally, the oilmen would make deliveries to the tank at the end of the garden, and Dad would advise me to stay in my room. On those days he said he'd had to gag Denise Norton and the child, so that they could make no noise. He said it was an embarrassment to have a mad wife and a stupid child. They were 'our secret'. That was strange. Who could I ever tell?

The long-haired man, wearing denim jeans and a black jacket, slid along the tall trees at the edge of our property, and then made a dart towards the back of the house, crouching low to the ground as he ran across. A burglar!

I stepped gingerly out of the room in time to hear glass breaking. I ran to the annexe to lock myself in my room but before I got there I heard her screeching, louder than ever before. She must have been lying on the floor, screaming through the tiny gap at the bottom of the door. 'My name is Denise Norton, I've been kidnapped! I'm locked in. I'm Denise Norton. Please, break down the door! Let me out!'

I heard brief scuffling from the kitchen and then ran to the sitting-room window again. The man must have jumped back out through the window, and I could see blood pouring from his hand as he sprinted across the lawn, dived into the hedge and over the wall. I ran back to the annexe. She was still shrieking her name over and over. I knew by now where Dad kept the key and I reached up to the kitchen cupboard and took the key out of the mug. As I opened the door, she was straining towards it, still chained by the ankle, clutching the small child by the hand.

'Oh, thank God!' she said, sobbing, and then she stopped abruptly. 'It's you? Peter? I thought they were different footsteps. You've got so tall.'

Her face crumpled and silent tears coursed down her cheeks. I looked at the girl by her side, who was staring at me from behind her mother's hip. She was silent, and thin too, with huge eyes, but paler than any child I had ever seen. Her skin had an almost blue tinge. She clutched the bear, my Toby, in her other arm. Denise was cleaner than the last time I had seen her. Still thin, but without the bulge in her belly. She was wearing an old dressing gown of Dad's. Her hair, though clean, was hanging limply down her back, tied with a rag. I looked around the room. She had a bright lamp now, and on top of the fridge there were a few potatoes and apples. She had three blankets, and the mattress behind her looked a little fresher than the one I remembered. There were no visible bruises this time.

'Peter –' her chest was heaving as she tried to get the words out – 'is he here? Whose were those footsteps? They weren't yours or his. And I heard glass breaking. What happened?'

I took a step backwards. She put her arms out to me. 'Please stay, please. You should meet your sister, Mary.' I stopped and looked back at the girl. Her mother babbled on. 'I promise I won't ask any questions. I must have been mistaken about the footsteps. I'm so sorry. I'll never do that again. Don't tell him.' I darted forward and grabbed the bear out of the girl's hands. The girl started to squeal and cry. Her mother raised her voice then. 'That's her only toy. It's the only thing she owns. Peter!' I edged backwards to the door.

'Please don't tell him! He'll kill me this time. He'll kill your sister!' She dropped to her knees.

I was stronger now than I was on our last encounter. I aimed a kick and connected with her face. 'Don't talk to me.'

'Oh God,' she gasped as blood poured from her nose. 'You're just like him. He'll kill me and you don't even care.' I was shocked at the blood, shocked at what I'd done. I turned and left, bolting and locking the door behind me.

I took the bear, stepped over the broken glass and went back into my room, slid the bear under my pillow and kept vigilant watch on the hedges until Dad came home.

Dad went into a rage when I told him what had happened. He made me repeat every part of the incident word for word. 'She definitely said her name?'

'Yes, over and over again, she kept shouting it.'

'You think he heard it?'

'Definitely.'

I had never seen him so angry. 'I'm fucked! That stupid bitch. The burglar will tell someone.' And then he ran upstairs and he shouted at me to pack a suitcase. I'd never heard him use the 'f' word before. I didn't have a suitcase. I followed him to his room upstairs where he was frantically rummaging through drawers. 'Where are we going?' I asked, my voice trembling.

'It doesn't matter.'

'What shall I pack?'

He threw a holdall bag at me. It glanced off my head. 'Stop whining like a girl. Pack what you need . . . No, wait, pack everything you own. Leave nothing behind. Don't just stand there. Hurry up!'

I ran to my room. 'How long are we going for?' I shouted. 'A long time.'

I had no idea how long that meant. The bag was small. I rushed around the room. I had three changes of clothes, four books, three copybooks. I hesitated and then grabbed Toby from under my pillow and stuffed him into the bottom of the bag. I had skipped telling Dad that I took Toby. Some instinct told me he would not be happy about that. There was nothing left in my room. I hoped that wherever we were going would have a bigger bed, because my feet stuck out of the end of this one.

'Quick!' said Dad. 'Get into the car.'

I opened the front door and, as I went to the car, I could see Dad pass through the hall towards the annexe. The next thing I heard was her screaming, and him roaring, and the child crying.

25

Sally

Conor Geary was forty-five years old when he fled Ireland in 1980. Thirty-one years old when he kidnapped my eleven-year-old mother in 1966 and thirty-nine when I was born in 1974. He would be eighty-three years old now. He had a sister, Margaret, who was technically my aunt. The guards told me she was living in the Killiney house where Denise and I had been held.

I wanted to talk to her. I wrote to her at that notorious address in June 2018.

She replied instantly. She wanted to meet me, to explain, and to apologize. Margaret came to meet Aunt Christine and me for lunch in Roscommon one day in August.

We looked alike. She had the same way of balling her hands into fists as I did.

She was annoyingly tearful throughout the lunch. I kept having to ask her to repeat what she'd said as she blew her nose. Aunt Christine whispered that I should be patient.

'I'm sorry,' I said to Margaret. 'I have emotional development issues because of him. I can't call you Aunt Margaret by the way. That feels wrong.'

'I understand. You don't have to explain.' Margaret said she was so ashamed of her brother. She admitted they'd had a strange upbringing.

'Our mother was tough on Conor. I'm not excusing him, but he didn't have it easy. Father died when we were children and it was as if she expected him to step into Daddy's

shoes . . . in every way. And he turned on me. He was . . .
aggressive with me, the way that she was aggressive with
him. It wasn't until I left home that I realized how screwed
up our upbringing was, how . . . perverse. I never understood
why he didn't leave too. I spent a few years in Canada as a
nanny and rarely came home. I used to write, but neither of
them replied, until Conor wrote to tell me that mother had
died. I was only twenty-seven.'

Conor inherited the family home and Margaret was left
with nothing. Conor refused to sell the house and share the
profits with her. She went back to Canada after her mother's
funeral with very little. They hadn't spoken in many years
before his crime was discovered.

'I let the house lie empty for a long time after Conor
absconded. I was afraid to come home because of the media
attention. I eventually returned to Ireland for good in 1990
and got a job managing a care home near the house. I had
made some money in Canada. Not enough to renovate the
whole house but enough to have the extension where your
mother and you were held demolished. My life was blighted.
How could I make friends, form relationships? As soon as
they found out who my brother was, they'd run for the hills.'

'Why did you come home then? Why didn't you stay in
Canada?'

'I don't know, the pull of home was always strong. It was
only when I'd packed up and come home that I realized there
was nothing here for me.'

'That is so terribly sad, the number of lives your brother
destroyed,' said Aunt Christine.

'But if he had never existed, I would never have been
born,' I said.

Aunt Christine and Margaret looked at each other and
smiled.

'What are you smiling at?'

'That's a unique point of view,' said Aunt Christine. This was the kind of answer that irked me.

Margaret said she had embraced the Church, and that she found comfort in God. She had friends now in a prayer group. She told me I was welcome to visit the old house, but the thought of it made me feel sick. I learned that Conor Geary had earned good money as a dentist. He had never had to pay rent or a mortgage in his life and had enough in his bank account before he emptied it and fled to start over anywhere he liked. I looked like his side of the family, there was no doubt. I, too, was antisocial and had few friends. Perhaps I had inherited those traits from him?

Aunt Christine was extremely kind. She came and stayed regularly, and twice she brought me to their large Victorian house in Dublin and I stayed with her and Uncle Donald. He was quiet and frail, and even though she said they were the same age, he seemed a lot older.

They had a piano in the house. I could tell by the dust that it hadn't been used in a long time, but they liked it when I played. Donald perked up and said it was 'soothing'.

I was doing my best to develop social skills in Carricksheedy. I went to the local pub with my old school pal, Stella, and we went to the cinema in Roscommon in the autumn, but even with earplugs, I was overwhelmed by the noise and spectacle. I had to leave early. Stella didn't mind. You wouldn't notice her stutter much at all any more. She showed me photos of her children and her husband and her dog. She suggested that I should get a dog for companionship. I wasn't sure that I wanted a companion who pooed anywhere he wanted and couldn't clean up after himself. Stella says I'm funny. I think she is. She sent me some romance novels to read. They were well-written stories, but I found it hard to relate to them. Stella thinks I should start dating. Like I said, she is funny. On my birthday she sent me a card and a woollen scarf and hat. They were soft and warm. I was forty-four now.

Martha was friendly too. She was always straight with me when I said things that were inappropriate. I asked her to point these things out. Tina thought that a great idea. I no longer assumed that people meant exactly what they said. 'Reading between the lines' was something I put into practice every day.

I went to dinner in Martha's house a number of times, and every time I saw Udo, he taught me some Igbo, which is his native language. He cooks great Nigerian food. I babysat for Maduka and Abebi a few times and they are the friends I like best. They say what they mean all the time. That year, they invited me for Christmas dinner. Aunt Christine invited me a few days later but I told her the Adebayos were more fun.

Tina was delighted with my progress and encouraged me to choose appropriate gifts for the family. I asked the children what they wanted and that was easy. For Udo and Martha, I bought a hamper of cheese from the big supermarket in Roscommon. I braved the crowds especially. Thank God for the earplugs.

26

Peter, 1980

As we drove out of the front gate, Dad said, 'Right, calm down and think. Think!' He was talking to himself. Fifteen minutes later, we parked directly outside the Allied Irish Bank. I had seen advertisements for it on the television. 'Wait here,' he barked at me. I had no intention of going anywhere. Dad was a long time and when he came back to the car he said, 'Bitch! I had to get the manager. It's my money. I'm entitled to take it all if I want, and no jumped-up little bitch is going to stop me.'

Next, we drove down a side street and pulled up beside a building. There was a door on the street and, beside the door, there was a brass plate which said:

GLENDALE DENTAL PRACTICE
TEL. 809915
CONOR GEARY
B. DENT. SC
DENTAL SURGEON

This was where my dad worked. I wanted to go in with him but he ordered me to stay in the car. A few minutes later, he came out with some files and a framed certificate. He dismantled the frame and threw it in the garden of an adjacent house and rolled up the certificate, opened the car boot and put it into the suitcase. I didn't dare ask any questions.

We swerved away from the kerb and drove off this main

street to a coastal road. He parked the car down on the pier and then we got out. Seagulls swooped low over our heads. He pulled a cap out of his pocket and put on a pair of glasses. I had never seen either before. 'Let's go to England,' he said, 'and then we'll think about how to get passports.'

We walked together and he smiled and nodded at every second person we passed, even women, pulling his cap lower every time. We walked ten minutes over to the ferry port and stood in a queue. I stood at a distance, afraid to touch anyone, but he yanked me towards him and gripped my hand. At the top of the queue, he bought two second-class tickets to Holyhead. I knew from geography books that Holyhead was in Wales. But I wasn't going to challenge Dad on anything. He was so tense. His grip hurt me and his jaw was clenched tightly.

I should have been excited. We were going abroad, for the first time ever. But it definitely didn't feel like a holiday. We were running away. But for how long? And who were we running from? Didn't Dad want to report the burglary to the guards? Dad always snorted at them on television. We watched *Garda Patrol* every week. He would laugh at them and call them 'incompetent lazy fools'. I tried to understand but my thoughts were scrambled. We boarded the ship and climbed what seemed like endless flights of stairs until we were outdoors on the deck.

'What's this town called, Dad?'

'Dún Laoghaire. Take a good look at Ireland, lad, it will be a long time before we ever see it again.' The anger was gone, and I could see his eyes glistening behind the clear lenses of his spectacles. Was Dad going to cry? Like a girl?

It was freezing on this deck, in the middle of March. Everyone else was huddled inside. Finally, the foghorn blew and the ship edged out of port, slowly at first and then picking up speed after we exited through the granite piers, one on either side, like outstretched arms, pushing us out to sea.

'We're going on our own odyssey,' he said, sadness in his voice.

'Dad.' I felt ready to ask him now that his anger had abated. 'I don't understand what's happening. Why are we going, so suddenly?'

He put his head in his hands. 'We have to. That's all there is to it. That burglar. If he were to tell anyone her name, people would come and take you away. They would put their hands on you, and you would die. I'm doing this for you.'

'But why would they take me away?'

'She's so crazy, she thinks I kidnapped her. Do you think that burglar isn't going to tell someone? The guards might believe her or they might believe me, but one thing is for sure, I wouldn't be able to stop them putting their hands on you, and that's not a risk I'm willing to take. We're going so that I can save your life. Your condition is so rare that most people don't believe it or understand it. Remember when I showed you the photos of the Boy in the Bubble? That's where you'd end up, if you were lucky, if they didn't kill you first.'

He lowered the spectacles and looked me in the eye. 'Do you understand?'

'I do,' I said solemnly. I remembered the story of the Boy in the Bubble. He was younger than me by a couple of years and his disease was so bad that the air could kill him, so he spent his whole life in a chamber in a hospital. Dad told me that my disease was similar, only that my death would be worse if I got infected. My dad loved me enough to run away to keep me safe.

'But once they discover that she's mad and dangerous, we can go home?'

'Maybe it's time we broadened our horizons. Don't you want to see the world?'

I nodded enthusiastically.

'Good boy. Now will we go down and get some food? We haven't had any dinner. Stay close to me.'

I can't remember how long the crossing took. Maybe three hours? I was tired by the time we arrived, but then Dad said we had to get a bus to London. We waited in a cold bus station, stamping our feet to get warm. I was too tired to be excited now. I had never been on a bus before. I revived a bit when we climbed up the steep steps. We found seats in the middle of the bus. It was too dark to see much outside. I fell asleep once we were in motion and barely noticed my surroundings when we stopped for a toilet break. It was approaching dawn when we entered London, but it was so big that it was almost another hour before the bus turned into a vast dirty-looking building. The sign at the entrance said 'Euston Station'.

'Is this the city centre?' I asked but he didn't answer. His jaw was tightening and he was looking keenly out of the window.

When we got off the bus, a woman bumped into me. I screamed, and Dad pulled me close to him, as the woman said belligerently, 'I barely touched him, what's he so hysterical about?' And I was hysterical, waiting for the pain to come, but Dad dragged me into a corner and said, 'It's okay, it's okay, she didn't touch your skin, just the back of your coat, you'll be all right.' But I was sure she'd touched the back of my head too. I was terrified, waiting for the pain to come, but it didn't.

'Peter, stop this now. You can't draw attention to us like this.'

Through my sobs, I told him that she'd touched my head. He reassured me that my hair would have protected me. A small group was staring at us. I threw my arms around Dad and snuggled into his shoulder. I could hear him saying to people, 'He's all right now, he just woke up, disorientated, you know. He's fine now. Nothing to worry about.'

'He's a bit old for that carry-on, isn't he?' The woman glared at us.

They dispersed quickly enough, busy people with places to go. I continued to hold on to him until I had calmed down. 'Don't mind that stupid bitch,' he said.

'Dad,' I said, 'remember you said that I might grow out of it, this disease? When will that be?'

'I haven't been able to find out if that's even possible. But I don't want you to worry, I'll keep you safe.'

'So, as long as I don't make contact with anyone's skin, I'll be all right?'

'Yes, that was what my research said.'

With all of the hundreds of people I could see milling around me, I was still worried. 'Dad, we're not going to live here, are we?'

'No. We need to go somewhere a lot quieter. Hopefully, we'll just be here for a few days.'

He took out a small book of maps and we began to walk. After an hour, my stomach growled and I asked, 'Is it much further? Can we have breakfast?' We stopped in a small and steamy cafe with dirty tables and muddy footprints all over the floor. Dad installed me at a table away from the window and went up to the counter to order. I wanted to go home. A man looked up and nodded at me. I looked away. Two women wearing short skirts, high boots and glittery sleeveless shirts came in and shouted their order at the man behind the counter, before taking seats at the window. I could see the dark-haired one's bra, and it was red. I had never seen women like these before. Weren't they cold, dressed like that? They wore glossy red lipstick and their eyelids were painted black. They blew plumes of cigarette smoke high into the air. Just as I began to feel an erection stirring in my pants, Dad grabbed my head and turned me to face him as he placed a bacon sandwich and a cup of tea in front of me. 'Don't look at them. Sluts,' he hissed. 'They have sex with men in exchange for money. They've probably come off the night shift.'

'Men pay for sex? Why don't they get married? Even if they married a crazy one, they could still have sex with her like you did.'

He stared at me, and I immediately felt embarrassed. 'What are you talking about, you little pup?' His anger was flaring.

'It's in the biology books you gave me, and the encyclopaedias. You must have had sex with her twice. Or how did I get here? Or that little girl?'

He picked up his tea and sipped slowly. We said nothing for a while and then he said, 'The girl was a mistake.'

I knew not to comment any further. But I didn't understand how he could have sex by accident. We ate our sandwiches and drank our tea in silence and I didn't dare to turn to look at those women again, though I could hear their cackling laughter and smell their cigarette smoke and perfume.

There was something else I had been thinking about. 'Dad, how are you going to earn money now? Are you resigning from your job forever?'

His brow furrowed. 'We have enough money for some time, but we will have to live frugally for the moment. No treats. All right? Just until I figure out a plan.'

I was alarmed. 'You don't have a plan?'

'Not yet, but I should have by tonight.'

We left the cafe and continued to walk. The streets got dirtier and the houses shabbier-looking. Eventually, we stopped at one which had a sign in the window advertising 'Vacancies'.

Dad knocked on the door. A small man answered, wearing denim jeans and a T-shirt. The T-shirt was stained and the carpet behind him was filthy.

'Hello,' said Dad, 'I'm looking for a room for my son and I for two nights, please?'

'You Irish?' said the man and, before he could answer, the man said, 'Fuck off home and take your bombs with you,' and slammed the door in Dad's face. Dad was furious.

'He must have thought I was in the IRA,' he said. 'Me? A terrorist?'

27

Sally

In the new year of 2019, my therapy sessions with Tina were going well. She was working on desensitization therapy with me, for anxiety and PTSD. When people shook my hand or patted my arm or even hugged me, I tried not to flinch. I was also having noise therapy to acclimatize me to 'normal' levels of sound. I still found this one difficult. Tina thought Martha's yoga classes were helping me to relax. Martha only ever touched me gently during the classes to guide me into the right positions. In the beginning, the stretching and bending felt unnatural, but I got used to it. I knew that centring myself and getting in touch with my body was calming when I was faced with difficult situations.

Tina thought I should get a job. She said I should have some purpose in my life. I explained that I had already been rejected as a childminder. But Tina asked me to think about what I like to do more than anything in the world. I guess I like to play the piano a lot. Tina wondered if I would consider teaching the piano. She asked me if I was patient. I didn't think I was. We did two sessions on patience.

I was good at Google and discovered a thing called regression therapy that could help me to remember. Tina was dead set against it and, after she explained, I understood. What was the point in remembering something so traumatic? And how likely was it that anything I recalled would help to capture Conor Geary now?

*

One day in February, I was talking to Udo in the Texaco shop. He told me the children were looking forward to their mid-term break. I indicated my umbrella and said I hoped the weather would improve because Abebi had told me she wanted to go camping. He thanked me for the information and said he was going to have to disappoint her. He said they would die of exposure in a tent. I told him about Stella's work with the homeless charity.

'A young man died of exposure in Dublin last week. You could tell her that,' I suggested.

'Sally, you can't talk about things like that with small children. It gives them nightmares. It should give politicians nightmares.'

'Thank you for letting me know, Udo, I'll add it to my list.' I had a list of things that I should not discuss with the children, written by Martha. I accepted a light hug and he exited the shop.

Caroline was behind the counter. We had swapped a number of recipes and my repertoire of meals was much improved. After Udo left, she said, 'First the lesbians and now the Blacks.' Her face was full of disapproval.

'What's the matter?' I asked her.

'They're taking over,' she said. 'Another three families of foreigners moved into the village in the last month. All because of that bloody meat factory at Mervyn Park.'

'It's good. More customers for you,' I said.

'They're not the sort of customers I want.'

'Why?'

'I'm not racist, but Ireland is for Irish people.'

'But Abebi and Maduka are Irish. They were born here.'

'They'll never be Irish,' she said.

'It's not good to be racist, Caroline,' I said.

'You don't understand a lot of things, Sally, and this is one of them.'

'I understand racism.'

'Stop calling me a racist.'

'Stop being one.'

Her face was getting redder.

'Look, you fucking weirdo, in the beginning I felt sorry for you, even after what you did to your poor father, because you were on your own, but now everyone feels sorry for you because of what happened when you were a kiddie. How do we know you're not exactly like your real father? You fucking psycho. Get out of this shop and don't come back!'

She was shouting now, and the two other customers in the shop were staring at us. I left as quickly as I could, without taking or paying for my groceries. I did my breathing exercises and remained calm but it was most inconvenient. From now on, I would have to shop in the Gala supermarket and I would have to memorize their shelves.

As I walked home, a car pulled up alongside me and the driver rolled down the window.

'Hey, are you okay? I saw what happened there in Texaco. What a cow. I gave her a piece of my mind after you left. You should report her to the manager.'

'She is the manager.'

'May I give you a lift? Sally, isn't it? I'm Mark. I've just moved here. Lucky I'm white, eh?'

'Is that a joke?'

'What? Yes . . . of course it is!'

He had pushed the passenger door open beside me. His eyes seemed kind and his face was pleasant. His hair was receding. His car was old. I could see he was wearing jeans with a shirt and tie. I couldn't see his shoes. But you can't judge a book by its cover, or a kidnapping rapist by the smile on his face.

'No thank you. I don't take lifts from strangers.'

'God. How stupid of me to even think . . . look, I'm sorry. I'm not . . . like . . . predatory.'

'And that is what a predator would say.' I walked on a little faster. The car stayed where it was for a long time. I got over the brow of the slight hill and down my lane and the car did not pass. Maybe he was not a kidnapper, but if there was one thing Dad was strict about when I was small, it was getting into cars with strangers. Now, obviously, I knew why. That's what my birth mother had done, and while Conor Geary was still out there, he could come back for me. That man though, Mark, was not Conor Geary. He was perhaps in his mid-fifties.

Despite more breathing exercises, I was a little shaken by my experiences of the day when I got home. I wanted to tell somebody what had happened. I thought of ringing Stella but she was at work and I was in the act of ringing Martha when I remembered what Tina had said about empathy. Maybe it would be hurtful to Martha to hear that Caroline was racist. But I could tell her about the man. Or could I? How would I explain how he started the conversation with me without explaining what Caroline said? I stopped the call. I needed more friends.

That was the day I decided to move house. I didn't like to feel unsettled on my own. For the first time in my life, I wanted to be around people.

I rang Geoff Barrington, the solicitor, who told me to ring an estate agent. He gave me a phone number for one and told me of a website where I could look at properties for sale. He also told me that I should start looking for a house, preferably before I put mine up for sale. He said that this was one of the big decisions and that I should seek guidance from someone. I thought I was seeking guidance from him. But he said he would handle the business end of things.

I guessed he meant that I should call Angela. I would wait until the weekend, when she was free. In the meantime, I logged on to the website and spent a happy few hours perusing houses in the county. I didn't want an apartment, although there was one for sale in the village. I wanted to be in the middle of things but I didn't want to share a corridor. Most of the houses available had three bedrooms but I only needed one, maybe two.

On Saturday afternoon, I called at Angela and Nadine's house and discussed my options. Nadine immediately suggested the run-down, derelict cottage on Bracken Lane, opposite Martha's yoga studio. 'It's been for sale for years.'

'I can't live in that,' I said.

'Use your imagination,' she said. 'Think of what it could look like.'

'Don't you ever watch home-makeover shows on TV?' said Angela.

'Yes, I love them, but I want a shower like yours. It would take up half that cottage.'

'But you could build an extension, double or triple the footprint of the property? I bet you could get the place for half-nothing. You'd need a surveyor and an architect. Look at our kitchen. You think it was built with the rest of the house in 1904? Do you think our paradise shower is a Victorian fixture?'

Nadine began to sketch on the back of a letter. She drew the front of the cottage. 'How far back does the property go? Probably fifty feet? Do you want a garden? Or maybe a small patio? Low maintenance? I've often thought that place could be beautiful, with skylights in the right places. You'd need to look at the drainage situation, though. There must be

a reason why nobody has touched it in twenty years or more.'
Nadine was excited. 'Let me ring the council on Monday. See
what they say. You'd be doing them a favour. The only reason it hasn't been condemned is because it's up a laneway
and out of sight. But you'd be in the middle of Carricksheedy. I wonder who owns it.'

Angela laughed. 'Uh-oh,' she said, 'Nadine's got a bee in
her bonnet. I always said designing furniture was too small
potatoes for her.'

'Sorry, sorry! I'm getting carried away. Loads of potential.
The other options are small three-bedroom terraces on main
street or the bland three-bed semis on the housing estate
beside Mervyn Park. I heard they're building more, though,
since the business park is expanding. Your own house could
be worth a lot Sally. You've a few acres, don't you?'

I thanked them and explained I had to go because I was
going to Martha's party.

'A party?'

'Yes, I haven't been to one since I was a child. I'm
nervous.'

'Don't be nervous, have fun!'

'But I don't know anyone there except Udo and Martha
and the children. They're holding a party for the new recruits
at Mervyn Park.'

'You'll be fine. Have a glass of wine or a cup of sugary tea
before you leave the house, to relax you. Remember, most of
those people will be new to the area too. You are part of the
welcoming committee. Make an effort to talk to the new
ones. They know nothing about you. Everyone else in the
village knows your story.'

'Most of it. Nobody knows all of it. Not even me.'

Angela looked at Nadine, who busied herself chopping
vegetables.

'What are you going to wear?' said Angela. I looked down at my black skirt and indicated the sweater they'd given me for Christmas the previous year.

'Ask one of your friends to go shopping with you some day. Your dad was tight with money, but you don't need to be scavenging in second-hand shops. You're well off, you know. Jean used to love her shopping sprees and you might enjoy one too.'

'I don't think so.'

'Really? Talk to Tina about it. You might find it therapeutic.'

'I might find it hellish.'

'Not necessarily. You won't know unless you try it.'

Martha and Udo lived in the new housing estate at the edge of the village. At the beginning of the party, I stayed on my own in a corner of the kitchen, pretending to take an interest in the plants on the windowsill. Gradually, people introduced themselves. I met the people that Caroline had been talking about. One couple was Brazilian, Rodriguo and Fernanda. There was a divorced Indian woman, Anubha, with two children, and an English Black couple, Sue and Kenneth, and their three children. The garden was large and, despite the grim weather, the children all played together at the end of it in a treehouse that Udo had built. They were extremely noisy. As a compromise, I inserted one earplug.

Remembering all the tips that Tina had given me about socializing in advance of this party, I told them one or two facts about myself: I live on my own and I like to play the piano. Debussy is my favourite composer. I was looking for a job.

The other challenge was to ask them something about themselves. I asked Rodriguo and Fernanda if they were planning on having children. Martha interrupted me and took me aside and quietly explained that I shouldn't ask personal questions. I wished Tina had written out some rules that I could memorize. Fernanda later told me that they were trying for a family. I knew that meant they were having a lot of sex and realized why the question was so personal. Rodriguo asked me what my work experience was. I told him that I had never worked. 'My mother died when I was young and I looked after my father until his death fifteen months ago.' They sympathized with me. Rodriguo's father had also died in the previous year. I asked what his funeral had been like and Rodriguo described Brazilian funeral traditions as a lot like Irish ones, though he was surprised that people brought food to the bereaved here.

'Who can eat at a time like that?'

'I can eat all the time,' I said.

There was a kind of lull then, and I thought I'd move on to Anubha, the small, pretty Indian woman. After my introduction, she said she'd love to learn to play the piano, but that she wouldn't have time, being a single parent with two little ones.

'What happened to their father?' I asked. Martha was behind Anubha, I think monitoring my conversation. She put her face in her hands and I thought maybe I'd asked the wrong question again.

'He left me for his fancy woman in Dublin,' said Anubha.

'Does he see the children much?'

'Yes, he's good with them, *shukar hai*.'

We then got into a conversation about languages. *Shukar hai* was the Hindi equivalent of 'thank goodness'.

'Did you say you were looking for a job? Mervyn Park is expanding. There's not just the meat-processing plant there. A pharma company is opening next month. If you have basic computer skills, you could get some admin role? It probably wouldn't pay a lot, though.'

'It's not about the money,' I explained. 'My therapist thinks it would be a good idea.' Anubha frowned slightly. I couldn't tell what she was thinking, but then she smiled at me.

A new arrival came out on to the deck with a bottle of beer in his hand. Udo said, 'Has everyone met Mark? He's just started in the Accountancy Department.' There were various greetings. Mark was the man who had pulled his car over the previous day and had witnessed my argument with Caroline. He was Irish. He shook hands with most people but approached me awkwardly.

'I'm Mark Butler. We met yesterday?'

'You tried to get me into your car,' I said.

'I know,' he said, 'I keep thinking about how stupid that was. No wonder you thought I was a predator. I mean, I sort of . . . I know your story. Someone here told me. I feel like such a fool. Please accept my apology.'

I sighed. He didn't seem threatening now.

'May I get you another glass of wine?'

'Yes please.'

I moved away and was approached by Sue and Kenneth. Sue was the new primary school teacher in the village and Kenneth was a Boning Hall Quality Controller in Mervyn Park and a vegetarian. I thought it was funny that a vegetarian worked in a meat plant. I asked them if we could swap recipes. I had enjoyed swapping recipes with Caroline but, now that she was no longer my friend and had banned me from the Texaco, I needed a replacement. Sue offered to lend me a whole book of recipes. We arranged to meet for coffee the following week. Kenneth was quiet. I think I spoke more than him. I'd noticed that wine made me more chatty.

I pointed out that their children were the noisiest of the mob in the garden. Sue said that living in an apartment cramped their style and she was delighted to hear them being boisterous with a garden to play in. I apologized if my comment had seemed rude. I explained that I didn't always say the right thing because of my mental development. Sue assured me I had not made her uncomfortable.

Mark came and sat in the seat she had vacated and presented me with my third glass of wine of the day. 'I want you to know,' he said in a low voice, 'I reported the Texaco manager to her Head Office. She should not be in that job if that's her attitude. They may try to contact you to verify the incident.'

'Thank you, I was going to do that on Monday.'

I tried to think of something to say.

'I'm putting my house up for sale.'

'That's a big decision. Where are you going to go?'

'I'm not sure yet, but it's a bit isolated where I am and my doctor and therapist both say I should be more social and be around people, so probably into the village.'

'You're being social today.' He grinned. His teeth were white and even.

I was delighted with the compliment but admitted that I found socializing a big effort. 'I often offend people without meaning to, because I say what I think. I like your teeth.'

He looked at me strangely.

'See? That's an example. I should never comment on people's appearance.'

'But that's not offensive. Maybe you shouldn't comment negatively on people's appearance.'

'That's not what Tina says. If, for example, I said that it was good that you were slim, it might imply that I would disapprove if you got fat. And if you then got fat, you would think less of yourself.'

He laughed. 'Oh yes, I learned a long time ago never to

congratulate anyone on a pregnancy until they're showing me the ultrasound scan.'

I laughed voluntarily at that.

'Is it wrong to say that you have a nice laugh?' he said.

'That's my real laugh. Dad always said that when people laughed, I should laugh with them, and I do when I'm sure they're not laughing at me, but sometimes it's hard to tell.'

'You're honest.'

'Yes, I think it's due to my social inexperience and isolation. Though I believe it's a good thing.'

'So do you still think I'm a predator?'

'I can't be sure, can I?'

'That's true. I find your honesty refreshing.'

'So where did you move to Carricksheedy from?'

'Dublin. I've been looking for an excuse to move to this part of the country for over a year.'

'Why?'

He turned away and looked towards the treehouse 'Oh, you know, fresh air? A quiet life.' The question seemed to discomfort him, so I tried something else.

'Do you have any children?'

'No, just an ex-wife, Elaine.'

'Did you cheat on her?'

He stared at me for a moment and I think he was annoyed.

'Yes. Yes, I did. I threw away a perfectly good marriage for a fling with a girl half my age.'

'You're honest too.'

'Your . . . vulnerability makes me feel like I have to be honest with you.'

'Will your wife forgive you?'

'She's moved on. She has a child with her new husband.'

'And what about the girl you left her for?'

'She left me. She wasn't ready to settle down. End of story.'

'You deserved that.'

'I suppose. What about you? From what I read and heard, you've never had a relationship, is that right?'

'Correct.'

'Don't you want one? Wouldn't you like to fall in love?'

'I don't know. I'm theoretically heterosexual. But I definitely don't want sex.'

At this point, the chatter had grown quiet. Martha grabbed Mark by the arm and led him out to the garden. Sue sat down beside me again. 'That sounded like a personal conversation, Sally. Are you sure you want to share details like that?'

I felt deflated again. I had somehow said the wrong thing and I noticed that people were glancing in my direction. I heard Anubha saying to Fernanda, 'What did she say?' and Udo said to Kenneth, 'I'm not sure about Mark.' Kenneth nodded, looking confused. I went over to Udo.

'I have to go now. Thank you for a lovely afternoon.'

'Did Mark say something to upset you?'

'Not today. I think I said something that should be private.' There was a buzzing in my head. 'Maybe I've had too much wine. Will you please explain to everyone about my deficiency and thank Martha.' I scurried towards the hall and grabbed my jacket.

I had failed the test of attending a party. I made a mental note to raise it with Tina at our next session.

28

Peter, 1980

We were luckier on our third attempt at finding accommodation. The house was clean even though it was on a filthy street, and the landlady was chirpy and friendly and brown-skinned. She introduced herself as Mona.

'Are you here on holidays? Going to do some sightseeing?'

'We're looking for property in the area.' Dad smiled warmly at her.

'Moving to London? From Ireland? Now? That's a brave move.'

Dad said nothing.

'What a lovely boy you have. What's your name, sonny?'

'Steve,' Dad said before I could answer. She reached forward, and I don't know if she was going to shake my hand or pat me on the head, but I jerked backwards.

'Don't mind him,' said Dad, 'he's at that awkward age. Steve doesn't like to be touched.' He winked at her.

'Oh well, that will change soon enough, won't it?' She laughed as I stared up at Dad. Steve?

'I'll pay cash up front if that's all right.'

'Well, you're my favourite type of guest. I don't mind. How many nights?'

'Two to start with and then we'll see.'

'Bed and breakfast, or would you like evening meals as well?'

'What's the rate?' said Dad.

'Ten pounds per night, my love, twelve if you take dinner too. You won't find cheaper.'

'Well, Steve,' said Dad, 'will we take dinner as well?'

I nodded.

Dad counted out the notes. 'I'll pay for two nights then, please, and I'll let you know tomorrow if I need to extend our stay.'

'Great, well, the toilet is down the hall on your left and there's a shower in your room. You can knock on my door if you need anything. Dinner at seven o'clock, okay?' She handed over the keys and told us we were free to come and go.

Once inside the room, we saw that there was a bunk bed and a plastic shower cubicle in the corner. I had always wanted to sleep on the top of a bunk bed. 'Dad! Can I go on top? Please, Dad?'

'Yes.' He put his finger to his lips then. We were both silent for a moment and we could hear Mona humming to herself.

Dad lowered his voice. 'The walls are thin, we'll have to whisper.'

'Why?'

'We don't want them knowing our business.'

'Who?'

'Women,' he said.

'Is that why you told her my name was Steve?'

He grinned. 'I think it suits you. Like Steve Austin. The Six Million Dollar Man. Shall we call you Steve from now on?'

'Yes!'

'And what will my name be? I'm bored with Conor Geary.'

'James? Like Captain James Cook!'

'James, yes, I like that. What about a surname?'

'Armstrong, like Neil Armstrong.'

'James and Steven Armstrong. I like it.'

For the first time since I saw the burglar, I felt at ease. Dad was smiling at me.

'Right, you should probably stay here for safety's sake. I'll go and take a look around and see what I can find out.'

'Where are we, Dad?'

'Whitechapel in the East End of London.'

'Are we safe here?'

'I'll always keep you safe, Steve.'

We grinned at each other. He rustled in his suitcase and took out some envelopes. 'I'll have to go and see a man about some passports.'

'What man?'

'I don't know yet.'

'Dad?'

'Yes, Steve?' I sniggered every time he said it in the beginning.

'Is my disease a secret?'

'It's up to you, but I'd be afraid if you told people, they might want to test you. Everyone else who has it lives in a hospital. I've kept you out of them all these years.'

'Wherever we go to live, can it be far away from a town or a city?'

He smiled. 'That's exactly what I was thinking.'

He left, warning me to lock the door after him.

We were thirteen nights in that B & B. Dad went out every single day. He didn't shave in the mornings any more. He said he was growing a beard. He always put on the spectacles and the cap when he left the house. Mona wondered why I wasn't accompanying him, and I told her to mind her own business. She didn't ask after that. Dad said something to her about my hormones. He was always cheery and smiley with her. I stayed in the room by myself and Dad would bring sandwiches sometimes. Dinner by Mona was always strange. Rice and spicy meat stews. It took a bit of getting used to,

Dad and I agreed, but by the end of our stay, we found that we enjoyed curries. Mona even told us how she made them and what spices she used.

'Dad,' I said one night, leaning over my bed to see him below, brow furrowed, 'do you like Mona?'

'Who?'

'The landlady.'

'Don't be ridiculous.'

I liked her, but I didn't think Dad would approve.

Dad would often come back exhausted and weary. One night, I couldn't avoid seeing bruises on his ribs as he was undressing for bed. He explained that he had tripped over a dustbin, and he winced as he put his arm into his pyjama top.

One day, he made me come with him. I was scared and excited. There were so many people around and I was nervous of bumping into them, so Dad sort of steered me by standing behind me and putting his hands on my shoulders. I liked that. It was a kind of game. We didn't go far. He led me to the entrance of Whitechapel tube station. I knew all about the trains that ran underground, but I didn't want to get on one. I'd seen them on TV, people packed like sardines hanging on to railings from the roof. I could not help tears springing to my eyes. We stopped before the barriers and turned to the left. Dad looked at me. 'What's wrong?'

'I don't want to go on the tube.'

'Neither do I, so don't be a girl and dry your tears, because we have to go and get our photographs taken.' I was confused and wiped my eyes with my sleeve, but he led me to a small booth in the corner of the station. There was barely room for both of us in there, and he said we had to go in one at a time. I waited outside while he went in. I could see flashes of blue light coming from underneath the yellow half-curtain. We waited three minutes and then a row of four photographs came out of a slot in the wall of the booth. They were blank at first, but then, as if by magic, Dad's image began to appear, his neat new beard appearing first and then the rest of his face. Then it was my turn. He adjusted the swivelling stool and I looked into a mirror that was to take my photo. 'Don't blink when it flashes,' he said, and pulled the curtain behind him. I opened my eyes as wide as I could when the flashes came, but even then, when my image appeared out of the blur afterwards, my eyes were closed in two of the four photos. 'That's all right, we only needed one good one.' He took me back to the B & B and I sat there reading *Tom Sawyer*, by now bored by the story I had read too many times.

On 31st March, Dad returned victorious with two passports in the name of Steven Armstrong and James Armstrong. They were small navy-blue booklets with our pictures and dates of birth in them. Dad's birthday was wrong in his one but he said it didn't matter. They said BRITISH PASSPORT at the top and then, underneath a royal coat of arms and at the bottom, in smaller writing, NEW ZEALAND.

'The day after tomorrow, Steve, we are going to embark on the most epic journey of our lives. We are going to sail across the world to New Zealand. Our new home.' I could remember New Zealand on our globe. Two long islands that looked like they might have fallen off the bottom of Australia. I knew that it was home to the kiwi bird and the All Blacks rugby team, that it had mountains and glaciers, and that the climate was not too different to Ireland's. I also knew that the population of New Zealand was roughly the same as Ireland, even though it was three times the size. There would be plenty of room for us there.

'Won't it take an awfully long time?'

'I expect it will, but you have no idea how expensive these

passports were and how difficult they were to get. I had to consort with some rough men, but I got them in the end. Air travel is too risky and I don't think it would be safe for you, with all that recirculated air from other passengers. We'll have to buy a house and a car when we get there.' His excitement was infectious. 'Look, I got you a few presents.'

He had bought me a pair of gloves and a hat with ear flaps that almost covered my whole head to keep me safe from accidentally touching another person. He presented me with three brand-new books. *The Flora and Fauna of New Zealand*, *New Zealand: The History and Culture of a Great Nation* and *New Zealand's Heroes*.

'Are we not Irish any more?'

'No, Steve, we are Kiwi natives, born and bred, members of the British Commonwealth. I have relatives in Ireland and went there on holiday after I left school. That's where I met and married your mother. I stayed there and qualified as a dentist. You were born when we went back to New Zealand a year later. Your mother died of cancer last Christmas, and we brought her home for the funeral in her family plot. Right now, we are going back home. That is our story. We are changing history, my boy.' There was glee in his voice.

'And another thing, the guards have found Denise and her brat. There's a search warrant out for me. They're looking here in England for an Irishman travelling alone but it's only in the Irish newspapers so far. They haven't picked up the story here yet. Your stupid mother seems to have forgotten about you. They don't appear to know you exist and, by the time they do, we'll be on the other side of the world.'

29

Sally

In March 2019, I finally got news from New Zealand. Detective Inspector Baskin from Dublin was in charge of the case, but he sent Detective Inspector Andrea Howard to my house with the information. She told me the New Zealand police could find no lead on Conor Geary. I wondered why it had taken so long, over a year.

'There were lots of leads in the beginning, when the photograph was circulated. They all had to be checked out and eliminated, and they all proved false. There were some leads which looked promising. A known paedophile Irish immigrant, but he's two decades too young and so was ruled out. A dentist who had spent years in Ireland and had lived not far from where a young girl was abducted in New Zealand in 1983. But he was a Kiwi citizen and died decades ago. And he had a son, older than you. Another dead end. And, finally, a dentist who was accused of molesting a young patient twenty years ago, but the woman in question has turned out to be a very unreliable witness. She has accused many men over the years, some of whom weren't even alive at the time of the alleged incidents. There were lots of other names thrown into the hat. People often think they're helping, when they are actually obstructing the investigation.'

'This is all useless information,' I said.

'Yes, well, I just wanted to keep you updated. Whoever it is may have posted the box in New Zealand but could have just been visiting. It wasn't much to go on.'

'Are you going to continue searching? Are they? In New Zealand?'

'Well, like I say, we have explored every avenue.'

I was dissatisfied with this outcome. It turns out that no news was not good news, like they say. No news was no news.

'I don't know who sent you that bear, Sally, but it's possible that it's a different bear, some idiot trying to mess with your head. There are all kinds of weirdos out there. It was reported in the newspapers at the time of your mother's abduction that she had a teddy bear with her.'

'It was my bear.' I was angry.

'If you say so.'

'I don't tell lies.'

I knew it was. I was absolutely sure, but I tried my breathing exercises and seeing it from Howard's point of view. I could understand her reticence, but I'd been waiting for over a year now and she had nothing.

Again, she asked me if there was anything I remembered from the period of my captivity. By this time, I knew why I remembered nothing at all. My dad's files had included lists of all the medication I had been given, both in the psychiatric unit with my mother and in the year or two after my adoption. Angela said that the dosages were highly irregular, that I must have been in a near-zombified state for the first year at least until I was eventually weaned off the drugs. I don't remember being given tablets. Perhaps they had been mixed in with my food. How dare Dad do that to me.

The next time I got to see Tina, I was seething. As usual, she helped me to rationalize my feelings. I wasn't wrong to be angry. It was a perfectly normal response. But she made me look at things from Dad's point of view. If I had come across a child who had lived through a horrific situation, would I not try to take those memories from her? I heard Tina out, but I worried that maybe those buried feelings could emerge one day, that I wouldn't be able to control them. Most days, I could put it all to the back of my mind, but that churning anger was becoming more and more fiery, particularly since Detective Inspector Howard's visit. Tina wondered if I felt threatened by the news, if I was worried that somehow Conor Geary would come back for me, but that wasn't what scared me. It was wondering what he might have done afterwards. Do paedophiles stop being paedophiles if they're not caught? I was not afraid of him, but I hated that he knew where I was. 'S' was out there somewhere.

'Sending Toby was his way of letting me know that he still thought of me, that he was still in control.'

I hated him. I told Tina that I would like to kill him. He had committed a horrific crime and got away with it. What was to stop him doing it again and turning up in Ireland?

'After the visit from DI Howard, I went outside the back door and smashed a vase in the yard. I've never done anything like that before. My anger scared me.'

Tina told me to focus on my breathing exercises and asked me if I was continuing my yoga practice at home.

I told her I'd decided to sell the house. It was even more urgent now, because I didn't feel safe there alone. She asked if a sophisticated alarm system would make me feel safe. I knew that it was impossible to hide in a small village, but I was also too scared to move to a bigger unknown place; even Roscommon town was too big and noisy for me. 'He will be able to find me, if he comes back here.'

'I don't think he has much interest in adult women, Sally. He's eighty-four now? He must be frail. I doubt that you would be in physical danger from him. And we still don't know for sure that he sent you the bear, though it seems likely. Is there anything else that worries you about him?'

I remembered my conversation with Mark at Udo and Martha's party. 'My fear of sex and relationships. That might come from witnessing things. I've found Google helpful, Tina, and I know you won't approve, but I don't think I'm socially deficient. Emotionally, I'm a child. Who says what they think all the time? Children. Who doesn't consider sex or relationships at all? Children.'

'Sally, it's never a good idea to self-diagnose, but there may be something in what you are saying. Though you are certainly not socially deficient or childlike.'

I told her about the party and my conversation with Mark.

She was quiet for a moment. 'This Mark, he knows your history, yes?'

'As much as everyone with Google does.'

'Do you think he might have been sounding you out because he was interested in you – romantically, I mean?'

'No.'

'Why not?'

'Well, isn't it obvious? I'm damaged.'

'That's not obvious at all, Sally. If I saw you in a bar or at a party, I would think you were a handsome woman. And since you started doing yoga, there is a lightness to your movements.'

'I'm more aware of my core, I've been working on that.'

'You have a lovely face. You look years younger than you are. Not a single grey hair. No wrinkles.'

I winced. 'Yes, like a child.'

'No, like a good-looking adult.'

'But I told him I didn't ever want to have sex, in front of the whole room. And I think people were shocked.'

She paused and asked me to breathe deeply for a minute.

'You seem to be comfortable with your asexuality. Do you now think that's something to be ashamed of?'

I hadn't thought of that. Asexual.

'But, Tina, I did imagine having sex with Harrison Ford, quite a lot.'

She smiled. 'I think we've all done that. Sally, I'm not a sex therapist but —'

'That's okay. I don't need sex or want it or miss it. I don't even masturbate. I think you're right. I'm asexual. That's a relief.'

'Why do you feel relieved?'

'I like labels. Socially deficient. Asexual.'

'You are not deficient. But maybe don't talk about your sexuality with people you don't know well. It's a personal thing.'

'Do you have a lot of sex?' I was curious.

'I'm not answering that. It's personal and private.'

'Okay, I get it.'

After that, we did some touch therapy. I allowed Tina to brush out my hair. It was surprisingly relaxing. She was shocked that I had never been to a hair salon. I always cut my own hair and tied it up in a bun. It was easier that way. Then she massaged my shoulders for a little while. I didn't see the point of that.

As I was leaving, she reminded me again about the breathing exercises, and managing my anger. 'Easier said than done,' I said.

'Don't break things. Don't strike out at anyone, unless you're in danger from them. Just breathe through it. Play your piano.'

We had run over our time but I had to ask her. 'Do you think I could be a piano teacher if I haven't got any qualifications?'

'I think so, but you would probably have to get garda clearance first in order to work with children. Teaching requires a great deal of patience, but you've been learning that, every time, in this room. Garda clearance might be tricky, though, because of the incident with your dad's remains. Let's wait a while?'

That afternoon, I went to meet Sue and Mark for coffee. The waitress took orders without having to write them down. I could do that, but I couldn't work in a place with such awful music playing. She smiled at everyone she talked to. I struck waitressing off my mental list of possible jobs.

Mark joined me first and, as he sat down, Sue came in. There was a lot of what I now know is called 'small talk' before the smiling waitress presented us with menus. Sue handed me a Jamie Oliver recipe book, and I gave her a sheaf of pages, recipes I had printed from the BBC Food website, plus the ones I'd copied from Caroline at the Texaco.

'So you like to cook?'

'Well, it passes the time, but it was better when Dad was alive, because there was someone to appreciate it.'

'You should have a dinner party!' said Mark.

I didn't know what to say about that, so I changed the subject.

'How is everything at Mervyn Park?' I asked.

Sue's husband, Kenneth, and Mark both worked there. Mark looked after the payroll systems.

'I keep asking him to give Kenneth a pay rise,' said Sue.

'You know I would if I could. I'm guessing the company will only turn a profit in the fifth year of operations if we're lucky.'

'I'm only teasing, Mark,' said Sue.

'How about your job hunt? Anything on the horizon?' Mark asked me.

'It's hard,' I said, 'I'm forty-four and I don't know what I want to be when I grow up.' That was my little joke, but neither of them laughed.

'Ten-year-old Mark wanted to be a detective,' said Mark.

'I wanted to work in fashion,' Sue said.

'I think I only want to play the piano. I'm good at it.'

'Really?' said Mark. 'Do you compose or just play?'

'Sometimes I make up short little pieces, but I prefer to play. Debussy, Bach, John Field.'

'Maybe you can play for us at your dinner party?' said Mark, winking at Sue.

'Oh, wouldn't that be lovely?' she said.

'I don't know. I've never had a party.'

'Never? Not even when you were a child?'

Mark blinked slowly and Sue put her hand over her mouth.

'Oh, I'm so sorry, I didn't mean . . . I wasn't thinking. I heard about . . . when you were a kid.'

'I know, I asked Martha to explain when I left her party on Saturday.'

Mark looked at me earnestly. 'I wish you hadn't left in a hurry like that. There was nothing to be embarrassed about.'

'Mark, are you interested in me romantically?'

Two red marks appeared on Mark's pale cheeks.

'Woah,' said Sue, 'should I leave you two alone?'

'No, please, I need to know. I discussed it with my therapist. And I think you're flirting with me. I'm not sure, though. I've never had this kind of attention from a man.'

Before Mark had a chance to reply, Caroline from the Texaco was banging her fist on the window and shouting something at me.

'What the hell?' said Sue as Caroline barged her way through the door and straight over to our table.

'You bitch!' she snarled. 'I've been fired from my job, because the woman who fucking incinerated her own father told my head office that I was racist.'

'I called your head office,' said Mark. 'I was there when

you said those things about our friends. Don't blame Sally. It was me.'

'I rang them to confirm the details,' I said.

Sue looked uncomfortable. Caroline glared at her.

'I see you've latched on to another one.' Caroline spat the words at me. The smiling waitress was no longer smiling. She appeared behind Caroline. 'Caroline,' she said, 'I'm going to have to ask you to leave. We don't tolerate abusive behaviour here.'

'Oh right, but you'll serve that one?' she said, pointing at Sue.

Mark jumped up, but the unsmiling waitress put her hand on his shoulder and spoke calmly. 'Get out of here, Caroline, you're barred.'

'Don't worry,' she screeched, 'I'm going to move out of this village anyway. I'm not staying with all of you freaks. I'm sick of this place. I'll go back to Knocktoom. And by the way, Valerie,' she said as she got to the door, 'your quiche is shite.' There was a silence after she slammed the door, and all eyes were either on Caroline as she stomped off down the hill or on the three of us. Then, they all looked towards Valerie and began to clap, including Mark and Sue, and then me. The mood turned festive in an instant. There was laughter. A number of people came to our table and assured Sue that she was most welcome in Carricksheedy. An old man said that we needed to mix up the gene pool as the complexion of Carricksheeders was pale blue. As he left a few moments later, he shouted, 'Best quiche in Ireland!' and there were cheers and laughter from the remaining customers.

Mark asked Sue, 'Are you okay?' and she wiped tears from her eyes.

'I guess I hoped it wouldn't happen here.' She was upset.

The waitress, whose name was clearly Valerie, approached

us. 'I'm sorry that happened in my cafe. Your meals are on the house.'

Mark and Sue protested and insisted that none of it was Valerie's fault. She was awfully kind. We thanked her and paid the bill, splitting it three ways (like Tina had suggested). Mark and Sue had to get back to work and left in a hurry.

As I exited, I thanked Valerie.

Mark hadn't answered my question.

Aunt Christine rang and told me that Uncle Donald was seriously ill.

'Is he going to die?' I asked.

'I think so,' she replied and broke into tears.

I thought about the right thing to say. 'I'm sorry. I hope he isn't suffering.' I tried to feel sad about Uncle Donald. It didn't work. But I did feel sad for Aunt Christine.

'They are keeping him comfortable for the moment but he's going downhill fast.'

I judged that this would not be the right time to tell her about my anger issues. 'I hope he dies peacefully in his sleep like my dad.'

'I think that's the best we can hope for.'

'How long have you been married?'

'Almost forty years.'

'That's a long time.'

I wanted to ask her how often they had sex, if she enjoyed it, if she was going to have him cremated, if I was expected to go to the funeral, but I didn't.

'I can't imagine life without him. It's stomach cancer, with secondaries in the lungs and liver. There's no hope. I thought we'd have more time together.'

'That is sad.' Privately, I thought forty years was plenty of time.

'Thank you, my dear. I'd better get back into his room now. Time is precious. I'll call you if there's any news, okay?'

I knew she meant news of his death. 'I'm sorry,' I said, again.

'Thank you, you are a good girl. Bye now.' Her voice trembled before she hung up.

I had handled that conversation well. Even though I am a woman and not a girl. I felt a little moment of triumph that I could tell Tina about next month. Empathy! I had felt it and expressed it.

30

Peter, 1982

On 2nd April 1980, Dad and I left England. We were able to sail from Dover to Calais as foot passengers and then to Genoa in Italy, but then there came the horrific, months-long voyage from there to Port Said in Egypt, through the Suez Canal to Colombo and then to Singapore, and to Sydney, and finally to Auckland, sometimes hidden away on freighter or cargo ships thanks to generous bribes and sometimes as regular foot passengers. Dad seemed to enjoy the expedition, 'seeing the world' he said, but I was scared and/or sick all the time. I hid in whatever cabin we were allocated, and rarely went on deck.

By the time we arrived in New Zealand, Dad had a full moustache and beard. He never shaved again, though he kept his beard neatly trimmed, 'like Sigmund Freud' he said. He also wore thick-rimmed glasses thereafter with clear lenses. Only people who knew him well would recognize him as Conor Geary, and I was the only person who knew him well.

We stayed in a small, rented house in Auckland for two months. Dad had changed the name on his dental certificates to James Armstrong and had registered with the New Zealand Dental Association under that name with some letter he had been able to forge from the Irish Dental Board. He had to take some kind of exam too, but he passed it easily.

Then we moved to Wellington and Dad got locum dentist work. He picked up the local accent quickly and urged me to do the same. It was harder for me, though, as I didn't see too many people.

The biggest change was that I was no longer a secret. Dad was proud to introduce me to people we met. Although he sometimes had to explain my disease, he played it down, later telling me that he didn't want people pitying me. But I began to talk with other people for the first time. It was very difficult. I never knew what to say.

Dad told our sob story about the poor dead mum and wife. This elicited sympathy and congratulations to my father for raising me alone.

We were invited to another dentist's family home for lunch. I wore the hat and gloves, and Dad did the usual explanation of my rare condition, but I couldn't take my eyes off Dad's colleague's wife and daughters. Girls a little older than me, who behaved completely normally. Their mum was normal too. She had baked a cake and roasted a chicken and she made her daughters show off their hand-knitted sweaters. I said little. Dad explained that I was shy as I'd had to be homeschooled in Ireland.

Afterwards, at home, I expressed my admiration for the mother and daughters. Dad looked at me strangely and then said that it was time to move on, to set up his own practice.

We moved to Rotorua, a cheap place to buy property. It was 1982 and I was fourteen years old. The whole place smelled of rotten eggs because of the hydrogen sulphide that hovered above the thermal water. Our house was on a back road three miles outside town. There was a small, ramshackle house next door, but apart from that, our nearest neighbour was miles away. Logging trucks passed our house fairly regularly, but there was almost no other traffic.

There were two bedrooms, a functional kitchen and a long dark sitting room, with a separate barn ten yards back from the house. The house was made of wood, and nothing like as grand as our house back in Ireland with its cultivated garden, wide driveway and stone pillars. Dad said it was an adventure, starting again. Neither of us believed it. He drove in and out to his new office every day. He had bought it from the widow of a recently deceased dentist. He had a young receptionist called Danny. I met him infrequently. I think he thought there was something wrong with me mentally, because I was unable to chat with him. I was desperate to socialize, but my inarticulation made it hard. When I said it to Dad, he warned me off interacting with other people. They could kill me without even meaning to, he said.

During the long days while he was at work, I explored our new territory. Our land wasn't fenced at the back, and it was three weeks before I discovered that there were natural hot springs about two miles back under a sharp cliff edge. I was nervous about testing my skin in such water, but when I told Dad, he was as excited as I was. We set off on a cold May day and swam in the hot rock pool before cooling off in the cold-water lake beside it. This was so much better than the beach back in Ireland. The water had no detrimental effect on my skin. Dad and I often went there at the weekends after that, summer and winter.

On the property adjoining ours, there was a boy who looked a few years older than me. He drove his own truck. I was fascinated. I could see him from my window and, when Dad was at work, I would spend time hanging around the adjoining fence, eager for some communication. As far as I could see, he lived with his mother. They went out early in the morning and he would come home in the afternoon, and then she would be dropped off around 9 p.m., later at the weekends. When he came home from school, he booted a rugby ball around his yard and tended to chickens I could hear from a coop on the other side of his property.

I watched my neighbour and concluded there was something gentle about him. He was poor, judging by his clothing and home, but I could hear him speak to his mother. And he was respectful of her. She seemed old. I then wondered if she was his grandmother.

Now that I was older, I was beginning to question the way Dad spoke about women. New Zealand had been the first country in the world to give women voting rights, a fact that enraged Dad when I told him. When I talked about the old lady next door, he closed his eyes until I stopped speaking of her. There were certain subjects that were off limits to Dad and that was how he expressed it. He shut his eyes to shut down the subject.

I wondered about my mother and sister in the room next door, years previously. I remembered kicking her pregnant belly. That could not have been right, even though Dad had encouraged me. If he was right about everything, why were we living with new histories and new names on the other side of the world?

Yet, my mother must have been the problem. He was my dad, he looked after me, he never raised his hand to me. I had seen evidence of my mother's madness and aggression. I had once asked him when my sister was a baby why he didn't take her and leave her on the church steps, but he said it was an act of charity to let her stay with Denise. 'She is all she has,' he said. 'I'm not so cruel that I would separate them. It was bad enough when I took you from her, I couldn't do it to her again.' Dad obviously had a kind heart.

31

Sally

Mark phoned me a few days after the cafe incident. I reminded him that I had asked him a question before Caroline's interruption.

'Why are you so interested in me?'

'Well, it's sort of complicated, but I would like to be your friend, to look out for you. I don't feel sorry for you, but I don't want to give the wrong impression either.'

'What's complicated about that?' I voiced my suspicion. 'Are you a journalist?'

'God no, I'm an accountant, and I'm new to town. I find you fascinating, your history. Did I do something or say something?'

'You asked about my relationship history. My therapist thought you might be interested in a relationship with me.'

'There is someone I'm interested in, but it's early days and I'm afraid I might screw it up. You remember Anubha?'

I breathed a sigh of relief. 'Anubha seems lovely and you're both divorced. You should ask her on a date.'

'I'd like to but, technically, I'm her boss, so it could seem like workplace harassment.'

'Maybe she's waiting for you to ask her out? She has two children, so she probably likes sex.'

He laughed. I was irked.

'I wasn't joking. She seems nice.'

'She is.'

'But why did you ask to meet me for coffee?'

'I wanted you to know that I wasn't uncomfortable about our conversation at Martha's party. Can't we be friends?'

I agreed to try it.

'I think you should be careful, Mark. Even if she does like you, her children might not.'

'You'd make a good agony aunt.'

'Does it pay well?'

'Not really.'

'I'm still looking for a job.'

'There's got to be something you can do. Would you like me to ask around at Mervyn Park?'

'Yes please. Mark?'

'Yes?'

'I'm angry about my birth father. The police have found no trace of him in New Zealand. Nobody knows where he is now.'

There was a pause.

'May I come to your house?' he asked.

'Why?'

'It's easier to talk face to face, especially about him.'

'Okay, come for dinner. I'll make spicy shepherd's pie. About six?'

'Great.'

'It's not a dinner party, though, okay?'

He laughed. 'It's not a date either, okay?'

I laughed.

Mark came over after work and I brought him up to date with how Toby had led us to New Zealand. 'Toby?' he said, alert. I explained about the bear. He asked if we could use Dad's computer to look up the New Zealand newspaper coverage. We pored over page after page, photofits and 3D models of what Conor Geary might look like now. There was nothing in the news reports that Detective Inspector Howard hadn't already told me. Mark's demeanour was grim. 'I saw the renewed appeal at the time but I didn't know it was connected to Toby. Are you sure you don't remember anything about him, about that time in captivity?'

'No, don't you think I'd help catch him if I could? Denise hardly spoke of him either.'

'How do you know?'

'It's all in my dad's notes.'

'What notes?'

I explained about Dad's diaries and medical notes.

'May I see them?'

'Why?'

'I want to help you, Sally.'

'I don't think that's appropriate. I don't need your help. I can read perfectly well. They're the private medical records of my birth mother and me.'

'But, you know, a fresh eye might see something that you missed. I could look at them more dispassionately?'

'There is almost nothing about Conor Geary in there.'

'But maybe there are clues?'

'There are no clues.'

'But how do you know? You have a literal mind. I might be able to see some subtlety that you missed.'

His persistence infuriated me.

'The guards have copies. They have investigated them thoroughly. Angela, my doctor and friend, has been through them with me. Mark, can you leave now, please? Your manner is making me uncomfortable.'

His smiley demeanour had disappeared. He opened his mouth, about to say something, but seemed to stop himself. Now, he was suddenly contrite.

'God, I'm so sorry. I get carried away. This case was such huge news in my childhood.'

'Everyone says that.'

He looked at me and I couldn't tell if he was sad or angry or happy. I definitely did not feel comfortable.

'Mark, will you please leave?'

'Yes, I shouldn't . . .' He didn't finish the sentence but grabbed his jacket from the back of his chair and left.

I couldn't decide whether I wanted to be Mark's friend or not. He seemed to have a dark side.

Next day, he apologized again for 'being so intense'. Tina said I should accept apologies if they were sincere. So I did.

I welcomed the distraction of the cottage. Nadine and I had visited the derelict building on Bracken Lane three times. It was a shell. The walls were intact, but the roof had caved in on the left side. Nadine made sketches of what she thought it could look like. Her enthusiasm was contagious.

The survey results returned a list of problems, the most prominent of which was that there was an underground stream which tended to swell in the winter. That explained why the floorboards were rotten throughout. Nadine saw this as a challenge to elevate the interior and expose the stream and make it a feature by having a thick glass floor panel running through the sitting room with underground lights that illuminated it in the evening.

Nadine said if I bought it, she would project manage the whole thing for 10 per cent of the cost. It had been vacant for twenty years. After three days of negotiations, the owners accepted my offer on 2nd April 2019. Nadine thought it would be ready to move into by late autumn.

Now there was the small matter of selling my own house

and land. My house was already clean so I didn't have to do much tidying, but the estate agent suggested that the site would be more valuable than the house and that I shouldn't bother repainting it. I was scared of change. Tina said it was progress: embracing change.

Mark and I met for coffee or a drink a few times with Udo and Martha, or Anubha and Sue and Kenneth, and once at a barbecue in Mark's apartment on Easter Sunday, 21st April. The barbecue was on the balcony. He lived in the same block as Kenneth and Sue. He was a perfect gentleman on all of these occasions although, annoyingly, he never failed to ask me if there were any further developments in the search for Conor Geary.

I liked the way he played with all of the children and did magic tricks to entertain them. He and Anubha seemed to keep their distance from each other. Mark confided that he didn't think she was interested.

I had started shopping in the small Gala supermarket on the village's main street. It took me a while to orientate myself and get used to what was on offer in each aisle. They had a surprisingly large range of goods, and when I asked for fresh curry leaves (for one of Jamie Oliver's recipes), the nice lady said they would order some in especially. 'You know,' she said, 'I think we need to expand our range of ethnic ingredients here. We don't want to lose all our business to the supermarket in Roscommon.'

I showed her another recipe and she noted all the ingredients and assured me that they'd definitely be stocking them in future. Her name badge said Laura. I began to introduce myself. 'Oh, we know who you are!' she said. 'You're famous around here.'

'Not infamous?' I said. I thought it was a good joke and so did she, because she laughed.

I told her about my attachment to routines.

'You figure out your routine here and I'll make sure I advise you of any changes. How about that?' she said.

I walked out of that shop feeling lighter and taller, and happy. I felt like I'd made yet another friend.

32

Peter, 1982

The neighbour boy's name was Rangi. I heard the old lady call him by that name. He never paid any attention to me until, one day, he kicked the ball awkwardly and it landed on my side of the fence. I ran from our porch to pick it up but, instead of throwing it back, I held on to it, standing by the fence, waiting for him to approach. After a minute of glaring at me, he did.

'What's wrong with you? Why didn't you just kick the ball back?'

'I'm Steve,' I said.

'Rangi.'

'I know.'

'Give me the ball, eh?'

I threw it towards him and, even though I fumbled the throw, he caught it deftly with one hand under his leg.

He didn't thank me and began to walk away. I had to stop him.

'Do you go to school? Is that where you go every morning?'

'Yeah?' He said it as if my question had been an accusation.

'You're lucky,' I said. 'I have a medical condition which means I can't mix with other kids. If they touch me, I could die.'

'Yeah? How did you get that? I'd love not to have to go to school.'

'It's bad,' I said, self-pity taking over. 'I have no friends.'

'You got a television?' he said.

'Yes. You can come and watch it if you like, before my dad gets home?'

'Where's your accent from?' he said.

I didn't think I had an accent. 'I'm Irish,' I said before correcting myself in line with our story. 'Well, I was born here, but I lived in Ireland since I was a baby. I came home two years ago.'

'Yeah? It's got a rugby team, right? That place where the war is on. You ever get bombed?'

He seemed disappointed when I admitted that I'd never seen a bomb or a gun and that the war was confined to one small part of Ireland that was under British rule. I could see he was losing interest so I changed tack.

'What age are you?' I asked.

'Fifteen. You?'

'Fourteen. Are you allowed to drive that truck?'

'Sort of. Cops don't ask. Why, is your dad the police?' Rangi was suspicious.

'No, he's a dentist. Is that your mum that you live with?'

'Nah, she's me Auntie Georgia. Where's your mum?'

'She's dead.' There was a pause. I expected him to express his condolences but he said nothing. I said, 'Do you want to come in and watch television? You can't touch me.'

'No, you freaking weirdo. Why would I want to touch you?'

This was going all wrong. He was walking away.

'See you later, maybe?' I called, trying to keep the desperation out of my voice.

He didn't look back.

Over dinner that evening, I nervously told Dad that I'd been talking to our neighbour.

'The brown boy?' he said, his nose wrinkling in disgust.

'Yes, well, his aunt is white, so I think he's mixed. He was unfriendly.'

'You shouldn't mix with them. I almost didn't buy this house when I saw who was next door. I'm guessing that's why it was so cheap.'

'I would like to have a friend, though, someone my own age?'

He put down his knife and fork.

'I've been thinking about that,' he said. 'Leave it with me.'

I was excited. In the weeks that followed, Dad began to do up the barn. I helped him run electricity from the main house in an underground trench we dug out. We pored over DIY books to figure out how to get water pipes from the mains into the corner of the barn. Dad installed a large sink, toilet and a modern shower. And then he bought a cooker and a fridge. He lined the walls with egg boxes. 'Soundproofing,' he said. 'They'll want their privacy. I'm going to look for a lodger, a young person who can work from home and keep you company.' I was delighted at the idea, but then disappointed when, months later, this young man had failed to materialize. 'It's hard to find just the right person,' Dad said, 'but don't worry, I'll keep looking.'

A few weeks after I first spoke to him, Rangi Parata turned up at the front door. 'Can I watch your television?' Dad wasn't due home for two hours.

'Sure,' I said, holding the door wide open and standing well back from him. I turned on the TV. There was a soap opera on. 'Can we watch the rugby?' said Rangi.

I switched to the other channel. 'Okay?'

'Yeah.'

'Ireland isn't as good as the All Blacks, but –'

'Ah yeah, I know that. Nobody is.'

At half-time, during the ad break, he asked, 'Have you got a beer?'

'We have Fanta. Would you like some?'

'Your old man doesn't drink?'

'No.'

Rangi watched the game and I watched him. 'Stop looking at me, you freak,' he said. 'Are you a queer?'

'No!' Dad had explained to me about gays and lesbians and I'd picked up other words for them from books and television. 'I rarely get to see people my own age.'

'Yeah? Well, stop it.'

'Sorry.'

'You got an indoor dunny?'

'You don't?'

'Nah. Just a long drop.'

I had wondered about the shed behind his house. I'd seen him and his aunt carrying pots to and from it. I had thought it was some kind of well.

'You want to use it?'

'Yeah, later.'

'What's it like in school?'

'It's shit. It's shit if you're me, anyway. They don't like my type there.'

I knew he meant mixed race, but I didn't know what the mix was.

'Are you half Māori?'

'Yeah. My dad was the full job.'

'That's cool.'

'Are you taking the piss?'

'No. I think it's exotic.'

'What's that mean?'

'Different, but good different, not weird.'

'Unusual?'

'Yes.'

'I like that. Exotic.' He looked at me and smiled for the first time.

The next time he came over, he brought his homework with him. It was extremely simple. The maths equations were ones I had mastered when I was ten. The reading material was *The Hobbit*. I had read that when I was seven. I saw corrected homework for the first time, and his teacher's critical comments written in red biro. Rangi's handwriting was barely joined up. He asked me to do his homework for him and I was tempted, to win his friendship, but instead I offered to help him. Rangi was going to be leaving school soon to start a building apprenticeship. He needed to pass his School Cert.

We sat at opposite sides of our kitchen table, while I talked him through the English comprehension tests and the maths problems. He was quick to learn.

'Why couldn't you learn that in school?' I asked.

'Too busy watching my back.' He explained that there was gang warfare in other parts of Rotorua and that he was try-ing to stay out of it. Even though he was only half Māori, the white students expected him to be involved and the Māori gang students hated him for staying out of it. He showed me fresh bruises on his arm where he'd been punched. School didn't seem that appealing any more.

'I turn up for my classes, talk to nobody and then I leave. I used to hang out at the dairy with this girl I liked' – the dairy was what they called the corner shop, I'd seen teen-agers sitting in there – 'but her brother found me in school and thumped me.'

'I don't think I'll ever be able to have a girlfriend or a wife.'

'No shagging? Ever? That's sucky, mate.'

'So, you have no friends either?'

'I guess not.'
I grinned.

Dad knew nothing of our new friendship. I made sure there was no trace of Rangi's visits, even flushing the toilet after him every time, since that was something he always forgot. I'd told him that my dad didn't want him in our house. He was unsurprised, but pleased that I still wanted him to visit.

On Friday 10th December 1982, Rangi got a half-day to mark the end of his schooling. He had a few days' study leave before his School Cert exams began. Christmas in the sun was still a strange concept to me, but one I liked. Rangi swerved into his driveway and then jumped the fence. He showed me a note from his teacher. 'Much improved,' she had written. 'Rangi has applied himself this year. This boy's future is bright.'

He whooped and hollered like a cowboy, kicking the dust with his bare feet. Rangi didn't wear shoes in the summer. From what I saw in town, a lot of kids didn't. 'Thanks, mate, look what you did for me! Teacher says I'm going to ace these exams.'

'You did it, Rangi, you did it.' And he had.

I had an idea. 'Let's go swim in the lake, to celebrate.'

He had an idea too. 'I'm not much for swimming but I got some beers. Let's go for a soak.' He went to grab my shoulder in some gesture of affection, I think, but I pulled back at the last minute. 'No touching!'

'Sorry, mate, I forgot.'

The trip to the lake was a mistake. The whole friendship was a mistake, and everything was my fault, but setting off that day, I felt happier than I ever had in my life. I had a genuine friend who was grateful to me for my help. We were going to have fun and act like grown-ups and drink beer. I had turned fifteen some months earlier and I knew that it was illegal to drink alcohol until you were twenty. Dad would have blown his top if he'd known about any of it, but in that moment, I didn't care.

When we got to the hot pools, we changed into our togs, keeping our backs to each other to reassure ourselves and each other that we weren't gay, though I couldn't help but notice Rangi's physique. He was built like a man. I was thin and scrawny and pale in comparison. He not only had bruises on his arm but lots of small circular scars on his chest. I couldn't help pointing to them. 'What happened there?'

'My mum's a bitch,' he said. 'That's why I can't swim. Couldn't take my top off in school without getting questions asked. Ciggy burns.'

'She burned you?'

'Yeah, crazy bitch, when I was a kiddo. I don't even know where she is now, probably in jail. Don't tell anyone. I figure I can trust you, Pākehā.'

I think Pākehā meant a white person. I was pleased that he trusted me.

'Who would I tell? Anyway, she sounds the same as my mother!' I said, delighted that we had this in common, mad and dangerous mothers.

'Yeah? I thought you said she was dead?'

I hadn't thought about her in months. Rangi was my best friend, my only friend. He had told me a secret. I could tell him, couldn't I?

'I suppose I wished she was. We had to leave Ireland because she told lies about my dad.'

I told Rangi the whole story as he cracked open two cans. I took a long slurp out of my can, assuming it would taste something like apple juice, but the taste was foul, like I imagined old men's feet to taste. I spat the liquid out on to the grass.

Rangi laughed at me. 'Seriously? You never had a beer before?'

I shook my head, but then attempted another sip. 'Chur, bro!' he said. I didn't want any more beer so left the other five cans to him.

'That don't sound right to me,' he said, when I told him what had happened when I'd stayed with my mother for the weekend. 'You shouldn't have kicked your mum, especially when she was pregnant.'

I shrugged. 'Dad said I could.'

'Don't sound right to me,' he repeated, and I felt uncomfortable. I regretted telling him anything.

'My Auntie Georgia says it's never right to hit a woman.'

I thought of his old aunt and her long days spent cleaning other people's houses and then her bar work in the evening. I suspected that Dad wouldn't think much of Auntie Georgia's opinions. Why did Rangi think women were so great? His auntie was a drudge. His mum was violent. I changed the subject and soon we were talking excitedly about the rugby as the Lions Tour was coming to New Zealand again that winter. I had begun to take a greater interest in rugby since I'd met Rangi. He would have loved to play for his school team, but it wasn't worth the hassle he would get from the other kids.

I got into the hot pools, which were shallow. At their deepest, they only came up to my neck. Rangi joined me and we bobbed around for a while. 'Sweet as,' he said. When we got out, the sun was hot on the surrounding rocks.

'We have to cool off,' I said. 'Let's go over to the cold lake.'

'Nah, Stevie, I'll stay here,' said Rangi. He was clearly uncomfortably hot as sweat poured down his torso.

'Come on,' I said, 'you'll bake if you stay here.'

'Can't swim, can I?' His voice was slightly slurred by the beer.

I felt special that Rangi had shown those scars to me. We were best friends.

'Right,' I said, 'so you can't swim and I can't drink beer. We're even, but at least I tried.'

He followed me to the cool water side of the cliff. I clambered down some rocks and slipped into the water. He followed me and sat on the edge, dangling his feet in the lake. 'Man, that feels good,' he said.

'Jump in!' I encouraged him. 'You can hang on to the grass at the sides.'

'How deep is it?'

'I don't know, deeper than me.' I dived under the water and swam around for a few seconds and then I saw and heard the surge of bubbles as Rangi entered the water, too close to me. I swam away.

I'm not sure what happened next. Maybe the beer made him brave as he tried to swim out from the safety of the rock to join me, but I was nervous that he was getting too close and I swam out further away from him. Then I noticed that he was in trouble. Less than three yards away from me, he was out of his depth and beginning to panic. I could see him underwater. His head craned towards the surface but he couldn't break it. I surfaced and tried to shout at him and point him towards the rocks just six feet away, but he never rose above the surface. If he'd pushed his body horizontally he could have touched the rocks and felt safe, but his eyes were scrunched closed. I wanted to help him. I wanted to guide him towards safety. It would have been so easy to lead him, grab his arm, but touching him would have meant my death, my agonizing putrefaction, and I was too afraid. There was nobody around to help. He thrashed around, gulping more water instead of the air he couldn't reach. I surfaced and dived, surfaced and dived, screaming at the top of my lungs for help, while his lungs filled with water. I watched my friend drown.

Later, I thought of all the ways I could have saved him. I could have broken a branch off a nearby tree and pushed it into his hands. I could have used one of our towels and pulled him in with that. I don't know how long the drowning took. It seemed like years. It seemed like seconds. It seemed like hell.

33

Sally

Uncle Donald died on 29th June. Aunt Christine asked me to come to the funeral in Dublin. She and I had been in regular contact. I had kept her up to date with all the news, my therapy, my new friends, New Zealand, selling the house, etc. She was so like my mum that it almost seemed as if she was back in my life. But I didn't know Donald and I didn't particularly want to go to the funeral.

Obviously, I had lived in Dublin in captivity for the early years of my life and I had been to Dublin once or twice when Mum was alive, and a few times to see Aunt Christine in more recent months, but when I went with Mum as a teenager, I was completely overwhelmed by the size of it, the noise of it and the masses of people. I watched lots of programmes set in cities all over the world, and even though Dublin is a small city in comparison to London or New York, the scale of it frightened me. I couldn't imagine negotiating it by car or bus.

Tina and Angela both said I should go to the funeral, and that I should go out of kindness, after all that Aunt Christine had done for me. Angela suggested I should ask a friend to go with me. Tina thought this was the perfect opportunity for me to put into practice all of the things I had been working on, touch, empathy, patience, diplomacy, self-control, etc.

I asked Sue to come with me. She offered to drive. She was on her long summer holidays from teaching and an overnight in Dublin was exactly what she needed. She said that she would deliver me to the church and then go off to meet her cousin. The day after the funeral she would collect me from Aunt Christine's and we could go on that shopping spree we had talked about in Dundrum. She said we could have our lunch there and then get straight on to the motorway afterwards and come home. I could bring earplugs for the noise, and we could go to the shopping centre first thing, before there were too many people around.

Sue picked me up from my house early on the Monday morning of the funeral. I was wearing my funeral outfit, the same one I had worn to my dad's funeral.

'Sally, please don't be offended, but the red glittery hat? It's not quite right,' Sue said.

'What? But Dad said I should wear it on special occasions.'

'I think he might have meant festive occasions, like wedding or party celebrations. It's not the right tone for a funeral.'

'But several people commented on how they liked it at Dad's funeral. Was everyone lying to me? Why would they lie?'

'Nobody wants to upset the chief mourner. Because of what happened with the incineration, everyone was probably delighted that the hat was a distraction? As far as I can tell, few people knew you well enough to say anything.'

I felt a flush creep up my neck. 'Do you think people were laughing at me?'

'No, but it is a little bit odd.'

'I am a little bit odd.'

'When we go shopping tomorrow, we'll pick out clothes mindfully.'

'Mindfully?'

'Yes,' she said.

Sue accompanied me into the church. We were a little late. It was more than half full of people. She advised me not to look at anyone but to go straight up to the front pew and stand beside Aunt Christine. She left then, saying she would collect me at Aunt Christine's in the morning. I had taken a tablet to deal with the strangers. Angela warned me that, in this case, I must not do anything to cause Aunt Christine any distress. It was better for me to be subdued. She was only giving me tablets these days on rare occasions.

Aunt Christine greeted me with a warm hug, which I was able to return. She introduced me to Donald's sister, Lorraine. Aunt Christine and Lorraine were weeping. The coffin was on the altar with a photograph of Donald on top. He was an old man with a jowly face. I did not turn around to look at all the people behind me but listened to the vicar talk about Donald's life in between all the mumbled prayers.

I perked up a little when she said that he liked to play jazz piano. Aunt Christine hadn't ever mentioned him playing the piano but they had one in their house. I had played it.

I zoned out again then. Lorraine was rigid in her expensive-looking black coat. Aunt Christine repeatedly blew her nose into her handkerchief and seemed at one stage to be almost choking on her tears. I did what I saw on television and put my hand on hers and she grasped at it. I let her.

At the end of the ceremony, the vicar said that all the mourners were invited back to Christine's house after the burial. Aunt Christine, Lorraine and I followed the coffin down the central aisle to the doors where the undertakers lifted it into a waiting hearse. I kept my eyes down. Way too many people. Outside, Aunt Christine and Lorraine were surrounded by other mourners. I felt stifled and retreated back towards the door of the church and was surprised to see Mark there, in a black suit and tie.

'Hi, Sally.'

'What are you doing here?' I asked.

'Anubha told me you were coming up for the funeral. I thought you might need some support.'

'But . . . how . . . did you take time off work? Sue drove me here.'

'You should have asked me.'

'Why?'

'I don't know . . . I – I wanted to be here for you.'

I was confused but grateful in this sea of strangers. Aunt Christine called me over to introduce me to some people. Mark grabbed my hand. 'Do you want me to come with you?'

'Yes please.'

I introduced Mark to Aunt Christine, but in the melee of people trying to offer condolences, it wasn't possible to explain properly.

'Would you like me to come back to the house afterwards?' said Mark, as I was being hustled into the car with Aunt Christine and Lorraine to go to the graveyard. I gave him the address and he said he'd see me there in an hour. He had driven all the way.

Few people came to the grave so that was more manageable for me. In the funeral car on the way back to the house, Aunt Christine asked who my friend was.

'That's Mark. He moved to Carricksheedy a few months ago, I think. I hope it's okay that I invited him back to your house?'

'That's fine. Are you . . . in a relationship?'

'No, not at all, he's a friend.'

Lorraine sniffed. 'He must be a very good friend to drive all the way here to come to the funeral of someone he's probably never heard of.'

Lorraine didn't like me, I could tell. I don't know why. I tried to put myself in her shoes. Who was I to her? The adopted niece of her sister-in-law who had no relationship with her deceased brother. She probably knew all about my background. She probably knew that I'd tried to cremate my dad.

'Lorraine, I know you think I don't belong here. I didn't know Donald well, but Aunt Christine asked me to come and my therapist keeps telling me that I should try to socialize with more people.'

'Oh . . . I didn't mean . . . sorry. It was a lovely service, wasn't it?'

'I didn't know Uncle Donald played the piano.'

Lorraine became chattier then and talked about the times that Donald had played the piano in jazz clubs in Soho when they were young. She was also widowed and lived in a small village in Sussex. She had a daughter who couldn't come to the funeral because her own daughter had just had a baby.

'So, you're a great-grandmother?'

'Yes, it's a privilege to live long enough to see your great-grandchild. I wish my granddaughter had been married first, but it's not like in our day, is it, Christine?'

Aunt Christine said she wished she and Donald could have had children and Lorraine apologized for being insensitive.

'I'm insensitive all the time,' I said, 'I can't help it. It's because of my upbringing.'

Lorraine looked out of the window and Aunt Christine put her hand on my arm. I guess nobody wanted to discuss my upbringing.

When we got back to the house, I helped to lay out trays of sandwiches and apple pies and sausage rolls, delivered by neighbours and friends. Those who had been at the grave-yard came in and were soon joined by others. I was delighted to see Mark.

'Are you okay?' he said.

'Better now that you're here.'

I introduced him properly to Aunt Christine and Lorraine.

'I'm sure Sally is grateful to have a friend here. So, how did you two meet?'

'He pulled over in his car and tried to get me into it.'

'What?'

'It was a misunderstanding,' said Mark quickly, 'but I was new to Carricksheedy and Sally was one of my first friends. You're her mum's sister, right?'

Aunt Christine talked a little bit about Jean. Mark offered his condolences on the death of Donald.

'So, were you and Jean close? You must have been a great support to her when she adopted Sally,' he said.

'Oh yes,' she said, distracted. She asked me if I could make sure that everyone had tea or coffee and to pass the sandwiches around. I swallowed my nerves. Nobody here knew me. None of them had met me before. I kept my eyes down as I did the rounds with the tea and coffee pots, and then with the platters of food. I could see that Mark was still engaged in conversation with Aunt Christine.

As the afternoon wore on, I went into the dining room and began to play the piano. I chose some Mozart sonatas. Nothing too sad or too upbeat. People drifted in and out of the room, and complimented me on my playing.

A short while later, Mark came in, a little agitated. 'I'm going to go now. Would you like a lift back to Carricksheedy?'

'No thanks, I'm staying tonight and then going shopping with Sue in the morning.'

He seemed disappointed. 'Right. I'll see you back in the village. I'll give you a call over the next few days.'

'Thanks, Mark.'

'Any news from New Zealand?'

'No.'

He leaned over and kissed me on the cheek. 'Take care of yourself, Sally.'

I felt okay. I drifted back and refilled platters and offered tea, coffee and wine for those who were drinking.

In the end, there was just Lorraine and Aunt Christine and me. As we cleared the rooms of plates and glasses, cups and saucers and napkins, they talked about Donald.

I was tired. The day had not been the ordeal I had feared but the tablet had taken its toll on my energy levels.

'I need to talk to you in the morning, Sally, before you go,' said Aunt Christine. 'Thank you for being here today. You were a great help, wasn't she, Lorraine?'

Lorraine nodded.

'You don't mind taking the box room, Sally? I have Lorraine in the main guest room.'

I did mind. A new bedroom always unsettled me.

'You'll have an entirely new house soon, won't you?' said Lorraine and that was not an unreasonable point.

I went to bed in a room with a lumpy mattress but slept well.

I woke early as usual and went downstairs to find Aunt Christine already at the kitchen table. As I filled the teapot, she gestured me to come and sit with her.

'This Mark fellow, how well do you know him?'

I explained that we had become friends through Martha.

'Do you know anything about his background?'

'He's divorced. He had an affair with a younger woman, but it didn't work out.'

'I see. You didn't say anything about inviting him to the funeral?'

'I'm sorry. I didn't invite him. He turned up at the church.'

'Does he . . . I'm sorry for asking, but what exactly is your relationship with him?'

'He's a friend. He's an accountant at Mervyn Park, the meat-processing plant.'

'Are you sure he doesn't want to be more than a friend?'

'Oh yes, I've told him it's out of the question. Because of sex and intimacy and all that. Besides, he says he fancies my friend Anubha. They work together but he's her boss so it's a bit tricky.'

'Sally, he asked me a lot of questions about you, about when you were young, about what Jean had said about your time in captivity. It was strange and, I have to say, inappropriate at my husband's funeral.'

'I'm sorry. But I always like it a bit when other people are inappropriate.' I laughed. Aunt Christine didn't.

'What's his last name?'

'Butler.'

'Do you trust him?'

'Yes. Tina says I should be more trusting of people and not assume that everyone is a predator.'

'Don't you think it strange that he would turn up to a funeral uninvited?'

'Well, I invited him back to the house.'

'But not to the church?'

'No, he heard about it from Anubha. He said he looked up the details online. He didn't want me to be on my own. He knows how difficult I find strangers.'

'Mark Butler.' She wrote down his name. 'Accountant. And where did he live before he came to Carricksheedy?'

'Dublin, I think?'

'You don't know what part?'

'No. Why are you asking me these questions?'

She brightened then and smiled at me. 'It's probably nothing. Maybe he likes you more than you think he does?'

I wondered about that.

'By the way, Sally,' she said, 'your piano playing was wonderful, everyone was moved. You play beautifully, and without any sheet music!'

'It calms me.'

'It calmed us, Lorraine and me, yesterday. It was thoughtful of you.'

'I was sort of doing it for me?'

'Accept a compliment,' she said. 'Donald would have played ragtime if he'd been here.'

'I expect you would have preferred him to be playing rather than me.'

Her eyes filled with tears. I moved awkwardly to hug her as Tina had suggested. She squeezed me tight before letting me go. I didn't mind.

I couldn't wait to tell Tina that I had passed this social test with flying colours.

34

Peter, 1982

After Rangi drowned, I gathered all my things and went back to the house to wait for Dad. Why didn't we have a phone? I knew Rangi didn't have one but we weren't poor. We should have had a phone. I knew Auntie Georgia wouldn't be home until late. I lay on my bed, unable to stop shaking.

I must have dropped off because the next thing I heard was my dad's voice. 'Who'd like some fush and chups?' It was our Friday evening treat and Dad liked to say it in a Kiwi accent.

I emerged from my room, wrapped in my blankets, and promptly burst into tears.

'What's happened?'

I told him the whole story, starting with the fact that Rangi and I had become friends, that he had watched television regularly in our house, that I had helped him with his school-work, all the way to his drowning.

Dad glared at me. 'What did I tell you? Didn't I tell you to stay away from him?' In the next sentence, he asked, 'What did you take with you, to the lake?' I told him about the towels, the chilly bin of Rangi's beer cans. 'You drank alcohol?' He was shouting now. 'Did you leave anything of yours behind, anything at all?'

'Dad, you have to get the police, an ambulance, you have to drive into town and tell his Auntie Georgia. She works in The Pig and Whistle.'

'Answer the question. Did you leave anything behind?'

'No.'

'Stop crying like a girl. We are going to do absolutely nothing. Do you hear me? Do you want to be accused of drowning your "friend"?' He said the word sarcastically.

'But, Dad, if he'd touched me, I would have died. It was him or me! I didn't know what to do.'

His voice softened now. 'I know that, but the police will see it differently. They believed that bitch Denise, didn't they? They can't be trusted. And your disease is so rare that most people don't even believe it exists. If they took you into custody, they would kill you within a matter of hours.'

'But, Dad —'

'That's enough. Get some plates. Our fish and chips will be cold by now.'

I stared at him. I didn't move.

'Now!' he roared.

I moved mechanically to the dresser and withdrew plates, knives and forks, and collected salt and vinegar from the cupboard beside the sink and placed them on the kitchen table.

He unfurled the newspaper and turned straight to the TV page. 'What would you normally watch on a Friday afternoon?'

I looked at the paper and picked out the programmes I was in the habit of watching.

'Right. If anyone asks, you stayed indoors today because it was too hot. You watched these TV shows. You noticed Rangi come home around lunchtime and you never saw him again. Okay? Where are the empty beer cans?'

'We left them at the lakeside. His T-shirt is still there.'

'Good. Accidental drowning because the stupid boy was drunk.'

'What about his Auntie Georgia?'

206

'What about her? She'll move away now because she can't drive. It suits us. I'll buy her property. Dangerous having neighbours that close. It's only a shack. I might even pay her more than it's worth – or maybe not, that wouldn't look right.'

I didn't understand what he was talking about. I tried to make him understand.

'Dad, my friend died. My only friend. Ever.'

He put his hand out and clasped mine. 'I know it's tough right now, but you have me. You'll always have me.'

My tears pooled with the vinegar on my plate. He didn't get it.

I went to bed about 9 p.m. as usual. It was still bright but I was looking forward to the oblivion of sleep. Sometimes Auntie Georgia got dropped off home by another bar worker around 9.30 p.m., 11 at the latest. Despite my exhaustion, I could not sleep.

At 10.15 p.m., there was a tentative knock on our front door. I heard Dad go out to the porch.

'I'm sorry to disturb you, sir, but my boy isn't home and I'm wondering if Stevie's seen him?'

'My son, Steven, is in bed, as he should be.'

'Oh, I know he's a good boy, but would you mind if I talked to him?'

'You want me to wake my son, at this hour?'

'Yeah, it's just that I'm worried, it's not like Rangi to go off on his own.'

'Rangi?'

'Yeah, that's my boy's name. Him and Stevie are mates.'

'Steven and Rangi are not friends. Steven has often com-plained that your son has come here uninvited. He has encouraged my son to drink beer. Steven is a quiet child and is easily intimidated. When Rangi does come home, please ask him not to bother Steven any more.'

I couldn't believe what I was hearing. How could my dad be so cruel? He knew that Rangi was dead, and yet he was allowing Rangi's aunt to think that he was some kind of bully who intimidated me.

Auntie Georgia scuttled back to her house.

I emerged from my room, furious. 'Dad!'

'Lower your voice.'

'Why did you say those things to her?'

'Those are the things I believe. He was a bad influence on you. Good riddance. It will be a few days before she does anything. Her type doesn't go to the police. When the body shows up, they might come around here asking questions, but you stick to that story, all right? Now, go back to bed.'

I did as I was told but I didn't like it. He didn't know Rangi. He had never even spoken to him. He'd lied about him.

The next morning, Auntie Georgia was picked up in a mini-bus as usual. She put a note under our door, asking us to call her boss if Rangi turned up. She assumed we would have a phone.

That Saturday night, after her shift at the bar, she knocked on the door again, asking Dad if we'd seen Rangi and then asking him if she could use our telephone.

Dad feigned a bit more concern this time. 'I'm sorry, Miss Sisterson, but I checked with Steven, he didn't see Rangi at all yesterday, though he did hear his truck pull into your driveway around lunchtime. He's sorry to hear that your boy is missing. We will keep an eye out for him, but I'm afraid we don't have a telephone. Who did you want to call?'

'The police! Rangi has been missing for more than a day now. It's not like him. He hasn't even left a note.'

'Didn't the children get their summer holidays yesterday? Might he have gone camping with some friends?'

'Without his truck? Without a bag? He doesn't have friends. He thinks your Stevie is his friend. Talks about him all the time.'

'Well, I'm sorry that Steven doesn't feel the same way. Goodnight, Miss Sisterson.'

Dad kept calling me Steven to Aunt Georgia, even though he called me Steve, and sometimes Stevie. I couldn't remember the last time he'd called me Peter. 'Steven' was a way of distancing me from Rangi, as if the name he called me was in some way illicit.

Dad came to my room again. 'She might call the police tomorrow. Just remember. Stick to our story. Stay indoors. She doesn't work on Sundays, right? Keep out of sight.'

The next day, early, she banged on our door again.

'I'm sorry to bother you, Mr Armstrong, but would you be so kind as to drive me into town? I don't know how to drive, see, and I need to report that my boy is missing.'

Dad played the good neighbour. He told me to stay put while he took Auntie Georgia to the police station. They returned three hours later. From my window, I could see that her face was tear-stained. She held my father's handkerchief to her eyes.

Dad told me that when the police realized from his name that Rangi was a part-Māori boy, they told her that he was probably off with some gang, up to no good, that he was probably trying to avoid the upcoming exams. Auntie Georgia showed them the teacher's note he had left on the kitchen table, to prove that Rangi wasn't a gang member. He was a lonely boy, she'd said. The police questioned where his mother was, why his aunt was reporting the boy as missing. When she was forced to reveal Rangi's mother's name, Celia

Parata, the officers looked at each other. Dad thought she was probably a prostitute because of the way the police smirked. They suggested Rangi Parata would show up, eventually. Dad said they didn't take it seriously. They didn't even write anything down or ask for a description.

Dad was gleeful, relating this to me. I was disgusted with him, with myself. I wanted to tell Auntie Georgia that Rangi was dead, that she should stop hoping, stop waiting for him to come home. He was never going to come home.

Before the week was up, Rangi's bloated body was found at the other end of the lake, closer to town. I was never questioned. The *Daily Post* reported a tragic drowning. Auntie Georgia didn't look me in the eye as she came and went. A police car dropped her home twice, once on December 18th and again the next day. I could hear her wailing aloud into the night from my bedroom and I wanted to console her, to confess and explain that it was an accident, that it was my life or his and that I had to choose mine, and that he had been my best friend.

Christmas Day in our house was strange. Dad pretended that everything was normal. We ate outside on the porch, toasting the day with Coca-Cola. Dad bought me a record player and I'd bought him a book on Māori culture. I found it in the bin a few days later.

35

Sally

My shopping expedition the day after Uncle Donald's funeral was not entirely successful. Sue parked in a vast underground car park and we emerged into this blindingly bright, dizzyingly high, cavernous building with neon signs everywhere, piped music and, for a Tuesday morning, lots and lots of shoppers. I had seen shopping centres on TV, but I hadn't expected this scale.

'I don't like this, Sue. Please may I go and wait in the car?'

'But the whole purpose is to get you kitted out with a brand-new wardrobe!'

'I don't like it.'

'Here, hold my hand,' she said, 'I have an idea. We will go to one shop with a huge range. You can go straight to the fitting room, and I'll bring you a selection of things to try on.'

I had recently found that hugging or holding the hands of friends was somewhat comforting. I allowed Sue to lead me into a shop called Zara. She spoke to an assistant while I stood, trying not to tremble, as people manically picked out random items on hangers, discarding them across the rail without re-hanging them, pulling at sweaters from the middle of a neatly folded pile and throwing them down again. I had once thought of working in a clothing shop, but my jaw hurt from the clenching of my teeth. I would not be able to stand this.

Sue came back with a young and beautiful shop assistant. They took me to a large changing room, with full-length mirrors on both sides. I sat dutifully and waited. Within ten minutes, Sue came back, laden with armfuls of clothing. I thanked her and began to try on sweaters, culottes, jackets, boots, jewellery, waistcoats, blouses, overcoats, T-shirts, skirts short and long, trainers, jeans, cardigans. Sue would check in with me every few minutes, exchange sizes for things I liked but didn't fit, and return things I didn't like. There were six times as many things in the changing room as there were in my wardrobe at home. The shop assistant took some of them straight to the till. I was dazed by so much choice, the silks and cottons and suedes and denim and sparkles and fur. I liked what I saw in the mirror. All the different versions of me.

I bought everything I liked. I passed over my bank card while Sue pirouetted with excitement. 'Just one more place I have to take you,' she said.

I was exhausted and the shopping bags were heavy.

We exited the lift on the top floor and Sue took me towards what turned out to be a beauty salon. 'Hair, nails, facial, lashes, eyebrows, make-up – I think you should do the lot.'

We were outside the door. I stopped. 'Why?'

'Don't get me wrong, you're beautiful, but wouldn't you like to see what you look like with a different hairstyle, a few blonde streaks or a curly blow-dry? I don't even know what your hair looks like when it's loose. Is it very long? Facials are so relaxing. This is a way to pamper yourself.'

'No thank you, Sue, I don't mind changing my clothes but I don't want to change the way my head looks.'

'Aren't you curious?'

'No.'

'Oh Sally, please? Let them style your hair. If you don't like it, you can pin it straight back up. Treat yourself.'

I could feel myself becoming agitated. I raised my voice. 'I said no.'

Sue's face flushed. She was annoyed. 'I booked us both treatments. I'm going in for a facial and to get my eyelashes done. Do you want to wait in the car?'

'Yes please.'

She threw the car keys at me. 'Level 1 in the elevator. Car Park A.' She swung open the door of the salon and disappeared behind smoked glass.

I couldn't tell how I had failed on this occasion. We had never mentioned hair and make-up and tinting eyebrows when we planned this trip. It was purely about clothes shopping. What did Sue mean about it being a 'treat'? How is it a treat if I don't want it and was never asked about it? Did she think my hair was awful? Were my eyebrows the wrong colour? I liked them. Tina said I was handsome and elegant. Sue had just said I was beautiful. I knew I was chubby but I didn't mind. Why would I change my appearance?

When Sue returned to the car, I was ready with my explanation, but before I could start it, I noticed her eyelashes. 'Wow,' I said, 'they're amazing!'

'You could have –'

'Look, Sue, I'm sorry but I think we misunderstood each other. I love your eyelashes and I'm glad it makes you feel good, but I'm different. All these clothes are enough change for me. I like my hair the way it is. I don't want to change my face or my nails or my hair. I hope you understand. It was kind of you to offer, but I'm not the same as you. I never will be.'

'It's fine,' she said, but in a voice that said it wasn't fine. 'I'm guessing you won't want to have lunch here either?'

I gritted my teeth and for a moment regretted the decision to undeaf myself. There were no misunderstandings when people thought I couldn't hear them.

'I'd prefer not to, if that's okay. Is there anywhere near here that would be quieter and less bright?'

'I know a place,' she said, and reversed out of the car space.

Five minutes later, we were in a cafe in the grounds of a city farm, Airfield House. It was bright, but suffused with natural light, not strobe and neon. The other customers were either elderly people or mothers with pushchairs and small children. I chose a table at the back.

Sue's face was still tight. I wasn't sure how I could fix this and I didn't want to lose another friend, although Caroline from the Texaco was no great loss.

For a minute or two we ate silently, and then Sue exhaled in a loud sigh. 'You're right,' she said, 'I don't understand, and it's unfair of me to blame you. I think the fault is mine, expecting you to want to change and experiment. I find it hard sometimes, to get a handle on you, to get inside your head.'

'Same here.' I nodded enthusiastically, and we laughed together, a voluntary laugh, because we knew that trying to 'be' each other was silly and pointless.

We chatted about the clothes we had both bought, and what occasions were most suitable for the many outfits I had.

'And that mini skirt and sparkly top, that's for flirting.'

'Sue, you know I won't be doing that.'

'You must open yourself to the possibility! Mark is obviously interested.'

'Well, I've made it clear to him that nothing's going to happen.'

'And yet he drove from Carricksheedy to Dublin and back so that you wouldn't feel uncomfortable at a funeral? Come on! He likes you.'

I had already confided my belief that I was asexual to Sue. I said nothing.

'How's the touch therapy going?'

'Good. I can offer and accept hugs now. Shaking hands is mostly fine, though I wish people wouldn't do it immediately after blowing their noses.'

'But this time last year, you would have thought that impossible. Has your therapist talked to you about masturbation?'

'She has mentioned it. Tina wants me to spend ten minutes looking at myself in a full-length mirror every night, and then next week, I think I'm supposed to start caressing all the different parts of my body, as long as I'm comfortable.'

'It's such a shame that you're asexual.'

'No, it's not. I've seen sex scenes on television. The moaning and screaming is off-putting. Have you noticed that in comedy films the women always scream and the men grunt, and in romantic films the women moan and the men breathe hard. Which one is right?'

'Oh God, I'm not qualified for this conversation, but I can promise you that there's no wrong or right way. When it happens, you go with the flow.'

'It's never going to happen, Sue.'

'Poor Mark.'

'He's interested in somebody else.'

'What a shame.'

'Not for me.'

Sue laughed again. I wondered how Mark and Anubha were getting on. I hadn't seen them together and Anubha rarely mentioned him when we met.

I paid for lunch and for petrol and chocolate when we stopped on the way home. Sue played some pop music and she taught me the lyrics to some songs by Adele and Hozier. I thought I'd probably be able to pick out the tunes on the piano later. They weren't Bach, but they were pleasant enough. 'You have a nice singing voice,' said Sue.

'Mum used to encourage me to sing when I was a teenager, but I'm out of practice.'

'You could take lessons or join a choir?'

'Honestly, between therapy and yoga and learning to caress myself, I've enough on my plate.'

'There's a great choral group in Roscommon. It's another way to meet people. Would you be afraid to sing in front of other people?'

'No, I don't think so. Easier to sing than talk about myself.'

'Mention it to Tina, I bet she'd encourage it.'

'I might.'

Sue reached across and squeezed my hand. 'Your future is so exciting.'

I squeezed her hand back and we grinned at each other briefly before she focused her eyes on the road ahead.

The estate agent phoned. 'Great news,' he said. 'We have had a lot of interest in your property, or as I suspected, in your site. Three main bidders at the moment: a developer, Morgan Homes, wants to build fifty townhouses. The pharmaceutical plant that's moving into Mervyn Park want a lower density housing development for their executives and employees, and a German supermarket are also keen. You have an acre of road frontage. I haven't had this much interest in Carricksheedy in my life!'

'That's good,' I said.

'Good? It's absolutely brilliant,' he said.

'Right.'

'Sorry if I seem over the top, but I don't think you understand the money you can make.'

Building was going ahead on the cottage. All I wanted was enough to make it as nice as it could be.

'But what will I do with it?'

'The money? You can do anything. Start your own business? Invest in shares? Your future is secure. We have a few investment opportunities ourselves that might tickle your fancy.'

'Do I get to choose which business buys the land?'

'Sorry?'

'I think a German supermarket would be a bad idea here. And a housing development? Will they all have gardens?'

There was a pause.

'Normally, we sell to the highest bidder. That's how it works.'

He tossed out some figures that frankly shocked me. The house would definitely be demolished, no matter who bought it.

'I think I'd like to speak to the potential buyers.'

'Why? I'm the estate agent. Between the solicitor and myself, we set it up so that you don't have to talk to them.'

'But what if I want to? Is that illegal?'

'Miss Diamond, I don't know what to say to you. It's not illegal, but . . . look, why don't you think about it? You shouldn't delay. These are serious bidders.'

'I'll think about it. Would you email me the details of all the buyers and I'll get back to you as soon as I can?'

He sighed deeply.

Angela said, 'You're dead right. A German supermarket would put the Gala out of business.' I thought of Laura in the Gala and how she was now stocking root ginger, garam masala, curry leaves and fenugreek seeds, how she had gone out of her way to accommodate the new community that was joining our village. She had just applied for planning permission to extend the shop.

'Well,' said Angela, 'you're mad not to take the best price, but if you can afford ethics, you should definitely stand by them. I admire you for it.'

The exasperated estate agent had asked the three interested parties to pitch their development ideas to me. The last developer was the best. Morgan Homes' plan was to build a mixture of social and affordable housing alongside private homes. They also had designs for a central green in the middle of the estate, on which there would be a children's playground. A lot of Mervyn Park's employees were on low wages, and the same could be true of the pharmaceutical plant, which was mid-construction.

The estate agent wasn't too dismayed when I told him I would sell to Morgan Homes. The price was still way more than I'd imagined. I felt bad for our neighbour farmer, Ger McCarthy, who had put in a tiny bid in comparison, to use the land for cattle grazing, but I was able to negotiate for him to get the back field for a nominal sum, and he was grateful for that. Morgan Homes were relieved not to be responsible for it. The same stream that ran underneath my new cottage sprang up in that back field and Morgan Homes would have had to bury it in some way. It was useless to them, but of great benefit to Ger McCarthy.

Nadine was busy with the cottage. She sent me emails with colour schemes and tiles, kitchen units, bedroom sets, wardrobe fittings, floor coverings, three-piece suites, shutters and curtains, shelving units, doors and windows. Again, I was blinded by so much choice and, in the end, I asked her to choose everything. Their house was beautiful and I trusted her taste more than mine. I was finally on the move.

36

Peter, 1983

Rangi's Auntie Georgia moved away into town. She couldn't stay this far out without being able to drive. Rangi had done all the grocery shopping. He had often dropped her and collected her from her various jobs. Dad bought her shack and patch of land for a pittance. On her last day in the house, weeks after the discovery of Rangi's body, I saw her go towards the side of the shed with an axe and, one by one, those hens fell silent. She left two plucked chickens on our porch, in gratitude to my dad for his help with the police and for taking the property off her hands, she said in a note.

Since moving to Rotorua, I had only been in the superette with Dad a handful of times, and to the library and bookshop more regularly. In the summertime, I could wear a baseball cap and long, oversized shirts with sleeves that came down over my hands to avoid touching people. I never wore shorts either. I told Dad that I was old enough to drive now, but he said he didn't have the patience to teach me. I regretted not asking Rangi. I know he would have taught me.

A couple of weeks after Auntie Georgia moved, Dad suggested that we go to a local wildlife park close to Lake Rotorua. It was January 1983, still warm, and holiday season was in full swing. Dad said we should take advantage of it. Despite the tragedy, I was eager to get out again and to see people.

We drove up as far as the northern part of Lake Rotorua.

A few families were camping by the lakeside. Dad didn't seem that interested in going into the forest or exploring the wildlife. Like me, he was looking at the people. Eventually, we walked off towards a forest trail. A small, slim blonde girl was climbing a tree. Dad stopped to look. We stood for a while, impressed. She got to the top and then looked back down, troubled.

Dad called up to her, 'Are you all right?'

'I don't think I can get down. There's a possum, right beside me. I'm afraid,' she said. We could see the fat-bodied animal two yards from her face on the same branch, fast asleep.

I looked up at her once again, dismayed that there was nothing I could do to help her. The easiest thing would be to climb up and take her hand and lead her from branch to branch. Possums were harmless but they were a scourge. They could hiss and spit when disturbed and had very sharp claws. Rangi had said everyone hated them.

'Why don't you jump? I'll catch you,' said Dad.

'I'm afraid,' she repeated, tears in her voice.

'Okay, we'll have to leave you up there, then,' said Dad and moved as if to walk away.

She began to sob.

'Dad, we can't leave her.'

'I suppose not,' he said. 'Where are your family?' he called up to her.

'They're on the other side of the lake. Mum told me to get lost until six o'clock.'

'Well, that doesn't sound fair. How about I come up and get you?'

Dad was surprisingly agile as he scaled the tree; a little unsure of his footing at times, but he reached her without any problems. He took her by the hand and led her from branch to branch, like I would have done if I could. The possum never woke up.

Eventually, she jumped a few feet to the ground, landing directly in front of me.

'This is my son, Steve. What's your name, petal?' Dad asked her.

'Lindy Weston. Hi, Steve.' She was shy and her face was dirty with tears, which she wiped away with her forearm.

'My name is Mr Armstrong, but you can call me James if you like.'

'Hi, Lindy,' I said.

'Where you from?' she asked.

'From Dunedin originally but I lived in Ireland for years.' This was our story.

Dad walked ahead while I chatted to Lindy. I was nervous, though I had no reason to be, not then.

'My neighbour is from Ireland, don't ask me where. She talks like you.'

I couldn't think of anything to say.

'Do you live around here now or are you on holiday?'

'No, we're not on holiday, we live in Rotorua.'

'You don't go to my school?'

'No, I don't go to any school. I'm homeschooled but I think I'm nearly finished. I've done all the schoolbooks up to Form Seven in every subject, but Dad lets me study what I want now.'

'You study when you don't have to?'

'He sure does,' said Dad, dropping back to join us. 'He's studying botany now and market gardening, aren't you, son?'

'Yes, I want to grow vegetables and sell them. The soil on our land is good.'

'Probably because of the rain here,' she said. 'It rains all the time.'

'It rains a lot in Ireland too,' said Dad.

'Have you got brothers and sisters? I got two brothers, they're always fighting. They're seventeen and eighteen.'

'No, I'm an only child. What age are you?' I asked.

'Fourteen.'

'Are you really?' asked Dad, and I saw a shadow cross his face. 'I thought you were younger.'

'Nope, fourteen. What age are you?' she asked me.

'Fifteen,' I said and she looked at me.

'I like your hair. My mum doesn't let my brothers grow their hair long.'

I felt myself blushing.

'Poor Steve has a rare medical condition,' Dad interrupted. 'He can't touch other humans, unless they're blood relatives.'

I knew straight away that Dad was warning Lindy not to attempt to touch me. It didn't occur to me until he said it. She inclined her head towards Dad as if he had a screw loose.

'Really? I never heard of that.' She turned back to face me. 'What about if you wanted a girlfriend?'

'I guess I can't have one.'

'Seriously? Ever?'

'No, he can't,' said Dad firmly.

'That's freaky. I never heard of such a thing.'

'Most people haven't. It's rare.'

'What's it called, this disease? I'm going to ask my dad, he's a doctor.'

'Necrotic hominoid contagion,' said Dad. 'I'm sure your dad will know plenty about it, but I'll bet he's never seen a case. Only one in six million people get it. I was only able to get some info about it from German medical journals and translate it.'

'Wow, that's grim. And yet, you can walk around, looking totally normal. What about pets? Can you have a dog or a cat?'

'I wouldn't like to take the risk with Stevie. He's a precious boy.'

'That's the saddest thing I ever heard.'

Hearing that from this strange girl made me feel sad too. I had never thought of what other people might think of me. Maybe Rangi had felt sorry for me too?

We had walked deep into the forest now, following Dad's trail map.

'Gosh, I better get back to the olds, I'm going to be late.' She checked her watch.

'Well, this trail leads us right back to where we've parked the car – we can give you a lift to the other side of the lake if you like? It's around this corner.'

'That would be great, thanks so much, Mr Armst– James. You know, my mum doesn't like it when I call adults by their first names. Why do you think that is?'

'Maybe she's a bit old-fashioned?'

'I'm going to tell her you said that.'

We all laughed. Lindy was a breath of fresh air.

When we got back to the car, Dad moved his seat forward so Lindy could sit in the back. We drove off and Lindy chatted amiably to both of us. She sat carefully behind Dad in case she touched me by accident. I appreciated her thoughtfulness. Then we came out on to the main road.

Lindy said, 'I'm sure we're going the wrong way, James. You should have taken a left back there. Want me to jump out here?'

'I think you should come back and have dinner with us. What do you think, Stevie?' said Dad, picking up speed.

'I'd love to, but I better tell Mum and Dad first? They'll be raging if I go off with two strange fellas without telling them.'

Dad said nothing. He took a swerve off the main road and we began to drive over the back roads towards our house.

'James, Mr Armstrong, what are you doing?'

'Don't worry, Lindy, we'll drop you back in an hour, okay?'

Lindy went silent. I turned around to look at her and smiled. 'It'll be fun,' I said, though I was thinking that Dad would be furious if I kept him waiting somewhere for an hour – not that I ever went anywhere without him.

But when we got to the house, instead of heading towards the porch, Dad put his hands on Lindy's shoulders and steered her towards the barn. She flinched away from his touch. 'I don't like this. I want to go home. I want my mum.' She began to cry.

'Dad, perhaps we should take her back. She's upset. It's not fair on her.'

He pushed her towards the barn door, opened it and shoved her inside, then he pulled the door closed again and turned a key in a padlock I hadn't seen before.

'You wanted a friend. I got you one. Now quit whining!'

I could hear her but only faintly, hammering on the door. The last thing we had done was seal the egg-box lining with another layer of sheetrock, even on the door. If she was screaming, I couldn't hear her at all.

37

Sally

A week after my house was sold, I heard from a lawyer that Conor Geary's sister, Margaret, had died two months previously. Margaret seemed to have managed to keep a low profile all those years. There was no publicity surrounding her death or her relationship to Conor Geary. Her solicitor had contacted me to say that Margaret Geary had willed her house to me. A large detached house in a salubrious part of Dublin. The house where I had been held captive with my mother. It was my natural inheritance.

The paperwork was handled quickly, and I put the house up for sale immediately. Nobody knew I was the vendor. Geoff Barrington dealt with the legal end of things. I didn't mention it to anyone, except Tina. This time, I didn't give a damn about the ethics of who bought it, I wanted that house to be demolished. I took the first offer. It was a very significant amount of money. What would I do with it all?

When news got out that I had sold my own house in Carricksheedy, I decided that I would have a party after all. All of my friends encouraged me. Who would have thought that I would have so many friends this time last year? Tina convinced me that it was a good idea too. I could ask everyone to bring a dish of food for sharing and, in return, I could offer them any of the furniture or household items I would no longer need. The only pieces I wanted to keep were my piano, my bed and perhaps my dad's office desk.

The party was planned for the afternoon of Saturday 14th

September. The guest list was long: Angela and Nadine, Aunt Christine (who would stay the night), Mark, Stella and her husband, Kieran, Kenneth and Sue, Anubha, Martha and Udo, Laura from the Gala supermarket, Fernanda and Rodriguo, Valerie from the cafe and Ger McCarthy, as well as all of their kids. Sixteen adults and seven children altogether.

I also invited Geoff Barrington, the solicitor, out of politeness, who thankfully declined, and Tina, who said that it was best if we kept our relationship on a professional footing.

I rented a marquee-style tent and a bouncy castle for the children. I also hired a security guard. A female one. I spoke to her on the phone and I looked her up on the internet. She was tall and strong-looking, lots of tattoos. When I told Sue and Martha, they were taken aback, but I reminded them that my mother was snatched from a garden on a sunny day. Also, at the back of my mind, although I tried hard not to think about it, Conor Geary was still out there somewhere. He knew where I lived. I didn't want to risk him or anyone like him abducting children from my garden.

Not content with designing my new home, Nadine arrived the day before the party with festoons of bunting and lights, which she hung from tree to tree. She helped me empty the cupboards of all the stuff I didn't want to bring with me to the cottage. We had marked everything that was up for grabs with yellow Post-it Notes. Guests could take what they wanted. Nadine suggested that we taste some of the wine to make sure it was okay. She was such good company, talking about the cottage. I would be able to move in in mid-October. 'There will still be a few finishing touches to be done,' she said, 'but it will be home.'

Although I didn't expect to, I slept well the night before the party. I woke with a dry mouth and a slight headache. I don't think we should have tested the red, white and the rosé. I struggled out of bed.

Sue arrived early to help, bearing several containers of bean salads, flavoured rice and empanadas. Two men came in a truck and took half an hour to inflate the giant castle on the site Nadine had designated. They were friendly and wished us a good time. They would return to collect it on Monday.

As the truck disappeared up the side lane to the road, Sue looked at me and looked at the castle. She kicked off her shoes, yelling 'Come on!' as she sprinted towards it and leapt into the interior, rebounding almost to the top. It did look like fun. I kicked off my trainers and ran towards it, and soon we were both jumping up and down, holding hands, bumping into the soft walls and each other, screeching with laughter.

Ten minutes later, we were lying on our backs, wheezing. 'Oh my God,' she said, 'you have this until Monday? Can my boys come back tomorrow? Please?'

'I guess all the kids should get the use out of it while they can.'

She beamed at me.

I showed her inside the marquee where the plates, napkins, cutlery and glasses were neatly stacked, ready for use.

'This is going to be awesome!'

'I hope so.'

Sue went home to collect Kenneth and the children to be back in time for two o'clock.

I chose a smart short silk dress that tied in a bow at the back. It had a heart-shaped neckline. When I had tried it on in Zara, Sue had said I'd need some fake tan for my legs. I didn't have any fake tan and my legs were the colour of legs, so I felt satisfied. The dress was comfortable. My body was comfortable. Yoga had made me more flexible. I could stretch and bend now without any groans or creaks.

Today I liked what I saw in the mirror. The short skirt swished and flared at the hem. I brushed my hair out and let it hang to see what it was like. It changed my face too much. I didn't like the feeling of it on my shoulders and twisted and rolled it into my regular bun. I liked my face. I liked the faint crinkly lines that came from the corners of my eyes when I smiled at myself. I was beautiful.

At 1.45 p.m., to calm myself while waiting, I played the piano. I remembered the Adele songs that Sue had played and sang to myself, softly at first and then louder to try and match her powerful voice. There was a knock on the front door. I went to meet Lina, the security guard. I gave her the guest list and asked her to make sure that nobody else got past her.

'You're that girl, Mary Norton, right? At first it didn't make sense, but then I googled you.'

'Yes, but please call me Sally. I don't wish to discuss the past.'

'Okay, right, so where would you like me?'

I showed her the spot where I wanted her stationed, to direct cars to the end of the lane, though most people would be coming on foot from the village as it was such a nice day.

'Watch out particularly for elderly men, please.'

'They never caught him. I read about it. But you don't think he's in Ireland, do you?'

'I honestly don't know. If anything strange happens, I want you to blow hard on this whistle.' I gave her a whistle alarm that Aunt Christine had given me all those months ago after Toby had arrived in the post. I slept with it beside my bed. It couldn't be heard more than a hundred yards from the house, but it might scare an intruder.

First to arrive were Rodriguo and Fernanda.

'Wow,' said Fernanda, 'you look great!' Rodriguo nodded in agreement.

'Thank you! I feel beautiful today. Fernanda, you look –' I stopped myself.

Rodriguo grinned. 'You're lucky that Fernanda is pregnant,' he said, and they laughed. I congratulated them and accepted a large tray of fluffy cheese bread rolls.

I brought them through the house, pointing at all the items they might like to take home with them.

Next was Valerie, who came around the side of the house with a giant bag of confectionary specially baked in the cafe that morning. 'I didn't even know there was a house down here, and I've lived in this village my whole life.'

'Well, it won't be here much longer.'

'So I hear! How exciting. You look smoking hot, by the way. Great dress! Do you mind if I grab a beer, then? It's a thirsty walk from the village.'

'That's why it's there. There are glasses in the tent if you need one?'

I popped open the bottle for her and she swigged straight from the neck. Dad didn't approve of people who didn't drink from glasses, but I knew now that he was old-fashioned. I tried to imagine what he would think of me now, in a short dress, hosting a party.

Ger McCarthy arrived with a sack of apples and potatoes. 'You can give them away as going-home presents,' he said.

People arrived one on top of the other then, and soon the garden was humming with chatter. The children ran towards the bouncy castle. Maybe later, I would change into my jeans and have another go.

Mark and Anubha arrived separately. I watched them but they didn't seem to gravitate towards each other, or indeed show any interest in each other at all. Abebi hugged me and sat on my knee while she placed a paper crown that she had made on my head. Everyone said I looked lovely and Stella made me do a twirl in the dress and everyone clapped. There was way more food than we could possibly eat and I knew I'd be asking people to take some home.

Martha had a small speaker gadget which she attached to her phone and soon the air was filled with music, not all of it to my taste, but some people started dancing. People pestered Fernanda and Rodriguo to dance the samba, but they admitted that, despite being Brazilian, they didn't know how to do it. Stella and Kieran stepped up and offered to show them. Sue and Kenneth and their children joined in, swinging each other around, shouting and giggling. Their noise didn't bother me today.

Aunt Christine was surprised to see me surrounded by so many people. 'But where did they all come from?' she asked.

'They're my friends,' I announced.

'Oh darling, that's wonderful. I'm so proud of you.' Her eyes filled with tears and I knew she was thinking of Donald. I handed her a napkin. 'Thank you, it's . . . I wasn't going to come. It feels wrong to celebrate . . . it's so soon after, and I'm much older than everyone else.'

Mark appeared at our sides. 'Christine, how lovely to see you. Come and take a seat in the shade here. May I prepare you a plate of food or would you like to come and see?'

'Thank you, Mark,' I said as Aunt Christine allowed herself to be led away to the catering end of the tent. I thought it was kind of him to make a fuss of her. She seemed a little suspicious of him after the funeral, but then I heard them laughing together in the tent. He arranged a chair and table for her and sat with her, filling her glass. The sun was high in the sky. I was drinking slowly, diluting my wine with water as much as possible. It seemed like it was the perfect day.

Later, a calm descended, which suited my mood. Rodriguo lit the outdoor citronella candles. It was still mild, but dusk was the time when the biting insects came out to play.

Mark sought me out and helped me ferry glasses into the kitchen.

'Before you ask,' I said, 'there are no further developments in New Zealand. I think Conor Geary is no longer there, or he never was, and maybe he had the parcel sent from there to confuse me.'

'Bastard. And he was free to kidnap another child, wherever he went.'

'I try hard not to think about it. I want you to stop talking about him.'

'Right. Sorry.'

'By the way, if you like Anubha, you'll have to try a little harder with her.'

'What?'

'Didn't you tell me you liked her?'

His face flushed. 'I suppose I did. But . . . it's hard when you work together.'

I don't understand romantic relationships. I let it go.

I heard loud laughter outside and when I went out Angela and Nadine were having a go on the bouncy castle. Sue winked at me. 'Sal! I knew this would happen!'

Angela came back, breathless. 'Jesus, I should know better. Do you have any idea how many injuries I see as a result of drunken adults on bouncy castles?' She clapped me on the back. 'Damn good party, Sally. I didn't think I'd ever see this day. This is what Jean wanted for you. Friends and fun!'

Was this what happiness felt like? Laughing and smiling came easily to me today.

Until I heard the high-pitched whistle.

38

Peter, 1985

Dad kept Lindy locked in the barn, the same way he'd kept my mother locked in the annexe. Her ankle was shackled to the wall. Her disappearance had been on the TV news for weeks afterwards, but nobody mentioned seeing her get into our car. I guess Dad had parked a little outside the main car park for a reason and, if anyone did see us, we looked like a normal family. Lindy wasn't forced into the car. There was no screaming or crying. We were all nondescript. Dad had told me that day to leave the hat at home, so there was nothing unusual about us.

The police theory was that she had fallen into the lake but, obviously, divers had not recovered a body. In the weeks afterwards I was worried sick about what we had done. Dad kept the barn key with him at all times. He told me that if we let her go, we'd both go to prison. He reminded me that I wouldn't survive the arrest because the police would manhandle me. I would die in terrible agony. He acted like he had kidnapped this girl to do me a huge favour, to give me a friend. But why a girl?

After the first few weeks, I visited Lindy every day once he got home. He unlocked the door and then locked me in with her for an hour or two. In the beginning it was terrible because she was so hysterical and distressed. She tried to escape so many times that first year. She threw boiling water at both of us. Dad was badly scalded, but I got out of the way in time. After that, Dad disconnected the gas to her stove and she got no hot food for a month, and that was a cold winter. But each time Dad put things further out of her reach or discovered a new tunnel site and blocked it up, I would try and make things easier for her. I was saving up to get her a television. I used to watch her soap operas so that I could tell her what was going on with all the characters. I installed new lights to make the place brighter. I gave her Vaseline to ease the chafing of the chain around her ankle.

Dad let her go outside sometimes, behind the house, but each time, she tried to run, even though he was holding one end of the chain. I wished she would learn to accept it, that her place was here with us. It was too late after two years to release her. She was stuck with us. She hated me too, until she realized that I didn't hate girls as much as Dad did. She begged me to release her and I asked Dad, several times, but he got angry each time, and I learned not to bring it up.

The older I got, the more I felt my isolation. What must Lindy have felt? I was earning some money from my market gardening. Dad and I had flattened Rangi's house and tilled the land. I grew vegetables and some fruit: potatoes, carrots, silverbeet, string beans, broad beans, parsnips, strawberries, cabbage and lettuce. I sold my vegetables to Kai, the manager of the small Clayburn superette in town. It was best to keep as many crops going as possible. It meant that if one failed for whatever reason, I'd always have something else to sell. I wanted my own money and it kept me busy while Dad was at work.

Dad had finally relented and taught me how to drive. I was a quick learner and it didn't take long to get my driving licence. I had to explain to the examiner why I was wearing gloves in summertime, and he was understanding, although very curious about my disease. He sat up against the passenger door of the test car so as not to touch me. I sailed through the test. Once I had my licence, Dad seemed happy for me to be independent. After that, we rarely went anywhere together. I ran errands for him at the weekends. I often did the shopping for all three of us. Occasionally, I dropped him at his dental office and collected him afterwards. I wanted to buy things that Dad didn't know about. Things for Lindy.

I found that old teddy bear when I decided to repaint my bedroom. And I thought about Denise again, and that little girl. I was so small when I spent those two nights with her all those years ago. Why did she have Toby, a toy? If she had married Dad, what had she brought to the marriage apart from an old bear? Dad had always said she had no family.

I tried to recall what age she might have been. She was certainly an adult, a pregnant adult when I met her, but what age was she when I was born? Were she and Dad really married? Wouldn't she have been better off in a psychiatric hospital? Dad seemed to despise her. He hadn't given her new clothing or much food, definitely didn't like her, but he had sex with her. Did she want to? My mother seemed to hate him too. And if she didn't want to have sex with him, did he force her? I didn't want to think about it. Dad was such a good man in so many ways. But then there was Lindy.

I bought Lindy basic groceries that she could prepare herself and I got her books from the library. Dad insisted that she get no writing or drawing materials, no pens, pencils or crayons. I bought her gifts, though, some chocolate or clothes from the op-shops, nice soap and shampoo, new towels. Dad said there was no point being sweet on her because I couldn't ever touch her. I knew that. But the more vulnerable and scared she was, the more I liked her. I buried my physical desires for her. I wondered if Dad was having sex with Lindy. I was afraid to ask her because I was scared of what the answer might be. One time, in the morning, Dad had scratches on his face. He said he'd tripped into the brambles when coming back from delivering Lindy's breakfast. That was a lie because Lindy made her own breakfast. Another time, I could see dried blood pooled in his ear. Why did it take me so long to realize that my father was a paedophile?

There was one occasion when I joined her in the evening and she was particularly subdued. I laid the bag of groceries within her reach, and then backed into the corner and began to chat about the day. There was blood on the front of her T-shirt. As she silently put her things away, I noticed that one of her front teeth was missing.

Lindy had to spell it out for me, and the words rang bells that echoed right back to my early childhood. It was March 1985. I didn't comment on her tooth, or the blood. I tried to pretend I hadn't noticed. She waited until I was sitting in the only chair and sat down on the floor, right in front of me, and looked up into my face. 'Steve, he said he'd kill me if I told you, but your dad isn't keeping me here so that I can be your friend. You're seventeen years old and you can't be that bloody innocent. Your dad is a rapist shit. He's been raping me twice a week since I arrived here. And if I resist, he punishes me.' She pulled up her sleeves so that I could see bruises on her wrists.

I told her to shut up.

'You think my tooth fell out?' she said, and I remembered my mother's gums. Lindy was only voicing what I had long suspected. I had worked it all out and she could tell.

'You know, Steve, you've known all along. If it wasn't for your disease, you'd be raping me too.'

I was horrified by this. 'I swear, I'd never hurt you, I didn't know anything.'

'I don't believe you. You definitely know now. What are you going to do about it?'

I couldn't look at her, couldn't think of what to say. I locked the door behind me as usual, and ignored her tears and frustration.

My mother was another Lindy. I remembered all the things she had said to me. She was eleven when he had kidnapped her. I remembered my little sister, Mary. What had happened to them? I had kicked my mother when she was pregnant. My own mother. Lindy was telling the truth.

I had watched enough TV shows, real-life shows and not just dramas, to see that women could be smart and funny, sweet and kind. I had met them in town occasionally, Kai's wife and sister. They were Polynesian. Dad had made derogatory comments about them.

I had never confronted my dad before. I had never needed to. I had lived in denial. He had always been gentle and kind and protective of me. But there were times when we had arguments. For example, I had begged him to get a telephone installed, but he'd refused, claiming it was a waste of money. I'd told him he was stubborn.

Lindy's situation was something I could not ignore any longer. I had a sleepless night, my mind in turmoil. I didn't join Dad for breakfast the next morning. I stayed out in the vegetable garden. That evening, it was my turn to cook dinner. When I heard his car come down the road, the knot in my stomach tightened. I had burned our pork chops and overboiled the potatoes. I put the plate down in front of him and sat at the other end of the table. I watched him pour water from the jug into his glass. I was too nervous and stomach-sick to eat.

'Are you feeling all right? You look a little off-colour,' he said, concern in his voice.

'I was thinking about my mother and how you raped her.' I choked on the words.

His knife clattered on to the table.

'I'm seventeen years old, Dad. How old was she when you got her pregnant? Was she older or younger than Lindy?'

He slammed his fist down on to the table so hard that everything jumped. His glass of water fell over. 'I will not have this –'

'You kidnapped her. You took her from her family and imprisoned her in that room next door to mine. You starved her and beat her and punished her, and you raped her. You're beating and raping Lindy, knocking her teeth out. Do you do it with extraction forceps or pliers?'

The water glass rolled sideways on the table.

'That lying little bitch! You can't believe a word –'

'She didn't tell me anything. I worked it out. I think I always knew, but I didn't want it to be true. I can't believe a word you say, Dad. You ran away from Ireland and you dragged me with you and now I'm complicit in kidnapping Lindy.' The water from the glass was dripping on to the floor.

He snarled at me, 'And what do you want me to do about it? Let her go? What do you think would happen to you? Who will protect you like I have? Like you say, you're an accomplice.' He pushed his chair back from the table and stood up, facing me. The toppled glass rolled sideways off the table and smashed on the wooden floor beneath us. I was terrified at the thought of being imprisoned, I was terrified at the thought of being left alone, I was terrified of dying an agonizing death. But I thought I knew right from wrong.

'Dad, you have to leave her alone. You're a paedophile and that's the truth.'

'And what do you get up to with her every evening, ha? Talking, reading?'

'Yes! What are you suggesting? You know I can't touch her.'

The high colour drained from his face. He held on to the table with both hands. He shook his head as if he had water in his ears.

'If I go to prison, you go too. You're not too young to go to an adult prison. Do you know what they'd do to you there?'

I'd read many prison books over the years. *Papillon* was vivid in my mind.

I ran from the kitchen and grabbed the car keys off the hook. Dad came after me, shouting. 'You can't do anything without killing yourself, you stupid boy!'

I took the car that night and drove for hours, but where could I go, and who could I tell?

39

Sally

As soon as I heard the whistle I felt like I was going to be sick. He was here. I had asked Udo and Nadine to run to the aid of Lina, the security guard, if the whistle blew, and they both sprinted around the side of the house. Everyone paused, wondering what was going on, except for the children, oblivious on the bouncy castle. I immediately did a head count of all the children attending. They were all there. I exhaled, but there was a lull in the chatter. I asked everyone to stay where they were. I went through the house and collected a poker from the fireplace on my way. A rage boiled up inside me. Finally.

As I opened the front door, I heard a woman's voice screeching. 'That freak murdered her father and you don't even care!' Lina had her in a headlock, but I couldn't see her face. Udo called over to me. 'It's fine, it's only that racist nutter who used to work in the Texaco. She's refusing to leave.' Caroline.

'You don't belong here. Why don't you go back to your own country?' she screeched at Udo.

Lina was hustling her backwards down the lane. 'My wife is a doctor,' said Nadine, 'we should have you sectioned.'

'Lezzer! —'

Lina clamped her hand over Caroline's mouth.

'Shall I call the guards, Miss Diamond?'

The poker in my hand seemed to take on a life of its own. I was so wound up and enraged by the thought that it might be Conor Geary, I didn't know what to do with my anger. I ran towards Caroline with the poker raised. Nadine grabbed me around the waist. 'Sally! What the fuck?'

Udo wrestled the poker from my grip.

Lina pulled Caroline out of my reach. She dropped her hand from Caroline's mouth but kept a firm grip on her neck and shoulder.

'You all saw that! She was going to attack me with that poker. That's attempted assault. You're witnesses. If anyone's going to the guards, I am!' screamed Caroline.

'I didn't see anything,' said Nadine. She turned to Udo and Lina. 'Did you see Sally try to attack anyone?'

'Definitely not,' said Udo, and Lina shook her head vigorously.

'You're imagining things, see?' said Nadine. 'You should be sectioned. Now, are you going to fuck off or are we going to call the guards?'

Everyone was lying now. My head started to buzz.

Caroline ran back up the lane, shrieking about liars and freaks, while Udo and Lina watched her go.

Nadine led me into Dad's office, which I'd labelled with a notice that said 'Private'. 'Wait there,' she said, 'I'll get Angela.'

Angela always seemed to have appropriate tablets to hand in her bag. 'Take this and tell me what happened.' She passed me a glass of water.

'You know why I hired Lina. When I heard the whistle, I assumed it was him. I felt a fury and couldn't control my anger. I was ready to kill him, and even though it was only Caroline, I . . .'

'You need to tell Tina about this. You must learn to manage that rage, Sally. Now, stay in here until you have calmed down and then rejoin the party. Nobody back there heard what happened. As far as they're concerned, Caroline tried to crash the party. They're all delighted that she has been dispatched. Nobody likes her. She's clearly a bit deranged.'

'Like me?'

'Not like you at all. Take a little time and do your breathing exercises. No more alcohol on top of that tablet, okay?'

'Yes.' I took a deep breath. 'Angela? What if I had killed her?'

'You didn't. No point in catastrophizing. Would you like me to stay with you?'

'No, I'll be fine. Thank you.'

I waited fifteen minutes in there before I emerged, and while the party outside was still in full swing, the joy I had felt was gone. I felt numb. I helped myself to some food and sat for a while with Aunt Christine.

'I heard about the gatecrasher,' she said, 'the brass neck of her! And she's the one you had trouble with before.'

'Yes, she lost her job because of me.'

'Sounds like she deserved to.'

I felt flat. Lifeless.

'Are you tired? Goodness me, it's seven thirty already. What time do you think it will finish up?'

'I don't want to stop people enjoying themselves.'

'It's a fabulous party, Sally, what a success. I've met lots of your friends. It seems like you're well liked here.'

I wondered if I would be well liked if everyone knew that I had almost attacked Caroline with a poker. I wondered if Udo and Nadine saw me differently now. Udo was watching me. I didn't want him to tell Martha what I had done. Eventually, he approached me. 'Are you okay? That was intense.'

'I'm so sorry.'

'You really scared her. You were fierce. You scared me a bit.'

'I hired the security guard in case my birth father turned up. When she blew the whistle, I thought it must be him.'

'But you saw that it wasn't?'

'I know, but I was so angry. I didn't know what to do with the anger.'

He was silent for a moment.

'Thank God you were there, Udo. I could have hurt her.'

He laughed then.

'It's not funny. You know I'm seeing a therapist? I still have issues because of my childhood.'

'Look, it's over. You didn't hurt anyone. And who knows what Caroline is capable of? She's terrifying too. She's going to have one hell of a hangover.'

'Was she drunk?'

'Very. Lina couldn't get rid of her. That's why she blew the whistle. She won't bother you again. I imagine the shame will be too much.'

'I have shame too.'

'Look, you shocked us, but it's over now. Relax.'

The pill Angela gave me was doing its work. I began to feel more at ease. This was something I would process next week with Tina.

Back out in the garden, Ger McCarthy took an accordion out of an ancient-looking case and began to play some old traditional tunes. Valerie, Angela, Nadine, Stella and Kieran (who had left their children with his brother), and Laura gathered in closer and we made a circle with our chairs and rugs.

Just then, Aunt Christine tapped me on the shoulder. 'Sally, I don't want to worry you, but I think there's someone in your dad's office? I heard noises in there. Furniture being moved. But there's a "Private" notice on the door. Are any of the guests missing?' I looked around and counted in my head.

'Mark.'

'Let's go and see what he's doing.'

Aunt Christine and I excused ourselves. We crept along the hallway and I swung the door open. Mark was sitting at the desk with a flashlight reading through Dad's old files.

'Mark!' said Aunt Christine. 'What on earth are you doing?'

He dropped the file and papers went all over the floor. These files were about to go into storage. The guards had the originals, and these were all copies.

'You wanted to see these files before. Why?' I demanded to know.

He brushed straight past us, pushing me against the desk, and left through the front door.

'I don't like this, Sally. I don't like this at all. He is way too interested in your history. He didn't say anything today, but at Donald's funeral he pestered me about what had happened.'

'He told me he was fascinated by the case.'

'He told me the same thing,' said Aunt Christine. 'I was so sure he was a journalist then, I looked him up on Google, but his background is all in accountancy. But this is crazy, going through Tom's old files. How dare he? What's he looking for?'

I grabbed my phone and called him. It went straight to voicemail. I left an angry message, demanding to know what he thought he was doing.

I declared that the party was over. Some of my guests were drunk. Stella threw her arms around me and declared that I was her best friend. I told her that Sue was my best friend and she thought that was hilarious. Nadine and Angela were both a little unsteady. Sober Kieran said he'd take them home. The others all wanted to walk. They thanked me again for a fabulous day.

Valerie and Laura left together, leaving Aunt Christine and me on our own.

'I don't think you should contact Mark again. If he leaves an apology message, fine, but don't respond. I'm going to tell Angela tomorrow,' said Aunt Christine.

'Why Angela?'

'His behaviour is extremely peculiar. He watches you and talks about you all the time, and I know you told me he was interested in that Asian girl, Anubha? But he didn't even try to talk to her today. He's obsessed with you, Sally. And not in a healthy way. Angela is your unofficial guardian in the village. She needs to know.'

I became emotional. I admitted to Aunt Christine what had happened earlier with Caroline and my attempted attack on her.

'I cannot imagine the anger you must have inside. You were lucky there were people there to stop you. Your experience was so unique, Sally, and even though you don't remember, you know what he did. It's horrific. Still, Caroline is a different matter.'

'Poor Udo and Nadine. And Lina. I didn't even think about how Caroline's words would have affected them. I'll call them tomorrow to apologize.'

'Good girl.'

'Aunt Christine?'

'Yes?'

'I'm a woman, not a girl.'

'I'm sorry, it's because I've known you since you were a little girl.'

'What was I like then? The first time you met me.'

'Honestly? Silent. Jean and Tom treated you as if nothing

had happened. They didn't enrol you in school for the first year. You slept an awful lot. Jean and Tom argued about that. She didn't think you should be sedated. If you don't mind me saying so, Tom was arrogant, insisting always that he was better qualified. You didn't like it when Donald visited with me. It upset him, you know. He would never have harmed anyone in his life, but you ran from him. Jean was the only one who could hold you or hug you, and even then, you struggled a bit, though I suppose that's not so unusual for six-year-olds.'

'Didn't I ever ask about my mother? My real mother?'

'No, Tom was determined that you would forget she existed.'

'It worked.'

'Maybe it was for the best? We'll never know.'

My head nodded to my chest.

'Let's go to bed. We're both exhausted. And we have children coming back tomorrow.'

The children arrived promptly at twelve. I'd said they could stay from twelve to three. Udo volunteered to keep watch at the front of the house and I gladly accepted. I warned him not to let Mark down the lane either. I said we'd had a disagreement and I didn't want to see him. Udo didn't ask any further questions. I tried to apologize for Caroline's racist abuse of him, but he said I didn't owe him an apology.

I made some lemonade for the children and put out plates of leftover cake. Angela arrived, admitting a hangover.

'Don't you have tablets for that?'

'They don't take away the embarrassment. I sang. In front of people. In front of patients. I had a go on the bouncy castle, despite all my dire warnings, at my age.'

'I noticed that,' I laughed.

'Nadine is still in bed. She's worse than me.'

Aunt Christine and I told her what had happened with Mark.

'Oh God, what the hell is his problem? When did he first turn up here, Sally, in Carricksheedy?'

'Around February or March, I think? The first time I met him, he tried to get me into his car, but after that he was apologetic. And he was so polite, concerned. But he was always asking about what was going on with the investigation into Conor Geary, and about what I remembered from childhood. I asked him to stop more than once. He'd asked to see those files before.'

'Maybe he's one of those true crime geeks?'

'Do you think he might have deliberately got a job here to get close to Sally?'

'It's possible.'

'Where does he live?'

'In the same apartment block as Sue and Kenneth.'

'What about his family?'

'He has an ex-wife, Elaine. He's never mentioned parents or siblings. From Dublin originally.'

'Have you ever googled him?'

'I did,' said Aunt Christine. 'I found nothing suspicious. Worked in various accountancy firms but seemed to be in a more senior position than he is now. A few photos here and there, some old ones from about fifteen years ago which included the ex-wife, Elaine Beatty.'

'What about school?'

'I didn't find anything that went back further than twenty years.'

'Does he have a LinkedIn profile?'

I was familiar with LinkedIn. I had registered when looking for a job. They sent me annoying notifications about jobs I couldn't possibly do or in which I had no interest.

'Yes, but there was nothing about his school on there.'

I was confused. 'Why would it matter what school he went to?'

'I don't know,' said Angela, 'but I'm going to do some digging.'

'There's another thing,' I said. 'I asked him ages ago if he was romantically interested in me and he said he was interested in Anubha, but yesterday, she told me that she practically ignored her at work.'

'Playing hard to get?'

'I don't think they even like each other.'

'It's all very odd.'

Sue came to collect her children and joined us in the sitting room. She asked me if I knew anything about Mark going on holiday.

'Why?'

'I saw him throwing suitcases and boxes into his car. I asked him where he was off to and he mumbled that he was in a hurry and drove off.'

'I have a bad feeling about this,' said Aunt Christine.

Sue wanted to know what was going on. Angela explained calmly that we were a bit worried about him, that his behaviour had been erratic. 'I'm sure there's an explanation,' said Sue. 'He's always nice to us, but he was definitely peculiar this morning.' She went out to summon her children.

Angela suggested that we keep this quiet. No point in causing a fuss or maligning Mark if he was just a true crime fanatic. It wasn't against the law.

They all left together. I felt strange in the house on my own. I couldn't wait to move out of it. The unpleasantness with Caroline and then Mark made me feel unsafe.

What happened the next morning terrified me.

I didn't sleep well. I put on my dressing gown over my

247

pyjamas and went down to the kitchen to turn on the kettle for some tea. After breakfast, I went through the house making notes of whose Post-it was on what item so that I could arrange collection. I heard the flap at the front door go and went out to collect my post. There was an envelope addressed to Mary Norton, my birth name. It had a New Zealand postmark. I opened it with shaking hands.

It was a birthday card. Fluffy kittens on the front, something appropriate for a child.

It's your real birthday, Mary. 45 today, 15th September. Not sure if this will arrive on the right day, but I think it's important that you should know.

S

It was a day late. I rang Angela but it went straight to voicemail. This was an emergency. I rang Detective Inspector Howard. She said not to touch the card. She would send somebody over.

The doorbell rang five minutes later. I hid in the sitting room, but peeked out of the window to see if it was a guard. I saw that it was the men who had come to take the bouncy castle away. They made their way around to the back of the house and packed it up. I didn't go out to them. They left in their truck. They didn't need to see me. I'd already paid up front.

Half an hour later, the doorbell rang again. I heard Angela's voice. 'Sally, it's me!'

I let her in and, before I could even show her the card, she said, 'Sally, Mark Butler is not who he says he is.'

40

Peter, 1985

After my confrontation with Dad, I had driven around aim-
lessly for hours through the night before realizing there was
nothing I could do about Lindy's situation without risking
my own life. I went home eventually, arriving at breakfast
time. Dad said nothing on my return. He knew I had nobody
and nowhere else, and that my disease would stop me reaching out, in any way.

The next evening when I visited Lindy, I told her about
the confrontation.

'So now you know, why haven't you gone to the police?'
Her voice was high, hysterical. 'You can let me go right now.
What is stopping you?'

I tried to explain that there was nothing I could do, that
the risk to me was too high. I told her that Dad had implied
that I'd been having sex with her too, which made no sense
because of the disease. She was silent for a while and then
she said, 'This disease you have, necrotic whatever, it's very
convenient, isn't it?'

'What do you mean? It's not convenient to me. I have no
bloody life.'

'He has lied to you about everything else, everything . . .'

A few months earlier I had asked my father to find any
new research papers he could on my illness. He brought
home printouts with photographs of deformed dead bodies
and people in hospital beds, mummified in bandages in isolation rooms. There was mention of research in a German

clinic, but that progress was slow and underfunded because of the rarity of the condition. There was no cure on the horizon.

'I bet you don't have any disease. He used it to keep you away from people. You've never been to school. You've never had a mother in your life, have you? What happened to her?'

I didn't want to tell her about my mother. 'I don't know.'

'So, for your whole life, it's been you and your dad. Do you know how crazy that is? Take off those stupid gloves and come here and touch me, just my hand or my arm.' She reached out as far as the chain would let her. I shrank back.

'He wouldn't lie to me about that.'

'He hasn't even told you where your mother is. You know now what he does to me. I've never heard of this disease. At the very least, it's suspicious.'

'Stop it!' I shouted at her.

'You have to let me go! We both need to escape,' she screamed as I locked her in.

I thought of all the life I had missed out on, if what Lindy said was true. And then I thought of Rangi. If I didn't have necrotic hominoid contagion, then I could have saved him easily. If I didn't have necrotic hominoid contagion, I was responsible for his death.

I said nothing about this to my father that evening. He acted as if nothing had happened after our big reckoning the day before. He cooked and I set the table. Eventually, when we were both at the table, he began to speak.

'Peter,' he said, and it was the first time he had called me that since we had left London, 'you have your disease and I have mine.'

'What?' I said, sullen.

'Let me speak, please. I'm not proud of what I am. I know it's a sickness, this attraction to young girls, but it's a disease I have no control over. Like your disease. We are what we are and –'

'You have control,' I interrupted him. I wasn't prepared to let him paint himself as the victim. 'You chose to take my mother out of her garden when she was a child, you chose to kidnap Lindy from the lake, and worse than that, you pretended that you were doing it for me.'

I didn't challenge him about my disease. I was going to research that myself.

'I'm sick, Peter, what do you expect me to do about it?'

'You should hand yourself in to the police. Tell them who you are and what you did in Ireland.'

'And what would become of you?'

'I'd manage. What about my sister?'

'Who?'

'The baby that was born in Ireland, in that room!' I raised my voice.

'I had no use for her, Peter. I wanted a son, but not a daughter, and I wasn't cruel. I could have taken that child from Denise, but it would have broken her.'

'You don't think she wasn't broken already? Shackled to a radiator for God knows how many years? You told me to kick her and to hit her when I was too young to know better. And you knew she would never retaliate because she loved me.'

'I love you,' he said, and I could see tears in his eyes. He put his hand on my arm, and I let it stay there, so starved was I of human contact. We had always had a tactile relationship when I was younger, but once I'd hit my teens, it seemed less appropriate. I took my cues from television and grown boys did not walk hand in hand with their fathers. They did not hug them or hold them close. I withdrew from Dad, physic-ally, though I missed the touch dreadfully. In that moment, I felt sorry for him. But not so sorry that I didn't spend the next week at the library.

At home, Dad and I reached an understanding. He didn't know how I was spending my days once I dropped him at his office. He thought I was working the land. We didn't talk about Lindy. He had left the key out on the kitchen table. I could visit her while he was at work, but I found it hard to face her. Apart from dropping off groceries, I left her alone.

In the library, I asked for every medical journal they had, but they only had their own *New Zealand Medical Journal*. I went through every edition of the previous five years. There was no mention of my disease, but I thought perhaps New Zealand was too small. Dad had said it was incredibly rare. The library agreed to order back issues of the *British Medical Journal*, *The New England Journal of Medicine* and the *Journal of the American Medical Association*. All of these journals had been cited in the New Zealand one. I remembered the Boy in the Bubble. Was he the only child in the world to have Severe Combined Immuno Deficiency? How different was my dis-ease? How did Dad have me diagnosed in a small country like Ireland?

Ever since I had started going to the shops, the library, selling my vegetables, I had carried out all transactions wear-ing hats with earflaps as well as gloves and several more layers of clothes to protect myself in spite of the discomfort in summer months when every other boy was in shorts and a singlet. My hair was deliberately long to cover my neck. I planned on growing a beard, but my facial hair was still sparse. I knew the people I dealt with thought I looked odd, but Dad had told me there was no point in explaining any-thing as nobody would understand. I had been bumped into by people a number of times despite how cautious I was, and had been terrified each time, but there was never any skin-to-skin contact. Dad had carried out any dental work, so my teeth were fine. I had recurring tonsillitis, but Dad always managed to get me antibiotics to treat that. I had never seen a doctor. Maybe it was time.

41

Sally

'So, who is Mark Butler?' I asked Angela as she made me sit down at the kitchen table.

'Let's wait until you have a cup of tea in your hand,' she said, and flicked on the kettle.

The doorbell rang. I went to the door with Angela hot on my heels and opened it to see a young guard in a uniform that was too big.

'I'm Garda Owen Reilly, here to collect a piece of evidence,' he said.

'It's there, the card and the envelope,' I said, pointing to the table that had Martha's Post-it on it. I quickly updated Angela on the birthday card. The guard picked it up with a pair of tweezers and put it into an evidence bag.

'Should we tell him about Mark Butler?' I asked her. Garda Reilly looked at us quizzically.

'I don't think it's anything to do with the guard's enquiry,' said Angela. 'Let's let the man go on about his business.'

'If there's anything funny going on, you should tell me,' he said.

'It's private family business,' said Angela. He looked miffed not to be let in on the secret.

I was annoyed too. As I closed the door on Garda Reilly, I turned to her and said, 'Tell me!'

She steered me back to the kitchen, pushed me down into the chair and went back to filling the teapot.

'For God's sake, Angela, I'm not a child. What do you know?'

She placed the two mugs on the table and sat down opposite me.

'I'm sorry, I don't mean to scare you. If I thought he was a danger, I'd have told that guard, but it's probably completely unrelated.'

'What is?' I had never known Angela to be this irritating before. Her eyes were almost dancing in her head.

'Okay, where will I start?'

'Just start!' I tried not to shout.

'I found Elaine Beatty on Facebook.'

I had deliberately not joined any social media sites. Tina had suggested they would not be good for my mental health. I wanted real-life friends and my name was well-enough known by now that it would attract voyeurs and, possibly, my birth father.

'Mark's ex-wife?'

'Yes, I sent her a private message asking to speak with her about Mark. I expected her not to reply or to ignore me, but she answered within the hour. We exchanged phone numbers so I called her. She's been worried about him.' She took a dramatic pause.

'Mark Butler is a troubled man. He changed his surname by deed poll before they got married, for a good reason.'

'What was his original name?'

'Mark Norton.'

'But that's my name, or rather, it was my birth mother's name.'

'Sally, he's your uncle.'

I was glad I was sitting down but I still held on to the table.

'He was four years old when Denise was kidnapped. He worshipped her. It destroyed his family,' Angela said.

'Wait, what? I didn't see his name in any notes anywhere.

In the recordings, Denise never mentions him – at least, I don't think so?'

'Maybe she couldn't connect with her childhood, pre-Conor Geary? She was kidnapped aged eleven, released aged twenty-five. She spent longer in captivity than free. It's possible that she didn't even remember him. And then she died in hospital a year later.'

'She committed suicide.'

'Yes. His parents both had breakdowns, according to Elaine. His father hit the bottle. His mother barely kept things together. His whole childhood and adolescence after that was spent chasing leads. Denise's disappearance dominated their lives. By the time he was sixteen, his parents had given up looking for her, and he couldn't forgive them for it. Then, when he was eighteen, Denise was found, with you. And he wasn't allowed to see her. You must remember, she didn't want to be around any adult male at the time, including her own father. Your dad – Tom, I mean – was the only man she saw.'

'And his wife told you all this?'

'Yes, they met in college in Dublin. As soon as people heard his surname, they wanted to know if he had a connection to the now infamous Denise and Mary Norton. His parents had moved to France, his sister was dead. He was a pitiful figure who drank too much, but Elaine thought she could rescue him. It was her idea to change his name, so that he could escape the constant questions. They married young, at twenty-two, and she thought that once they settled down and had a family, she could fix him, they could live a normal life. But he was still obsessed with finding his sister's kidnapper and furious with his parents for allowing you to be adopted. He was told, like everyone else, that you had been adopted in England.'

'I'm going to ring him. Why didn't he tell me any of this?' I said.

'No, wait, we have to think this through. Elaine said he refused to have children because he was terrified that history could repeat itself, that his child could be abducted and treated like Denise. That's what eventually ended their marriage after fourteen years. His obsession. There was no affair that she knew of.'

'He lied to me.'

'He and Elaine are still on good terms. She forced him to go into counselling and try to find new interests. And, for a while, he was stable. She has remarried and is happy with her new husband and son, but after your father's death, when you hit the headlines and were exposed as the baby born in captivity –'

'You make me sound like an animal in a zoo.'

'I'm sorry, I should choose my words more carefully. But, Sally, it was then that Mark became obsessed again. Elaine said he went to Tom's funeral. And then, against her advice, started looking for jobs in Carricksheedy. He was desperate to connect with you. Elaine even called his parents in France and discovered that his mother had died. His father, your grandfather, was shocked at the news of you, but he felt that the fact you had disposed of your father the way you did was proof that you were as dangerous as Conor Geary. He called Mark and told him to leave you alone, but Mark wouldn't be stopped. His father asked Elaine to intervene.'

'This still doesn't make sense. Why didn't he tell me who he was?'

'I don't know. But, Sally, you have to wonder what he wants. Did he merely want to get to know you? Or find out more about what happened to his sister, trying to read your dad's files? Or is he looking for clues to find Conor Geary? He was so capable of fooling us all.'

'What if he wanted all of those things? If he's Denise's brother, my uncle –' the word sounded strange from my mouth – 'well then, I think he has a right to see those files.'

'He'd be hurt to find that he's not mentioned in them.'

'Maybe. But he has a right to the truth, doesn't he? I'm going to call him and confront him with all of this.'

'Elaine is worried about him. He's not answering the phone to her either. I called Mervyn Park this morning. He's called in sick.'

'Tina talked to me about instinct and gut feeling. I think he was genuinely concerned for me, but there were times when he got intense and that made me nervous. What do you think, as a doctor?'

'I can't tell you as a doctor – first, because he was never my patient, and second, because even if he was, I couldn't tell you. But as an outside observer, and having had long conversations back and forth with Elaine over the last twenty-four hours, I think at the very least he needs professional help. He hasn't committed any crime. I feel sorry for him, if anything.'

'I'll text him. He probably won't answer my call.'

I sent him a message. *I know you are my uncle. We need to talk. Please call me.*

'Angela, I don't want to stay in this house any more. I don't feel safe. Nadine said the cottage would be ready to move into next month. Can't I move in sooner?'

42

Peter, 1985

Necrotic hominoid contagion did not exist. The doctor I visited in Auckland wanted me to go for a psychiatric evaluation.

'You're absolutely sure there is no such thing?'

'Where did you even hear about it?' the doctor asked me. 'Are your parents outside?'

'It's a rare disease, you might not have heard of it?'

'You believe that you cannot touch another human being? Seriously, where are your parents?'

'They're parking the car.'

'Did they tell you –'

'What about the Boy in the Bubble?' I interrupted her.

'That poor boy in Texas? I think he has an auto-immune disease. Your skin looks fine to me. Do you want to take off your hat and gloves and maybe your jacket, sweater and shirt, and I'll have a closer look?'

'No!'

'I promise I won't touch you. I'll put on surgical gloves, to be doubly safe.'

I was incredibly tense as I removed my hat and my long hair came spilling out of it, and my gloves revealed sweating hands. I pulled my vest over my head and she walked around me. 'I don't see any abscess, lesion, wound. No scarring anywhere. Do you mind if I check your heartbeat with a stethoscope?'

She pushed a cold metal disc to my chest and listened. 'A

little fast, because I guess you're nervous, but totally within the normal range.'

I persisted. 'But maybe you haven't heard of it? It's probably referred to as NHC?'

'Believe me, at med school, the weirder the condition the more interested we were. If this thing, necrotic something contagion, if it did exist, everyone would know about it.

'Peter,' she went on, using my old name, the one I'd used to make the appointment, 'have you ever been seen by a psychiatrist?'

'Do you mean that I won't die if I touch another person's skin?'

'I mean that nothing, *nothing* will happen at all. Want to try?' She took off her gloves.

'What if you're wrong?'

'Should we wait for your parents?' She gestured to the half-empty parking lot outside her window.

'I've had this condition since I was born,' I said.

'What did you say your address was again?'

I had given a false address in Auckland when I registered with the receptionist. Dr Bergstrom held the form out in front of her. In a hurry, I put my clothing back on, and my hat and gloves. 'I'm going to go and find my folks,' I said, backing towards the door. She tried to detain me, leaping up from her desk.

'Please wait,' she said. 'I do think you need help, but not the kind –' She reached out and touched my face with her ungloved hand. I contained my scream and shot out of the door, through the waiting room and ran down the street so disorientated that it took me ten minutes to find the car.

I immediately checked my face in the rear-view mirror, expecting to see molten skin. I could feel it burning, but in the mirror everything looked normal. I sat in the car for thirty minutes in a state of terror and panic but gradually realized that the burning sensation was what my mind had told me to expect. There was no feeling there at all. I pinched my skin to see if it had somehow been numbed by her touch, but I felt the pinch. Her bare hand on my face had no effect whatsoever. I could scarcely believe it.

I drove to the city centre, my mind such a jumble of confusion that, on arrival, I couldn't recall where I was. I parked on a side street and took off my hat and my gloves, even though it was cold. I left them in the car. I walked down a busy street and into Whitcoulls bookshop. The man behind the counter looked up and smiled at me. 'Hello there!' he said. I couldn't speak. I went to the Ngaio Marsh shelves and picked one out for Lindy, then turned to the counter. The man asked, 'Getting cold out there?' I shook my head, still unable to speak, and reached out a trembling hand containing a twenty-dollar bill. He took the note from my hand without touching me and turned to the cash register. When he passed me the change, he placed it into my open palm, again without touching my hand. I pocketed the change and then took his hand in mine and shook it.

'Thank you very much,' I said.

He seemed surprised and, as tears began to fall down my cheeks, he held me by the shoulder. 'Are you okay, sonny? Did something happen?' My hand tingled from the touch, but there was no burning, no discolouration, just the warm impression that was left behind by this man's hand. I wanted to bury my head in this stranger's shoulder but I turned and left the shop.

I drove back to Rotorua, my anger surging as I accelerated. I arrived in town just as it was time to collect Dad from the dental office.

He waved from the window and came out, locking the door behind him. He sat in the passenger seat and threw his briefcase into the back. I took off before he had fastened his seat belt.

'What's the rush?' he said.

'Tell me again about necrotic hominoid contagion,' I said, trying to keep the ice out of my voice.

'Funny you should mention that. I rang an immunologist in Melbourne today to see if there were any updates. I'm afraid there's no treatment on the horizon, but I suppose you're used to it now, Steve.'

'Yeah? What was the immunologist's name? I might want to talk to him myself.'

'I think it's best if you leave the medical end of things to me.'

'What's his name?'

'Dr Sean Kelly.'

'An Irish name. Interesting. And what hospital does he work in?'

'St Charles.'

'Right. And is that a general hospital or one that specializes in immune diseases?'

He stroked his beard, and as I glanced at him, I saw he looked me straight in the eye. 'It's a specialist hospital. All the funding now is going into the research of this new gay disease, AIDS.'

There was no hesitation at all, but then Dad was an expert at lying.

'And exactly when was I diagnosed? I mean, if I was born in that annexe, how did you know I had it?'

'Has that little bitch –'

I took my eyes off the road and stared at him. 'Don't call her that.'

'Oh, for Christ's sake, Steve, you can't believe anything Lindy Weston says to you. She's one of them.'

'I don't have any disease, you lied to me about that as well.'

'Well, if you want to take the risk –'

'What about Rangi? I was three feet away from him. I could have easily pulled him back to shore, but to save myself, I let him drown.'

'He was a half-breed and a bad influence. He had you drinking beer at your –'

'He was smart and kind. He was my friend!' I couldn't help shouting.

'Watch the road!'

We had veered off the back road that led up to our house on a slow-rising hill. I tried to correct the steering, but I overdid it and we were on the other side of the road, headed for a steep drop. I panicked and hit the accelerator pedal instead of the brake. The engine screamed for what seemed like a full minute and then we hit fresh air. I'll never forget the noise as we rolled over and over. Later, the police said that we'd only dropped fifteen feet, but it felt like rolling down a vertical cliff, hitting every boulder on the way, my head ricocheting between the roof of the car and the windscreen until the glass smashed.

I had never heard Dad scream before. What a strange sound. I opened my mouth but, like in a nightmare, no sound came out. Blood filled my vision and I could hear the loud twisting of metal and the cracking of bones as we fell until we stopped. The car was upside down. I wiped the blood from my eyes with my shaking hands. My door had been torn off. Dad's door was wedged against the earth, mud tumbling through the shattered windscreen on top of us. I unbuckled the seat belt that was tangled around my knees and fell on to the ceiling of the car before hauling myself out. When I tried to stand up and orientate myself, I felt a searing pain through my right ankle. I looked back at Dad. He was still screaming. His shirt was stained with blood. The car had crumpled around him and it looked like he was crushed against the door. The way he was positioned, he couldn't reach it. His right arm was mangled and broken. The smell of petrol filled my nostrils and I noticed a plume of flame in the undergrowth at the rear of the car.

'It's on fire,' I said, my voice trembling.

Dad lunged towards me. 'Get me out!' His head was pinned sideways to the roof of the car. It would have been easy for me to release him from the seat belt. I'm sure there would have been time. I could have pulled him out. But, instead, I scrambled up the incline with my elbows, dragging my useless foot, grunting with pain. Dad was screaming again, begging, 'Don't leave me here! Peter! Please!' and then in fury, 'I am your father. Get me out!' I heard the flames taking hold as I edged my way up the embankment. I heard my father's screams. I didn't look back.

I woke up on a stretcher at the side of the road in the dark as the ambulanceman lifted my right foot. Another one held my head with his bare hands. The shock was intense, but I wasn't sure if it was the fact that he was touching me or the pain in my ankle. My shirt and jacket lay in ribbons on the grass verge. My trousers had been cut open. I didn't dare to look down at my foot. The ambulancemen talked to me in soft and sorrowful voices. 'What's your name, kiddo?'

What was my name? I felt exhausted, too tired to talk. One of the men said, 'I think he'll be okay. Not coughing blood or clutching his stomach, so probably no internals. You think that was his dad?'

I raised my head long enough to say, 'Yeah, that was my dad.'

Everyone touched me in hospital, the nurses, the doctors,

the police, the social worker, the chaplain. In my haze of medication in the first two days, each touch was joyous. I shook hands with everyone, cried tears, laughed aloud at the craziness of everything that happened. My foot was operated on straight away. I had broken my ankle. They said it was a clean break. Six weeks in a plaster cast and using crutches and I'd be as good as new.

Every time a nurse or a lady doctor touched me below the neck, I got an erection. Most of them noticed and ignored it, but some kindly told me that it was nothing to be embarrassed about and that it was a totally normal reaction, especially at my age. I felt less like a freak by the day.

I had a laceration across my hairline where my head had hit the rear-view mirror. Nine stitches across my head made me look a little bit like Frankenstein's monster. The food was regular and about as wholesome as whatever Dad and I had cooked. I shared a ward with four other men, all much older than me. I had never shared a room with anyone before, not since those two nights when I was seven years old. These men spoke to me sympathetically. A nurse told me she had turned away a local journalist who wanted to ask me about my father's last moments. They were all disturbed when I explained that I had no living relatives. They referred to me as the orphan.

Everyone in the hospital felt sorry for me. I got anything I asked for, including a haircut and new clothing.

The police ruled that my dad's death was accidental. I said I had swerved to avoid a dog. It wasn't unusual to see dogs everywhere around Rotorua, so it was entirely believable. The police were kind. They handed me a bag of what they were able to recover from the car and from my dad's burnt corpse: his broken watch with its melted strap, his fake wedding ring, his large set of keys and a briefcase containing some tax forms and that day's newspaper that had been thrown from the car.

The *Rotorua Daily Post* did a fundraiser for me. The people of Rotorua were exceptionally generous. I allowed Jill Nicholas, the local reporter, to interview me. The social worker told me that while technically I was old enough to live on my own, she strongly recommended that I stay with friends for a while. I refused the offer, insisting that I had been living independently for years, that I cooked and shopped and earned my own money with my vegetables. She was surprised that I hadn't been to school, and that I wasn't registered with a local doctor. She arranged for a solicitor to telephone me in the hospital to discuss my dad's estate. When I was well enough, I could visit him in his office, but in the meantime, the generous donations from Rotorua's finest would keep me going. I could buy a replacement car, which was what I needed most urgently.

Ten days after the accident, I was discharged on two crutches with a recommendation to rest as much as possible. A district nurse would visit every day at 11 a.m. The social worker drove me back home from the hospital, stopping off to pick up groceries on the way.

She took a tour of the house, satisfied that there were no steps. Everything was conveniently laid out. She had no interest in investigating the barn, but she did take a walk around my vegetable plot. She asked me again if there was anybody I wanted to call. I asked for her help to install a phone and she registered surprise and dismay that we didn't already have one. She said that she would look into it 'as a matter of urgency'. She reluctantly left me on my own. The nurse would be there in the morning. The social worker patted me on the arm and told me I was a brave boy. I glowed under her touch.

I had missed Lindy, but I knew she had access to water. Her food might have run out but I was home now. She'd be okay. And she'd never have to face my dad again. He was the reason she wanted to leave. It was just going to be the two of us. She would be happy to stay with me.

As soon as the social worker was gone, I took the key off the latch on the back door and stumbled my way out to the barn, dangling the bag of groceries off one crutch.

43

Sally

I moved into the cottage the following week, the last week of September. All of the structural work was done. I had a working bathroom and kitchen, but no carpets or curtains. The walls were plastered but not painted. The patio area wasn't finished, and the floor tiles in the hallway had yet to be laid. Most of the furniture hadn't been delivered, but I hung sheets for curtains and took the old sofa and the kitchen table and chairs from the house. None of my friends had wanted them anyway. I bought some cheap rugs to scatter on the floor as a temporary fix.

Nadine introduced me to all the tradesmen and women who were coming to finish their various jobs. It was uncomfortable with people coming and going at all times of the day. I spent as much time as possible out and about.

I missed my piano dreadfully, but I couldn't install it in the cottage while the builders were still working because of the dust, so for one whole week, I went to stay with Aunt Christine in Dublin and played hers every day.

She was shocked to hear all about Mark Butler/Norton. But she had a vague recollection of Mum telling her that Denise had a brother. 'Jean was much more in touch with Denise's family than Tom was. I recall her saying something about the brother being too old, that Denise wouldn't have recognized him as the four-year-old she had last seen.'

Why had Dad thrown out Mum's files? Aunt Christine sighed. 'Your dad wasn't perfect, Sally.' I was beginning to understand this. I was always stubborn as a teenager, but Mum often forced me to do things I didn't want to do. Now, after nearly two years of therapy, I could appreciate that Mum had been trying to integrate me, encouraging me to join clubs and go to school discos and parties. Dad overruled her and allowed me to do what I wanted, taking notes all the time. I recalled overhearing a row once and my mother shouting at my father, 'She's not your case study, she's our daughter.'

In the meantime, Tina and I worked specifically on anger management. When I told her about the overwhelming rage I'd felt towards Caroline, she helped me to see that I was taking on anger that I had learned from my birth mother. Through her files, especially from those tapes, and possibly from repressed memories.

'You have often said to me, Sally, that you can't relate to her as your mother, but you must have witnessed things or at least seen some of the aftermath of the most extreme emotional and physical abuse. When you or someone or something you love is threatened' – she was referring to the time I attacked Angela when she took Toby from me – 'you want to lash out, like Denise probably did. Anger is a secondary emotion. Rage can be sparked by fear or any emotion where we feel vulnerable or helpless. But now you're an adult, you're not locked in a room. You can use different powers. You can use your voice and you can walk away. Two of the most important tools you have. Remember, you are not a child locked in a room. Violence is almost never an appropriate response.'

I had a lot to think about.

Mark never replied to my text, and when Angela put me in touch with Elaine, she hadn't heard from him either.

'I am worried,' she told me, 'but he has done this before, disappeared for weeks when he got stressed and then surfaced again, full of apologies and promises never to do it again. It's a pattern with him. I guess you're my ex-niece-in-law?'

She was friendly and offered to meet me.

'I don't think so. We're not properly related, you and I.'

'Okay, if that's the way you feel.'

'It would be strange, though, wouldn't it? All we need to do is exchange information. We can do that over the phone. You're not my family.'

'I guess not.'

'Mark is my uncle and he should have told me.'

'I couldn't agree more.'

Sue asked me if anything had happened after the party. Kenneth had told her Mark was the talk of Mervyn Park. Apparently, he was on stress leave, and wasn't in his apartment. They were full of speculation about what had happened. I told her, because she was my best friend. Sue was as shocked as Angela, Aunt Christine and me.

'Anubha thought he was mad about you. He talked about you a lot, always asking questions. She eventually told him to shut up one day at work when he was speculating about what you must have gone through as a child. She said it was creepy, but the rest of them thought he had the hots for you, like as if he was fascinated by your "little orphan Annie" story. God, that's so weird, Sally, and nobody knows where he is now?'

'No.' I paused. 'I hate that film. The sun rarely comes out tomorrow, not in Carricksheedy. Not in winter anyway.' Sue laughed. 'What are you laughing at?'

'I don't think musical lyrics should be taken so seriously.'

Before the builders left the cottage, I had a locksmith put bolts on all the doors and windows. And then they left, the first week of October, and I had my own beautiful space and my dream bathroom. The lines were sleek and straight. I could hardly believe that this gorgeous home was my own. The stream ran through the house under glass panels and emerged in a rockery in the back yard. Everyone who came admired it as if it had been my work. I gave them Nadine's business cards. When the piano moved into the cottage, I finally felt at home. I felt secure, I suppose, but sad and a little scared.

While I was concerned about Mark, I was far more worried about 'S'. The guards couldn't find out anything about where the card had been sent from except that it was processed through the main post office in Auckland, like every other piece of overseas mail from New Zealand. It frightened me. Conor Geary was still out there.

44

Peter, 1989

It took me a while to get over Dad's death. I felt the weight of the phantom disease lift off me. I missed him and I hated him and I loved him, but I could not forgive him. There was nobody with whom to be angry over all the lost years, the years where I could have gone to school, the years where I needn't have been so physically uncomfortable in hats and gloves, years of friendships, connections, sports and parties, and most particularly the decades of Rangi's life that were lost because I was gullible enough to believe what my father told me.

I missed the companionship, though, the care and consideration.

Jill from the *Daily Post* encouraged me to write an open letter to thank the local people for their generosity and wanted another photo of me at home. I agreed to the letter but refused another photograph. Years of hiding didn't disappear overnight; the feeling of escaping and hiding never left me. I wanted my anonymity back and so I went from being a minor local celebrity to being a recluse. I had a telephone, finally, but nobody to call.

The logistics of sorting out Dad's estate were overwhelming, and I was appointed a social worker and a lawyer who handled everything for me. I wasn't alone, but everybody thought I was. Money was transferred into a bank account for me. I was not rich and I would have to work hard to pay the bills, but I owned the house outright.

Questions were asked about why I hadn't gone to school, but I told the truth, that my father had believed I suffered from a disease and that socializing could put me at risk. I had to take some equivalent of their National Certificate of Educational Achievement exams. The authorities were dismayed, I think, that I scored so highly and was duly awarded the certificate. My social worker also made sure that I was registered with the Inland Revenue and explained that my income was taxable. She managed to persuade the authorities not to pursue me for revenue I had already earned. The weeks on crutches were difficult. I was dependent on social workers and district nurses to take me to and from physiotherapy and grocery shopping. In the superette, as I filled the shopping cart, they commented that I had a big appetite. They didn't realize that I was shopping for two.

Lindy had been half crazy with hunger when I unlocked the door for the first time ten days after the accident. She ate cheese out of the packet and stuffed potato chips into her mouth between screaming at me for leaving her alone for so long. I waited for her to notice my short haircut, the stitches on my head and the crutches I leaned on, and when she did, she sat back on the bed and looked at me. 'What happened? Where is he?'

I told her about the car accident, the argument that led to it, how I had let my father die. My eyes filled with tears and her eyes glistened too. When I finished explaining, she tipped her head back and her hair hung over her shoulders, her beautiful face pointed at the ceiling. Even with a missing tooth, she was still lovely. 'It's over,' she said. 'I can go home.' And then she looked at me suspiciously. 'Where are the police? Why aren't they here?'

I stared at her. It had never occurred to me that she might want to leave now that Dad was gone. She was all I had.

'You're mine, Lindy. I'm going to keep you safe.' I swore I would never rape her, never hurt her. I told her that I'd let Dad die so that he would no longer hurt her, and that was true. I wanted us to be friends and that could never happen if I let her go. She turned her face to the wall and howled and wailed like I'd never heard her before. 'Lindy,' I said softly, 'it's for the best. I'm in charge now. I'll look after you.'

'Fuck off, Steve!' she screamed at the top of her lungs. She hated me. If she ever did get away, she would tell them exactly who I was and where to find me. I had been complicit with Lindy's kidnapping for two years already so there were two strong reasons for keeping her: I loved her; and I didn't want to go to jail. The first one was more important to me.

I was given an old car by one of Dad's former patients. Eventually, the dental practice sold and my inheritance hit a bank account in my name and I could get on without social workers, lawyers or nurses. I got my independence back.

By 1989, when I was twenty-one, I noticed girls in town looking at me sometimes. I'd never paid much heed to my appearance before. The scar had faded into a thin white line on my forehead. You wouldn't notice unless you got close, and nobody got close. I ate well and exercised regularly. I had joined a gym and was lifting weights and bench-pressing. I'd leased a small shop in town and set myself up as a greengrocer. I still supplied to the superette but also to other outlets in surrounding towns. I'd studied what other producers were charging and undercut them. I was on nodding terms with some guys in the gym and in the shops I supplied, and a few customers. But now that I could have friendships, I didn't want them. I didn't want anyone getting too familiar because

I had Lindy. She was my secret. She wasn't my girlfriend, not yet, but I knew she would be eventually. I was prepared to wait.

I was good to her. I let her have the newspapers when I'd finished with them. I had installed a proper bed and a colour TV. I bought her favourite food instead of the essentials like Dad did. She loved Shrewsbury and MallowPuff cookies, so they were her weekend treat. I bought a plug-in radiator for the winter because she had always complained about how cold it got out there. When I went out of town on a trip, I bought her new clothes and jandals, women's magazines and lipstick. It was trial and error with the sizing, but I got it right in the end. When she asked for sanitary towels and tampons, I was shocked that Dad had never supplied those. I got them in bulk twice a year after that so that she would never have to ask and she would never run out. I gave her a clock and a calendar so that she knew what day and time it was. I bought her a record player and a radio. Everything I could do to make her happy. And yet, she was never happy. 'Why are you keeping me? If you don't want sex, what do you want? I'm never going to be your "friend",' she said, scorn in her voice. 'I'm never going to feel like you're anything other than my jailer, and you're an idiot if you think differently.'

45

Sally

I finally received a text from Mark: *Please do not contact my ex-wife. This is none of Elaine's business.*

I was furious. I had only spoken to Elaine twice. I had never met her, even though she had offered.

I texted him back straight away. *Fine. What did you want with me, Mark? That's what I can't figure out.* And then, as an afterthought, I sent another text. *By the way, I got another card from 'S' the day after you left. Could that be you? Are you playing mind games with me?*

My phone rang moments later.

'Mark?'

'What did the card say?'

'Well, hello to you too.'

'I need to know what it said.'

'I need to know why my uncle would turn up here in Carricksheedy, pretend to be my friend, and then vanish without a word.'

'I wanted to tell you, honestly, but I just needed to be sure. And I was about to tell you. I was going to, after the party. I wanted to tell you and your Aunt Christine together. But I thought you'd be like her, like Denise.' His voice cracked.

'Mark?' There was a muffled sound and then his voice was broken by tears.

'I thought you'd be like her, but you're like him.'

'What are you talking about?'

'Sally, you're violent and aggressive.'

'What? I know. I'm dealing with that side of things. Mark, I need to see you. I feel hurt and confused and angry.'

'I'm afraid of your anger.'

'Me too. Please come back and let's talk.'

He took a lot of persuading and was reluctant to come to the village, so I arranged to meet him in Farnley Manor, a country house hotel outside Roscommon town, at the weekend.

Farnley Manor was a beautiful converted castle on the banks of the Shannon. The first thing I noticed when I entered the impressive marble lobby was an unattended grand piano among the plush champagne-coloured sofas.

Mark stood up from one of the sofas and waved towards me. I approached him as if for the first time and, when we were standing face to face, I put out my arms towards him. He accepted the hug. I was filled with an unfamiliar emotion and, when I stepped back, I noticed him reaching for a handkerchief to dab his eyes. 'You're my uncle,' I said.

We sat, and he had ordered afternoon tea so a cake stand was soon delivered to our table. Eventually, he said, 'I saw you, from the sitting-room window. Lashing out. Violent. At your party, with Caroline . . . and then you reappeared as if nothing had happened.'

He saw me attacking Caroline.

'Oh, Mark, you have no idea. I was overwhelmed by fear. I was worried that Conor Geary would show up. Tina told me my fear was irrational, but my brain doesn't know it's being irrational at the time.' He just stared at me.

'Denise was like that too,' I said, 'violent.'

'My sister was the sweetest. She would never strike out –'

'She did after my birth father was finished with her. It's all in my dad's notes.'

'Please . . . tell me about her. My father won't discuss her, my mother died calling her name . . . you must remember something.'

I explained yet again that I had no memory of Denise, but I had a good impression of her from the taped interviews and my dad's written reports.

'They were going into storage, Mark, but I kept them once I discovered who you were. You're entitled to see and hear them all.'

One of the first things he talked about was Toby. 'He was my bear. I was four years old when Denise was abducted. I followed her around all the time. She would play games with me. Sometimes she would hide Toby in the front garden in a hedge. I thought you'd like to have these. I had the originals restored and copied.' He took out an envelope and handed it to me. There were only four photographs, all black-and-white. One of a small girl in a communion dress and veil, her hands clasped, eyes heavenward. A pretty girl with big eyes and freckles across both cheeks. In another, she was older, holding the hand of a toddler, Mark, who in turn was holding a small bear, brand new, but recognizable immediately as Toby. Her hair had darkened. Then there was a portrait photograph of her, smiling with cherubic cheeks. I had seen this one before but only from newspaper archives on the internet. The last one was a family photo. Mark was a baby, Denise was frowning. Her father's hands were on her shoulders. Her mother was grinning at the new baby in her arms.

I remembered the photographs in Dad's files. Denise as an adult, emaciated, almost toothless, thin, limp-haired and angry. Clinging on to me for life. Mark would have to see those too.

'This photo,' I pointed at the portrait, 'this was taken shortly before she was abducted, right?'

Mark nodded, his eyes glassy.

I thought of Abebi and Maduka, and Sue's children, and Anubha's children. Their smallness, their innocence. I felt anger again, but checked myself when I looked at Mark, Denise's brother. I wished I'd had a sibling. Someone to share these feelings with. Someone who missed me as much as he missed Denise.

'I don't understand,' I said, 'you were so young. How could you miss someone you knew for such a short time?'

'She dominated my entire life. Some of my earliest memories are of my mother crying, flashing blue lights outside our house, guards coming to our front door. In supermarkets, shopping centres, on holidays down the country, we never stopped looking. By the time I was sixteen, there was nowhere left to search. Our dining room was a shrine. There was even an altar with that photo in a silver frame in the middle of it. Candles constantly burning.'

'Oh, Mark.' I was imagining what it was like to be Mark. I was putting myself in his shoes. 'Weren't you angry?' I asked, thinking that I would have been.

'One day I came home from school and watched as Mum blew out the candles on the altar. She wanted to give up.' His face dropped into his hands. 'I tried to relight the candles, but Dad stopped me. The altar was dismantled the next day and the photo disappeared into a drawer. They stopped talking about Denise, they stopped talking about anything. Our home was silent and I couldn't think which was worse.'

I felt true sadness.

'When I left home at eighteen to go to college, I felt like I could breathe for the first time. I worked shifts in a petrol station and rented a tiny, dingy flat in Rathmines, and for six months, I lived a normal life. I made friends with guys who didn't know who I was, I had girlfriends, I played a lot of snooker. I was finally free of it all. And then . . . she was found.'

I let a silence fall between us, because I knew the rest of the story, or I thought I did. One question bugged me, though.

'It was an anonymous tip-off, wasn't it?'

'I think I know the answer to that one. It was on one of those true crime websites. A guy who ended up in Mountjoy Prison claimed he'd made that call to the guards to tell them where Denise Norton was being held. He'd discovered her while trying to burgle the house.'

'What? When?'

'The house in Killiney, where you were held. He boasted about it, apparently, to cellmates but was too stupid to realize he could have used it to get leniency on one of his many prison sentences. Word got around, though.'

'Is he still alive? I'd like to talk to him.'

'No, he died in 2011. It infuriates me that prison guards and police knew this for years and never thought that we might want to talk to him. I managed to verify it a few years ago with his sister.'

'So, you said she was found? But we were found together.'

'I know, sorry. My parents' interest was in Denise. It's not that they didn't care about you, but they didn't see you as Denise's child. And for me . . . it was . . .' Mark put his hand over his eyes again. 'I'd spent my whole life living in the shadow of this ghost, and I had just found my life. My sister's rescue was all over the media. I was in the limelight again. My new friends wanted to know everything about her and all that had happened. Part of me wished we'd never found her, because after that, it was worse.'

'What do you mean?'

'I wasn't allowed to visit her and nobody would tell me why. I thought Denise would be able to give statements to the police and then she'd be able to come home, but then . . . there was you.'

'I was her daughter.'

'But you were his daughter too.'

I closed my eyes.

'I don't mean to . . . look, try and put yourself in my parents' position.'

I tried, but this time it wouldn't work. I was a child. A victim. And their own grandchild.

'I wanted my parents to take you home and raise you. I offered to move home and help them, but they said there were so many issues with your development. I'm so sorry.'

'What does your father think now? Have you told him that you found me?'

Mark shook his head. 'He saw the story about what you did to Tom Diamond. That was enough for him. He didn't want to know any more. I tried to tell him that I'd connected with you, that you were good and kind . . .'

'Am I?'

'But then I saw you attack Caroline, outside your house.'

'I'm angry, Mark. Most of the time, I can keep it hidden, but sometimes, when I feel threatened or vulnerable, the rage bubbles up. I'm working on it, I promise you, with Tina.'

'Sally, you were out of control.'

'I know. I frightened myself. I'm sorry. But you know why I'd hired a security guard that day, right? I was terrified that he might turn up. Conor Geary. There were children in my garden. He knows where I live.' I thought for a moment. 'Mark, did you ever think that maybe I get my lack of empathy from your side of the family? How could your parents abandon me?'

He looked anguished. 'I don't know.'

He was upset, too, when I told him there was no record of him at all in Dad's files or on Denise's tapes.

'Are you sure? My name never came up? Never?'

'She didn't mention you. I'm sorry.'

'I have to listen to those tapes.'

'Come back to Carricksheedy,' I said. 'I'm sure they won't have replaced you at the factory yet.'

'I took sick leave, but I didn't think I could ever come back.'

'Mark, you have a life here, you have friends. You have . . . a niece. I want to hear about my birth mother too. Do you think your dad would understand now? He could like me. He's my grandfather.'

'I'm not sure. He's so old now. Almost ninety. I don't think he'd be able for such upheaval.'

I was annoyed that my existence was such an inconvenience to my own grandfather.

'I think we should see my therapist together. You're the same generation as me. You could think of me as your sister?'

'Like Denise?'

This time I was emphatic. 'No, not like Denise, not like Mary Norton, like Sally Diamond. That's who I am now. Do you want a sandwich?'

Mark laughed. I don't know why, but it broke the tension between us.

'I'll go back to the village. I'll tell the office I'll be back on Monday.'

'I'll explain to our friends. Most of them know now that you're my uncle. They were surprised but sympathetic. You'll be welcomed back.'

I asked him about Anubha. He admitted that he'd only said he was interested in her in order to put me at ease. I voiced my disapproval. He said he was still in love with his ex-wife.

'I think Elaine cares about you too.'

'She feels sorry for me, Sally.'

'She's been supportive of you, though. You married young, didn't you?'

'Too young. I was so desperate for a family connection that had nothing to do with Denise.'

'You changed your name.'

'That was Elaine's idea. One of her best.'

'Hasn't she remarried now? She has a son?' He nodded.

Eventually, we stood up and hugged for about two seconds longer than was comfortable for me. Mark sensed it. 'I'm sorry, Sally, I'm sorry about everything.'

'I'm sorry that you lost your sister in such a terrible way.'

'But I found a niece, and a friend.'

'Absolutely.' I smiled.

He left then and I lingered, eyeing the grand piano. Nobody had played it while we had been sitting there. I drifted towards it and pulled out the velvet-covered piano stool. I flipped open the lid and placed my hands on the keys. I played a number of soft pieces, orchestrations to calm my mood. I closed my eyes and lost myself in the music.

I felt a tap on my shoulder as I finished the Moonlight Sonata. A man wearing a suit with a name badge that told me he was Lucas the manager stood behind me. I should have asked his permission to play.

'Excuse me, madam, we have enjoyed your playing, you are obviously a professional,' he said, and indeed, there was a ripple of applause. When I looked out over the lobby, many people were clapping and nodding towards me. 'I don't know what your situation is, and I hope you don't find this insulting, but I wondered if you would be available or interested in a little part-time work?'

46

Peter, 1996

There were many renewed escape attempts in the five years after Dad died. Lindy had given up, but now her campaign to break out started again.

I had given her writing materials, something she had often begged from my father. She'd said she wanted a pencil, crayon, pen, anything with which to write.

'What are you going to write?' he had asked sarcastically.

'I want to write stories,' she said.

She told me she desperately wanted to write memories of her family, her friends and her home because she was afraid she would forget them. When I'd asked Dad on her behalf, he said it was better that she forget the past because, that way, she'd find it easier to accept the present. As soon as he was dead and gone and I was back to full health, I bought her a whole packet of coloured felt-tip pens, and a sketch pad, biros and notebooks. I told her that I'd never look at them and I respected her privacy. She could draw or write or do whatever she wanted with them.

The same week, I was returning her library books. She liked books by women. I wasn't much of a reader. I had grown out of the adventure stories of my boyhood. All the books I had now were non-fiction, how-to books on crop rotation, DIY, marketing, entrepreneurship and occasional biographies of important men. On the way to the library, I leafed through the books, out of suspicion, and there I found her notes written in the margins of the pages and in the blank pages at the back, giving her name and my name and my father's name, detailing what he had done to her, the date on which she had been kidnapped and a haphazard description of the route from the lake to our house.

I had to buy replacement books for the library and explain that I had damaged them by accident. I never told Lindy what I had discovered, but her mood certainly improved in the days after that. She smiled more and laughed when we watched TV together. As time moved on and nobody came to release her, I could see her confusion and anger grow. She was short-tempered with me. I didn't react. I waited for things to get back to normal, and eventually they did. I bought her random books from the op-shop sometimes after that, told her it would be good for her to build up her own library. She glared at me then. She knew.

I had replaced Dad's chain with a soft but strong rope. She sawed her way through it with a bread knife in two days. I kicked myself for not predicting that. She was waiting behind the door instead of at the other end of the room when I entered that evening. She lunged at me with the knife but my reactions were quick, and I turned to the side so she only stabbed me in the thigh instead of the stomach. I wrangled her back to the bed and she screamed like a banshee. She thought I was going to rape her. I was not my dad, but I did have to reinstate the chain. I wrapped the shackle in foam. I also allowed her to move the shackle from one leg to the other every week as she had developed a severe limp from carrying it on one leg for so many years.

Another time, she threw boiling water again, but I was always wary and out of her reach. She tried to poison me, too, by putting bleach or detergent in my food (she cooked for me sometimes), but the taste was obvious. I explained to her how foolish that was. If I died, she would die. Nobody would come looking for her because everyone thought she was already dead. She would die alone of starvation. I tried to protect her from herself. She wasn't thinking straight.

I had made some adjustments to the barn over the last few years. I added another layer of insulation, sheetrock and corrugated iron on the outside of the building. Three years earlier, I had discovered that Lindy had clawed her way through the interior wall behind the fridge. She had pulled out a number of egg boxes that provided the soundproofing. I caught her in the act. I didn't punish Lindy. I held her in my arms until her weeping subsided, and then I let go of her. I was not my dad.

No sound would ever escape, and nor would Lindy ever hear the outside world. That was her last escape attempt. She gave up. We settled into a less fraught relationship. She stopped asking why I was keeping her and when I would release her. She stopped fighting me. We had most dinners together in the barn. She sometimes sat beside me on the sofa I had bought, but we didn't touch. I told her everything, about my childhood in Ireland, my mother, my sister, our escape to New Zealand. She made sympathetic noises and then said, 'Maybe a burglar will try to break in here?' I wished I hadn't told her anything.

I let her outside a lot during the summers, a bit less in the winter, for sunshine and fresh air and exercise. I even brought her down to the hot springs and the lake behind the house. In all the years we'd lived there, I'd never seen another soul. I didn't dare buy her a swimsuit but she had shorts and vests and T-shirts. She complained that she couldn't swim with the chain attached, but I held the weight of it so that she could. I tried not to look at her body when she emerged from the water, but it was impossible not to notice her sleek shape, the nipples standing out from her chest. We lay on the rocks afterwards and shared a picnic. Still, I did not touch her.

Then one night, in midwinter 1990, we were watching some horror film on TV, side by side on the sofa, and she buried her head in my shoulder as the axe murderer approached. I instinctively put my arm around her and squeezed gently. She looked up at me and I gazed down into her perfect face. She reached forward and kissed me on the mouth tenderly. I kissed her back. My first kiss. As she leaned forward and positioned herself in front of me, she did not stop me when I ran my hand down her back. She did not stop me holding the back of her neck. She nuzzled her face into my shoulder and kissed my mouth again, her tongue finding mine, and I felt myself stiffen.

She noticed too, and immediately detached from me. 'We . . . I can't . . .' she said. 'Your father –'

'I'm nothing like him.'

'I know you're not. I never kissed him. I mean . . . he forced me, it wasn't like . . . this.'

We kissed again, passionately. Our mouths a perfect match. And then I moved away.

'Goodnight, Lindy.'

'But –'

'I love you,' I said as I locked the door behind me.

It took six years but by 1996 I was sure she loved me. I was 99 per cent certain of it. By the time we consummated our relationship in 1992, I was twenty-five and she was twenty-four. She had been terribly traumatized by my father, so I let her set the pace and, though it was glacial, she slowly learned that I could not and would not hurt her, and nor could I let her go. She trusted me with her life. I trusted her with mine. I removed the chain when we were indoors. But I still locked the door every time I left. And when we went down to the hot pools, I used a rope rather than a chain. She no longer seemed to mind. Part of me thought that, if I released her, she wouldn't run away, but I couldn't be certain.

When I wasn't working, we spent all our time together. I had almost moved into the barn with her, only going into the house to change my clothes and shower, and occasionally I cooked in there and brought the meal out to Lindy. I thought about the practicalities of bringing her into the house but the risk was too great. I got visits occasionally from the boiler repair guy or a mechanic and from one persistent creditor.

Business was bad. The superette had been replaced by a large supermarket chain that got all their vegetables from a central supplier elsewhere. I'd had to relinquish the lease on the shop. The only retail I did was a weekend market. I had struck a deal with the local hospital to supply all their fruit and vegetable needs, but it wasn't a big hospital and I'd had to bargain so hard to get the contract that it was hardly worth it. Lindy helped out. She knitted scarves and hats with wool I ordered for her from a catalogue she'd seen advertised in a magazine. She added tassels and triangular ends to the scarves and earflaps to the hats, like the ones I used to wear. I sold them alongside my produce at the stall. In the winter, I made more from her wares than mine.

I had insisted on contraception. Lindy desperately wanted a baby but that would mean so much trouble and I was barely making enough money to pay our bills. We couldn't afford a kid. And besides, what would I do with it? Bring it up with me in the house like I'd been brought up or leave it in the barn with Lindy? There wouldn't be room for three of us in there. What if she liked the kid more than she liked me? I insisted on condoms and she eventually conceded. I never forced her or pressured her. I didn't trick her into taking the pill. I thought about it, but I had no way of getting it and I wanted our relationship to be open and honest.

When she told me she was pregnant four years later, early in 1996, I was taken aback. She had missed two periods. I hadn't noticed. That was the only time I ever got angry with her. Had she pierced the condom with a pin? Had she saved the used condoms and somehow inseminated herself? She swore she hadn't. 'The condom must have burst. It happens. I've read about it.'

'We can't afford a kid, Lindy, you know that.'

'I'll cut back on everything. I can start knitting other stuff. Sweaters, waistcoats. I'll do it twice as fast. I promise, we can make it work, Stevie, really we can.' Her begging was futile. The baby was on its way and there was no way I could stop it without hurting her.

I agonized for the following months about how we could cope as I watched Lindy's belly swell and watched her excitement grow with it. She knew she wasn't going to a maternity hospital but she used me as her yardstick. 'Your mother gave birth twice by herself. If she can do it, I can do it.' I drove to Auckland to buy books on pregnancy and childbirth. We both read them cover to cover. I ordered medical textbooks on obstetrics.

My biggest fear was that Lindy would die giving birth. I did my best to pretend to be happy about it and I think Lindy did her best to believe me. She speculated endlessly, deciding one day that it was a girl and then another day she was sure it was a boy. She talked about the days when we could take the baby to the hot pools together and the nursery rhymes we would teach him or her. All the time, the pain in my chest got tighter and tighter.

It was late August 1996 when Lindy went into labour. Her

waters broke conveniently while she was in the shower. I was staying around as much as possible because I was afraid of what might happen if she had to cope alone. When I walked into the barn and found her squatting on the bed on all fours, I knew exactly what was happening. I tried to block out the memory of my mother going into labour in that dingy room twenty-two years earlier. I was too young to understand what was happening then.

Now, I was prepared. I had a kitbag ready and waiting. I used the sterilizing fluid on everything; spread plastic sheeting on to the bed while Lindy huffed and puffed during a contraction. In between times, she turned over on her back but found that more painful. There seemed to be no position in which she could get comfortable. Eventually, she settled on her side until the next wave of pain broke and a film of sweat covered her whole body. 'This is normal, right, Stevie? All this is normal?' I tried to assure her that it was.

Seven hours later, as dusk was falling on that late winter evening, Lindy gave a final push and a scream that was unlike any I had heard before, and I had heard plenty. The baby's head was forced out. I delved my hands inside her and managed to place them around its tiny shoulders and the rest of the baby plopped out on to the plastic sheet. A perfect girl. She was covered in a film of almost violet slime. I had been expecting this, or so I thought, but nothing can prepare you for the reality.

Lindy was almost delirious with pain and fear and joy, and reached for the child. 'Is she breathing? Is she breathing?'

I couldn't tell. The baby was squirming and shuddering in my arms. I wanted to wipe her clean, but Lindy reached greedily for her daughter. At the moment when I placed the little girl on Lindy's chest, her tiny mouth opened and she squealed like a kitten. I was overcome with wonder and awe.

I snipped the cord with the sterilized scissors. Lindy and I both cried. She shuddered with more contractions until, with a final push, the placenta was ejected. I made her some tea and began to clean up the bloody mess. I helped Lindy into the shower and together we washed our daughter in a large basin of water. I washed Lindy too, delicately. She was exhausted.

I waited until Lindy and the baby were asleep and then I lifted the tiny girl from her mother's arms and crept out of the barn, locking it quietly behind me. It was past midnight. I took her into the house and wrapped her tightly in the blankets I'd bought from an op-shop in Auckland and placed her in the wooden crate I had thickly lined with old newspapers. I took the crate out to the car and placed it in the footwell of the passenger seat where nobody ever sat and drove to Auckland. She didn't stir.

PART III

47

Sally

Everything was back to normal in the village. And I had a job that was perfect for me. At weekends, I would drive out to Farnley Manor and play the piano. Sometimes on weekdays too, if there was a wedding on. I also got unlimited tea and coffee and dainty sandwiches and pastries during my breaks. I couldn't have asked for a better job.

By mid-November, I had over €2 million in my bank account from the sale of Conor Geary's house. It would have been €3 million, if it hadn't been for the taxman. Geoff Barrington urged me to seek financial advice regarding how best to invest it, but it felt like dirty money to me. I made a large anonymous donation to Stella's homeless charity and to the young people's mental health charity that Aunt Christine had been involved in and left the rest in the bank until I could think how to deal with it.

Mark found it hard to settle back into the village. Despite my assurances, both Martha and Angela regarded him with suspicion. Tina was shocked when I brought him to our next therapy appointment but, once I explained, she said she would help us both. Mark cried a lot in that first session. It was distressing to me, and we all agreed that Mark and I should see Tina separately for a while before we did a family meeting again.

Mark was obviously distressed, particularly when I handed over all the files and he saw those photos of his emaciated, toothless sister for the first time. Tina told me to be honest with him, but to give him time to come to terms with his own feelings. She warned me that he might be angry. But I knew that, and I understood. He loved my new home and soon became my most regular visitor.

Life was going well until I got a call from Mrs Sullivan in the post office the day after I closed my house sale on 28th November.

'Sally,' she said, still shouting at me. She had never understood that I wasn't hard of hearing. 'The sorting office in Athlone had a letter addressed to Mary Norton at your old address. They've left it with me. Shall I drop it in to you?'

I put on my coat immediately and went around the corner to the post office. I took the letter from Mrs Sullivan with a pair of tweezers. 'It might be evidence,' I said. 'The guards might want your fingerprints.'

She was amused. 'Oh, Sally, you are funny. What are we playing at now? CSI Carricksheedy?' She hooted with laughter.

When she realized I wasn't smiling, she started to explain, shouting, 'It's a television programme, Sally, about forensics.'

'Thank you, Mrs Sullivan, I know the concept.'

I left without smiling. The handwriting was familiar at once. It was 'S'. It had an Irish stamp on it. When I got home, I rang Mark. It was 4 p.m., but he said he'd come straight over.

We looked at the envelope together. It was thicker than the others. I wondered if we should call the police first, but neither of us could wait. Mark had brought some surgical gloves with him from the factory. He opened the envelope carefully and I pulled the letter out. A small box came out with the letter as well as another larger box, which was labelled DNA ACTIVATION KIT.

Dear Mary,

*My birth name is Peter Geary, and although my birth was never
registered in Ireland, or anywhere, I was born there. My mother was
Denise Norton and my father was Conor Geary. I am your brother.
I was born seven years before you in a house in Killiney. Our father
took me away from Denise as soon as I was toilet-trained. I was not
allowed to see her, or you, even though my bedroom was next door to
yours in an annexe our father built.*

*I was allowed to enter the other parts of the house as I got older.
You and our mother were kept under lock and key. In the early years,
I never saw another human except for on the pages of his newspapers
and, later, on television.*

*I have no recollection of meeting my mother until I was seven years
old, when I spent a terrifying weekend in that room with her. I realize
now that she had been terribly mistreated and brutalized. She was
heavily pregnant with you and was frightening to me. I won't go into
detail here as I don't want to upset you. I know that you were born
the day after I left the room and I didn't see you again, except once,
on the day my father escaped, taking me with him. Do you
remember? You must have been five years old.*

*I do not understand why nobody was looking for me. I know you
and I were separated, but I believe that my mother missed me, at least
until you were born. Did she simply forget about me?*

*In London, our father arranged to get us fake passports and we
moved to New Zealand. My life there has been difficult. I was
homeschooled and, even after that, he continued to keep me isolated
for a long time. The good news for both of us is that he died many
years ago. He is no longer a threat to either of us.*

*And yet, I do not feel free of him. My life has been blighted and
destroyed. It is only because of the age of the internet that I was able
to get any information about you or him, or my mother. I finally
learned that my mother was dead. After you hit the headlines when*

*you disposed of your adoptive father's remains two years ago, I began
to investigate what happened to you and where you had been. Previous
reports gave the impression that you had been adopted in England.*

*When the newspapers subsequently confirmed that you had not
murdered Dr Diamond, and that you were 'different', I realized that
you were probably like me. That's why I sent Toby to you. I thought
he might bring you some comfort at such a difficult time.*

*It didn't cross my mind when I sent you the teddy bear that it
would lead to a police hunt for our father in New Zealand. I didn't
think it through at all, but obviously you must have thought that he
had sent it to you to torment you. The police tracked me down and
questioned me, but I lied and denied everything. I was a coward. I am
so sorry, but I did not want to be dragged into a public scandal. I
showed the police Dad's fake passport. I guess they didn't investigate
that too much, because they didn't come around again. And anyway,
they weren't looking for a man with a son. I don't understand that.
They didn't seem to be aware that our father had a son?*

*This year, I realized that you would probably not know your date
of birth so I sent you the birthday card, but I did not know how or if
I should reveal myself to you. I hope that my existence is merely a
surprise rather than a shock. Or perhaps you have always known
about me?*

*The main reason I am contacting you is because I have nobody in
my life. I have never had a friend or a colleague, but now I find a
sister who might understand me. Do you think that is possible?*

*I am currently in Dublin in a hotel. I bought a pay-as-you-go
mobile phone and even though I am not used to talking on the phone,
I will make an effort if you would like to talk to me.*

*The only thing I beg of you is not to alert the media or the police. I
cannot stand for people to look at me, I am noise-averse and I hate
fuss and attention. As it seems that nobody knows I exist, I would
like to keep it that way. I therefore include my saliva sample and a
DNA test kit which you may use to confirm that I am who I say I*

*am. You may send off the kit and wait for the results before calling
me. I promise I will not come to your village unless I'm invited.*

*I will understand if you do not want to call me at all. I have
taken three months' leave of absence from my job as Head of Cyber
Security at Aotearoa National Bank. I have a return ticket to New
Zealand and can only stay here for a maximum of ninety days. If
things don't work out, or if you don't want to see me, I can go back
and continue to live my life in isolation. I guess it's not so bad when
you're as used to it as I am.*

Steven Armstrong
086 5559225

'Wow,' said Mark and, unconsciously, I began to pull at my
hair. Mark knew me well enough to steer me towards the
piano. My hands, on autopilot, found Bach's Partita Number
2 in C Minor.

'Tea or wine?' said Mark.

'Tea,' I said. Tina had advised that turning to alcohol in
times of stress was not a good idea.

As soon as I took my fingers off the keyboard, they trembled, until Mark pushed the hot mug into them.

'Wow,' he said again. 'Should we call the police?'

'No,' I said. 'I have a brother.'

'We don't know that yet. He could be anyone, chancing his
arm,' said Mark.

'Why though? Why would anybody do that? What would
he have to gain?'

'I don't know. Unless he's a journalist?'

I lifted the small box and opened it. It contained a sealed
cellophane bag, inside of which was a plastic tube containing
a viscous liquid, his saliva. The larger box contained a full kit
for me to use. There were no names, just code numbers.

I held up the DNA test information leaflet. 'It's easy to find out. Doesn't it seem true to you, Mark? I believe him. He says he won't come unless I invite him. Mark, why would he come all the way from New Zealand if he wasn't sure I would want to meet him?'

'How do we even know he was in New Zealand? This guy could be –'

'Toby. He sent Toby.'

'But Denise never mentioned him – unless . . .' Mark's eyes widened.

'What?'

'At one point, in the taped interviews, she mentions "my boy".'

'I don't remember that?'

'Yes, I've been listening to them over and over. I hoped it was a reference to me, but it didn't add up. She said something about not letting go of you, because "he took my boy". Your father quizzed her about it, but she clammed up. The recording was full of static. I thought she was talking about Toby.'

I remembered it now. I had also thought she was talking about Toby. There was nothing in the written files to note this reference. Dad had missed it too.

'Oh God,' I said, doing the maths in my head. 'She was twelve years old when she gave birth to him.'

'You're right. Fucking hell.'

'I have a brother –'

'But he sounds so damaged, he could be dangerous.'

'You're describing me, exactly two years ago.'

'Fine. Fine. But I'm doing a DNA test too, to make doubly sure. If you're my niece, then he's my nephew.'

'Mark!' I said.

'What?'

'Conor Geary is dead!'

'Let's not jump the gun, Sally. According to these DNA instructions, we may have to wait up to a month, and then if the results prove it, you have a phone call with this guy, okay? Not until then. You must promise me. I'm speaking as your uncle now, okay?'

I poured more tea from the pot. After the initial shock, I felt elated. Conor Geary, the bogeyman who loomed over my entire life, was dead. And I had a brother, someone who sounded exactly like me. Someone who might completely understand me.

The waiting was agony. We sent off our samples as soon as Mark had ordered his own kit. Mark did it all online. He labelled us all with initials rather than surnames. 'Who knows what other relatives might be out there, Sally? Conor Geary may have fathered other children. We don't know what Peter is like. We need to protect our privacy.' I was SD, Mark was MB and Peter was PG.

After two days, Mark found the audio that contained the reference to 'my boy'. These recordings had been made in the pre-digital era. Dad was asking Denise about her extreme attachment to Mary (me).

Tom: Denise, I notice that you watch little Mary all the time. You know that you're safe now, right? Nobody will hurt you ever again?

Denise: [*unintelligible*]

Tom: Sorry, Denise?

Denise: I'm still afraid.

Tom: What are you afraid of?

Denise: He'll take her away.

Tom: Denise, he's not here. You will never see him again.

Denise: He took my boy.

Tom: What?

Denise: It doesn't matter. I didn't want him.

Tom: [*a tone of exasperation in his voice*] Denise, do you
    understand that it's not good for Mary's development
    for you to be so close to her? The child needs to learn a
    little independence. Mary?

[*Sound of whispering*]

Denise: Don't talk to her.

Tom: Why not? Do you think I could hurt her?

Jean: Tom, perhaps –

Tom: Hush, Jean. Denise?

[*A hissing noise, followed by silence and then the tape shuts off*]

'I wonder what she meant by "I didn't want him",' I said.
'Why wouldn't she want him?'

'We can't be sure that she was talking about Peter.'

'Who else would she be talking about? She said, "He took
my boy."'

'It's weird, isn't it?'

Mark was annoyed with my dad. 'Do you think Jean
guessed something?'

'I'm not sure. Perhaps she was hinting to Dad that he needed
to be more patient with her. The way he said that about hurting me, Denise could have interpreted that as a threat.'

'Was he like that with you? Impatient?' said Mark.

'Not at all. He was kind and indulgent with me. But I guess
I was always compliant. That tape is dated almost a year after
our rescue. I'd say he was exhausted. He hadn't made any
breakthrough with Denise. She wasn't exactly cooperative,
was she?'

'After what she'd been through? Are you surprised?' Mark
raised his voice.

'I'm sorry. I forget that you knew her. She was your big sister. I wish I remembered her.'

'Another thing we can thank Tom Diamond for,' Mark said, a bitter tone in his voice.

'He was doing his best, what he thought was right for me.' I was fed up with people talking badly about my dad. He might not have done everything he should have, but what he did do, he did for the right reasons. I'd had plenty of time to put myself in his shoes and imagine what I would have done if I had been him. Tina made me see it. I had forgiven him. 'We can't change the past,' I told Mark.

'One thing I can't understand,' he said. 'If Peter has known all this time about you and about Denise, if he remembered what Conor Geary said and did, why didn't he ever go to the police? Being afraid of publicity is a lame excuse for shielding a paedophile, especially after he's dead.'

'I get it, Mark. I would be the same as him. He hasn't done anything wrong. Why should he be associated with his – our psychopathic father?'

I ignored his glare.

48

Peter, 2012

It took Lindy five years to forgive me for giving the baby away. She had called her Wanda. Throughout the pregnancy, I had pretended to go along with it. I thought it was easier to let her have this fantasy. It made her so happy.

I had taken the baby in the box to the front door of St Patrick's Cathedral in Auckland in the middle of the night. It was cold. I hoped she would survive and tucked her as tightly into the blankets as I could. As I walked away, I heard her begin to mewl. I kept walking through the deserted streets until I got into the car and drove home.

Lindy was beyond hysterical when I got back. At first, she thought I'd taken the baby to the hospital because there was something wrong with her. I didn't tell her anything.

During the following years Lindy attacked me so often that I had to put the shackles back on. She stabbed me with knitting needles, knives and scissors, scarred my arms badly with a solution of sugar and boiled water, attempted to strangle me with a home-made noose. I ended up in the hospital's A & E twice. The staff there assumed I'd got into fights with my peers. I let them think that. One matron threatened to call the cops, but when she looked at my medical records and saw that I was that Steven Armstrong, who had been orphaned so young, she relented and instead gave me a lecture about mixing with the wrong crowd.

Lindy stayed angry for years. We went back to the old ways. I lived in the house and dropped her groceries inside the door once a week. I still visited every day. I'd make idle conversation about stories in the news. She did not respond. The abandoned baby at St Patrick's Cathedral made national news and, with radio and TV, I followed the story, up to the point when the baby was adopted six months later. I breathed a sigh of relief. I hoped that Lindy might accept our circumstances now, but without uttering a syllable, she made it clear that our relationship was over.

When I tried to touch her, she violently repelled me. She barely spoke full sentences and, when she finally did, it was to renew her demands to be released. 'I'm never going to touch you again, Steve, never. You might as well let me go and get my baby, or kill me.'

She had refused to do any further knitting for the stall too, and money was becoming an even more pressing issue. I needed to do something else for a living. I was clever. I should have gone away to college and made something of myself. I had studied so many books in my younger days, I could have been a scientist or a doctor or an engineer. The reason I didn't was because I couldn't leave Lindy. So, I became a gardener, and now we were living on the breadline. I still couldn't let her go. I held on to the hope that one day she would forgive me.

I signed up for computer classes in the local community centre and got some basic skills. I got a job as an office junior in a real estate agent's office. They liked that I kept myself to myself and didn't ask any questions. I didn't want to go for a beer with them on a Friday after work. After three months, they wanted to promote me. It meant more money, but I would be showing people around houses. I didn't want the promotion. I knew from TV how normal families worked. I'd never had one and I didn't want to be confronted with them in somebody else's domestic setting.

I moved on and got a job working for a cancer charity. It involved cold-calling businesses all over the Bay of Plenty region and asking them to sign up to a monthly donation. I was not good at this. I was so unused to talking to people, and the manager said that I sounded like I didn't care. I was supposed to tug on these people's heartstrings. The job was commission only. After the first month, I'd made less than I had with the real estate agent. I kept going back to the recruitment agency.

A job had come up in a bank in town. It was full-time, cataloguing accounts for their new computer system. The interviewers were impressed by my self-education. One of them remembered my father's death being in the papers; he had contributed to the fund for me. They treated me like a minor celebrity: 'You're that kid?'

I admitted I liked to keep to myself, and I'd prefer to work alone. They seemed delighted with that answer. The job I was applying for was one I'd be expected to do on my own after some initial training. I was offered the job a week later, which I was glad to accept in September 1999.

The training on their computer system was a residential course in Wellington. There was no way I could commute there and back. I'd have to leave Lindy on her own. The day before I left, I brought her the usual bag of groceries, but when I tried to talk to her, to tell her that I would be gone for a week, she turned up the radio full blast to drown out my voice.

The course could have been done in a day. Most of the other attendees were younger. They seemed to be slow on the uptake. It was incredibly easy to learn the system. At the end of the week, they gave us booklets that explained the whole process anyway. In the evenings, we went back to the low-grade hotel. The girls went to dinner together. Several of them turned up every morning with hangovers. I got sandwiches and ate them in my room and watched TV. I shunned their requests to join them. One of the course instructors warned me that my social skills could use some improvement. But she praised the speed of my learning.

I was frustrated to be away for so long. Even though I was sure Lindy hated me, my feelings for her had not abated. I often thought of the look of ecstasy on her face when I placed the baby on her chest. She had never looked at me like that. But she had told me she loved me. Until the baby came, that was enough for me. I often thought of setting her free and then disappearing, but where could I go? I didn't have the money to get on a plane, though I had kept my passport renewed, in case. Originally, I had kept money aside for escape, but I'd had to use that to pay the bills. Lindy knew my real name and my whole history. She would tell. I'd spend the rest of my life in prison. She might truly have loved me once, but she certainly didn't now. I had changed the locks on the barn door many times in the previous years. I knew she would never be able to get out.

When Friday came and the course was over, I drove the six hours back to Rotorua at top speed. I got home at midnight and went straight to the barn.

She was lying on the bed but sat up immediately. 'Where were you?' she asked. Her face was tear-stained and her voice was subdued.

'I tried to tell you on Sunday night, but you didn't want to listen.'

She burst into tears. 'I thought you were dead. It was like the last time when your father died, but I . . . I missed you.'

I moved towards her and held my arms out to her. She collapsed against my chest.

In the weeks that followed, we talked more than we ever

had before, almost as if we were making up for the silences of the past years.

'I was so angry with you. I accepted that you had taken my freedom. I gave up trying to escape. I fell for you against my will. You were always so kind and so considerate. The opposite of your father. But then, all I wanted was a baby. I didn't trick you into it, I promise. That's why, when I did get pregnant, it felt like a miracle. I'd never asked you for anything, not for years. A baby would make us a proper family. Someone to love unconditionally.'

That hurt me and I told her. 'Look,' I said, 'babies get sick all the time. I could never take her to a hospital or a doctor. Would you want your baby to grow up here? Like this?' I indicated the windowless room.

She looked around, a puzzled expression on her face, and I realized that this barn had been her home for longer than anywhere else. She had lived here for sixteen years, and once Dad was gone, she felt safe here. She was thirty years old. This windowless room, as nice as I had tried to make it, was normal to her. I regretted reminding her of how abnormal her situation was. Her escape attempts had been nothing to do with finding her home, but everything to do with finding her baby. I knew that keeping her captive was wrong, but she was no longer aware of it.

Gradually, we became close again until finally she let me return to her bed. She didn't ask about having a baby and, as soon as I could afford it, I had a vasectomy, a relatively painless day procedure. Once again, I took away the chain and she was full of gratitude. I felt like a monster. That's the word my mother used to refer to my father. I remembered that.

At work, I got through the digital cataloguing of accounts quickly. I wrote to the head office IT department and suggested improvements to the programme they had developed to make it more user-friendly. I taught myself how to use other software programmes, and then after I had turned down the offer of promotion to Assistant Head of IT in the bank's head office in Wellington, I began to look for other jobs. I went from one to the other – a year in a small stock-broking firm, two years in an insurance company – but never far from Rotorua. In 2004, I became an IT specialist in the Rotorua Rabobank. This time, I had my own office. Things were looking up.

During the crash of 2008, the bank downsized and I took a pay cut but I was needed and kept my job. In 2009, after a massive credit-card fraud was perpetrated in America, I applied for a job in our cyber security department. I was successful. My earnings were now good enough to support Lindy and myself comfortably.

As I gradually rose through the ranks and found myself on interviewing panels, I tried to hire every Māori applicant I could. The casual racism of the past was now rightfully seen as shameful. Māori culture was being embraced by the Pākehā population. Now, the Māori language had been incorporated into our everyday correspondence and every email was signed off with *Ngā mihi* as well as *Kind regards*. I often thought of Rangi and his potential to take any of the jobs we were advertising. He had been naturally good at mathematics, something he only discovered when he applied himself to it. Times and attitudes had changed for the better.

I'd installed skylights on the roof of the barn so Lindy had natural daylight. I'd lined the walls with bookshelves at the far end of the TV area. I upgraded her bathroom. She didn't ask for anything but she laughed with delight at every gift or improvement. When we walked to the hot pools in the summer, I didn't need to use the chain any more. She put her hand in mine and we walked side by side. I applied suntan lotion to her soft skin so that she wouldn't burn. We made love in the grass. She began to knit again.

It was all building to something, and one night in the spring of 2011, I did not lock the door. Then, for a whole weekend, I did not lock the door.

'Why aren't you locking the door?' she asked me.

'I trust you. I love you. You can come into the house.'

'No, it's okay, I'm happy here.'

Wasn't she even curious about the house? When we walked towards the lake, we never passed the house. She couldn't see it from the barn door. I invited her again, the following weekend. I unplugged the phone that never rang and hid it in the car. She tentatively stepped inside the front door and went from room to room. 'There's so much space,' she said, and I guess, compared to the barn, there was. I asked her to stay the night, but she couldn't get comfortable in my bed and eventually nudged me to tell me she was going back to the barn. I nodded my agreement and pretended to go back to sleep. I watched from the window as she made her way. I followed at a distance until I saw her pull the door of the barn open and disappear inside. She closed it behind her. I stayed up all night, watching the door, waiting for her to sneak out. She didn't.

The following week, I called the office and told them I was sick. Every morning, I'd drive out on to the dirt road and park the car out of sight. I walked back to the bushy area opposite the house and watched with binoculars to see if she would try to escape. Every evening I'd come 'home from work' to find her contentedly watching TV or knitting or preparing dinner. The most she had done was walk around the outside of the house, looking in the windows. She didn't even try the door, though I'd left it open. She greeted me cheerfully every evening, her gap-toothed smile broad and her blue eyes twinkling.

Eventually, I persuaded her to come into the house for dinner sometimes, but she was always nervous there. 'It's the ghost of your father,' she said, and indeed, some of his belongings were still around the house. I don't know why I'd held on to his spectacles and his dentist's bag. I threw them out immediately. I password protected my laptop, not that she had a clue how to use it. I had a mobile phone for work. Lindy had seen them on TV but wouldn't know how to turn it on. I kept it hidden anyway.

A few months passed. Lindy was free to go anywhere she wanted. She presented me with a handmade quilt for Christmas 2011. We celebrated in the house together for the first time. I'd bought a tree and decorations and she festooned the tree with tinsel and fairy lights. I'd also bought a bottle of wine. Neither of us was used to alcohol and got drunk quickly. It was a pleasant feeling. We sat on the porch in front of the house shaded from the blazing midsummer heat and toasted each other like a real married couple.

I thought about whether it would be wise to bring Lindy into town. I dismissed the idea quickly. She had never asked about it and we would both have to agree on a new name and backstory. Lindy seemed to have forgotten that she had been kidnapped. I didn't want to remind her. And I guessed she might behave strangely around other people. No, Lindy was mine. I did not dare to share her with the outside world. I was happier than I had ever been. So was she.

I came home from work one day the following March, and went straight to the barn because she still preferred it there, but realized she must be in the house. I called her name and went from room to room. I found her, passed out on the bathroom floor. Her face was clammy and hot to touch. There were pools of vomit on the floor around her.

The previous two nights, she had complained of stomach pains and I'd asked her to describe her symptoms exactly. I always did this when she was unwell. Then I'd go to the chemist and describe the same symptoms and bring home whatever they wanted to sell me. She had described it as a rumbling pain across her lower belly. I assumed it was period pain and she agreed that her period was due but she said this pain felt different. That morning, she'd felt worse, and she did look pale.

After work I'd gone to the chemist and described the pain. The chemist asked me to press the right side of my abdomen, and when I didn't express any further pain, she gave me some Domerid for nausea and paracetamol for pain. 'It's not appendicitis. It might be something you ate,' she said, 'or a stomach flu – there's one going around, you know.'

In a panic, I doused Lindy with cold water to reduce the temperature and wake her up. She screamed in pain and clutched her right side. 'Shit! It must be your appendix, I need to get you to a hospital.' I didn't hesitate. It would be quicker to take her myself than to call an ambulance. She screamed again as I lifted her and vomited over my elbow.

'I'm scared,' she managed to say.

'Don't be, they'll fix you right up.'

'No,' she said, 'I'm scared of them. People.'

She passed out again as I carried her to the car. I no longer cared what the consequences were. I didn't even think of a name or a backstory or the jail sentence that awaited me. I laid her on the back seat on her left side. She began to shiver violently but appeared to be unconscious. At every corner, I reached for her. I was approaching the main road when she made this strange gurgling sound. Her whole body stiffened and then she went limp. I pulled over to the side of the road and climbed over the back seat. Her eyes were wide open in shock, but she wasn't moving. I held my hand over her heart but could feel no heartbeat. I shook her and held her close to me. A spill of bile fell out of her mouth, but I kissed it anyway. 'Please, no,' I whispered. 'Please, please, come back.'

I brought her home and washed her in the bath. Her skin took on a mottled colour. I washed and combed out her hair, careful not to let her head fall below the waterline. When she was clean and dry, I dressed her in her favourite clothes, a green cotton skirt, rubber-soled boots and a soft blue sweater. I wrapped her carefully into the sheepskin rug from the barn. Before I could put her in the car again, I had to clean it out with disinfectant.

It was about 2 a.m. when I drove to Lake Rotorua and parked in the deserted car park. It was a particularly chilly autumn evening. I carried her to the part of the lake that was closest to the forest trail where I'd first seen her, a brave little girl climbing a tree. I unfurled her stiffened body from the rug and gently folded her into the water. It must have been deep in that part, or maybe it was because it was dark, but she disappeared from view almost immediately.

49

Peter, 2019

When Lindy died in 2012, I was distraught. She was the person I was living for. I took extended leave from work. I had plenty of colleagues who had never turned into friends and, even if they had, how could I tell them that the love of my life, my only love, had died. I could not explain this to a bereavement counsellor; the intensity and length of our relationship, the co-dependency. Who would understand it, even if I told the truth? And I could not tell the truth.

I saw no reason to shower or change my clothes. Twice, I went to the lake with the intention of drowning myself, but when I hit the bottom of the lake, Rangi was there, pushing me back up. 'It's not your time, *e hoa*,' he said, or I think he did. Three deaths on my conscience, Dad, Rangi and Lindy, *kēhua*, and all three of them came out to play, both in my nightmares and in my waking hours. All of them pleading with me to save them, and I could have saved them all.

I dismantled the barn bit by bit. I took the pieces of furniture and left them on the side of the road in remote areas all over the North Island. I was left with a pile of sheetrock and corrugated iron. I couldn't be bothered to have it taken away. At least it no longer looked like her home. In the house, though, her presence remained.

The mystery of the unidentified woman found at Lake Rotorua three weeks after she died was a big story. The media reported that she had not drowned, that she had died of appendicitis, that she was fully clothed, that she had been in the water for less than a month. They made much of her missing front tooth. It would be a significant identifying factor, according to the police. Reports commented on the fact that the body of this woman was discovered at the same lake where a young girl had gone missing almost thirty years earlier.

I needed to get away from Rotorua. I had turned down job offers in Wellington and Auckland before but when I eventually went back to work after five months, I put myself forward for those jobs. There was nothing to tie me to Rotorua. Maybe a fresh start was what I needed. Another reinvention. I was appointed Head of Cyber Security at the Aotearoa National Bank in January 2013 in Wellington. The pay and conditions were excellent.

In preparation for the move, I removed what remained of the barn, and scrubbed the house clean with bleach from top to bottom. I kept very little of my father's belongings, apart from his old fake identification documents. I had lived under a false name for so long, but I needed some back-up in case anybody ever questioned it.

I had promised Lindy that I would never read her notebooks. I tore them up and scattered them on long journeys in the middle of the night.

I sold up in Rotorua and rented a waterfront apartment in Wellington Harbour and tried to settle in, but I could hear people in other apartments, talking, laughing, watching TV together. I could smell their family meals. I bumped into so many people on a daily basis that I felt ill. After just a month, I moved out and bought a small detached house on South Karori Road. I had no neighbours that I could see. My commute to work was a thirty-minute drive.

Work kept me occupied. As usual, I kept my distance

from my workmates, and refused their invitations to parties and after-work drinks. I did not join in the water-cooler conversations.

I was desperately lonely. I did some internet dating but I never forged a relationship. I slept with some of the women anyway, if they wanted it. Sex was hasty, physically satisfying but emotionally empty. The need for connection could never be satisfied by strangers.

Almost a year after her death, in January 2013, DNA tests definitively linked Lindy to her surviving brothers, Paul and Gary Weston. Both of her parents had gone to their graves never knowing what had happened to their daughter. Her brothers were left with the burning question of where she had been for twenty-nine years.

I thought about my mother and my sister in Ireland. I googled them regularly. There was a lot of information. True crime websites compared my father to Lord Lucan but my father had not killed anybody. Not directly. Denise Norton had died in a psychiatric hospital a year or so after she was freed from my father's house. My sister, Mary Norton, had been adopted in England. Conor Geary had gone on the run. I looked everywhere for mention of Conor Geary's son. Had Denise not told them about me? Had she forgotten about me? Was she mad? Or just terrified? How brainwashed I had been. My father was evil. And I was half evil, at least. I had to live with that. It became my habit to check on updates to the Denise Norton story at least once a month.

In December 2017, a story broke in Ireland. Mary Norton, my sister, had tried to cremate her dead adoptive father. I saw a photograph of her. Tall and strong in a black coat with a jaunty red hat, at Thomas Diamond's funeral. She looked like me, her nose, the shape of her eyes. Thomas had been my mother's psychiatrist and he had secretly adopted my sister after Denise's death. I knew where Mary was, her village, her new name.

A spark lit inside me. I had a chance to do something good. To right a wrong. I remembered tearing that teddy bear from her tiny fingers. I could return it to her. I packaged it carefully in an old shoebox and sent it anonymously with a short note.

Six months later, my father's real name started popping up in internet searches, and then on the pages of the *New Zealand Herald*. A very old photo of my father, clean-shaven and without spectacles, taken back in Ireland. An artist's impression alongside it of what he might look like now in his early eighties. Why were they looking for him now? How had they tied the missing paedophile Conor Geary to New Zealand? Who told them he had been here?

And then I realized – it was me. Sending Toby had alerted them to a Kiwi connection. How stupid of me. I was a cyber security expert. I had always been able to hide my Google search history by setting up privacy software and I wasn't dumb enough to have any social media presence, but I was the person who had alerted the Irish authorities to New Zealand. Now the police were looking for him. A retired Irish dentist. No mention of a son.

But in August 2018, I got a phone call from the New Zealand police. They wanted to interview me about my father, James Armstrong. They came to my home. It wasn't hard to pretend to be upset about the circumstances of his death in 1985 in a burning car. They asked me where I'd been born and where he had been born. My story was so well rehearsed after thirty-eight years, they hardly pressed me on any issues. They asked if the name Denise Norton meant anything to me. Had my father ever used any other name? Where had he studied dentistry? Where had I lived in Ireland? Had my father taken any special interest in other children? Why had my father homeschooled me?

I was able to paint a picture of a strict but indulgent father, in deep mourning for my mother ever since we left Ireland. His distinct lack of interest in other children and his belief that the New Zealand education system was sub-par. I was able to produce his Irish dental qualification document on which the name Conor Geary had been expertly replaced with James Armstrong.

My father, I said, was an eccentric but a loving father and an excellent dentist as any of his patients might testify. I missed him every day. I teared up at the hypocrisy of my words. The detective apologized for the intrusion and said they would not bother me again. They implied they knew they were on a wild goose chase. The man they were looking for did not have a son.

I continued to monitor any news of my sister, Mary Norton, living as Sally Diamond in Carricksheedy, Co. Roscommon, Ireland. I felt some warmth towards her. All of the reports I had read described her as 'a loner' or 'a misfit' in school or her village. I couldn't find any record of her having a job or a career. I felt for her. Was that kinship?

Her date of birth was recorded as 13th December 1974, but I knew it was earlier, the 15th September of that year. I remembered that date very clearly. As the New Zealand police had ruled my father out of their enquiries and had no link between either of us to Denise Norton, I risked sending my sister a birthday card in September. I thought she should know when her birthday was. She would never be able to guess who sent the card.

*

In early November, I received an email from a team of pod-casters to my work email address.

Dear Mr Armstrong

We run a podcast company, Hoani Mata Productions, based in Christchurch, making documentaries about true crime cases in New Zealand.

I am trying to track down a Steven (Steve) Armstrong who lived in Rotorua between 1981 and 2013. Did you and your father live in Rotorua at the time that a child, Linda Weston, was abducted there in 1983? Was your father James Armstrong? We know he was recently ruled out of a case regarding an abduction in Ireland in 1966. We know that James Armstrong was not involved in either case, but we are looking for his son to appear as a 'talking head' in our series investigating the disappearance of Linda Weston and the subsequent recovery of her body as an adult woman in April 2012. Are you the Steve Armstrong who lived in Rotorua during this entire period?

We are aware that this James Armstrong died in a tragic car accident in 1985, but if you are his son, we would love to get your thoughts or memories of the time when Linda went missing and what it felt like to be a child in Rotorua and how your father came to be a suspect in the kidnapping of an Irish child. I understand the Steve we are looking for was homeschooled, and that is of interest too, as it was so unconventional. Also, if it is you, and it's not too personal, we might talk briefly about the abduction in Ireland? You may not know anything about it, and I'm not sure if we will use the Irish angle in the final cut, but we are gathering as much data as we can.

It is not public knowledge yet but it has recently come to light that Linda Weston had a daughter who was abandoned at a church in 1996 as a newborn baby. Linda's daughter, Amanda Heron, has agreed to present our podcast and I am hoping to develop it into a TV documentary at a later date. Please let me know your response at your earliest convenience, and of course, apologies if we have the wrong person. Alternatively, if you are that Steve Armstrong, we will fully understand if you do not wish to take part. The police are not co-operating with our investigation at this time, so our search for information has been frustrating to stay the least.

Ngā mihi from Christchurch
Kate Ngata

I took a deep breath and cancelled my schedule for the rest of the day. My daughter, Amanda Heron, was out there, looking for answers. I googled her and found a glut of information. Young people have no idea how available their data is. Within minutes, I had her address, her phone number, her school records, her Master of Arts in Music qualification from the University of Auckland, photographs of her with her adopted family going back to when she was a baby. Photos of her singing with a choir. Photos of her with two different boyfriends, Amanda on a motorcycle crossing the Golden Gate Bridge in San Francisco, Amanda in a camper van in Montana. And very recent photos: Amanda in an evening gown just last week at a New Zealand Symphony Orchestra performance.

Amanda was twenty-three and stunningly beautiful like her mother. I was startled by the sight of her lovely grinning face, with its intact teeth. Our daughter, Wanda. I stared at the photos, wondering how I would begin to have a conversation with her, before realizing that it would not be possible. I had to get away.

I sent a very polite reply to Kate Ngata, wishing the company well with their series, but 'as head of Cyber Security with New Zealand's premier bank, it would be entirely inappropriate for me to comment on any personal matter. I'm sure you understand.'

I knew this would merely add to her frustration, but I was grateful that the New Zealand police was not sharing information with amateurs.

I did not exist on the internet, except as an employee of the bank. There were no photographs or entries except for the ones from the *Rotorua Daily Post* in 1985, detailing my survival of the horror crash that killed my father and the subsequent fundraising on my behalf. Hoani Mata Productions must have sent the same email to every Steve Armstrong in the country.

I sent a note to the COO of the bank, saying that I had to take leave as a matter of urgency on a private medical matter. It would require three months, I said, but I would be contactable by email. I briefed my second-in-command on issues relating to the bank's relationship to bitcoin and crypto-currency, which was becoming a problem for us. I then left.

I went home and used my laptop to book flights to Ireland. I needed to go back. I needed to find my sister. She was the key to the connection I needed.

50

Sally

The results, when they came within twelve days, were unequivocal. Peter/Steve was my brother. Mark was our uncle, but there was something else that showed up in the results on the ancestry website. I had a niece called Amanda Heron and she was Peter's daughter. He hadn't mentioned a daughter or a wife or girlfriend. His letter had led me to believe that he was a loner, possibly like me. But he wasn't asexual like me.

It was time to call him. I wanted to have this conversation on my own. The ancestry results had come to my home and Mark didn't yet know.

Peter's phone rang once before he picked up.

'Mary?' he said.

'It's Sally, it's been Sally since I was adopted so I'd prefer if you called me Sally.'

'Okay.' There was a tremor in his voice.

'Are you still in Dublin?'

'Yeah, I'm in a park now beside a church in the city centre.'

'Right. So, I got the DNA results.'

'Yeah?'

'You are my brother.'

'I knew that. I've known about you all my life.'

'So why did you never get in touch before?'

'I explained it in the letter. I didn't know where you were. You didn't show up on any internet searches until Thomas Diamond's death.'

'Sorry, yes, you did explain. But if you knew about me and my mother and you knew what our birth father had done, why didn't you ever go to the police?'

'It's hard to explain. He had me brainwashed for a long time. He told me I had an illness. I hardly knew right from wrong – I can't say it all over the phone. Will you come and meet me?'

I had discussed what would happen with Mark if the results proved that we were siblings.

'Peter, we have an uncle, Denise's brother.'

'Really?'

'Yes, he'd like to meet you too. He will collect you in Dublin and bring you to my home.'

'When?'

'Tomorrow?' The next day was Saturday. I would cancel my weekend piano playing. Lucas would have to find a replacement.

'That would be good. Thank you. Mary – I mean, Sally, do you remember me?'

'I'm afraid not.'

'Did my mother, Denise, did she talk about me?'

'We have so much to talk about, Peter, let's wait until we're face to face.'

There was a pause. 'I'm not very good at talking.'

'Oh well, we're definitely siblings. It's taken me nearly two years of therapy to get over that.'

'Yeah?'

'Yes. Do you have friends? A wife? Girlfriend?'

His voice trembled. 'No.'

It wasn't time to ask him about his daughter. 'I can't believe I'm talking to my own brother.'

'You haven't told the media, or the police?'

'Absolutely not.'

He gave me the address of the hotel and we ended the call. Mark wanted to vet him, to make sure he wasn't violent or threatening in any way, and he arranged to collect Peter early the next morning. Peter wanted to know how he would get back to Dublin afterwards. Mark told him not to worry. We could put him up in the Abbey Hotel in Roscommon for a few nights. We had no real plan for what would happen.

I was on tenterhooks the next morning, constantly going to the window at every noise to see if Mark's car was parking. I received one text from Mark.

Stopped at a service station. He seems normal but extremely quiet.

Sue and Martha called to the door to see if I was okay. I'd missed my yoga class that morning. I didn't invite them in for coffee the way one is supposed to do with friends, but I didn't tell them a lie either. 'Sorry, I should have told you I wasn't coming. I have some family business to attend to.'

'Are you okay?' said Sue. 'You seem a little agitated?' and indeed I was looking behind her down the lane, hopping from foot to foot.

'Yes, yes, I'm fine, thank you. I'll see you during the week, okay?' I closed the door and went back to the kitchen. I had prepared sandwiches way too early. They had dried out. I set about making fresh ones, chicken, ham, tomato and coleslaw. Peter could be a vegetarian. I knew nothing about my brother.

51

Peter, 2019

It took me twenty-eight hours to get to Ireland, compared to the three-month ordeal it had taken to get to New Zealand almost forty years earlier. I ordered DNA test kits to be sent to the hotel in Dublin I had booked. I wrote my letter to Mary. Then I wandered around the city on foot. I bought some winter clothes. I'd travelled light. I'd never been in the city centre before, even as a child. Dublin was modern and multicultural and unfamiliar in every way.

The pay-as-you-go mobile phone rang over two weeks after I sent the letter. Mary had not alerted the police. There was an uncle, Denise's brother, Mark. He collected me in Dublin on 14th December and drove the two hours to Mary's cottage. He grilled me in the car about his sister. What did I remember? Had she ever mentioned him? What was she like? The questions were like an assault, and I avoided answering as much as I could.

We drove across the country mostly on a motorway. The day was dark and grey and wet. The sun did not appear. The land was flat. We stopped at a service station for fuel and we had bad coffee. I didn't know what to think of Mark. He seemed way too young to be my uncle, but we discovered he was only five years older than me. He said grimly that Denise was twelve when she gave birth to me. Neither of us said much for the rest of the journey.

52

Sally

Peter said he was seven years older than me but he looked much older. His wrinkles were deep and his face was weathered. His hair was short and grey, receding. He was clean-shaven. There was a faint white line across his forehead. An old scar? Inflicted by Conor Geary? But his eyes – the shape, the hazel colour – and his nose were identical to mine. My brother.

We didn't have an immediate connection. It was more gradual than that. Mark and I knew it would be awkward. It was hard to know what to call him to start with. I was adamant that I was Sally Diamond. He had been Steven Armstrong for most of his life, but now, he asked us to call him Peter. He was not forthcoming in conversation, and I was nervous at first. It was the Christmas season, so I was called on to play at the hotel a lot. I paid for Peter to stay in the Abbey Hotel in Roscommon and we would meet in my house whenever I was free. Mark always tried to be there too.

On the first day, there were long silences and occasional small talk. But Peter's small talk was even smaller than mine. It was only on the second day that we broached the subject of our father and who he was. Peter insisted that he wasn't physically harmed by Conor Geary in the same way my mother was. Peter lived most of his early life in solitary confinement, fearing that a made-up disease was going to kill him. A disease designed to keep him away from everyone and to make him entirely dependent on

Conor Geary. Our birth father was cruel and manipulative. My brother was as isolated as I had been, but not through choice. He had desperately wanted to go to school and make friends but, by the time his father died, it was too late and he didn't know how to be social. It was hard to get this information from him, but Mark was good at coaxing him, and later, after Peter had gone back to the hotel, Mark would come back to the house and parse what Peter had said and what he didn't say. Mark was good at reading between the lines.

Peter still felt guilt about Conor Geary's death because he'd been driving the car. The scar on his forehead was a result of that, and the terrible burns on his arms, from when he had tried to pull his father from the burning car. We assured him that his father, my father, was not worth saving, but he looked out of the window, refusing to meet our eyes.

We clashed over that. Despite everything Conor Geary had done, Peter felt loved by him, as if that cancelled out the horror he had visited on our mother, on me, and on Peter himself with this terrible story of a deadly disease.

'How can you defend him? I'm so glad he's dead,' said Mark.

'Don't you understand?' said Peter. 'People aren't one hundred per cent anything. You say he was a monster, and yes, he did terrible things to all of us.' He looked towards Mark. 'He took your sister, destroyed her in every way. He kept Sally locked up. He went on the run and dragged me to the other side of the world with him, took my name from me, lied to me, isolated me, but I know that he cared about me. I know he did.'

Mark used sarcasm, I think. 'Oh well, that's all right then. As long as he cared about you.'

I felt distressed. I went to the piano and they both shut up then. I played for a while and then asked Mark to take Peter back to the hotel. It was so difficult, but Peter was like me in so many ways. I couldn't help feeling drawn to him. Over the course of a week, we were able to get a fuller picture of Peter's life in New Zealand.

On the internet, Mark and I found the archive from the *Rotorua Daily Post* that told the story of the death of a respected local dentist, James Armstrong, and the survival of his poor orphaned son, Steven. Conor Geary had lived in New Zealand for the best part of five years working as a dentist under a fake name. Peter's passport was in the name of Steven Armstrong. He was wary of getting his status regularized, although Mark and I both felt that he should reclaim his name and nationality officially. He was here in Ireland on a ninety-day holiday visa. We suggested looking into the practicalities of doing it through my solicitor but Peter was reluctant and terrified of the media. This had to be handled with kid gloves, or not at all. We agreed that Peter should take his time and decide for himself when he wanted to go ahead with it.

After the first week, I invited Peter to stay in my home, for Christmas, and as long as he wanted thereafter. He smiled for the first time that day. We shook hands. That was as close as we had dared to be physically. I drew up a roster for use of the bathroom and breakfast and bedtime. We would take turns to cook for each other. He balked at the idea of being introduced to my friends. 'Please,' he said, 'I'm not used to people. Maybe one at a time?' and I understood that too. Mark was no longer present for all of our conversations. He found it more upsetting than I did.

On Christmas Day, Mark and Peter and I had lunch together. There was something I had wanted to ask Peter about, but Mark had said we should take things slowly, so I waited until Mark cut the Christmas cake and I poured us all a glass of port.

'Peter, you know, when we got the DNA results, there was a record of your daughter, but you've never mentioned her?'

'I don't have a daughter,' he said. I opened the laptop and showed him the website and there it was clearly stated:

PG [his initials]

Amanda Heron

Parent/Child 50% DNA shared

I clicked on Amanda Heron's name. Her date of birth was 1996.

'You definitely have a twenty-three-year-old daughter. I thought you said you didn't have any relationships or girlfriends?'

He knocked back the glass of port and refilled his glass, and the silence grew.

'Peter?' said Mark. 'What's going on? Did you know about her?'

'I never knew her name,' he said. 'I had a few, you know, one-night stands, and one of those women came and told me she was pregnant, but I didn't believe her, or at least, I thought anyone could be the father.' All the time he spoke, he was looking at the floor, ashamed, I think.

I was perturbed. He was not asexual like me. Tina had told me it was not the kind of thing I could quiz Peter about. People's sex lives were private, she insisted.

'My . . . encounters were drunken. I was never able to talk to women sober,' said Peter.

'Well, I guess you got more family than you bargained for,' said Mark, 'but let's take one step at a time. Everything must be overwhelming for you now.'

Peter nodded and when he looked up his eyes were full of

tears. That was another difference between us. He cried. I didn't.

'I reckon she'd be better off without me. I'm not good with people, especially strangers.'

'But maybe she'd like to get to know you.' Mark pushed it.

'I wouldn't be a good dad, it's too late for me. I don't even remember who her mother is.' He wasn't interested in his daughter. Mark wanted more answers than me, but I told him to leave it.

Over the following weeks, I noted that Peter was as anti-social as I used to be. I could empathize with him. He seemed so alone in the world, but he was never aggressive or threatening in any way.

I asked him to come and see Tina with me, but he didn't want to. He always made an excuse to go to his room if I had visitors, and refused second-hand invitations from my friends. We told everyone he was Mark's cousin, my second cousin, and that he was visiting from Australia, which was almost the truth. We didn't want to mention New Zealand because too many of my friends knew about the weird post I'd been getting from New Zealand. But we didn't fool everyone. Angela asked me if there was something going on with us.

'With who?'

'With you and that Australian fellow. Is he your boyfriend?'

'No. You know I don't have boyfriends.' The thought horrified me, but I was sworn to secrecy that he was my brother.

'It's unusual for you to welcome a strange man into your home.'

Sue had said the same thing. And it was definitely awkward even though Peter and I liked each other. He got up at dawn and went walking for hours, and eventually would turn up at dinner time. We stuck to our bathroom rota. And we did not enter each other's bedrooms under any circumstances. He only showered every second day, even though my shower was beautiful. I couldn't understand that. He stopped shaving shortly after he arrived and looked generally unkempt. Conversation was often stilted. He didn't seem to like it when I played the piano. As soon as I started, I heard the front door bang. It was rude. But it was my house and if I wanted to play the piano, I would.

We continued to talk, though. Why had my birth father chosen to keep Peter by his side and abandon me? Peter described a loving, benevolent, indulgent dad, clever and hardworking, and yet, we both knew what he had done to my mother, and how he had manipulated Peter.

The hardest thing for Peter to learn was that my mother hadn't spoken of his existence. We gave him the tapes and files but we kept from him the tape on which she said, 'It doesn't matter. I didn't want him.' He read through everything and listened to all of the recordings.

'She was screwed up,' he said.

'Yes, by your loving father.' Mark was increasingly annoyed by Peter's defence of Conor Geary.

'What about other "relationships"?' said Mark.

'What do you mean?'

'I mean, you were living with him there for five years. Did he have access to other children? Didn't you worry that he might kidnap another little girl?'

'I only really worked out what had happened with my mother not long before he died. We fought about it. But Dad only took adult dental patients. In New Zealand, kids' dental care is subsidized by the government but adults are more lucrative, and even the receptionist that Dad hired in the dental office was a man, and that was unusual. He never went after another kid. I'm sure of it.'

'I find it strange that a paedo who had been so active would just stop and change his ways, especially when he'd got away with it? Maybe he found a way to hide it from you.'

Peter looked away. 'Look, I know you don't like me defending him. I don't think he ever went after any other kids. But he was a misogynist. He always referred to women as stupid or ugly or opinionated. He didn't like them, that's for sure.'

'You know,' I said carefully, 'I think Conor Geary might have been messed up by his mother at a young age.'

'Yeah?' said Peter. 'I asked him about his parents once or twice. I was curious about my grandparents, you know? He got tight-lipped and changed the subject.'

'Why do you think that? About his mother?' Mark asked me.

'It was something his sister said.'

'His sister?' said Peter. 'You mean I have an aunt as well?'

'Yes, sorry, I should have mentioned her before. She died a few months ago. I only met her once with Aunt Christine, after I hit the newspapers. She got in touch. I don't know why. She was distressed. I suspect Conor Geary ruined her life as well.'

'What did she say about their mother?'

'It was kind of an off-the-cuff remark, but I've thought about it a lot. She said their father died when they were young and that their mother expected Conor to fill his shoes in every way. She said it was perverse. It was the way she said it.'

'Jesus Christ,' said Mark.

Peter was silent for a moment. 'Was she . . . normal?'

'Margaret? I guess so. But I think she met me out of some sense of duty?'

'Don't you feel anything . . . about her death? You never mentioned it before,' said Mark.

'Why should I? I met the woman once. She seemed nice. Isn't it amazing how different two siblings can be?'

Peter looked at me. 'We're different.'

'We're not that different. Two years ago, I used to pretend to be deaf so that I could avoid talking to people.'

He smiled at that. 'That's a good idea.'

On another evening, Peter told us about the two nights he had spent in the room with Denise. Mark wanted to know every detail, but Peter was only seven at the time, he reckoned. His memory was hazy. All he remembered was that she was terrifying and heavily pregnant. Mark pressed him for details but the only other things Peter remembered were that she didn't appear to have any front teeth and that she was in pain. She seemed old to young Peter. When the internet came along and he was able to start researching, he was shocked to discover that our mother was only nineteen years old at that time.

I contacted the guards and asked for the return of Toby, my teddy bear. They agreed, saying he was of no further evidentiary use. Now that I knew Peter had sent him to me, I was happy to have him back.

As we moved into mid-January 2020, Peter became morose and silent. He more or less stopped talking. When I pushed him to explain what was wrong, he said something about missing the summer in the southern hemisphere. I asked him if he intended to stay in Ireland, if he would look for a job with his experience and qualifications. He reluctantly admitted that he didn't know what to do. I offered to teach him how to play the piano, but he shouted at me then. 'You can't solve every problem by playing the fucking piano, Mary.'

I was taken aback. He slammed the door behind him as he took off, leaving me upset, shouting, 'My name is Sally!'

I didn't want to tell Mark because I think he didn't fully trust Peter. When Peter came back later, he went straight to his room. The next morning, he muttered an apology. I thought of all the coping mechanisms Tina had taught me. I calmly told him that I needed to be respected in my own house, that I was also dealing with anger issues, and that if he didn't seek therapy, he would need to leave my home.

For weeks, we were careful around each other. He kept making promises to see a therapist, but when I pressed him for details he gave me the silent treatment. As much as I cared about him, he infuriated me. Tina said that was normal for siblings.

I finally realized what I had to do with the money in my bank account from the sale of Conor Geary's house. It was Peter's inheritance too, though Margaret never knew it. He was entitled to 50 per cent of it. When he asked me for a loan one day, I told him all about it.

'You can start over, Peter, here in Ireland, where you belong,' I said as I started to explain where the money had come from. 'You can afford a comfortable home here in the village, and there'd be enough to start your own business too. You don't have to work at all if you don't want to.'

'I don't understand,' he said.

'That's your inheritance from the sale of your father's house.'

'What do you mean?'

'Margaret left me that house in her will.'

'You sold the house?' His voice was raised.

'Yes, but I'm giving you half of the proceeds from the sale.'

'If I'd known . . . I'd have kept that house. It's the only place that ever felt like home. I lived there with my dad, happily, until you came along.' Tina would have said his anger

334

was irrational. I hadn't known he existed when I sold the house.

'But your mother was chained to a wall, you never saw her. You never saw me.' He didn't answer.

He was even less communicative with me than before, but he was businesslike about the money and, after all, he worked in banking so he knew what he was doing. He suggested that I transfer the money into cryptocurrency as he had no way of setting up an Irish bank account yet. I assured him that I could give him as much cash as he needed until such time as we were able to regularize his citizenship and identity, but he was afraid of the publicity that would inevitably follow if the media were to get a sniff of the fact that the infamous Conor Geary had a living son in Ireland. I could see his point. It would be impossible to keep a big story like this private.

I didn't know anything about bitcoin, but Peter already had an account. All I had to do was go to my bank and direct them to make the transfer. The bank made a fuss and the bank manager was called to talk to me and tried to persuade me that my transaction was most unorthodox. I reminded her that it was not illegal and that it was my money.

The day after all of his money was transferred, Peter said he wanted to go travelling around Ireland for a while. I thought it was a good idea. We had spent nearly ten weeks cooped up together and, much as I enjoyed getting to know my brother, his resistance to any change or progress frustrated me. I'm sure I had been that bad too before therapy, but I made an effort with people when Angela asked me to. He made none.

Strangely, he didn't say goodbye. He was gone when I woke up the next morning. The night before he left, I was playing the piano when he came in from one of his walks. He said, 'Dad used to play the piano, you know? When we lived here, in Ireland. He was as good as you are. I'm sorry, but I can't bear the sound of it.'

I slammed the lid shut.

He had left the place spotless, although I thought it was strange that he had taken all of his belongings with him. He had also taken Toby. I was annoyed about that.

Mark thought his sudden disappearance without a word was alarming. I hadn't told him about the money.

As usual, I defended Peter. 'He's gone travelling. You could see how overwhelmed he was by everything. Maybe he's looking around for a place to live. His holiday visa expires at the end of the month. He'll go to the guards soon. I think he's decided to stay in Ireland. I hope so.'

I saw so much of myself in him. I was full of warm feelings for him. Maybe I loved my big brother.

I called Peter a few times but he never answered his phone. Mark grew more concerned.

A week later, I got a text from Peter.

Mary, I've thought about it a lot. I don't fit in here and I don't feel like your brother or Mark's nephew, no matter how hard I've tried. I'm in Dublin Airport. I'm going back to New Zealand. It's best for everyone if we don't keep in contact. I don't want to hurt you and I'm grateful for the money. I will put it to good use. I wish you and Mark all good things. You did your best. I'm not right in the head and no therapy is going to fix me. I'm better on my own.

I wrenched clumps from my hair and screamed until Martha came running from across the road.

53

Peter, 2020

When Mark said 'cottage', I imagined a small thatched one-room place like you saw on Irish tourism posters in New Zealand, and although it had a slate roof and small enough frontage, everything was new and modern and clean inside. There was a stream running under glass bricks all the way through the house. I'd never seen anything like it. Mary was not what I expected at all. She stared into my face until I looked away. We didn't know what to say to each other and then she shook my hand and went into another room and played the piano. It brought back memories of Dad when I was a small boy, locked in that bedroom, listening to the music he played. Mark told me that it was the shock, that she'd be okay in a few minutes. He seemed to be comfortable here. He'd pointed out his apartment on the way into the village, but Mark and Mary seemed close, I guess like family should be.

We had sandwiches and tea and, later, wine and a pasta meal. I wasn't used to talking so much but they had endless questions, about Denise, about what Mary had been like as a girl. She kept correcting me: 'My name is Sally.' I couldn't help getting it wrong, but I got the hang of it. I was relieved when they finally said that a taxi was on its way to take me to the hotel in the next town. I was exhausted from the talking and all the withholding of information. I had to be so careful about what I said and what I didn't say.

Back at the hotel, I slept fitfully. In the hostel in Dublin,

I hadn't dreamed at all and thought it was a sign that I was finally in my rightful place, but having spent the evening with Mark and Sally, they all came back to haunt me, Lindy, Rangi and Dad.

Sally came to collect me the next day and we went to a cafe in her village. This time, I asked her the question that had bothered me. Why did she not remember me? Hadn't our mother told her about me? She explained something about her psychiatrist father medicating her. She had no memory of our mother. I was relieved and jealous. Relieved she didn't know what I'd done to our mother but jealous that she could forget it all. There were so many things I wanted to forget. She asked about our father, and I could see she was upset that he had treated us so differently. 'He hated women,' was the only explanation I could give. It seemed inadequate but the only thing I could say.

Over the following week, we spent a lot of time together and with our Uncle Mark. I liked her. She said the weirdest things sometimes. She wanted me to see a therapist but I was afraid of someone being able to see into my head. Sally was the only woman I'd talked to properly since Lindy and, when she invited me to stay in her house, I was relieved. I could tell she was pleased with me. Sally seemed to have plenty of money but it wasn't my business where she got it. She wanted me to meet all her friends but pretend to be a cousin. I couldn't do that. I had so many lies to juggle that I couldn't cope with any more.

As much as I liked her, I couldn't help feeling envious. She had grown up with a mum and dad, gone to school, played sports, all the things that had been denied to me. And by her own account, she had squandered all of those opportunities to live in a solitary way until just the last few years. Now, she had friends, now she had some kind of job playing the piano.

I had nobody in my life except her, and I could never be fully honest with her.

The connection I yearned for was not in Ireland. Neither Sally nor my Uncle Mark could give me the feeling I craved. Sally was so pleased to have me there, Mark less so, but I couldn't relax. The tension in my head never dissipated, even for a moment. I needed Lindy, or someone like her.

I checked in with work regularly on my laptop, and said I was dealing with my medical issues. They knew me well enough not to pry. Several problems arose that I could handle remotely, often in the middle of the night. I needed to stay on the payroll until I figured out what I was going to do next. I couldn't stay with Sally indefinitely, but could I stay in Ireland? Should I go home to New Zealand? Where was home?

Over Christmas lunch, Sally mentioned Amanda Heron. It hadn't occurred to me that she would show up on the ancestry website. In the beginning, I denied all knowledge of her, but Mark was so suspicious, I lied and said I'd had some short affairs. They showed me the website. There she was, the baby I had delivered, '50% DNA shared'. I told them I didn't want to know. My initials that were connected to her on the website were PG. That, at least, was some comfort. If anybody went looking, my initials in New Zealand were SA. Mark and Sally had provided no other information, not even their birthdates.

But I had underestimated those amateur podcasters. On 12th January, an email landed in my inbox.

Dear Mr Armstrong

I apologize for bothering you again. By process of elimination, we believe you are the son of Conor Geary, also known as James Armstrong.

339

Some information has recently come to light which has made us focus more particularly on your father. It has not been possible to find a birth certificate for him in this country, nor is there any record of a James Armstrong studying dentistry in Ireland in the years he might have qualified. We believe the certificate he had was a forgery.

We heard from a retired cop who met James Armstrong when he accompanied a woman to the police station to report the disappearance of her teenage nephew, Rangi Parata. Parata drowned in a lake a few miles from your home in Rotorua. I believe you lived next door to Parata? The circumstances of his death were not deemed suspicious at the time, but in the light of recent events, we wonder if your father might be connected not just to the abduction of a girl in Ireland, but also to the drowning of Rangi Parata and potentially to the disappearance of Linda Weston.

There is something else. As you know, this podcast story was originally all about the disappearance of Linda Weston in 1983 and Amanda Heron's quest to find out what happened to her mother. Just in the last few weeks, Amanda's birth father has appeared on an ancestry website. We know nothing about him but for his initials – PG – and the fact that his DNA shows him to be 98 per cent of Irish descent.

We know that James Armstrong could not be Amanda's father as he died eleven years before she was born. But he lived outside Rotorua at the time Linda disappeared. He lived next door to Rangi Parata. He did, as far as we know, live in Ireland for some period, and he also practised as a dentist for five years in Rotorua. The man wanted in Ireland was a practising dentist, and a father of one child, Mary Norton, born to the girl he kidnapped there.

I know that this is a lot to take in for you and I apologize for presenting you with such potentially upsetting information.

Is it possible that you were also abducted? We would really like to gain as much information about your father as possible. This may all be a misunderstanding but one we would love to be able to clear up, with your help.

I understand that you are currently on leave from the Aotearoa National Bank and, understandably, we cannot get any information as to where you live or even a mobile phone number for you. If you are monitoring your email, please get in touch at your earliest convenience. All of my contact details are at the top of this email.

Ngā mihi
Kate Ngata

I stared at the screen, reading and rereading the email. The amateurs were far closer to the truth than the police. Kate Ngata had not mentioned going to the police with this new information but surely it was only a matter of time before she did?

A cursory look at Hoani Mata Productions website showed that it was a one-woman operation. But Kate was clearly smart. She had found a retired cop from Rotorua, and knew we lived next door to Rangi.

I felt a tightness in my throat. I was trapped. I needed to decide what to do. I wondered what Sally would say if I told her that Dad had abducted Lindy. I could lie that she had escaped, that I never knew what happened to her. Sally might believe it. She seemed to accept things as fact, but Mark was always suspicious of me. It was obvious he didn't trust me and he never believed that Dad stopped being 'an active paedophile' the day he left Ireland. They would force me to go to the police. I couldn't let that happen.

A week later, I responded to Kate's email. I had to throw her off the scent and buy time.

Dear Kate

Thank you for your email. I am away from Wellington at the moment, dealing with a personal medical matter.

I am shocked by the information you have gathered. But I'm afraid you have the wrong suspect. My dad certainly wasn't connected to the death or disappearance of any of these kids. His only name was James Armstrong and I have a copy of his birth certificate at home. I was very young when I lived in Ireland and I have good memories of my mother. They were very happily married. We lived in Donegal in the north-west of Ireland. I was an only child. In fact, my mother died in childbirth along with my baby brother six years after I was born.

When we moved back to New Zealand after my mother's death, we did indeed buy a house next door to Rangi Parata. I remember the time he went missing. I can confirm my dad drove his aunt in and out to the police station. As far as we knew, Rangi drowned because he was drunk. Weren't empty beer cans found nearby? I didn't know him well.

As for Linda Weston, I remember her story dominating the news for a long time. But she disappeared from Lake Rotorua around Christmastime that year when Dad and I were on holidays in Wanaka on the South Island. I can't remember the name of the motel we stayed in, but I'm sure it could be verified too. Any of Dad's old patients might remember he took two weeks off every Christmas, and we would travel around the country together.

I am happy to meet with you when my medical ordeal is over, though that may not be for another month or two. I'm sorry that your research has led you astray and I wish you every success in your quest.

Kind regards
Ngā mihi
Steven Armstrong

Once again, my freedom was on the line. All of the facts that I presented were vague on detail, hard if not impossible to verify as almost nobody would hold records from 1983, certainly not digitally. I made my 'medical ordeal' sound like a cancer battle so that she would be disinclined to harass me any further, particularly when I was so adamant that she had got her story wrong. I was alert enough to block my IP address so that nobody could know I was in Ireland.

Still, she was dogged. I didn't know whether she would take my word for anything I'd said. She could ask to see my father's birth certificate. But I knew from my job that you could obtain almost anything on the dark web, including a fake birth certificate. She did not seem to be in any way suspicious of me, but was it a lure? Was she feigning concern that I was also an abductee? Did she suspect that I was Irish and that I was Amanda's father? If I did engage with her, she was sure to ask me to take a DNA test, and that would be harder to avoid. I thought about going to the dark web to look for a new passport for myself, under a different name, a different nationality. I downloaded the Tor search engine, and spent the rest of the day searching through sites, shocked by what was on sale. Some users warned that the FBI were all over the dark web, but their focus was on drugs, guns and people trafficking.

I assumed that I would get an apologetic response from Kate the next day after New Zealand had woken up. And I did get a response, but it wasn't as apologetic as I had hoped, and it came almost five weeks later, weeks in which I barely slept and lost my appetite.

Dear Mr Armstrong

I am sorry to hear you are going through medical issues and I wish you a speedy recovery. I hope you don't mind, but I have just a few very simple questions for you. Where and when in New Zealand were you born? Do you know the name of the hospital? That information would be really helpful to my enquiries.

Ngā mihi
Kate

She didn't address any of my assurances. She may still have thought that I was an abductee, but the curtness of the email convinced me otherwise. I didn't reply.

I went to the dark web and looked into getting myself a new identity. It was way more expensive than I had guessed, NZ$170k or €100k. I could just about afford it, if I could get some kind of a loan from Sally, but I would have nothing left. I couldn't sell up in Wellington from Ireland, not without attracting attention. And how would I explain to Sally why I needed money?

All this time, Sally was going about her business. Mark came for dinner twice a week. She desperately wanted me to get to know her friends, particularly her adoptive mother's sister, Christine. I shut down every time she brought it up.

Mark continued to ask inconvenient questions. He was very keen that we all go to the guards and that I should come clean about everything, at least everything he knew. I knew it was only a matter of time before he alerted them himself.

The day after I got the email from Kate asking for my birth details, I asked Sally if she could lend me a sum of money. I didn't even have to name the sum because she started talking about Dad's house in Dublin, how she had inherited it and sold it. She said I was due half of the proceeds. It annoyed me that she'd been sitting on this money all along and hadn't said anything. I was astounded to find that my share of the house was worth over a million euro. More than enough to start over somewhere else and to buy my new identity.

I made sure to get the money in cryptocurrency. As soon as it was transferred, I left Carricksheedy, telling her I was going travelling for a week or two. I left before she got up that morning in order to avoid what I knew was a final farewell. I stayed in a good hotel in Dublin. My new passport, along with my California driving licence and social security number, was delivered there by courier within four days. This time I was American and my name was Dane Truskowski. I flew to London without incident. In Heathrow, I looked at all the destinations on the flight board. I posted my parcel. I texted a farewell to Sally. Where could I go from here? Anywhere.

54

Sally

I couldn't tell Martha what had happened. She pulled my hands from my hair and asked if I was injured and I said no. I admitted to having had a shock. She made me a cup of tea and tried to put her arm around me. I went to the piano and tried to play a little Einaudi but my fingers refused to cooperate.

'I loved him,' was all I could say.

'Who?'

'Peter.'

I gripped the mug with trembling hands.

'The weird guy who's been staying with you?'

'He's not weird. You don't –'

'Was he your boyfriend? I haven't seen him for a while.'

'No!' I shouted at her. 'He was not my boyfriend. And he's not weird.'

'Sally, calm down.'

'Why do you think he's weird? Why must you judge everyone according to your own smug, perfect life? You thought I was weird until you got to know me. You didn't even know Peter. How dare you, Martha?'

'Smug, perfect life? You have no idea. And this guy? Despite you introducing him to me and several others, he never acknowledges us on the street. Never even answers us when we say hello. Nobody believes he's Mark's cousin. Who is he, Sally?'

When I refused to tell her or explain why I'd been screaming, she said she couldn't help me.

'If he's your boyfriend and he's left you, well good riddance. He's not good for you. You didn't keep secrets before he arrived. I hope he never comes back.'

'Get out, Martha, I never asked you to come!' I yelled at her.

She stopped on her way to the door. 'You know, I went out of my way to make allowances for you, Sally. I welcomed you into my home and I let you into my children's lives. But your tragic childhood and weird upbringing does not give you any excuse to be a bitch!' She slammed the door on her way out.

I didn't want to see Mark. I knew he would be angry. I decided to go and see Aunt Christine in Dublin and tell her everything. There was still no way I could face city driving and motorways. I got the evening train to Dublin by myself and Aunt Christine met me at the station. The journey was just about bearable. Strangers sat beside me and in front of me, but I looked out of the window at the rolling green fields and pretended to be deaf.

I began to tell Aunt Christine the story of Peter when we were in her car, but she seemed stricken by the news and asked me to wait until we got to her house. When we settled down with a pot of tea, I began to tell her who Peter was.

'Oh my God,' she said. 'I think Jean knew.'

'What do you mean?'

'She suspected that there was another child. She always said that it didn't make sense that Denise would not let go of you if you'd had separate bedrooms in the Killiney house. She said Denise insisted that she had always slept by your side, but we knew there was that bedroom next door.'

'What? But why wasn't that information anywhere in Dad's records?'

'He didn't believe it. Denise refused to answer any

questions about having another child. Tom said if she'd had a son, she would have been screaming about him too.'

'Screaming?'

'Look, Sally, I've kept my mouth shut for so many years, but your dad could be a tyrant. He could also be misogynistic. Jean's opinions were never as valid as his. There is something I need to tell you. I have tried to be honest with you as far as I can, but there is no need for me to hide information from you any more. I'm not telling you any of this to hurt you, but you should know the truth.'

'What truth?'

'The truth about Jean and Tom, your mum and dad.'

'Go on.'

'Jean was a lot more intelligent than your dad. She strongly objected to the way he treated you. She said that he never saw you as a daughter, but as a patient. He experimented on you, trying out different treatments and medications, evaluating everything. When you left school, Jean was adamant that you should go to college. You had brains to burn and you could have studied anything, music obviously, but she thought you'd be a good engineer too. You have a very mathematical mind. You didn't want to do anything.'

'I remember.'

'But it was so bad for you, Tom insisting on the move to an even more remote village, becoming more and more isolated. Jean was desperate for you to meet other people. No matter how you resisted, you must understand now that it would have been best for you.'

'Maybe.'

'Tom disagreed. He wanted you to do exactly what you wanted so that he could study you. Jean was on the point of leaving him when she had a stroke.'

'What?'

'She suffered from high blood pressure, and the stress of fighting with Tom and you over your future was too much for her. He wasn't . . . kind to her, Sally. Thank God you never saw that side of him. She had planned to leave him, but she didn't know if you would come with her. You were over eighteen then, technically an adult. I don't suppose she ever discussed it with you?'

'No, I would remember that. But the weekend before she died, she wanted me to come and visit you with her. Does that mean –'

'She knew you didn't like change, and she'd planned to make the move gradually –'

'But then she had a stroke?'

'Yes.'

'Why are you telling me this, Aunt Christine?'

'Because I don't want to go to my grave harbouring secrets that are more your business than mine. How he treated your birth mother, well . . .'

'What do you mean?'

'If Denise's behaviour didn't match his own interpretation, he dismissed it and called her hysterical. There were those toy soldiers . . .'

'What toy soldiers?'

'Everything that belonged to Denise and you was brought to the unit in St Mary's Hospital, to your living quarters. There wasn't much. You didn't have any toys except for these toy soldiers. Denise said they weren't yours. Jean quizzed her about who they belonged to, but she stayed silent. When Jean queried the guards, they said the soldiers had been found under the bed in the small white bedroom.'

'Why didn't you tell me this before?'

'What was the point in telling you something that didn't make sense? I never even thought about it when that teddy bear arrived. Did your brother send it to you? Did he sleep in the small white bedroom, Sally?'

'Yes.' Peter had taken Toby with him when he left. I couldn't imagine what he wanted with the bear.

'How strange that evil man was, to separate mother and son, brother and sister, and yet have them living a room apart. Did you like him, your brother?'

'Peter? Yes, I really did. I understood him. He was moody and silent a lot of the time, but it must have taken so much courage to get on a plane and cross the world to come and tell me the truth. I think he was very brave. I'm so upset that he's gone.'

I felt a shuddering in my chest, as if all the air was being squeezed out. I began to sob real tears for the very first time I could remember. Aunt Christine held me and I put my head on her thin shoulder, and it seemed like every sorrow I should have felt for decades came pouring out on to Aunt Christine's kitchen table. She stroked my head and made soothing noises, the way mothers do to small babies.

She wanted to know why he had never gone to the police and I explained about his anxiety, his social isolation, his fear of strangers, the brainwashing over years with my birth father. She wanted to know if he had succeeded in life, at least professionally.

'Yes,' I said. 'He was head of cyber security at a bank head-quarters. I think he'll probably go back to that job.'

'So, he's okay financially, then?'

'Oh, he certainly is.' I told Aunt Christine about Marga-ret's death and the inheritance and how I'd shared it with Peter before he left.

'Hold on,' she said, 'how long after you gave him the money did he leave?'

'Straight away. There was a lot of fuss about the money and I had to transfer it to him in cryptocurrency –'

'So, wait, he came, stayed for two months, you gave him a million euro, and then he disappeared?'

'He didn't disappear, he went home. He said he didn't feel like he could fit in.'

She was quiet then for a few moments.

'Sally, did you ask anyone's advice before you gave him this money?'

'No, I didn't. I'm an adult and it was my money.'

'You don't think that might be why he came?'

'Absolutely not. Nobody knew I had that money. I didn't tell anyone.'

'But he knew you didn't work for a living; he knew you lived in a beautiful new home.'

I was annoyed now. Why did she think I was a fool?

'He was entitled to the money, Aunt Christine. Ever since I started going to therapy, I've been told to work on my trust issues and to give people the benefit of the doubt. Now you're telling me that Dad was terrible, you're implying that my brother only wanted money from me. Dad loved me.'

'Didn't you just tell me that Peter said the same thing about your birth father?'

'Are you comparing Tom Diamond with Conor Geary?' I could feel the anger within me. I jumped up and stood over her.

'Of course not, I –'

'Don't you dare speak to me about them in the same breath. They were nothing like each other . . .' I stopped myself, appalled at my own temper taking over again. Aunt Christine had stumbled backwards out of her chair and was now standing behind it, as if she needed to protect herself from me.

I took a deep breath. 'I . . . I'm going to bed.'

Aunt Christine was silent. I should have apologized but I was still incensed by her words. Was my mum, Jean, also a victim of domestic abuse, physical and emotional? It was all too much.

It was not yet 10 p.m. Next day was Saturday. I was due to play in Farnley Manor.

Aunt Christine stayed in her room while I had breakfast alone on Saturday morning. I was distressed and sat at her piano, but I couldn't bring myself to lift up the lid. Eventually, I left the house without saying goodbye and hailed a taxi to take me to the station.

On the train, my phone rang. It was Angela. 'Sally, you have terrified Christine, she just rang me in floods of tears.'

I didn't say anything.

'Can you hear me?'

'Yes,' I said.

'And that guy who was staying with you is your brother? I can scarcely believe what she told me. Why didn't you come to me? And why didn't you go to the guards with him?'

'It was none of your business and it wasn't Aunt Christine's business to tell you.'

'Who else knew about this? Mark?'

'Yes, he's family. It's our own private business.'

'You are supposed to tell me when . . . You gave this guy a million euro?'

'What about you, Angela? What about the truth you never told me?'

'What are you talking about?'

'Is it true that Mum was going to leave Dad? Was he violent towards her?'

I heard her deep sigh at the end of the phone. I desperately wanted her to deny it. But she said nothing. I hung up. Every-one in the train carriage was staring at me.

In the taxi from the train station to Farnley Manor, the radio was on and the taxi driver tried to engage me in conversation about the headlines: '*First case of coronavirus confirmed in the Republic of Ireland. The man, from the eastern part of the country, recently travelled from Italy. A statement from the Minister for Health is imminent.*'

I turned up for work just in time. I had never needed the piano more. Lucas asked me if I was all right. I guess my eyes were puffy and I was not communicative. He sent me a pot of hot coffee and some cake and insisted that I eat something before I started, but I carried the tray to the piano and forced myself to play. I started with the last move-ment of Beethoven's Piano Sonata No. 14, a fast and fiery piece, my fingers flying up and down the keyboard in a frenzy, trying to work the anger out through my hands. It was the first time I'd played since I learned that Conor Geary had been an accomplished pianist.

Lucas interrupted and asked me to play my usual reper-toire, soft, soothing music. The rage within me took over. I swept the tray on to the deep, pale carpet, coffee splattering the sofa and the guests nearest to us. Everyone stopped to stare. Lucas went immediately to the guests. I went to the staff cloakroom and retrieved my bag and coat. I called another taxi to take me home. It arrived mercifully fast because if Lucas had attempted to reprimand me, I know I would have hit him.

I cried again on the journey home. I tried the breathing exercises, I tried putting myself in Aunt Christine's shoes, in Angela's shoes, but my rational self asked why they couldn't put themselves in my shoes. Was anger never justified?

I took a hammer from my toolbox and was in the act of smashing my piano when the doorbell rang. I ignored it and swung the hammer harder, but then I heard loud knocking at the window right behind me. I turned in irritation to see who it was. Mark.

'What's going on with you? I must have left ten messages and voicemails. Did something happen? Martha said –'

'Mark, please go away, I don't want to talk to anyone right now. Please?'

I tried to keep my voice calm. While Mark stood in the open doorway, a garda squad car pulled up behind him. Detective Inspector Howard approached with a uniformed guard. She was smiling.

'Sally, I think we finally have news for you regarding Conor Geary. May we come in?'

She looked at Mark, expecting him to go away.

'I'm Mark Butler, Mark Norton, I'm Denise Norton's brother, Sally's uncle. I'd like to hear what you have to say.'

Detective Inspector Howard looked at me. 'I . . . is it okay with you, Sally?'

I felt drained of all emotion and utterly exhausted. I had not renewed my prescription for Valium as it was so addictive, but I needed something. To hell with what Tina said. Alcohol.

I let them all in and fixed myself a glass of Jameson. Mark was shocked that the piano was in pieces but I told him I was not prepared to talk about it. The guards exchanged looks.

I didn't offer anyone anything, but Mark did, as if my house were his own, and set about making coffee.

Detective Inspector Howard began to tell me so much I already knew. Only I knew more. They had good reason to believe Conor Geary died in 1985. He'd lived in New

Zealand under an assumed name. He had a son, named Steve Armstrong. Mark stepped in and corrected her. I said nothing as Mark told her everything about Peter and how he had been staying in this house. That stopped Howard in her tracks.

'Here? When?'

'Since, I think, mid-December, up until just over a week ago, right, Sally?'

'What? How did he make contact?'

I let Mark do all the talking. Howard and her associate took copious notes. She asked the inevitable questions about why we hadn't alerted the guards. Mark told them I had insisted on Peter's privacy.

'And where is he now?'

'He's gone travelling around Ireland. Sally is in touch with him, aren't you, Sally?'

They all looked at me, and here came the tears again, rolling down my face. Mark moved over and put his arm around my shoulders.

'What is it? What did he do?'

With shaking fingers, I found the text I'd received just two days previously.

I passed the phone first to Mark and then to DI Howard.

Mark said nothing but breathed what I think was a sigh of relief.

Detective Inspector Howard asked us to come to the station on Monday morning.

'He's not a criminal. He's a victim, as much as Denise or I am,' I wailed.

They stood up to leave.

'Did he ever mention Linda Weston or Rangi Parata?'

'No, not to me. Sally?'

I shook my head.

They were at the door when Detective Inspector Howard turned and said, 'Did he ever mention Amanda Heron?'

'Yes, that's his daughter. We did DNA tests before we met him. He said he'd never met her. She was the result of a one-night stand,' said Mark.

55

Peter, 2020

Like father, like son. Peter Geary and Steve Armstrong vanished. I guess that podcaster was taken seriously by the police after all.

I landed in Chicago as Dane Truskowski. Everything was so much easier for me than it was for Dad, thanks to the dark web and my inheritance. These masks are a blessing. I flew from city to city within the United States, but I think I'm going to stay here in Nutt, New Mexico. I grew a beard. I've bought a house. It's way up a dirt track off a road that you wouldn't know existed. It hasn't been lived in for a while, but I'm fixing it up nicely.

When I've finished with the house, I'm going to build a barn behind it. Sound-proofing materials are available on Amazon, like most things, even shackles. I realize now that the only way to make that connection I seek is to take a woman and keep her until she submits. I'm prepared to wait. I won't force her to love me. I haven't found her yet. She won't be a child. I'm not my father.

56

Sally

The country is in lockdown. Despite the two-kilometre limit on movement, Mark and I were called to the garda headquarters in Dublin twice.

The coronavirus has knocked most other stories off the news agenda so little has been said about the discovery of another child of Denise Norton and Conor Geary, or of my birth father's death in New Zealand in 1985 and his links to the drowning of a boy called Rangi Parata and the abduction of Linda Weston. It is not yet public knowledge that Peter is the father of Linda Weston's child, Amanda Heron, though there is an international search for him. New Zealand's borders are closed. Peter never allowed us to take photographs of him but we spent hours at Dublin Airport going through CCTV footage from 22nd to 28th February. We found him in Terminal 2, in the departure lounge, but we couldn't tell which gate he was going to. He disappeared into the throng. Nobody by the name of Steve, Stephen, Steven Armstrong or Peter Geary went through the airport that day. He must have had a different passport.

Some podcaster called Kate Ngata has contacted me via email. She and my niece, Amanda, are making a podcast series and are badgering me to contribute. Sue, my ex-best friend, has talked to her via Zoom apparently, and has told her how suspiciously Peter behaved when he was in the village. I don't want to know Amanda Heron. My uncle and my brother have been so disappointing. I'm better off without family.

Aunt Christine doesn't call at all since I 'turned aggressive' in her home. Stella is annoyed that I didn't tell her anything about Peter.

'Why didn't you tell me who he was?' she complained.

What's the answer? I finally had someone who was mine. I loved him, I wanted to protect him and keep him to myself.

I couldn't have known what he was capable of. The idea that a man could inherit a sickness like that from his father, from my father, and that I could welcome him into my home makes me want to scream all night long.

Linda Weston was twenty-seven years old when Amanda was born. I keep telling them that there's no proof she was raped, no proof that she and Peter didn't have a consensual relationship. She wasn't murdered, she died of appendicitis. Mark told me to get a grip. Why had Peter disappeared? Why did he want us to keep everything quiet when he was here? Why did he travel on a false passport? I cling to the belief that he was innocent, in some way. I cling to my sanity.

Angela phones and texts me regularly but I rarely answer the phone, except when I need a new Valium prescription. I take quite a lot to stop me screaming. I also drink a lot.

I had to tell the guards about the money I gave to Peter. Mark was furious about it. He said I should have discussed with him what to do with the money. He thinks he was entitled to some of it, as it was he who had suffered the most. We argued over it. Margaret left that money to me. I haven't spoken to him in weeks. Angela left a voicemail to say he had the virus and was in hospital. He's very sick. No visitors allowed. I don't care. I don't want to see him.

Tina was wrong about everything. I was right to trust nobody. They all let me down in the end. Keeping secrets or telling secrets behind my back. I'm deaf again. I don't speak to anyone and I pretend I don't hear their whispering. This lockdown suits me very well. The village pub and the cafe are closed. So is Martha's yoga studio. I've given up going to the Gala supermarket because every time I went in, Laura tried to chat to me. I've gone back to shopping in the Texaco. Everyone keeps two metres apart and there is no handshaking, never mind hugging. We all wear masks and I avoid eye contact where possible. The piano is still in pieces in the sitting room, a reminder of my heritage. I can't get anyone to take it away.

I saw Abebi on the street yesterday. She is growing tall. She must be eleven years old now. I waved at her, and she saw me, but she put her head down and walked faster down the street, away from me. She is the same age as my mother was when my father kidnapped her. I pull at my hair again, taking a fistful from my head.

Epilogue

Amanda, May 2022, Auckland Town Hall

I am happy. New Zealand is finally coming out of lockdown and I'm performing in public for the first time. God knows I have practised so hard for the last two and a half years, but my rapid antigen test is negative, the hall is fully booked, and Mum and Dad are here from Christchurch.

My two new uncles have come from Rotorua. I am nervous about meeting them, but we have had Zoom calls and they seem like pretty decent blokes. Mum and Dad are keen to meet them too. Kate is not coming. She is annoyed that I withdrew from her podcast series after all the work she put into it, but my backstory is so ghastly that I would rather keep it private. I never wanted to know the gory details. If I'm going to make it in life, I want to be known as a composer, not as the daughter of an abductee and a kidnapper. It's all in the past.

The police have confirmed all of Kate's research. I don't know where my father is but I'm certainly not going to go chasing him. I'm not his victim, I never was. Kate can tell the story if she wants but she cannot use my name. The last thing I need is drama. To be a composer, I need peace and a piano. And that old teddy bear that randomly arrived in the post a couple of years back. He has become my lucky charm.

The house lights go down. I hear a hush descend in the auditorium. The spotlight appears on the piano. I step out on to the stage. No nerves. I place my bear on the lid of the piano. He smiles at me with his one eye. I smile back and nod to him, and there is a ripple of applause and laughter from the audience. I settle myself on the velvet-covered seat and raise my hands. It is time.

Acknowledgements

Thank you to the fabulous Marianne Gunn O'Connor, agent, mentor and friend; to Vicki Satlow, who has worked to ensure I am published in territories I couldn't find on a map; and to Pat Lynch, who ensures smooth transactions with great diligence.

At Penguin Sandycove in Dublin, praise is due to my editor Patricia Deevy, the best in the business, who always sees the bigger picture and, with this book in particular, afforded me the time to get it right; Cliona Lewis, publicist extraordinaire, Michael McLoughlin, who helms a tight ship, and I'm also very grateful to Brian Walker, Carrie Anderson, Issy Hanrahan and Laura Dermody.

In PRH London, I am hugely grateful to Amelia Fairney, Ellie Hudson, Jane Gentle and Rosie Safaty in comms; copywriter Zoe Coxon; Sam Fanaken, Ruth Johnstone and Eleanor Rhodes Davies in sales; and Richard Bravery and Charlotte Daniels in the art team for coming up with this beautiful cover.

Karen Whitlock has proven yet again that I am barely literate. Her excellent copy-editing skills make me look good. Thank you.

For research assistance in so many areas, Christine Pride and Lynn Miller-Lachmann, retired State Pathologist Professor Marie Cassidy, CEO of Tallaght Hospital Lucy Nugent, vascular surgeon Bridget Egan, psychologist Aisling White, solicitor Peter Nugent, barrister John O'Donnell, educational psychologist Dr Mary Nugent, and fellow writers Kate Harrison, Adrian McKinty and Alex Barclay. If I asked for your advice, and then ignored it, please forgive me. I'm afraid the story had to come first.

For New Zealand expertise, I am indebted to Vanda Symon, Liam McIlvanny, Sonja Hall-Tiernan, Craig Sisterson, Jill Nicholas, Steve Duncan, Fergus Barrowman, and Faran Foley at the Irish Embassy.

To my emotional support people over the last two difficult years, I thank Sinéad Crowley, Jane Casey, Marian Keyes, Kate Beaufoy, Sinéad Moriarty, Claudia Carroll, Tania Banotti, Maria O'Connell, Bríd Ó Gallchóir, William Ryan, Ed James, Clelia Murphy, John O'Donnell, Lise-Ann McLaughlin, Anne McManus, Zita Rehill, Moira Shipsey, Val Reid, Sharon Fitter, Fiona O'Doherty and a special mention for Colin Scott.

To my emotional support place, the Tyrone Guthrie Centre and all of the fantastic women there who afford me the time and space and nourishment to write.

And definitely, deserving of a paragraph of their own, thank you to the superb booksellers, book bloggers, festival programmers, moderators, fellow panellists, TV and radio producers and presenters, librarians and audiobook narrators. If I named you all, there'd be no room for the book.

Readers, you have no idea what your loyalty means to me. I hope I get to meet you at virtual and real festivals now that the world seems to be open for business again. Thank you for waiting a whole extra year for this book. Life got in the way of writing for a while, and I'll try not to let that happen again.

And of course to my large, ever-extending family, in-laws and out-laws and particularly my mother, you only have yourselves to blame. And remembering my lovely Dad who is probably strolling around an astral bookshop, turning my books face out.

LYING IN WAIT

LIZ NUGENT

WINNER Crime Novel of the Year, Irish Book Awards 2016

Richard and Judy Spring List 2017 – Winner of the Reader's Choice Award

Lydia Fitzsimons lives in the perfect house with her adoring husband and beloved son. There is just one thing Lydia craves to make her life complete, and she is determined that her husband will get it for her. The last thing she expects is that her obsession will lead to murder.

However, not even a dead body can stop Lydia in her tracks. If anything, it makes her more determined to get her own way – whatever the cost . . .

'A tense, taut, almost gothic thriller . . . I devoured it in one sitting'

Marian Keyes

'Mothers don't come more wickedly drawn . . . the wit is sharp and the plot full of punishing twists. Horribly hilarious'

The Times

'It twists, it turns, it is a compulsive pulp triumph'

Stylist

'Deliciously twisted . . . the denouement is truly chilling'

Sarah Hilary

'An exquisitely uncomfortable, utterly capitvating reading experience'

Publishers Weekly

SKIN DEEP
LIZ NUGENT

WINNER Crime Novel of the Year, Irish Book Awards 2018

WINNER Dead Good's 'Cancel All Plans for the Book You Can't Put Down' Award 2019

Delia O'Flaherty is as wild, remote and dangerous as her island home off the west coast of Ireland. Her adoring father tells her that one day she will be the Queen of Inishcrann.

However, tragedy leaves Delia alone in the world to make her way relying on her wits and her rare beauty. But Delia's beauty is deceptive – as anyone who cares about her eventually finds out.

What is the truth behind Delia's tragic past? And what happens when a face from that past turns up on her doorstep?

'Pure genius. Absolutely brilliant writing'

Shari Lapena

'Monumentally good. Liz Nugent is a beautiful writer and among the very best storytellers in the world'

Donal Ryan

'Every bit as amazing as her first two . . . She deserves immense fame and fortune'

Lisa Jewell

'For those who like their escapism on the darker side. If Patricia Highsmith were Irish she might well have come up with this tale'

Ian Rankin